HER PREGNANCY SECRET

BY
ANN MAJOR

MILLS
BOON

Published in Great Britain 2014
by Mills & Boon, an imprint of Harlequin (UK) Limited,
Eton House, 18-24 Paradise Road, Richmond, Surrey, TW9 1SR

© 2014 Ann Major

ISBN: 978-0-263-91471-9

51-0714

Harlequin (UK) Limited's policy is to use papers that are natural, renewable and recyclable products and made from wood grown in sustainable forests. The logging and manufacturing processes conform to the legal environmental regulations of the country of origin.

Printed and bound in Spain
by Blackprint CPI, Barcelona

Wakefield Libraries
& Information Services

This book should be returned by the last date stamped above. You may renew the loan personally, by post or telephone for a further period if the book is not required by another reader.

"Now who's seducing who?"

Michael pushed Bree back against the wall, and his lips found hers. He kissed her hard and long. Glorious heat rushed through her veins as she kissed him back.

He lifted his head. Dazed, her heart racing, her eyes met the wildness in his gaze. He was the father of her unborn baby. In spite of all the walls she'd tried to erect against him, she still felt connected to him.

What she really wanted was for him to love their child and maybe someday love her, too. And when he kissed her like this, some idiotic part of her believed that could happen, that he might change someday, that he might see her as she was and be capable of respecting her...of loving her.

Ann Major lives in Texas with her husband of many years and is the mother of three grown children. She has a master's degree from Texas A&M at Kingsville, Texas, and is a former English teacher. She is a founding board member of the Romance Writers of America and a frequent speaker at writers' groups.

Ann loves to write—she considers her ability to do so a gift. Her hobbies include hiking in the mountains, sailing, ocean kayaking, traveling and playing the piano. But most of all, she enjoys her family. Visit her website at www.annmajor.com.

To Ted
I love you more

One

Michael North awakened with a violent start in the middle of the night.

His first thought was for the safety of the exquisite woman curled trustingly against him. She was warm and soft, beguilingly beautiful in the moonlight with her dark golden hair spilling across his pillow. He wanted to touch that hair and kiss her lips again, wanted it so much he had to clench his hands.

Ironically, he'd enjoyed his evening with her more than he'd enjoyed being with anyone in a very long time.

Maybe that was why his gut twisted as he experienced an uncustomary pang of conscience. After all, he'd seduced her for very deliberate, self-serving reasons.

Careful not to disturb her, he sat up and brushed a lock of thick black hair out of his eyes. Everything he'd done tonight—the seductive dinner at her failing bistro, the lovemaking in his penthouse, all the shared laughter and smiles—had been a lie.

He'd set her up so he could protect his naive younger brother.

But at some point Michael had forgotten about Will. His dinner date with Bree had begun with champagne served in sparkling flutes at Chez Z, the intimate French bistro she'd inherited from her famous brother, Johnny Z. She loved to cook and to eat, and Michael had loved watching her indulge.

She'd blushed when she'd drunk champagne. She'd sighed when she'd licked chocolate off her fingertips, and his. The wet, warm tip of her tongue against his flesh had almost been as good as having sex with her. *Almost.*

He'd loved the sound of her laughter, the glow of her cheeks when she teased him, the flash of intelligence in her slanting eyes when she'd made him feel clever and her wildness in bed. When had he had such a good time with anybody?

Surprisingly, Bree had given him more pleasure and tenderness and amusement during their evening than he'd ever imagined possible.

Because, first, she wasn't his usual type. He went for cool, sophisticated glamour, for sleek, slim blondes who made heads turn and other men envy him. Bree was lush and earthy and wanton. She loved color and baubles and cheap scarves and probably didn't bother to carry a comb in her purse.

And second, Bree Oliver, for all her seeming innocence and charms, was a gold digger. She'd targeted his foolish brother, thinking Will was the chump she needed to keep Chez Z from going into bankruptcy.

For Will's sake, Michael had to finish her off. No matter how much he'd enjoyed being with her or how fabulous she'd been in bed, she deserved it.

If only Michael had been as smart five years ago when he'd fallen for Anya Parris. But, no, like a fool, when Anya had lied about being pregnant, he'd married her. He'd suffered through a hellish marriage that had included infidelity, scandal and a very public divorce.

Never again would Michael forget the cynical truth about the North wealth. It attracted women who pretended a genuine interest in him when all they wanted was the use of his penthouse, his ranch, his helicopters, his private jets, his invitations to the right clubs, the best restaurants and the A-list parties. Unlike his brother, Michael wasn't above enjoying the women his money lured, but only for brief intervals.

Never again would he believe any woman wanted more from him than his luxurious lifestyle. Never again would he make the mistake of forming a serious attachment. Unfortunately Will, who'd had a more indulged childhood than Michael, was too trusting for his own good. It was up to Michael to save Will from Bree.

Soft summer moonlight turned the high ceilings of his loft and his large bed to shades of silver and gray. Bree's body felt warm; treacherously so as she nestled closer against him. Her cheap silver bangles and necklaces on the bedside table glittered. Her colorful, filmy clothes and scarves lay in tangles on the floor beside her sandals where he'd stripped her while she'd swayed to music, laughing.

The cozy heat of her satin-soft body lured him. He wanted to stay beside her, to see the shy warmth of her sweetly crooked smile and the flirtatious glow that lit her amber eyes every time he kissed her.

No, he had to finish her off—now—even if her sweet strawberry scent filled his nostrils and made him weak with the craving to bury his lips in her thick, satiny hair, to kiss her throat, to taste her mouth and other parts of her sexy, feminine anatomy just one more time.

Intoxicated by her soft, sensual allure, he lingered in

the bed beside her, torturing himself as he savored her warmth and remembered all the ways they'd made love.

She'd been so silky and tight the first time, like a velvet glove. When he'd pushed eagerly inside, holding her against the wall, she'd cried out. But when he'd stopped out of concern for her, she'd pressed her palms into the small of his spine and pleaded with him to stay—to stay forever if that was possible. Slowly her small body had accommodated itself to him. Driving into her, the pleasure of each stroke had been so total in its visceral thrill that fierce pleasure unlike any he had ever known had saturated every cell in his body.

She'd been a damn good actress, playing at virginal innocence, enticing him, then surrendering like a wanton. She'd nearly undone him. She'd almost made him believe that he alone, not his fortune, was special to her.

"Who knew?" she'd whispered with him sheathed inside her. "I like it. No, I love it." Then she'd stroked his cheek lovingly, her eyes shining with wonder. "I'm glad it's you. I never thought it would be half so nice. I always wanted to date someone as handsome and smart as you. I…I just never thought anybody like you…would look at a girl like me."

It had been nice for him, too, being with her. More than nice.

Special.

His world could be so cold, and she seemed so sweet. For one forbidden moment, when she'd kissed him as if she'd wanted to consume him, he'd lost himself in the searing hot, torrid welcome of her body. He'd almost forgotten to protect himself.

Every time he'd made love to her, even with a condom, the sex had gotten better. And each time afterward when she'd clung to him, she'd seemed sweeter. Whatever this thing was between them, it had shaken him to the core.

Hell, just thinking about her and what she'd done to him made him hard again, even as he lay beside her icily plotting his next step.

"Will said you were cold and uptight," she'd whispered.

He hadn't liked her comparing him to Will, but with every kiss and unassuming glance her power over him had increased. A connection to her built deep inside him and morphed into something that felt more than physical.

What had been going on?

Her mysterious white-hot appeal had fueled a compulsion that no other woman had ever aroused in him. She'd made him ravenous. Together their writhing bodies had burned and soared. His out-of-control excitement had felt addictive, tempting him to forget everything he knew about women like her. She'd provided some deeply needed comfort he hadn't known he'd craved until he'd experienced it in her arms. He had never known a real home, or felt at home with anyone, not even with the Norths, who'd given him their name and had claimed him as family. Not until tonight…with her.

She was dangerous. He had to rid himself of her quickly.

If he stalled for even one more night, she might have him totally in her power. He might even sink his own money into her bistro.

If he invested enough, would she favor him over Will?

Hell, he had the money. A part of him wanted her to prefer him to all others.

He swore. Such thoughts could derail him from his purpose. Just as he was about to throw off the covers and escape her so he could get his head straight, she whimpered. Clutching at his arms, she seemed to expect him to protect her from some mysterious terror.

"Michael…"

His heart throbbed. Oh, God.

Her voice was feminine, helpless. When her feather-light fingertips brushed his skin, he burned, aching for her all over again. No way could he resist her plea.

How old was she? Twenty-five? Ten years younger than he was? Or even younger? Whatever her age, with her thick, dark gold hair tumbling about her face and bare shoulders, her wild beauty dazzled him. She had a classic brow, a long, thin nose, high cheekbones, an incandescent complexion and full, voluptuous lips.

Not that she had the money or sense of style to dress properly. Her baggy, overlarge clothes had concealed and distracted more than they'd enhanced her beauty. But naked—with her tiny waist, curvy hips, soft breasts and those pert nipples exposed—she was perfect.

More than anything he wanted to roll her over, take her in his arms, hold her and pet her hair, and whisper that everything was all right. But nothing was all right. Not when he knew what she was—and what he had to do—and yet still felt so powerfully attracted to her.

Careful not to disturb her, he arose. He had to get a grip. But the minute he broke their physical connection, she sensed it and seemed to miss his presence as much as he missed hers.

"Michael," she purred in a sexy, sleep-blurred tone. "Darling, come back to bed."

"I'm not your darling," he growled, hating that on some level he wanted to be.

"Michael, I… Have I done something…?" At his harsh tone, her voice grew shy and uncertain before it died in the silvery darkness.

The powerful need to comfort her from the hurt he was determined to inflict wrapped around him.

Hell. He had to finish this—or he would go crazy.

"I'm not your darling," he repeated ruthlessly. "To-night, everything, all of it—it was all lies."

"Lies?"

"I seduced you to protect Will. From you. When you came on to me while I was with him at the fund-raiser, I knew what you were and saw how you intended to use him. You made my job easy when you made a play for me, too."

"What are you saying?"

"I'm saying I sought you out tonight and slept with you so I could use it as leverage to make you stop seeing my brother. Tonight was all about Will."

"Will?" She sounded confused. "Wait a minute. You think Will and I...that we're a couple? That we're dating? You...you don't like me?"

"How could I like you, knowing what you are?"

Having been poor himself, he knew all about wanting more, about using people to get what he wanted. He'd worked damned hard. Still, he'd done a few things he wasn't proud of to get where he was.

"You were after him, and then after me, because you needed our money for your failing restaurant."

"No," she whispered.

"Do you deny Will is one of your investors?"

"No." But her beautiful mouth trembled just a little, and her eyes were now glistening with unshed tears. "You... deceived me? You didn't really want me?"

He shook his head.

"Why? How could you do that? I would never use Will...or anybody. Will's a friend, and yes, he's an in-vestor. He's been an investor right from the beginning. But I'm not after his money! I'm not!"

"Then why did you hit on me so blatantly the night we met at the fund-raiser when you were with Will?"

"Maybe I flirted. But only because I thought you liked

me...." She sucked in a breath. "Will is just a friend. He was a friend of Johnny's first, and an investor in Chez Z when my brother first opened it. That's how Will and I became friends."

"Friends? That's all you were?"

The night of the fund-raiser she'd worn a silver backless gown and a transparent shawl that had left very little of her sensuous shape to his imagination.

Her family history hadn't helped his opinion of her. Six months ago, Johnny Z, her celebrity-chef brother, had been found dead in bed with a prominent plastic surgeon's wife, another of the bistro's investors. Everyone presumed the surgeon had shot Johnny, but the husband, who'd hired lawyers, wasn't talking to the police, and his wife had vanished. Thus, the investigation had stalled. Still, the scandal, coupled with Z's absence in the kitchen, had been devastating to Chez Z's bottom line.

"Will asked me to go with him to the fund-raiser, so he could introduce me to some people who might be interested in investing. When he introduced me to you, I thought you might be one of those people."

Her eyes were so brilliant with innocence and outrage he almost believed her. Then he remembered Anya and how gullible he'd been. He'd wanted to believe her. Capable as he might be in the business world, apparently he was an easy mark when it came to women he wanted in his bed.

"Bottle the performance! If you think I'm as big a fool as my little brother, you're wrong. I want you to dress and leave. If you stay away from Will, I won't tell him I slept with you tonight. If you don't leave him alone, I'll tell him about us."

"Tell him for all I care. Better—maybe I'll tell him myself. He needs to know how far you'll go to control his life. Maybe he'll resent you even more than he already does."

Her reaction caught him off guard. He'd expected her to care more, to bargain, and what she'd said about Will hurt.

"He can't afford to resent me," Michael bluffed. "I write his allowance checks."

"So everything's just about money and control to you? And you think I'm like you—"

"I know you are! So, leave my brother alone, and I won't make him think the worst of you by telling him about us. You bet on the wrong horse this time. Pick another. Someone who isn't naive. Someone more like you and me."

"Tell him. I'm not like you, and you can't blackmail me, either."

"You are like me. Greed isn't the only thing we have in common," he replied coldly. "If Will didn't desire you, I'd be willing to set you up as my mistress. I'd keep you and your bistro afloat for as long you excited me."

"*Do you ever listen?* For the last time, your brother and I are just friends. That's why he won't care if you slept with me. He was just an investor in the bistro. He already has someone in his life."

"Really—who?"

Michael knew she was lying when she faltered and said, "Maybe you should ask him."

If only Will did have someone, then Michael could have Bree for himself. He could afford her a helluva lot more easily than Will, couldn't he?

Suddenly Michael reconsidered the situation. Where was the harm in keeping her, if she wasn't serious about Will? As long as he understood what she was and was willing to be generous to her?

"Okay, then, *if* Will doesn't want you because he has someone else, there's nothing to stop me from having you. Here's a new deal for you. If you cut Will loose as an investor and become my mistress, I'll keep your bistro afloat for as long as you please me in bed."

"What?" She stared at him as if she was having a hard time comprehending him.

"You heard me. Be my mistress, and your money problems will go away for as long as you keep me happy. Like you did tonight."

"I can't believe this. First you sleep with me to destroy an imagined relationship with your brother. And now you want to buy me for yourself? I'm sorry I ever met you."

"I'm sure you'll feel differently after you shop for the right apartment in the neighborhood of your choice and we settle on your generous allowance."

"Now you wait a minute!"

"You want to save the bistro, don't you? We enjoy each other, so why not?"

She pushed herself up from the bed. "You can't just buy people!"

"You'd be surprised what money buys."

"Well, I'm not for sale."

"I doubt that. I just haven't made you the right offer. Tell me what you want, and we'll negotiate."

"I can't believe I ever thought for one second that you were a decent human being." Her expression twisted in utter misery. "And I did. I really did. I can't believe I've been such a fool…again." She sighed. "This just proves what I told you earlier—I don't have very good instincts about men. I think you're the worst of them all…and I have to tell you, that's pretty low."

Her rejection stunned him. Too late Michael saw that he should have flattered her, that he should have seduced her into the deal as he had seduced her into his bed. Obviously she was like all the criminals in prison who proclaimed their innocence; she really didn't see that she had done anything wrong. That's where they were different.

At least he knew when he'd crossed the line and was willing to accept the inevitable consequences.

"I'll call my chauffeur," he said coldly, hiding his disappointment. "He'll be at the front door downstairs in five minutes to escort you out of the building. He'll drive you anywhere you wish to go. After tonight I don't ever want to see you with my brother again. Do you understand?"

"You can't order me around…or your brother, who is an adult, and who is, whether you like it or not, one of my key investors. I fully intend to see him as often as I like! He has every right to invest *his* money where he chooses."

"You're very wrong."

Michael turned his back and strode out of the room because the sight of her shimmering, pain-filled eyes, her quivering lips and her bare breasts were more than he could bear. Damn it, in spite of her rejection, in spite of what she was and how she was using Will, he still wanted her.

Only when he heard her rushing down his spiral staircase to the lower floor—she never used an elevator unless she had to because she was afraid of them—only when he heard his front door slam downstairs, did Michael return to his bedroom.

For a long moment he stood in the dark and stared out at the city that sparkled beneath a full moon and a starless sky. It was a beautiful night, he supposed, a night made for romance, if one believed in such things. He wondered if his failure to do so was due to the many flaws in his soul.

Growing bored with the view he left the window and turned on every light. Never had the vast marble bedroom in his penthouse apartment blazed with such cold and terrible brightness.

Only when he saw the bright splashes of red staining

his sheet did he realize that maybe he'd been wrong about at least one thing.

Had she been a virgin? His heart, which usually felt so solid behind its frozen walls, began to beat with vicious, guilty pain. Surely no virgin would have shown such a wild, uninhibited response. And yet…

When he remembered her little cry when he'd first entered her, and her sweetness, and the admiration in her eyes when he'd discussed some of his projects with her, he recoiled. What if she had been an innocent? What if he, who'd been raised so roughly, had failed to see goodness because it had been such a rarity in his life?

"If I could succeed at even one thing, I'd feel so proud of myself," she had confided. "And look at you—you turned the family investment firm around right after the last global financial meltdown. Now you're opening banks and hotels in China and power plants in Malaysia. You conquer worlds—and accept such feats as your due. Your family must be so proud of you." Her shining eyes had warmed him through.

If he'd been wrong about her virginity, had he been wrong about other things? Had she truly admired his accomplishments? Had she liked him, at least a little? Had he wounded her? And what was she really to Will?

No.

Damn it. He was sure of her ulterior motives. With her famous brother dead, his image trashed and their once popular bistro on the Upper West Side in trouble, she'd been after Will for his money. Then she had zeroed in on Michael at the fund-raiser when she'd seen a better mark. The only reason she'd turned down Michael's second offer was because he'd wounded her pride.

As he yanked the sheets off his bed, he remembered her radiant complexion and the wonder in her eyes and his own intense pleasure. Sheathed to the hilt, he'd felt all male and powerful and yet happy in a bone-melting way he'd never known before.

If she was what he believed, why had she turned him down? Why?

Michael tried and failed to push his gnawing doubts aside. Damn it, he had to know why. But he couldn't face her tonight.

They both deserved a few hours to recover from his brutal offer and her rejection. Tomorrow morning would be soon enough to confront her again.

But by morning she was gone.

After he bribed the doorman to let him in to her empty apartment, he stomped about flinging her cupboards open while he dialed her cell phone, which went to voice mail. For more than an hour he searched for some clue as to where she'd gone and found none. His texts were ignored. When he went to Chez Z, her steely-eyed French mother, Bijou, had been in a meeting with the waitstaff.

"She said she had to go somewhere," her mother said coolly, when he'd insisted upon interrupting her. "She said it was an emergency. She looked upset. I didn't pry. Now, I wish I'd asked more questions. Are you the problem? Is she in trouble because of you?"

"No."

"Well! She is no good with men. In fact, that's an understatement. She's *pathetic*. She took after me, you see. Her father did everything he could to ruin my life. If you aren't going to treat her right, stay away from her, yes?"

What could he say to that? Despite the circumstances, he envied Bree for having such a mother. He hadn't been so lucky.

When Michael went to his brother's to warn him about Bree, Will refused to let Michael into his apartment.

"She already told me what you accused her of," Will said, standing with the door half-closed to keep Michael in the hall. "I don't know where she is, and frankly, I wouldn't tell you if I did. You've overstepped the line."

"She said you were seeing another woman? Are you?"

Will, who usually had an easy nature, scowled. "Right now, maybe you can guess why I don't choose to discuss my personal life with you."

Then he shut the door in Michael's face.

Michael felt guilty and uneasy. What was Will hiding? Not only had Bree rejected him, she'd turned his brother against him. Will wouldn't even confirm he was dating someone else, so did that mean he was still interested in Bree? If Will was involved with another woman, what the hell had Michael accomplished by bedding Bree other than becoming obsessed with her himself?

The odds were he was right about her character. Maybe she was gone, but what good was that if Will felt more protective of her than ever? Instead of turning his brother against her, all he'd done was make his brother angry with him.

Despite everything, Michael burned for her. No matter how hard he tried to bury himself in his work during the weeks that followed, no matter where he traveled or how many glamorous women he publicly dated in the attempt to prove to himself and to her how little she mattered, he couldn't forget her.

Even when he left on what proved to be a month-long business trip to Shanghai to solve a crisis at one of his hotels, memories of her sweetness and outraged innocence lingered, haunting him.

The perfection of their night together drove him mad—especially after he learned that the same day he'd left New York, she'd returned to her bistro and had lunched with Will.

Had she deliberately remained hidden until he was gone? Was she that afraid of him?

What was her game? How could he stop her and save Will?

Two

Eight weeks later

Will has to be okay. He has to be.

As his heart beat in panic, Michael slammed through the heavy steel emergency-room doors with his dripping briefcase. When Pedro, his assistant who'd notified him about the accident, wasn't at the entrance, Michael had rushed inside and hurried down a crowded hall that was a blur of nondescript floor tiles and pale green walls, beds, patients and visitors.

Michael had been trying to call Bree from his limo on the drive through thick rain from JFK airport into the city. When all he could get was her voice mail, he'd decided to stop by Chez Z on the way to his office to confront her again. He'd just pulled up at the curb outside the bistro when Pedro had called him to tell him Will had been in an accident.

"Where's Will North?" Michael demanded of the

nurses in dark scrubs at the nurses' station. "I'm his brother. I got a call a while ago that he was in an accident and that he'd been brought here by EMTs."

"North?" Nurses looked up from their papers and stilled. When they didn't answer him, maybe because they had to choose their words carefully, he sensed the gravity of his brother's condition.

Oh, God. It was bad.

"Where is he?" Michael demanded in a hoarse voice he didn't recognize as his own. "What happened?"

Ask a tough question....

An older nurse with a kindly face gave him the bare facts.

A head-on collision in the heavy rain. Tony Ferrar, who was apparently his brother's friend and the driver, died at the scene. The driver of the SUV that struck them, a twenty-four-year-old woman who'd possibly been drunk or texting, had flown across the median of the interstate and collided head-on with Will's Mercedes. She'd died at the scene. Will had removed his seat belt and thrown himself in front of his wife. As a result he'd suffered back injuries, head injuries and multiple fractures. He needed immediate surgery.

The nurse's words buzzed in Michael's head.

"Wife?"

Was that what Will had wanted to tell him over lunch today? Had he married his secret girlfriend?

On some level Michael's numbed brain faced the harsh reality of his brother's injuries. On another, he refused to accept that his younger brother could be so seriously injured.

Not Will. Michael had called him from Shanghai last night. When Michael had asked him about Bree, Will had refused to discuss her.

"I have some big news. I'll give you an update over lunch tomorrow," was all he'd said.

"Can I see my brother...before his surgery?" Michael demanded of the nurse.

"Of course. But don't say much or you'll tire him."

Only when he saw Will's gray face washed of all color, and Will's body shrunken and as still as death did the gravity of Will's injuries finally hit Michael.

"Will. Can you hear me? It's me. Michael," he said gently.

Tubes hissed and gurgled. His brother, whose bruised face was swathed in bloodstained bandages, stirred faintly. His mouth quivered, and he seemed to struggle to focus on Michael's face.

"Don't talk," Michael commanded.

"Have to... No time... You know, they're wrong about your life passing before your eyes." Will's voice was so thready Michael had to lean close to his brother's lips to hear it. "It's the future you'll never have...that matters."

"Don't waste your strength trying to talk. You're young. You're going to be okay. I swear it."

"Not even you can fix this. But you can do one thing for me...."

"Anything."

"Take care of Bree."

"What?"

"Bree... She's...my wife," Will gasped.

"Bree? You married Bree?"

"She's pregnant. No time to explain. We didn't want to tell you like this. Just promise me...that you'll take care of her and...the baby."

"The baby?"

"She's pregnant and hurt. I don't know how badly. We were in the backseat. Tony was driving. Tony's dead.... Tried...to save her...for you."

"For me…"

"You care about her."

Sweat broke out on Michael's forehead. His hands opened and closed in fists as fury and concern for her and grief for his brother tore at him.

One thing was very clear. She'd lied about her relationship to Will. They had been involved. After she'd slept with Michael, she'd gone back to Will as easy as you please, gotten herself pregnant by him so he'd marry her. They'd kept it all a secret from Michael until he'd gotten back from Shanghai.

Will had been so dazzled by Bree he'd removed his own seat belt to protect her.

Then Michael remembered that Will would receive a million dollars from the North trust when he married, as well as a sizable increase in his allowance. He would receive even more once the child was born.

Had Will informed Bree about all those benefits? Probably.

Her treachery didn't matter right now. Only Will mattered.

His brother's glazed eyes read Michael like a book. "I know you don't think you like her. And I knew you wouldn't approve of our marriage, but she's been through a rough time. She's a wonderful girl. Not a gold digger like you think."

Michael swore silently. His brother was so hopelessly naive.

"What you did to her…was all my fault."

"Whatever I did, I did it for you," Michael said.

"Understood. So, promise me…you'll take care of her. If you'll do this one thing for me, we'll be square."

No way could Michael promise that.

"Promise me," Will insisted.

The room felt stale and airless. His brother looked so

pale—Michael couldn't say no to him. He yanked at his collar and tore at his tie that was damp from the rain. He wanted to run out of the room, to get outside, to breathe fresh air.

Through gritted teeth he said, "I promise I'll take care of your wife." Carefully Michael took his brother's limp hand and pressed it lightly. "I'll even shake on it."

"And her restaurant. Help her save it."

Michael nodded.

Satisfied, Will's heavy eyelids drooped shut.

A few seconds later an older male nurse in blue scrubs rushed up to the gurney and flipped through Will's chart. Without a word, he bent over his patient.

Michael stood in the doorway and watched the man wheel his brother away, watched until they vanished down the long hall. The sounds of people rushing past him died. All he could hear was his own heart. Would he ever see his brother alive again?

Suddenly he felt very cold, and very much alone, as alone as he'd been as a kid. Since he couldn't stand forever in an empty hall staring at waxed floor tiles and feeling sorry for himself, he turned and headed back to the nurse's station where he found Pedro, who took Michael to Bree.

Two women, probably family, hovered over Bree. She lay on a narrow bed that had been curtained off from the other beds in the large room.

Michael held out his hand. "I'm Michael North, Will's brother. Her brother-in-law."

The older woman took his hand. "I'm Bijou, her mother. Wait! I never forget a face. You're that handsome rich guy that came to the restaurant looking for her, yes? I thought maybe you gave her some trouble, yes?"

Heat washed through him. "Yes."

"I'm Marcie," the pretty blonde beside Bijou said. "I wait tables for Bree and Bijou. Bree's just the sweetest person in the whole world. So is Will. I can't believe that two such super people…"

"Marcie! You need to be strong, *oui!*" Bijou turned to Michael. "We'll give you a minute with her," she said. "But only a minute."

When they left, Michael moved closer to Bree's bed. Her thick lashes were still against her bloodless cheeks, so she didn't see him at first. Dark circles ringed her eyes. More than a dozen bruises and livid cuts covered her arms and cheeks. At the sight of her injuries, he choked on a breath.

She looked so slim and fragile in her hospital gown, he felt a stab of fear. She was carrying his brother's child, and Michael had sworn he'd take care of her.

Despite the money she must have been after when she'd married Will, Michael's resentment toward her faded. If Will died, her child would be Michael's last link to his brother.

"Bree? Can you hear me? It's Michael. When I got in from Shanghai I heard about the accident. I came at once."

"Michael…" Her lashes fluttered weakly, and for an instant her face lit up with pleasure…and with some other more luminous emotion that thrilled him. Her eyes had shone like that when he'd first entered her.

In the next second she must have remembered what he'd done because her gaze went flat and cold. "Where's Bijou? What are you doing here? I want my mother back."

"Your mother's right outside. Will asked me to check on you, so I'm here," Michael said softly.

"Will asked you…" She let out a harsh sob and turned her face to the wall. "I don't believe you! He's as fed up with you as I am! Go away!"

Michael felt conscience-stricken and confused, which wasn't like him.

"I don't need you here," she said to the wall, her tone so

low he could barely hear her. "Will knows that, so you're lying if you say he sent you."

"He did. He was facing surgery, and I think he was afraid."

She sucked in a breath. "Oh, God… I'm being so selfish. Tony's dead and maybe Will won't…and he's in there scared and alone…and thinking of me. He's so good."

"Yes, he is." Michael's voice was hard and condemning.

When she jerked her head around to stare at him again, he noted how the soft blue fabric of her hospital gown molded against her breasts. "They told me how badly Will was hurt. They didn't want to. But I made them. If he dies, it will be all my fault. He took off his seat belt…right before that SUV shot across the median and rammed us. Will saw it coming and threw himself in front of me…to protect me and the baby. Poor Tony never had a chance."

"Who's Tony?"

An odd, almost sorrowful expression passed swiftly over her bruised face. Clutching her sheet, she looked away. "Will's best friend. He was driving."

"Funny. I've never met him."

She chewed her bottom lip. "I imagine you were too wrapped up in money matters to really involve yourself in your brother's personal life—except when it came to me—because you saw me as a financial threat."

Her words hurt more than they should have. "Will said you and he were expecting a baby."

Her face went even whiter, if that were possible.

"H-he had no right to talk to you about the baby. He swore to me he wouldn't."

"He asked me to take care of you…and the baby…in case…"

She shuddered. "It just gets worse, doesn't it? You and me—stuck together…maybe without Will?"

"It's probably just a precaution. I promised him I would. If…if the worst happens. I intend to keep my word."

"Really? Your word?" She tipped her head back and frowned, studying him. "As if that means something." She took a deep, stabilizing breath. "Just go away."

"I intend to honor my promise—whether or not you want me to," he said.

"You deliberately deceived me, to get me to do things I find truly humiliating now. How could I have been so foolish?"

Sensual, erotic things he'd dreamed of her doing to him again.

"I thought I'd found the one person—never mind!" she snapped. "You made it very clear how you really felt about me at a moment when I was most tender and open and vulnerable to you. I don't know how all those other women feel, the ones you date for a night or two, but let me be very clear. You are the last person I would ever want in my life, even casually. I don't care if you're Will's brother and my baby's…uncle, or that you feel a duty to keep your promise. I do not want to see you. I do not want my child to know you. Do you understand?"

Her words cut Michael deeply. Curiously, he felt guilt, as well. Why should he feel that when he'd been trying to protect his tenderhearted brother who had proven time and again he was too trusting when it came to people who were after his money?

Not that Michael showed his pain at her words by even the flicker of his dark eyelashes. Having grown up poor, in a rough Houston neighborhood near the ship channel, he'd learned to put on a tough mask whenever he felt the slightest weakness. His mother had barely eked out a living as a masseuse before Jacob North had married her and adopted him.

Until Jacob, his mother had gone from man to man,

taking whatever they offered to survive. Michael had worked on the docks so he wouldn't be dependent on such handouts. He'd hated having nothing and being treated like nothing and feeling ashamed of how they'd lived. He'd learned early on that when you didn't have it, money was everything.

Will, on the other hand, had grown up a rich man's adored only son. Will had loved everybody, especially his older adopted brother, whom he'd accepted right from the first. Maybe Will was the only person who'd ever loved Michael. He'd promised Jacob, to whom he owed everything, that he would look out for Will. Those feelings of profound responsibility carried over to Will's unborn child, even if that child's mother was someone he could never trust.

"If Will dies, Will's child—your child—will be a North heir. Then there's the promise I made to my brother. Whether or not you want me in your life, I intend to take a very active interest in that little person from now on."

"So this is about money and control? My child is nothing more to you than the possible heir to the North fortune."

Why should he let her know what Will's child meant to him when she would only use such knowledge against him?

"A fortune does carry a huge responsibility."

"I'll bet you're used to getting your way."

She was right about that.

Her eyes darkened. "Well, you won't. Not with me. Never again."

"We'll see," he said. Then he let it drop. He fully intended to win this battle, but he wouldn't bully the pregnant wife of his injured brother.

"I want you to go," she said.

"Too bad."

When he sank down into the chair beside her bed, she glared at him. At his thin smile, she shut her eyes and twisted her face away. As he stared at her stiff back, he knew she couldn't force him out of her thoughts any more than he could force her out of his. Just being in the same room with her, even when she was injured, disturbed him.

An hour later, she was still rigid and seething when Will's grim, hollow-eyed surgeon found them.

"Mr. North? Mrs. North?"

When she opened her eyes and met Michael's, she blushed.

"I'm Will North's wife," she said. "Michael North is my brother-in-law."

"I see. Sorry about the confusion."

Michael had only to look into the surgeon's shadowed eyes to know the worst. Will was gone. Slowly Michael stood and shook the man's hand, listening, asking the appropriate questions, thanking him even as ice closed around his heart.

Bree let out a hoarse sob midway through the surgeon's detailed explanation.

"Your brother lost a lot of blood at the scene...."

Michael's vision blurred. He felt himself near some fatal edge. Maybe to steel his own nerves, he concentrated on Bree, whose face had gone as white as her sheets. Leaning over her hospital bed, he took her trembling hand. At his touch, she stiffened. Then, to his surprise, her fingers tightened around his, and she tugged him closer. Grabbing fistfuls of his jacket, she threw her wet face against his broad shoulder and burrowed into it. Clinging to him, she wept soundlessly.

His suit would be a mess tomorrow, but he needed to hold her, needed it more than he had ever imagined needing anything. Despite his own hideous sorrow and the profound gulf that separated them, he was glad Bree was here, glad not to be completely alone with his grief.

"Bree," he murmured. Careful not to hurt her, his arms closed around her. "It's going to be okay."

"You don't know, so how can you say that?"

"Time has a way—" He broke off, unable to repeat the usual trite phrases people offered one another for comfort.

Strangely, holding her seemed to be enough. Never had he felt more powerfully connected to another human being as her tears rained down his cheek.

After a long time she said, "Tell my mother and Marcie… about Will. Please…" Her voice was choked. "I just can't."

"Anything," he murmured as he let her go. "I'll do anything you want."

"Really? Excuse me if I find it hard to believe that the man with no heart is now willing to do anything for me."

"You're pregnant with Will's child, and he's gone. Everything's different between us now."

"Yes. Will's child," she repeated softly.

"There's nothing I wouldn't do for Will's baby, and, therefore, for you."

Three

The pain meds must have made her daft. Why else would she have agreed to spend the night—no, seven nights—at Will's loft with Michael?

Because your Victorian brownstone has stairs—three tall flights of them—and no elevator, remember?

The fact that her building had no elevator had never been a problem before. Okay, so she didn't like elevators or any small, boxy room. With her history, who would?

When she'd been a kid, an older cousin had locked her in a closet and left her there while he'd gone out to play. She'd been hysterical by the time her mother, who'd been busy in the kitchen downstairs, had found her. Every time the doors of an elevator closed Bree remembered Jeremy's gloating smile right before he'd shut the door and turned out the light.

Bree chewed a nail as Michael jammed the key into the door of Will's loft apartment in the Village. Maybe if she deliberately goaded Michael, he'd decide looking after her wasn't worth it.

"I can't believe, that as frequently as you saw your brother, you've never been inside his place before now," she said.

Michael's mouth tightened. "What do you know about it?"

She smiled. "Oh—did I hit a nerve?"

"He used to have me to his place on the Upper East Side all the time," Michael snapped, "but for some reason he didn't want me dropping by anymore when he moved here. Usually we met at my penthouse or somewhere in the city. I did stop by a couple of times, but he was either just going out or his roommate was home and they were busy. I didn't understand why he needed a roommate when he could have easily afforded to live alone. When I asked him about it, he said the guy was a good friend who needed a place to stay."

"R-right," she said uneasily, deciding to back up Will's lie. "He…he was still living here when we married."

"Must have been crowded, you two being newlyweds and all."

She didn't like his tone but refused to comment.

When Michael finished unlocking the door, he caught her elbow to usher her inside.

Startled by the fire in even that brief touch, Bree jumped back. How could she feel anything for a man who'd used her and had lied to her? He was the last person she wanted helping her. But he *was* Will's brother.

"This really isn't necessary," she said, hoping she didn't sound as nervous as she felt. "You don't want to be stuck with me any more than I want you here. Why don't you make it easy on us both and just leave?"

"I'm staying," he said in a tone that was raw and intense. "You can fight about it. Or you can make the best of it. Your choice."

The carved lines of his face looked powerful and strong—implacable. She was much too weak, exhausted and woozy from the pain meds to fight him. When he nudged her inside, she let him.

"Whoa!" Michael said, obviously taken aback by the dramatic design of the apartment and its furnishings. "This is truly amazing, totally different than his other place. I didn't know Will had something like this in him."

There's a lot you didn't know about him.

Strangely, the thought made her feel sorry for Michael.

Tony, who was a top designer and world-famous in certain circles, had put the apartment together. Not Will. The airy rooms with their skylights and soaring ceilings, and dramatic art collection and colorful, minimalistic furnishings screamed Tony.

Not Will, and not her. It wouldn't be long before Michael picked up on the fact that she hadn't really lived here.

Maybe there was a piece of paper from city hall that said she and Will were married, but there was very little of her here. A chipped coffee mug or two, a pair of her jeans and panties and a favorite sweater with a cat on it in the single drawer Will had emptied for her.

She'd slept on their couch for a couple of weeks wondering how she'd ever forget Michael and get clear of the mess she'd made of her life because of him. The only two things she'd been sure about were that she wanted her baby and she wanted to get Z's bistro back on its financial feet. Will had promised to help in every way he could, both personally and financially.

"I really think I'll be fine on my own here."

"Hey, we've been over that. You heard what the doctor said," Michael murmured in the same gentle, mesmerizing tone he'd used to seduce her. "You're pregnant. You have a nasty bump on the head. Your blood pressure is a little low, and you shouldn't be alone for the next week."

He *almost* sounded concerned.

Reminding herself that he didn't care about her, she also reminded herself that she was okay with that. She refused to care about anybody as cold and unfeeling as him. She stepped farther inside, only to feel truly trapped when he slammed the door, stripped off his expensive jacket and flung it toward the sofa.

"I don't want you here. You are the last person I want to be with tonight when I feel so utterly miserable."

"Understood. Ditto."

"Underline ditto," she cried.

"But here we are—together." Grimly, he bolted the various locks from the inside. "It might be dangerous for your baby, my niece or nephew, if I don't stay. Like you said, your mother has cats, and you're allergic to them."

Why was he acting as though he cared?

"From what the papers have said lately, I'd think you'd surely have some gorgeous supermodel waiting in your bed to welcome you home from China," she muttered, dragging her gaze from his wide shoulders.

After the fund-raiser when she'd been so dazzled by him, she'd researched him online. She'd been dismayed to learn about all the glamorous women he dated. After her one night with him, he'd gone right back to dating those women. How could she have thought he was interested in her that night? The eagerness she'd felt for him and the things she'd done in his bed still mortified her.

His jet brows winged upward in cynical surprise. "Jealous?"

Despite her grief and exhaustion, hot indignation that he'd hit a nerve flared inside her. "Only you, who are so arrogant and sure of yourself, would take it like that."

"Yeah, only me—the number one ogre in your sweet, innocent life." His grin was savagely ironic. "You didn't answer my question, sweetheart. Are you jealous?"

"Don't be insane! It's just that I couldn't help noticing an item or two about you and several models in the gossip columns. Did you go out with them to destroy them, too?"

When a muscle jerked in his jawline, she almost wondered if she'd hurt him. Then she remembered he didn't have a heart.

After an ominous pause, he said, "There's no supermodel…if you must know. Hell, there's nobody waiting, which is pretty normal. So, tell me about you and Will. I was shocked when he told me you were married, especially after you'd told me you weren't interested in him that way. How did it happen? And when?"

She turned away to hide her eyes, lest she give something away. "He asked me. I said yes. Unlike you, he's a really nice guy."

"Which made him perfect prey for a woman like you."

"You're wrong. About him and me." She stopped. There was no way she could defend herself without getting into deeper trouble.

"Forget it," she said. "I don't care what you think."

But she did.

Frowning, Michael paced the length of Will's dazzling white room with its grand piano and splashes of paintings and sculptures. He stopped abruptly to look at the photographs of Will and Tony on Tony's piano.

Panic surged through her when he lifted one.

"Who's the big guy in leather?"

She moved toward the shiny black piano. Not that she had to see the picture up close to know that it was Tony in his trademark black biker attire with rings in his ears. In the photograph, he and Will were toasting Johnny and her at a party at Chez Z. It had been only a few months ago, to celebrate the restaurant's success. Will had been ecstatic to be part of a successful venture and to share his happiness with Tony.

Tears misted her eyes. How could so much change so fast? How could they both be gone?

"It's Tony," she said

"The driver? He was Will's best friend who died at the scene? He was Will's roommate, too?"

"And our best man," she said.

And so much more.

Michael slowly set the picture back on the piano beside the others of Tony and Will with different friends. "Tell me again why you married Will."

She backed away. "Do we have to talk about this?"

"You asked me about *my* love life." A dangerous edge had crept into his soft voice. "Did you want him, my brother, as much as you wanted me?"

It made her sick to remember how much she'd wanted Michael; sick to think that even now he wasn't entirely unattractive to her. She wanted to believe he wasn't the man she knew he was, wanted to believe he cared, at least a little. But he'd told her in no uncertain terms how he felt about her, so she steeled herself.

"I married him, didn't I?"

"Why?"

Because of what you did to me. Because your wonderful, caring brother wanted to help me and take care of me, which was something he knew you'd never do. Because I didn't know what else to do.

He seemed to sense her vulnerability. Her heart skittered as his large, tanned hand closed over hers, making escape impossible. His dark eyes flashed with alarming passion as he drew her to him.

She averted her gaze from his handsome face. He'd been so cruel, and she'd fought so hard to forget him.

Why couldn't she? He'd only had to walk into her hospital room this afternoon to make her remember how he'd dazzled her.

Then he'd accused her of being a gold digger and worse.

"I've thought about you," he muttered. "Thought about that night, about everything we did and said, even though all I wanted was to forget you. Even now—when I know you were lying about your relationship with Will all along, you still get under my skin."

Ditto.

Feeling on the verge of a meltdown, she tried to wrench free. It was clear that he'd hated his involvement with her, that he wanted nothing to do with her. And it still hurt—more than it should have, even now when she knew how cold and cruel he was.

When his burning eyes stared into hers, she began to shake because she was terrified he would see her pain and understand how gullible she still was.

He held on to her and drew her closer. "How the hell could you marry my brother?"

Her pulse thrummed. As always when she was in his arms, he aroused forbidden needs.

She had to remember he'd deliberately used her, not caring how he hurt her. He still despised her. She couldn't trust anything he said or did.

Michael certainly did not deserve the truth.

"Why did you marry him?" he asked again.

"It's complicated."

"I'm good at complicated, so tell me. Or better yet, show me," he whispered.

"I don't know what you mean."

"Don't you?"

Suddenly his hands were in her hair, stroking the dark silken gold that fell against her nape. His fingertips followed the sensuous curve of her neck before he cupped her chin and lifted her slender face to his, his touch as gentle and seductive as it had been that night.

Frantically, because it would be so easy to lose herself to the emotions that blazed in his eyes, she fought to resist him.

If only he had a real heart. If only she could truly depend on him and didn't have to be afraid of how she felt. But she knew, and even so, he aroused her.

Her skin burned and her knees went weak. He had only to touch her to make her yearn for his tenderness. Had there been a night since she'd seen him last that she hadn't ached to have him hold her like this and make her feel loved again? To look at her as he was looking at her now, with eyes that devoured her, adored her?

The craving for all the things only he could make her feel became too much to resist. Without thinking, she arched her back and opened her lips, inviting his mouth to claim hers. His tongue entered her. In an instant, the rightness of his searing kiss, and her hunger, were a thousand times stronger than what she'd experienced before.

She had to fight him. She knew what he was about. But the room was spinning and she was clinging, melting, falling. As he pulled her closer, every feminine cell pulsed with the desire to surrender to him in the hope he felt something deeper than he could admit.

All that mattered was that she'd longed for him, and he'd returned. She felt him, erect with a fierce masculine need he couldn't hide as he pressed against her. No matter how he'd denied his feelings, there was a raw, elemental truth in his kisses. In that moment she believed he was as helpless as she to fight the explosive chemistry between them.

Again and again he kissed her, leaving her shaken from the bittersweet joy of being with him again. His tongue dipped deeply inside her mouth and sent a tremor through her. When his grip tightened around her waist, she realized he was trembling even more than she was.

Time seemed to slow as he made love to her with his mouth and tongue, as his hands moved down her curves. She'd missed him, though she'd denied it.

She couldn't deny it now as his hands slid downward to cup her bottom and bring her closer to the powerful, masculine heat of his arousal.

Throwing caution aside, her hands traced over his hard body before sliding inside his waistband. In her desperation she ripped his shirt out of his slacks. But when she caressed his hard abs, he shuddered, let out a savage cry and then tore his lips from hers.

Cursing her softly, he took a step backward, even as he retained a grip on her arm to steady her when she began to sway.

"What's wrong?" she whispered, aching for more.

"You answered my question," he said, his cold, flat voice reducing the tenderness and warmth that burned inside her to ashes. "You still want me—which means you married Will for cold, calculating reasons. You are every bit as low as I thought. I'll never forgive you for using my brother like that. You didn't care how you were going to hurt him, did you? Not as long as you got what you wanted."

"What?" In shock, her wild eyes met his icy ones.

Who was using who? How could Michael kiss her like that and then shut her out again just when she felt so passionately aroused and open to him? Just when she believed there might be feelings beneath his passion. Had he really kissed her like that only to prove a point?

She swallowed and fought to find some control within herself, but she was too close to the edge, too vulnerable. She had been through too much today. She wanted Michael, and he despised her.

"I don't want you. My resistance must be low because they gave me painkillers. I—I didn't know what I was doing."

"Well, you can believe that if it makes you feel better," he began with a calm disdain that chilled her to the marrow. "But you want me, all right."

Because I'm a human being, and I thought you cared.

"So, do you need help undressing or running a bath?"

"What?" His curt, dismissive change of subject hurt.

Surely she would lose all self-respect if he stripped her and touched her and made her even more aware of him as a man while he regarded her with such cool contempt.

Never again would she let him arouse her deepest feelings and play her for a fool. *Never again.*

"I can take care of myself," she snapped, furious. She was weak and injured tonight and that had made her highly susceptible. He'd taken advantage of her.

"Then I suggest you get started," he said.

"I don't want to bathe with you here."

"Then pretend I'm not here."

"Impossible."

"The only reason I'm looking after you is because I made a promise to my brother. Trust me, I'll leave you alone. I didn't kiss you because I wanted to. I kissed you to find out if you wanted my brother, the poor bastard. You didn't. So, go in the bedroom, shut the door and get ready for bed."

How could she stay here with him? How could she pretend he wasn't here while she undressed, when awareness of him still buzzed in her blood despite his icy disdain?

"While I'm waiting for my turn to shower, I'll see what there is to eat and make some business calls."

"Right—the all-important CEO who's always so busy looking after the North fortune he doesn't have time to be human."

"Damn you, I've got other things to do besides baby-sit you. I've got work," he growled. "Lots of it." Turning his back on her, he pulled out his phone and sank down on the couch.

Infuriating man.

Whoever answered on the other end must have begun by offering his or her condolences immediately because Michael lowered his voice and hunched over the phone, his expression haggard as he talked about Will. So, he wasn't totally unfeeling. He just didn't care for her.

Her heart constricted as she heard him going over some checklist about funeral arrangements, and Bree imagined he'd forgotten her. Surrendering to his will, partly because she couldn't bear to listen as he finalized the details of Will's memorial service, she padded softly toward Will and Tony's bedroom.

As she entered it, Michael cupped the receiver. "Don't lock the door," he ordered. "If you faint, I'll need to get in. If I can't open the door, I'll break it down. Do we understand each other?"

Exhaustion and frayed nerves and what was left her desire had her so close to the edge she felt like screaming. Or weeping hysterically. "You're such a brute! I don't want you here. And I don't have to do what you say. I don't! I can't stand you!"

"We've already had this discussion. The doctor released you on the condition you'd remain under my care until your checkup next week because you were spotting. You agreed."

As if he cares about the baby, she thought dismally.

"*Next week!*" she moaned aloud. "I was in so much pain, I was out of my mind to agree to a week with you."

"Bottom line—you agreed," he said. "So, you'll damn well do what I say, or I'll make you!"

She shut the door. Then, thinking about the way he'd

kissed her and rejected her—as if she was nothing—she opened the door and then slammed it so hard its frame shook. Not that the childish action gave her any satisfaction.

Her gaze ran over the guys' bright, modern bedroom. Being in Will and Tony's private space brought the loss she felt for them to the surface again. They'd been so sweet to her. Feeling confused, grief-stricken and concerned about her unborn baby, she went into their bathroom where she stared at her white, bruised face in the huge, carved mirror they'd told her they'd bought on a recent trip to Oaxaca.

Cuts and purple bruises covered her gray skin. Blood stiffened several locks of her hair. How could she have imagined Michael desired her?

He didn't want her. He never had, and he certainly didn't care about her. No, he disliked her. He'd seduced her to drive a wedge between her and Will. Tonight he'd kissed her and used his expertise at lovemaking merely to prove that he had her where he wanted her. His only interest in her had always been using her to protect the North fortune. For that same reason, he was interested in the baby. The baby was his heir.

If only she hadn't agreed to Will's plan. Then Michael wouldn't be here, and she wouldn't have kissed him again and relearned how powerfully she still felt about him. Nor would she have had to endure realizing how much he despised her.

Choking back a sob, she began to strip.

Michael couldn't stop thinking about Bree alone in Will's bedroom.

Had she and his brother been happy in that bed together? Even though a part of Michael hoped she'd made his brother happy, another more selfish part resented any connubial bliss, however short-lived, she might have shared with Will. Because the idea of her in any other man's bed, even his brother's, felt like sacrilege.

She was Michael's. He wanted her. Kissing her again had taught him how much.

Why was he always attracted to users like her? God, what a mess.

How many endless, bleak hours had passed since she'd slammed the door? With his arms pillowed under his head, he felt restless on this couch from hell that was too short for him. He stared up at the bar of moonlight shifting on the ceiling.

Michael had promised his brother he'd look after Bree. He'd come here intending to honor his promise. What had he done instead? He'd mauled her just because he'd had to know if she still desired him.

She did. Her molten response had almost brought him to his knees.

He had no right to touch her. No matter what else she was, she was his brother's widow. She'd been injured in a car wreck that had claimed three lives. She was pregnant, and her condition was precarious. For her protection and the baby's, he had to keep his hands off her.

His eyes grew heavy, but just as he was about to shut them, she screamed. His heart racing with fear, Michael bolted to his feet and raced across the shadowy apartment.

He pushed the door open. "Bree?"

She'd kicked her sheets and blankets aside and was shivering. When she neither cried out nor answered him, he realized she was having a nightmare. His fault, no doubt. She'd been through a lot, and he hadn't made things easier for her.

His anger forgotten, he rushed to her. The masculine, long-sleeved dress shirt she'd chosen to wear had ridden up to her knees. When he saw the paleness of her bruised

face and the dark shadows under her eyes, his concern
and the self-loathing for his callous treatment of her grew.

Instead of awakening her, he pulled the covers over
her gently. When she continued to tremble, he went to
the living room and grabbed his jacket. He draped it over
her shoulders. Then, unable to leave her, he sank down
onto the bed beside her. After a long moment he began
to stroke her hair.

Asleep, she looked young and innocent and completely incapable of deceit. He remembered the blood on
his sheets that first night and how virginal she'd seemed
when he'd made love to her. He'd never been with anyone who'd seemed so young and fresh and eager for him.
Although he'd told himself she'd been a clever actress,
he'd been enchanted. He'd almost forgotten that he'd ever
considered her opportunistic and out to deceive his naive
brother.

When she cried out again and then, drawn by his
warmth, cuddled against him, he hardly dared to breathe
for fear he'd startle her.

Then her hand slid across his thigh and a flame went
through him. In an instant he was as hard as granite.

With her soft body lying against him, it was much too
easy to forget why he should dislike her, much too easy
to remember the heat of her response.

"Michael," she whispered. "Michael."

"I'm here," he said, worried that he'd awakened her
somehow.

"I'm…baby…I'm having a baby. Wanted to tell you…
but didn't know how."

"It's okay." He looked down at her.

Her lashes were shut. He relaxed when he realized she
was only talking in her sleep.

"I know about the baby," he said. "It's all right."

"I wanted you to be happy about it."

"I am happy about it."

He was happy his brother had left something of himself behind. At the same time, illogically, he wished she'd never been involved with Will.

Unable to resist the temptation to touch her and reassure her, he placed his hand on her shoulder. Then very gently he brushed his lips to her forehead.

"Don't be afraid," he whispered. "I won't let anybody hurt you...or your baby. I swear."

In her sleep, she smiled. "I know. You just pretend... to be mean and awful and greedy."

The wistful tenderness in her voice touched his heart. As before, she smelled of strawberries, making him remember how slick and tight she'd been, how she'd cried out at his first stroke—just as a virgin would have—but then had refused to let him stop. She'd felt so perfect. She'd been so sweet.

The memories had him burning up. His every muscle felt tight. The blood on his sheets had been real. He'd been her first. She hadn't been lying about that as he'd tried to make himself believe. No matter what she was, that had to mean something.

He wanted to pull her closer, to hold her, to ask her why she'd never slept with anyone before him. But more than that, damn it, he wanted to make love to her again.

What was he thinking? Why did he care so deeply for this woman who'd only wanted his brother's money?

He had to get up and separate himself from her before he lost all control and kissed her and woke her...and risked jeopardizing her health and the baby's.

Gritting his teeth against the pain of leaving her, he eased himself to the other side of the big bed. Then he got up and went to the window where he stood for a long time, staring down at the glittering rooftops of the Village. Not that he really saw the sparkling lights or the buildings in the moonlight.

He couldn't let himself feel so much for this woman.

When his breathing eased, he walked over to Will's easy chair beside the bed and sat down. He intended to stay only a minute or two, but Bree's sweet nearness eased the savage demons that rode him.

No matter what she was, no way could he leave her alone to deal with her nightmares.

Before he knew it he was fast asleep.

An alarm buzzed in her ear. When she moaned and rolled over onto soft, downy pillows, her throbbing head felt foggy. Every bone in her body, indeed every muscle she had, screamed in pain. Where had this headache from hell come from?

She let out a smothered cry and sat up. What was wrong with her? Why did everything hurt?

"You okay?" growled a deep, protective voice from above her.

In confusion she blinked up at the tall, broad-shouldered man towering over her. "Michael?"

What was he doing in her bedroom?

Confused, she scanned the bright paintings on the walls. No, she was in Will and Tony's bedroom.

As Michael's black eyes continued their blazing appraisal, she blushed at the intimacy of awakening in yet another bedroom with him.

How long had he been watching her? What was she doing here with him?

In the next instant his tense, brooding expression had her flashing back to him sitting beside her in the hospital. She remembered the SUV careening across the median straight at her. Tony had been unable to maneuver into another lane. They'd been hit and had rolled. Will's limp body had crushed hers.

He hadn't made it.

The loss of Will, as fresh as yesterday, slammed into her anew. Sinking into Will's pillow with a shudder, she groaned and buried her face in her hands. Dear, dear Will, who'd become her best friend after Johnny's death, was gone.

Will had been closer to her than most brothers were to their sisters. And now, because desperate circumstances had forced her to agree to marry him, she was stuck with his brother.

"It was so nice before I saw you and remembered… about Will and Tony and everything that's happened," she said. "Reality sucks," she said mournfully.

Michael's black eyes darkened, if that were possible. "I know. There's always that first moment when you wake up…before you remember. Before the horror hits you."

"I don't want to get up and face a day without them," she said. "I don't want to be in their apartment."

"*Their* apartment?"

"I…I mean Will's apartment," she corrected quickly. "*Ours*. I don't want to remember…any of it or try to go on. It's too hard."

"Tell me about it. But we don't have any choice. We have responsibilities."

He sounded nice, almost human. But he wasn't. She had to remember that.

Michael must have grabbed her phone from the nightstand and shut off her alarm because the noise suddenly stopped.

"Do you want coffee?" he asked abruptly.

When she nodded, he vanished.

She was rubbing her eyes when he returned a few minutes later with a steaming mug. "What time is it anyway?"

When he held out the mug, she sat up straighter, causing something to fall from her shoulders.

His jacket. What was his jacket doing wrapped around her? The thought of him worrying about her and watching over her was oddly unsettling.

"It's 9:00 a.m.," he said, picking up his badly wrinkled jacket and folding it under his arm.

On a normal day she would be at the bistro, preparing for the day, but because of her injuries and the spotting, she wasn't supposed to work for a whole week. Her mother had volunteered to take over for her. So, here she was, stuck with Michael.

"I never thought I'd sleep till nine. But since I've been pregnant, it happens fairly often." How could she be talking to him in this normal way?

"You're growing a baby. I don't know much about pregnancy, but I think it wears you out." His deep voice was oddly gentle. "Think how tired little kids get. You've got to take care of yourself."

His desire to protect her for her baby's sake made her soften toward him, which was a dangerous reaction. If she wasn't careful, she'd start believing he was capable of treating her decently.

But that wasn't going to happen, and she couldn't allow herself to wish he could be different.

Last night she'd actually dreamed Michael was a nice guy. In her dream she'd been afraid, and he'd come running to comfort her.

Ridiculous fantasy. He was a ruthlessly cold money machine who believed the worst of her. He'd bedded her solely to protect his brother—and the North fortune. When she'd said she wasn't interested in Will, he'd offered to set her up as his mistress—but for a price. He saw her only as a threat or as a sexual commodity for his own pleasure.

"I've been thinking," he said. "This place is too small for the two of us."

She nodded. "And I hate it here because it reminds me of Will and Tony so much."

"Since we're stuck with each other for the next week," he said, "I think we'd both be more comfortable at my penthouse."

Her heart skittered in fear as she remembered their first wanton night together in his glamorous apartment where he'd seduced her and then broken her heart.

The last thing she wanted was to spend a week in the place where she'd experienced such devastation.

"I can't go back there. Your penthouse isn't exactly neutral ground. Besides don't tony Fifth Avenue buildings like yours have dictatorial boards? Would they approve of a woman, a nobody like me from the West Side just moving in?"

"Leave the board to me. If they exact a price, I'll pay…"

"You think you can buy anything you want."

"I can—most of the time." He stared into her eyes. "I have three floors and five bedrooms. Believe me, you'd be able to avoid me there much more easily than you would here. And vice versa."

"I suppose that does have its appeal," she agreed gloomily, hoping to wound him. For some infuriatingly illogical reason the thought that he wanted to avoid her as much as she wanted to avoid him stung.

He smiled. "For once you see reason. So, pack your bag, and we'll get the hell out of here."

She stared at the single drawer where she kept her things. "I…I can't."

"What is it now?"

"My stuff is still at my old apartment," she confessed.

When one black brow arched quizzically, she had to think fast.

"We…we got married so fast, Will was still in the process of moving things out to clear space for me." Flushing, she looked away.

The trouble with lies was that if you told one, you had to keep stacking more on top of the first. How long would it be before he discovered her secret and her house of cards came tumbling down?

"Okay, then," he said. "What do you say we do breakfast, and then we go to your place? We have to feed the baby, don't we?"

She couldn't believe she was nodding and almost smiling, or that she was agreeing so easily to move in with him, when he'd behaved so terribly last night, and would probably do so again. She should be furious. If only she could hold on to her anger and stay on her guard around him.

"Can we eat at Chez Z, so I can see how Bijou is holding up?" she asked.

He nodded much too agreeably. How would she stand a whole week with this man? She didn't trust herself to be around him when his every nice gesture made her want to trust him again.

What if he caught her in a weak moment? What if she stupidly confided her secret? What would he force her to do then?

Four

No sooner had Bree led Michael through the doors of Chez Z than she regretted it. Not that anything particularly worrisome was going on in the intimate dining room jammed with yellow chairs and tables, and paintings of sunflowers cheerfully aflame on fire-engine red walls. It was simply that being here with Michael brought back *that* night—the one that had changed her life so irrevocably and compelled her to marry Will.

Marcie looked up from setting the tables, smiled and then went back to her work as if having her battered boss show up on the arm of a devastatingly handsome man the morning after she'd survived a fatal car wreck was nothing unusual.

Bijou rushed over to ask how Bree was feeling. After giving her a concerned once-over, her mother must have felt reassured because she thanked Michael for looking after her. Then Bijou left to check the online reservations for the day, the availability of staff and the status of a delivery that was late.

Bree didn't want to think about the first night Michael had come to Chez Z, but with his strong hand gripping her wrist, it was impossible not to. His mere touch made the bright walls squeeze closer and her breath come faster.

Again she saw him striding through the doors alone on that warm summer evening, his black eyes purposeful as he looked for her. She knew now his sole intent had been to seduce her so he could neutralize her importance to Will. But that night, fool that she'd been, she'd felt flattered that he'd sought her out and had rushed up to him with pleasure.

Will had warned her about Michael, of course, saying that he was a real bastard when it came to business and could be rude and overbearing in his dealings with family and his lovers.

"He's a coldhearted genius who ruthlessly annihilates our foes. He'll do or say anything to win. Dad said he's what our family needs in this competitive world—so he put him in charge. Even though he's adopted, we all have to answer to him. Believe me, Michael interferes in everything. He says it's because he cares, and it is. But he can be rough and difficult."

"And you don't mind?"

"I mind, but he grew up hard. He once told me he was raised by wolves, so I sort of understand. He thinks he's protecting me. He really does, and he'll destroy anybody he sees as a threat to me. He worries about any woman I get close to, so stay away from him."

"But that's ridiculous. We're just friends."

"Believe me—he won't see it that way."

Had she listened?

Despite Will's warning, when his darkly handsome brother had flirted with her at the fund-raiser, she'd fallen fast and hard, maybe because he'd exuded way too much masculine power, confidence and charm for an innocent like her to resist.

And, oh, how foolishly she'd exulted when he'd walked into Chez Z looking for her. *For her,* when he could have had a gorgeous supermodel.

Tall and fit in his perfectly cut gray silk suit, his brilliant gaze and quick smile had dazzled her.

Mark, the maître d', had bowed and stepped aside when she'd rushed up to Michael, saying she'd lead him to his table.

"Hello again," he'd whispered against her ear as she picked up a menu and a wine list for him. "I wasn't sure you'd remember me."

As if any woman could forget…least of all her, who had zero experience with men like him.

"Will's brother? Even if you weren't my dearest friend's brother, how could I possibly forget *you?*" Realizing how eager she must have sounded, she'd blushed. "I—I didn't mean," she'd stammered. But she had. He was gorgeous. "Welcome to Chez Z."

His hard, sensual mouth had curved in amusement as if he considered her blushes and stammering his due. "I want a table in your section."

"I'm afraid I'm off tonight. I was just about to leave." She felt a pang of acute disappointment at this admission. "I'm going to see a movie with a friend."

"Too bad," he said with such genuine regret her tummy flipped. "Perhaps I can tempt you into joining me for a glass of champagne." He grinned down at her gently. "If I promise to select a very good year, maybe you'll decide to go to a later show."

Bree knew she was in over her head and that she should say no and leave to meet her friend, but when he looked at her in that intimate way, she wanted to be with him too badly to deny herself. Never in her whole life had she felt so excited. Cathy would have to understand.

"I guess I could stay for one glass…if it's a very good year."

He took her hand and squeezed it. As his thumb casually stroked the inside of her palm, thrilling warmth flooded her. He laughed at her blushes. Heads turned to regard them. The feminine gazes lingered on him before resting quizzically on her.

When she called Cathy, her friend suggested they postpone the outing until later in the week, which suited Bree even better.

She'd never been with anyone like Michael. Truthfully, she hadn't dated much at all. Oh, she'd loved a boy in college, but he'd broken her heart when he'd fallen for her best friend. Others had been interested in her, but she would have been settling if she'd let any of them make love to her. So, here she was, a virgin in her twenties, flirting with a man she should have run from.

Champagne, coupled with the aromas of garlic, duck and foie gras, had heightened her senses until she'd become giddy with conceit at finding herself the companion of such a virile and attractive man.

The heady pleasure of his company, of eating and drinking with him, had quickly proved too much. Food was like an aphrodisiac to her, and she wasn't much of a drinker. One glass of champagne had led to another because she hadn't wanted him to think her an ingenue.

She couldn't get enough of the cool pale liquid that tasted so bubbly and sweet. She'd basked in Michael's teasing and flirting. Suddenly there had been only him filling the dining room. The murmur of the other diners' voices and the clatter of their plates and silverware had soon died to nothing.

Soon she'd forgotten her shyness and her amazement

that such a stunning man was interested in her. With such chemistry between them, of course he was interested, she'd told herself, as she'd allowed him to draw her out.

When he leaned across the table, questioning her as if he found her fascinating, she'd told him all about her brother, Z, and about the strong-minded Bijou, who had adored Z more than anyone or anything in the world. Next Bree told him about the rest of her colorful family who had supported Z in his efforts to garner fame and respect with his cooking skills.

When their frogs' legs came, Michael picked one up with his fingers, and she watched him eat it. She picked up her own frog leg and nibbled at the rich, succulent flesh as gracefully as she could. He smiled when she sucked at the juice dripping down one of her fingertips. At the same moment they both dipped their fingers into the bowl of warm water tartly scented with lemon. When their fingers accidentally touched, a hot dart of excitement made her tummy turn over.

"I wanted to go into publishing," she said, quickly yanking her hand from the bowl. "To be an editor, but the family needed me here to help Z, who was bringing us all such glory. I couldn't resist them even if I always felt a little lost and colorless around all of them. They are all people of such grand passions and ambitions."

"Don't sell yourself short," he murmured.

When he looked at her, she felt alive, special—every bit as exciting as her relatives. It was a new and heady experience.

"I'm a book person. They love being center stage. They love the television shows shot in the bistro's kitchen. But Z left me the bistro, maybe because I shared his passion for food and was the most faithful about showing up whenever he had an emergency. Ironically, my exciting family works for dull me now."

"You are not dull. Far from it. Z must have realized you cared for the bistro."

Maybe she hadn't known how much she loved it until Z was gone and he'd left it to her. Michael had a point. She did care. She didn't want to lose the bistro and all Z and her family had worked for.

"Well, I'm not doing well in business, so dull or not, I'm in trouble with them for failing Z."

Michael picked up another frog leg. "Can't you quit? This wasn't your dream."

"But it is now," she said, realizing for the first time it was true. "The bistro means so much to all of them... and yes, to me. Investors, family, friends—they've sunk money into the restaurant. It's not just about a livelihood. It's about respect and family honor. It's for Z...and all the people I love. I'll do anything to save it. *Anything.*"

His eyes had darkened. "But what about you? Are you sure this is what you want?"

"It wasn't at first, but it is now."

"I envy you, having a family, a real family, and the goal to help them."

She paused. "I'm sorry. I shouldn't have gone on like that. I've done all the talking. You know, I don't normally do this."

"Do what?"

Once more he took her hand and turned it over in his, and again she felt the sharp sizzle of sensual excitement.

"*This.* I don't date much. I don't have the time right now. I'm sure you'd have more fun with some other girl... I mean, some other woman."

"You're very wrong." When he ran his thumb over her wrist, she gasped.

His eyes lit up, and she wondered if he sensed the intensity of her response.

"Don't apologize for being who you are," he whispered. "I like you. I came here because I wanted to get to know you better."

"Why?"

"I think you know why."

Did he feel something, too?

As he continued to run his thumb over her wrist and the inside of her palm, the hot current of desire throbbed with an ever greater force.

"Will said you're adopted."

A shadow passed over his face and his eyes grew bleak before he looked down.

She felt so stupid. Why, oh, why had she said that?

"Yes. I'm adopted." Then he was silent so long she grew uncomfortable.

"I'm sorry. I shouldn't have pried."

"No, it's okay. It's not something I talk about often, but I want to talk to you. I grew up poor. Poor enough to know what it feels like to be nothing."

"I'm sure you were never nothing."

"Well, I felt like I was. My father, who worked in a refinery in Baytown, died when I was a baby. So, I never knew him. My mother was a masseuse and earned just enough for us to scrape by. She had boyfriends. Too many boyfriends. I didn't like them or the gifts they gave me to bribe me into accepting them. I was in the third grade when I got my first job—on the docks. Not long after that I bought a used lawn mower and started mowing lawns. I had to put myself through junior college and the University of Houston. My life was tough until my mother married Jacob North."

"How in the world did she meet him?"

"He was a client. I was nineteen and just out of college when they married. I asked him for a job, and he hired me as a stockbroker. I didn't know much back then, but I guess he saw something in me because he took me under his wing.

"With his help I advanced rapidly, which a lot of people resented, including most of his family who disliked my mother. Right before my mother died, perhaps to please her, Jacob adopted me legally—because he said he needed somebody strong he could trust to run his businesses and look after the family interests. He said Will, his only son, was too weak because he'd been spoiled. Strangely, Will, who had no interest in the business, took to me in a brotherly way, and I took to him.

"When Jacob died, Will was all I had. The rest of the Norths tried to get rid of me. They sued, tried to break Jacob's will—but they lost—big-time." His grim expression should have warned her.

"At least they're not blood kin, so there's a reason you don't fit in."

He'd smiled and pressed her slim fingers tightly. "Except for Will, I feel like I've been alone my whole life."

"That's sad."

"It's just the way things are."

When he'd drawn her closer, she'd felt powerfully connected to him when he'd said, "It's a little hard for me to trust anyone."

Why hadn't she *listened?* Too late she'd learned the man annihilated those he didn't trust.

The waiter had come, and they'd elected to share crème brûlée and raspberries. The combined flavors of caramelized sugar, crème and tart berries had proved to be sheer perfection. Looking back, she couldn't believe she'd let Michael spoon-feed her. The memory of how warmly she'd felt toward him that night, of how deftly he'd used the sensual delight of food to seduce her, chilled her. Now she knew his interest in her had been based solely on his desire to destroy his brother's feelings for her.

Pushing back from the excruciating memories, she stiffened and marched ahead of him toward the kitchen. Even though it was still too early for lunch, her mother had already done most of the prep work, so the rich aroma of sautéed onions and garlic and other herbs flown in from Provence lingered in the air.

"I'll make you a soufflé," she said.

"You don't have to."

"Cooking relaxes me." Better than that, it would distract her from him and the reality that she was moving in with him.

She put on her apron and took four eggs out of the refrigerator while he wandered about, opening her drawers and investigating her cupboards. Just when she was about to object to his nosiness and tell him not to touch anything, his phone rang. Instantly, he was all business as he left the kitchen to discuss stock trades and a real-estate project in Mumbai.

He didn't return until she told him the soufflé was done. Then they sat down together to enjoy it with warm, buttery croissants thick with fresh, homemade raspberry jam and rich black coffee.

As always the lush flavors of even such simple fare put her in a better humor—which meant, she'd better be on her guard. She was eating with him again.

"Thanks for letting me come here," Bree said as he sank his fork into her luscious soufflé. "I needed to see that Marcie and Bijou have everything under control."

"Where's your chef and waitstaff?"

"Bijou's here. Mark's running late because he has some family issues, but he'll be here in a few minutes to cook. We do a lot of takeout orders, and we don't need waiters for that."

"Your mother can cook?"

"Yes…and no. She loves to cook, so she cooks. But…

no! Z and I were lucky to survive her cooking. Some of her guests were once hauled away from our house in ambulances after a family dinner when I was a child. We used to watch her in the kitchen, so we'd know what dishes to avoid."

"You're kidding."

"I wish. She used to throw anything that was about to spoil into a casserole or soup and then invite people over."

He laughed.

"We only let her start working here when she promised not to cook. Since Z died, she says she feels his spirit here. We need her, and when she's busy helping us hold Z's dream together, she feels better. Z was her favorite, you see."

"And you know this how?"

She wasn't about to tell him *she* was the reason her parents had felt obliged to marry, or that her mother had blamed Bree for the loss of her career as a concert pianist as well for her unhappy marriage.

Instead Bree said, "Z was their long-awaited son. The only thing my parents agreed on was how perfect Z was and how much they loved him. After he was born, I sort of ceased to exist."

There was a bread crumb on his lower lip. She clenched her fingers to resist the impulse to brush it away.

"Did you hate him for that?" Michael licked his lips, and the tempting bread crumb vanished.

Just the opposite. She'd felt relieved. "Z was just always so gifted, so charming and confident. He looked up to me and adored me, so how could I hate him?"

"So, when you were younger, you wanted to be an editor."

She wished she hadn't told him that, wished that he hadn't asked her so many personal questions. Her secret longings were none of his business. But talking to him like this touched her somehow, made her think that if they tried, they could have a normal relationship.

Unable to resist opening up to him, she began to babble. "I loved reading. Stories offered a safe escape from our family dramas. I wanted to do my own thing, though I hadn't figured out what that was. But when Z became famous and had to go shoot shows in foreign lands or do book tours, he needed someone to run the restaurant, and he asked me. None of us could ever say no to Z. Mother would have helped, too, but she broke her hip and was down for six months.

"The busier Z became, the more he needed me here. And I liked being needed. Unfortunately, he died at a very bad time for the business. He'd just expanded and taken on a lot of new investors."

"Like Will," Michael said in a grim tone that made her wish she'd avoided that topic.

"Will was already an investor." She took a bite of soufflé before continuing. "The restaurant is saddled with debt. If I fail, my family will never forgive me any more than I could forgive myself. To them, closing Chez Z would be the end of Z's dream. For them, he's still alive here, you see. I feel the same way."

"I know a thing or two about dealing with family issues and business," Michael muttered as he sank his fork into the airy perfection of her soufflé again. "It's rarely easy."

"But I've got to make it work, now more than ever, and not just for my family. I need to pay off the debt and earn a decent income so I can support my baby."

"Your baby's a North. You must know you won't have to worry about money. You're Will's widow. I'll take care of you."

"Do you think that, knowing what you think of me, I want to be dependent on you or the illustrious North money?"

His eyes hardened. "Will's dead and you're his pregnant widow. We're stuck with each other whether we like it or not."

With a coldly withering glance, he shut down on her.

He was impossibly controlling. How would she endure living with him for a week? He was an arrogant beast who thought awful things about her and was determined to control her life and her child's. Why the hell had she cooked anything for him? Why had she talked to him, told him about her family, shared her dreams?

Steamed, more at herself than at him, she stood up. Just as he was about to sink his fork into her soufflé again, she grabbed his plate.

"Hey!" he cried.

At his yelp of dismay, she grinned wickedly. When he leaped to his feet, she whirled and scraped the last of his soufflé into the sink. While he sulked, she turned on the faucet to wash it down the drain.

"That was cold," he said.

"You deserved it. We've wasted enough time on idle chitchat. I have a bistro to run. Why don't I pack, so I can get back here?"

"The doctor said you're to take the week off."

"I will. I'll just sit around here and supervise, juggle a few bills."

"The hell you will. If you think I'm going to let you stress yourself and endanger your baby just because you're stubborn, you don't know me at all."

"Look—you stress me out more than anyone or anything here ever could. I need a break from you. Okay? The last thing I need is a bullying babysitter. Don't you have an empire to run, or someone else to boss around?"

"I have quite a lot to do—as a matter of fact—but nothing matters to me more than Will's child."

"The North heir."

"*My* heir."

"Exactly," she whispered. She felt her stomach twist. "The only reason your heir matters is because he stands to inherit your precious fortune. Money is all you care about."

"You know me so well."

As Michael's gaze followed the steep, Victorian staircase up several stories into the gloom, he heard Bree struggling to get her key out of the heavy interior door that had closed behind them.

When she caught up with him, he whirled on her. "You are not climbing these stairs."

"I promise, I'll take it very slowly."

"Not in your condition! Your doctor said no to subways because of all the stairs, remember?"

"I don't remember all that."

"Well, I do, so you're to sit down on the stairs and make me an itemized list of everything you'll need for next week."

"Michael, it will be so much easier if I just go upstairs and grab—"

"You're going to give me your key, and wait here while I go up and pack for you."

"You couldn't possibly find—"

"I run an empire, remember."

"Hey, maybe I don't want you going through my things."

"You prefer to risk the baby?"

"You're making me feel like a child."

"The sooner you stop acting like one and start writing that list, the sooner we get out of here." He pulled a pen and a pad out of his pocket.

Sulkily she sat down and scribbled out a list. Then she told him that she hid her key outside her door in the bowl of potpourri. As he climbed the stairs, she dutifully stayed where she was.

Three Victorian flights were more like five modern flights, he thought as he let himself into her apartment. It was tinier, messier and much shabbier than he'd imagined for someone who had such a flair for color. He had to call her cell to ask her where her duffel bag might be when it wasn't in its proper place. Once he found it, he charged into her bathroom and pulled panties and bras and a transparent nightgown off hooks where they'd been drying. Next he scooped up toiletries and a large bottle of prenatal vitamins. Then he made his way to her bedroom so he could rummage in her chest of drawers and closet.

With an eye for what he thought would look best on her, he chose several outfits and pairs of shoes. When he was through packing he even watered her plants, a task she'd forgotten to put on her list.

"You're very bossy," she said after he'd rejoined her at the bottom of the stairs and she'd checked the contents of her duffel bag.

"I get that a lot. Mind if I take that as a compliment?"

"No. And you're fast. What you picked out…will do."

"That last's definitely a compliment."

"You're grasping at straws."

"With you, I have to. So—how come you didn't have a single picture of Will in your apartment?"

She paled. "They…they're all on my computer. I needed to print one and frame it. I just hadn't gotten around to it, I guess."

When she lowered her eyes, he sensed there was more, way more.

But what? What was she hiding?

Michael stared at his lawyer before flipping another page of the legal document in disgust. What had he expected?

Feeling acute betrayal on behalf of his trusting brother, Michael flung the papers down onto his desk.

Nothing like a legal contract in black-and-white to spell out the truth.

No doubt about it, just like his own ex-wife Anya, Bree's sole motive for marrying Will had been getting her hands on his money.

"You're saying the day Will married Bree, *on his wedding day,* he signed documents to set up a million-dollar trust fund to care for her baby? And his new bride was with him in this office when he did it? She cosigned?"

His attorney ran a hand through his shock of silver hair and then nodded. "I wasn't there when they came in, but that's her notarized signature. They had new wills drawn up, as well."

When inspired, a conniver like her sure worked fast.

"You knew about all this, and you didn't tell me?"

"I didn't draft the documents myself. You were still dealing with that mess in Shanghai when Will told me he'd hired an independent attorney who would be sending the documents over for me to review before Will and his bride signed them."

"Can we break them?"

"You can take anything to court, but if she puts up a fight, which she probably will, it will cost you more than it's worth," Roger said. "I don't have to tell you that family lawsuits are very unpleasant emotionally as well as financially. When I expressed my concerns about these documents, Will made it very clear that this was what he wanted. In fact, he insisted that I promise to tell you that very thing if anything should happen to him. He seemed very anxious to take care of his child."

"He mentioned me, did he?"

"He did. As for the new will, he left the bulk of his estate to his friend Tony. But in the event of Tony predeceasing him, which is what has happened, you still get everything as in his old will."

Now that was odd. Michael would have thought a man anxious enough to sign his will on his wedding day would have left his brand-new wife everything.

"Except Bree gets her million dollars," Michael said.

"Not exactly. He left her nothing. She's merely the trustee of her baby's fund."

"Which means," Michael said, "that she can do exactly what she wants with the money."

"There will be a second million deposited into the trust when the baby's a month old."

"Thanks for clarifying where things stand," Michael said coldly.

"Anytime. Is there anything else I can do for you?"

"Do you know how much my brother had sunk into Chez Z?"

"I have it here." Roger handed him another document. "My best guess is, he'd given her close to a quarter of a million dollars."

Michael whistled as he studied the document.

"Anything else?"

Michael shook his head. "I can't thank you enough for coming by."

When the other man stood, Michael arose and extended his hand. He didn't sit down again until the older man shut the door behind him.

Bree made Will sign the documents on their wedding day. *On their wedding day.* And she'd called Michael cold.

On top of the will, his brother had given her bistro nearly a quarter of a million dollars.

Michael found the whole situation oddly disturbing. Why had his brother left everything to Tony, a man he'd never even bothered to introduce to Michael or to the rest of his family, instead of to his new wife? And how had Bree felt about that?

Still puzzled by the documents, Michael buzzed Eden, his secretary, who filled him in on his various meetings for the day. Before ending their conference, she reminded him that he was having drinks at a midtown bar with a Mr. Todd Chase at 6:00 p.m.

"Oh, that's right. Todd."

"Who's Todd?" she asked.

"An old friend from the University of Houston," Michael said. "I completely forgot he was in town." Todd had taken a job as the CEO of a huge investment-banking firm that needed a genius at the helm, and Michael had invited him for drinks to celebrate.

"You had me make a notation that he's bringing his wife, and you're taking a date. Someone named Natalia."

Damn. The last person he felt like dealing with was Natalia. Although she was beautiful, she was extremely high-maintenance. A model, she always made sure the media knew her every move. He'd seen her a couple of times before he'd left for Shanghai, mostly to send Bree a message that he was through with her.

He'd forgotten all about his "date" with Natalia tonight. Knowing her, she'd have a media event planned.

"Do you want me to call and remind her for you?" Eden asked.

"No." There'd be hell to pay with the needy, supersensitive Natalia if he didn't make the call himself—especially since he hadn't been in touch with her for nearly a month.

Even though she was one of the world's most beautiful and celebrated women, she was riddled with self-doubt. A perfectionist, she saw only her imperfections and needed vast amounts of reassurance. Strangely, disillusioned as he was with what he'd discovered today, he would have much preferred to go home early to Bree.

* * *

Bree didn't do helpless well, so she felt guilty doing nothing as she sat in her tiny office amid piles of paper she very badly needed to organize, one eye on the nightly news and the other on Bijou and their undermanned kitchen staff. Several people had begged to be off tonight, so Bijou was dashing about shouting orders and screaming ineffectively at the waiters and prep cooks.

The closer it got to the dinner hour, the more pressured Bree felt to help. But she had promised Michael she'd go to his place at 6:30 sharp. She knew that was the bistro's busiest time, and didn't want to be tempted to pitch in. Glancing at her watch, she realized she'd be late if she didn't leave immediately.

Just as she was about to grab her purse and turn off the television, Michael's tall, dark image blazed on the screen. He strode out of one of the city's flashiest hotels with a beautiful blonde dressed in a sheath of skintight silver who smiled as reporters swarmed them.

While the newscaster babbled excitedly about Natalia's seven-figure contract with a major cosmetics company and Michael's multigazillion-dollar project in Shanghai, Bree couldn't take her eyes off the sexy supermodel, whose hands were all over Michael.

Bree turned the television off and flung the remote aside so roughly it smashed against her desk, causing its back to pop open and its batteries to spill out.

She caught them before they hit the floor. With shaking fingers she grabbed the remote and stuffed the little suckers back inside.

She didn't care who Michael dated…or how damn beautiful the woman was. He was nothing to her, nothing other than her bossy brother-in-law who'd used her doctors to bully her into moving in with him so he could run her life for the rest of this week.

He was nothing to her.

He's the father of my unborn child.

That was an unfortunate fact she would have preferred to forget.

No way was she going back to Michael's stuffy building and endure the snooty stares of his doorman and then sit in her suite behind his kitchen all alone while he was with the incredibly beautiful, immensely successful Natalia. No way. She'd stay where she was, with people who loved her and approved of her.

Just because he was her brother-in-law and a North, just because he was immensely wealthy and lived in a palatial building on Fifth Avenue, just because he was the father of her baby didn't mean he had the right to dictate to her.

He would have to earn that right.

It was well after 8:00 p.m. when Michael let himself into his dark penthouse. He'd worked with a vengeance at the office and had been five minutes late to pick up Natalia. Then she'd embarrassed him by sulking in front of Todd at the bar because he hadn't called or texted or sent flowers during the past month. When he hadn't invited her to dinner after they'd said goodbye to Todd and his wife, she'd thrown a fit.

Unfortunately, Michael had been so exhausted from his sleepless night in that chair beside Bree's bed and his long day at work, he'd exploded.

Forgetting how sensitive she was to even the slightest criticism, he'd said something about beauty, even hers, being impermanent and had advised her to let him or someone like him invest her money for her.

"My money! Is that all you care about? You don't think my beauty will last. Are you saying you don't love me, either?"

When he hadn't argued that point, she'd puffed up in hurt and indignation and slapped him. "You don't love me!"

"You don't love me, either."

"Why, oh, why does everybody hate me?"

Then Natalia had broken up with him.

She was such a child. He'd hurt her, and he hadn't meant to. Tomorrow he'd send her a note apologizing and proclaiming her beauty along with roses and a parting gift.

Okay—so he was buying her off.

But the only good thing that had come out of their unpleasant night together was that she'd taken his mind off Bree and Will for a little while.

Still, no matter what had happened today or what he'd found out about Bree, she was injured and pregnant and he'd sworn he'd take care of her and the baby.

So here he was, home early to check on a houseguest he would have preferred to strangle.

He removed his jacket and threw it on a chair. Crossing his great room, he went to the bar where he poured himself a single shot of vodka. As he bolted it, the silence of the immense room ate at him.

Earlier, before he'd left for the office, Bree had his stereo going as well as her television because she said his penthouse felt like a tomb.

Where the hell was she?

He needed a night's sleep to calm down from the attorney's news. The last thing he wanted to do was deal with Bree and risk more feminine drama, but he strode across the living room, down the hall and past his vast kitchen until he reached the guest suite.

The space was on the lower floor and had originally been designed as a maid's quarters. Since he didn't have a live-in maid, and since Bree had a thing against elevators and he had a thing against her climbing stairs in her delicate condition, he'd suggested she use the suite.

He was about to raise his hand to knock when he realized her door was ajar. Slightly alarmed, he pushed it open.

Her suite was dark. Flipping on the lights, he tore through the rooms, calling her name, first in anger, then in mounting concern.

Her duffel bag was open. Colorful, silky clothes and sparkly costume jewelry that she hadn't bothered to put away spilled onto the floor. Lacy bras and panties littered the top of the dresser. It didn't take long to determine she was out or to figure out where she probably was—Chez Z.

Damn it. She had a baby to think about. What didn't she get about her condition and the gravity of her injuries?

Did she want to lose Will's baby?

Slamming his glass down, he spun on his heel and tore out of his penthouse.

Five

When Michael didn't see Bree in the noisy, crowded dining room of Chez Z, he found Bijou, who was pouring ice water into stemmed glasses.

"Is she still here?"

Bijou's brows shot upward. "I told her to go home an hour ago, but she's in a mood."

"In a mood?"

"Everybody says she's super-dedicated to saving Z's restaurant for the family and the investors, but I call it stubborn. Still, she did take it easy all day…until this evening…around 6:30. I don't know what set her off. I told her to go home. When she was obstinate, I thought about calling you, but I misplaced your business card. And then things got busy."

He gave Bijou another business card for future reference. "Where is she now?"

"We had several plates returned to the kitchen because the scallops were soggy, so she's in the back teaching

Mark how to dry scallops properly before he sautés them so they won't taste as if they've been steamed. The poor thing's nearly dead on her feet, but will she listen?"

Dead on her feet.

A pang of sympathy shot through him. Then he grew angrier. Whose fault was it, if she was tired?

Irritated, he swept past Bijou, banging through the kitchen doors in his impatience to find her.

When a startled Bree looked up, her eyes blank and shadowed with exhaustion, another wave of concern hit him.

"You're coming home with me now," Michael said.

"Your penthouse in that stuffy building is so not home."

"I'm not here to play word games," Michael said firmly.

She turned her back on him and faced the line of people in white behind her. "Ignore him. Don't let him break your concentration."

"If you don't get your purse and whatever else you think you need tonight in two seconds flat and come with me, I swear I'm going to pick you up and carry you out of here."

She whirled. "Just because you think you rule the world, and you practically do, you aren't the only one who has a job to do, you know. I have one, too."

"This isn't about our work. You're pregnant. You're the only survivor from a wreck that killed three people yesterday. You were injured."

"Minimally. I'm young and strong."

"Young and strong? You're exhausted and grieving. A corpse has more color and life than you do."

"Your heir is perfectly safe," she said.

"Step away from that stove," he ordered.

"He's right. Go on home, darlin'," Mark said behind her. "We've got your back. I swear. We won't let you down."

With Mark's betrayal, the last spark of resistance in her eyes dulled. "Okay," she whispered wearily to Mark, and then to Michael she said, "You win. I'm coming. Just don't touch me. Don't you dare put a hand on me or try to pick me up."

Although she was trying to stand up to him, she looked like she was about to shatter.

"Wouldn't dream of it," he drawled softly.

He felt close to some edge himself, dangerously out of control. Why was it that only she affected him like this?

It was a beautiful night. The moon was big, the air crisp. Not that either of them was enjoying the loveliness of the black velvet sky lit by starlight.

No, the air in the dark interior of his silver Mercedes fairly crackled with white-hot tension as Michael whipped through the crowded streets. He hadn't spoken to her since they'd left the restaurant, and he was driving so fast, Bree was almost afraid to say anything for fear of distracting him. His hands clenched the wheel. His eyes narrowed as he focused on the flying vehicles on all sides of them and the changing traffic signals ahead.

Suddenly the silence felt so thick and smothering she couldn't breathe. Reaching forward, she turned on his radio, moving the dial instinctively until she found hard rock, hoping the heavy beat would make it impossible for her to think about Michael's pulsing fury.

With a hard jerk of his wrist, he switched the radio off.

"So—do you want to talk to me or not?" she said after a long interval of unendurable, hostile silence.

"No. I just prefer silence to your insane music."

"Well, I find your bullying and your rage oppressive."

"Deal with it—since you're the cause of it."

"You didn't need to drive all this way to get me, you know. You could have called me or something."

"Right," he growled. "And just like that, you would have come running."

Glad she'd goaded him, she fought not to smile.

The big silver car shot through the dark like a missile, narrowly missing a biker, who shot the finger at them.

When she heaved in a breath and clenched her door, she realized how shaken she must still be from the accident.

"Hey, shouldn't you slow down before you kill us or some innocent courier?"

"You're so self-destructive I'm surprised you care," he said, but after glancing at her, he lifted his foot off the accelerator fractionally.

"Oh, because if I don't do exactly what you say, I'm self-destructive?" she persisted, trying to ignore her fear of the other cars.

"How long were you at the bistro?"

"All day."

"Exactly." His single word punched the air with such force it took all her courage to dare a shocked glance at his broad-shouldered profile.

"Quit sulking. Everybody works better if I'm there," she said. "I owe a lot of people a lot of money. I don't want to let them down."

"Right—you're so *dedicated*."

His scowl told her he was still furious.

"What's the matter with you? I thought you were on a date, enjoying yourself with that model. Having the time of your life."

"*What?*" The single word ripped into her like an explosion.

Before she knew what he was doing, he'd jerked the car across two lanes, to the curb, amid a barrage of blaring horns. Once they stopped, he engaged his warning lights.

"What's wrong with you?" she cried.

"*You!* Do you think I want you in my life? Want you

haunting my every thought? I drove myself all day at the office in the hope I could forget about you and the way you used your charm to blindside my brother. The poor fool took off his seat belt to save you. *He's dead because of you!*"

His cruel words hit their intended mark. She'd tormented herself with the same thought, but she swallowed tightly and held her head high.

"Hey," she said, "while I was in my office—resting *obediently*—who should I see but you? On TV. With one of the world's most beautiful women. Natalia Somebody Or Other."

"I had a late business meeting. She was my date."

"Right. Well, you didn't look the least bit haunted to me. You weren't going to be at your penthouse, so why should I go over there and sit around all by myself dwelling on Will and Tony when you were out having fun?"

"Fun? You think you know everything about me, do you?"

"I know you want to be seen with women like her, that you date them or collect them…probably just to enhance your image because you don't have a heart."

"Collect them? No heart? So—now I'm inhuman, too?"

"I know that the only reason you slept with me was to make Will hate me because you were protecting his precious money…and your own."

When he thought about the trust fund she'd acquired the day of her marriage, her holier-than-thou attitude grew intolerable.

"With sharks like you out there, someone had to protect it."

"See—you don't care about me at all! Why are you so concerned about what I'm doing?"

"*I don't care?* You think I don't care?" He felt out of

control, on dangerous ground, but he couldn't back down. *He cared too much.* That was the problem.

"I felt lost and miserable. The restaurant took my mind off things. So what if I didn't go to your penthouse? You had Natalia to distract you, didn't you?"

"Shut up. Forget Natalia. She means nothing to me."

"Well, she had her hands all over you, and you seemed to be eating it up."

"You don't know anything about me. About what I feel."

"What do you feel then?"

"Disappointment. Disillusionment…that you're as bad as I believed you to be."

"Oh…." She *so* didn't like him.

Then why did his assessment crush her?

Unsnapping his seat belt and then hers, he yanked her toward him roughly.

"Quit it! I don't want to be manhandled by someone who dislikes me."

"I wish I disliked you," he muttered. "Even though I know what you are, on some level I fell for the sweet innocent you pretended to be that first night and can't get her out my head."

"The last thing I want to think about is that night!" When she balled her hands and pushed against his massive chest, his mouth closed over hers.

"I don't want to kiss you when you're angry like this, when you say such awful things," she whispered as his hard, determined lips took hers again. "Don't do this."

His breath came in harsh rasps. "I don't want Natalia, you little fool," he said. His tongue pushed inside her mouth. "I want you," he said. "In spite of everything that's hard and cold about you, I want you." He kissed her again.

Beneath his anger, Bree felt the fierce desire inside

him. Natalia or no Natalia, he was as lonely as Bree was and driven by needs he fought but couldn't deny.

It was as if they were both two lost creatures hemmed in by this crowded city where neither could find a haven anywhere but with each other. Which was ridiculous. She wasn't lost; she had a family. And he hated her. He was a heartless money machine who dated gorgeous super-models for show. She didn't even like him.

So why was his mouth fused to hers, and why had she stopped fighting?

Why was he kissing her like a man who would die if he couldn't have her?

Her hurt over his poor opinion of her, her hurt over Natalia, was forgotten. Dazed, her arms closed around his neck, and she pulled him closer, communicating with her seeking lips and tongue that she wanted him as desperately as he wanted her.

He kissed her until she couldn't breathe. Until his anger dissolved, and his kisses grew sweeter. Then his lips moved lingeringly down her throat.

After an infinite time of shared kisses and feverishly whispered love words passed between them, he dragged his mouth from hers and stared at her in the dark. Again, the intensity in his gaze communicated his need. The same wildness that pulsed in his blood, pulsed in hers. Confused, she didn't think she'd ever seen so much mis-ery, shock or passion in anyone's eyes as she saw in his.

How could he, of all people, blow away everything she knew to be sensible and logical and make her want him with every fiber of her being?

What if he's not as bad as I thought or as bad as he thinks he is? He came after me tonight, didn't he? He came after me because he cares.

If you think that, you're a fool—you never want to see the truth about people when your heart's involved.

But my heart's not involved. I won't let it be.

She didn't know what to say or do. Apparently neither did he. Without offering an apology or explanation, he turned off the warning lights, snapped on his seat belt and ordered her to fasten hers. Too shaken by what had happened to protest, she obeyed him.

They drove through a tangle of Manhattan traffic, most of it jostling taxicabs, in tense silence until they reached Fifth Avenue. Then, even as he was racing around the front of his Mercedes to open her door, she jumped out. Slamming it, she stalked silently past him and his uniformed doorman, although she did blush when the man's eyebrows rose in what she imagined to be disapproval.

She'd forgotten how impossibly stuffy Michael's building was with its rules that had been dreamed up for decades—to keep out the wrong *elements*.

Michael caught up to her at the elevator. "Behave," he whispered, "at least, while we're in the lobby."

Ignoring the splendor of marble and chandeliers, she shut her eyes and swallowed a deep breath. When she opened her eyes she focused on the bronze elevator doors.

Wrong move.

Elevators! Why did he *have* to live in a penthouse? Why had she ever agreed to stay here? Even for one night?

Her wild eyes must have betrayed her fear because he said, "You ever going to tell me why you're scared of elevators?"

"Maybe someday," she said trying to make her voice light.

After her cousin Jeremy had locked her in that dark closet for hours, she'd disliked all closed spaces, but a second childhood experience had further refined her phobia so that elevators had become her number one terror.

When her mother had taken Bree along to sign a paper at her attorney's office, Bijou had gotten off on the attorney's floor while talking to another woman. Bree had dropped a bunny and rushed back inside the elevator for it. Unfortunately, the doors had closed and the elevator had whooshed upward. She'd become too hysterical to punch the buttons, and the thing hadn't stopped until she'd reached the top floor. By then she'd been lost and alone and terrified she'd never find her mother.

Michael must have sensed her desire to bolt when the elevator doors opened because his hand closed gently over her elbow and he nudged her inside. When the bronze doors shut them inside, she clenched her hands and shut her eyes and tried not to think that they were shooting up dozens and dozens of stories in a closed box at rocket speed.

Sensing her growing panic as the elevator ascended, he muttered something that might have been meant to reassure her, but she felt too on edge to comprehend anything.

She didn't realize she'd begun to shake until his arms closed around her, and he drew her close to steady her. She should have fought him, but instead she clung gratefully.

Then the doors opened, and she came back to herself. Pushing free of him, she all but jumped out into his elegant hall. When he caught up with her at his door and unlocked it, she raced toward her suite and shut herself inside. Sagging against the door, she waited for her heart to slow down.

No sooner could she breathe normally than she heard him in the kitchen, slamming cabinet doors. When the rich aroma of bacon and eggs frying and bread toasting wafted into her room, she realized that even though she'd been at the bistro, she hadn't eaten in hours.

Her stomach growled. Why couldn't he have gone upstairs so she wouldn't have to think about him out there enjoying eggs and bacon while she was trapped in here?

When he kept stomping about, she removed her phone

from her purse and attached it to a set of external speakers. Soon the suite was flooded with pulsating rock. She'd shower. By then maybe he would have finished his meal and gone upstairs and she could safely raid his kitchen.

Hearing the roar of her rock music, Michael's thoughts turned to the woman in his guest suite.

Hell, why couldn't he forget the taste of her sweet mouth in the car? Forget the sharp bite of her nails digging into his back?

He wanted her, his brother's pregnant widow, this woman he'd sworn he'd protect.

But she was injured, and a gold digger, so he fought not to think of her stripping in her bathroom, showering and then slipping into her bed wearing the transparent nightgown he'd selected. Or maybe she'd wear nothing.

It drove him crazy to remember how warm and soft she'd felt curled against him that night after they'd made love. He'd wanted to hate her, but he hadn't been able to. The truth was, he'd give anything to hold her close like that again.

Who was she? The gold digger or the sweet voluptuous siren who'd enchanted him with her innocence?

Who had seduced who? He still didn't know.

Had Michael really been her first? *Had he?* Why did he care? She'd wasted no time getting herself pregnant so Will would marry her.

But Michael's questions wouldn't stop. Something was wrong with his picture of her. The pieces to the puzzle didn't fit.

Was she dedicated to the bistro for noble reasons? Or was she as low and conniving and greedy as he kept telling himself? She'd damned sure signed those documents on her wedding day. Did she kiss him in the car merely because he was rich?

Hell, she'd damn sure responded when he came on to her.

Michael's mind and emotions raged as he tore his hand through his hair. He had to get a grip.

When he finished his dinner, he rinsed his dishes and left them in the sink for Betsy Lou, his cleaning lady, who came every morning to tidy up.

Long after he'd climbed the stairs and endured a long, icy shower, he thought about Bree. Only in sleep did he have what he craved, when she came to him in his dreams and lowered her naked body over his and did everything that he desired.

Just as he was about to find his release, he heard a scream from two floors below.

Six

One minute Bree was sound asleep and happily dreaming that she was back in Michael's Mercedes wrapped in his arms as he whispered such sweet words.

Then her dream twisted, and she was shut out of his Mercedes. Standing on the sidewalk. Feeling lost and abandoned, she watched him inside his car kissing the beautiful Natalia whose slanting eyes glittered in triumph as she stared at Bree over Michael's shoulder.

Hurt washed over Bree. Thrashing against her sheets and pillows, she came awake in Michael's moonlit guest suite.

Sitting up amid tangled covers, she gave herself a minute to settle. Then she forced herself to think about her dream because she believed that dreams were a form of truthful self-talk. If she didn't think about it immediately the most telling details would recede.

She chewed on her bottom lip. The dream was worrisome. It told her that she wanted Michael even though she couldn't believe he really wanted her.

So what else was new?

As she lay there feeling frustrated and unable to sleep, a fierce craving for sardines—for anything salty and fishy—compelled her to arise, shrug into the enormous man's robe she'd found earlier in her closet and pad into his kitchen.

Remembering seeing a can of sardines sitting right by a big jar of peanut butter in the pantry, she found them easily. Smiling, she grabbed the can.

A sandwich would be good. A sandwich with mayo and pickles and maybe mustard and onions. Now that she thought about it, a white creamy cheese…Camembert. Almost tasting the rich, gooey French cheese, she headed toward his refrigerator. Her head buzzing with food fantasies, she wondered if Michael had chips, as well.

Disappointed when she found only an old onion, some cheddar and a jar of mayo but no pickles—she could never be with a man who could live without pickles— she grabbed the mayo. But as she turned to close the door the overlong sleeve of her borrowed robe snagged on the handle. The mayo jar along with the cheddar cheese and onion slipped out of her hand and smashed to jagged bits on the granite floor. Off balance, she grabbed for the counter and dropped everything else into the mess. When she moved to start picking up after herself, a shard of glass sliced into her heel and she screamed.

She froze when she saw the pool of scarlet oozing out of her torn heel. Just when she spotted his paper towels on the far side of the kitchen, a bare-chested Michael, wearing only blue pajama bottoms, stepped into the kitchen.

Why did he have to be so heart-stoppingly sexy? "Stay where you are," he ordered in that tone that made her feel gauche and then bristle defensively. His black eyes darkened dangerously at the sight of her blood as he strode toward her.

"I don't want to be a bother. I can take care of myself," she protested.

"Right," he grumbled testily as he stared at her bloody foot. "I can see that."

"I was just about to get the paper towels—"

"Do think I would risk you cutting yourself again before we even know how bad it already is?"

"I'll be fine."

"I intend to make sure of that."

Lifting her into his arms as if her weight was nothing, he crushed her against his chest as he carried her out of the kitchen and then down the hall.

Pressed so close to his hard bare flesh, she couldn't help but inhale his clean male scent. The smell brought back the night she'd spent in his arms when they'd made love. He was too virile and too sexy when he was being so nice, and she was a sucker for nice.

"Put me down," she whispered even as he headed for the stairs. "Blood is dripping behind us."

"Good thing I have stone floors and a maid coming in the morning."

"Only one maid for this place?"

"I'm not nearly as messy as you are."

Stung, maybe because she could see that about him, she rushed to her own defense. "My apartment isn't always the way it was when you saw it. I…was sort of… preoccupied last month."

"I wasn't criticizing you. I was stating a fact. Do you think I care about your apartment?"

"Put me down. Where do you think you're going? What are you doing?"

"I need to clean up your foot, and the nearest bathtub

is on the second floor. Since you don't like elevators, I'm carrying you up."

"But I can handle elevators," she said testily, perversely annoyed at his thoughtfulness.

"Right." He grinned down at her. "You do them so well."

"I practice."

"How? Like one would a piano?"

Her lips twitched. She fought not to smile. "Sort of."

He wasn't nice. She didn't like him. She didn't find him amusing. He was making fun of her neurotic fear, a fear that was perfectly logical considering what had happened to her. She should be furious.

But it felt much too marvelous to be in his arms, much too nice to have him pretending that he cared.

Be careful. He's tricky. He was nice the night he seduced you. And here you are—pregnant.

As he climbed the stairs, he went more slowly at the top, and she noted with satisfaction that his breath came a little harder.

She smiled. So he was human after all.

When he reached the lovely white marble bathroom accented with gold, he helped her sit down on the edge of the tub. Kneeling, he ran his hands over her ankle before he lifted her foot and examined it.

"It's not too deep," he said as he gently removed a couple of pieces of glass. "I think I got them all. Don't watch, or this will hurt more," he said.

"What?"

"Shut your eyes. I need to make sure I got all the glass."

"Ouch," she cried when he yanked out a third sliver.

"Sorry about that. It was a little deeper than the others. But I think that's it. I'll just wash your foot now and bandage it."

She'd never imagined a man stroking her foot could

make her feel so sexy, especially when she was bleeding, but apparently he could make any activity sexy.

"If you give me your first-aid kit, then I can take it from here."

"No," he snapped in that forceful tone that could so annoy her. Only it didn't annoy her now.

Turning on the water, he held his hand under the stream until it was cool enough to suit him.

"That's too cold," she cried when he stuck her foot into the flow.

But his grip on her ankle remained firm. "Hold still. Cold water helps blood clot."

"I think you just enjoy torturing me—Dr. North."

"That, too," he teased. Ignoring her, he let the icy water stream over her heel for another minute. Then he found towels. After drying her foot, he deftly applied ointment, butterfly stitches, and a bandage.

"There," he said, after he'd finished. "I don't think we need to go to the E.R."

Feeling a little chagrined, she studied her expertly bandaged foot and then the wreck they'd made of the lovely bathroom. But after the car accident, she felt truly grateful that he'd taken care of her. The last place she wanted to visit was an E.R.

"Thank you," she whispered.

"You're welcome. Now what exactly were you doing in my kitchen in the middle of the night?"

It started with a dream about you kissing Natalia, she thought. Aloud she said, "It couldn't possibly matter."

"Tell me."

For no reason at all she found herself staring at the black hair on his bare chest in fascination. "I woke up with this…er…craving."

When he turned, she couldn't resist watching the play of his muscles as he folded the towels.

Brilliance flashed in his black eyes when he glanced at her lips. "For what?"

Heat crept up her throat before she could avert her eyes. "If I tell you, you'd better not laugh at me."

With some effort he made his handsome face severe. "I won't—I promise."

"A sardine sandwich."

He struggled not to laugh, he really did, but he couldn't help himself. The rich rumble of amusement made him seem slightly less formidable.

"You promised," she whispered.

"Well, since I broke my promise—I owe you. After all that you've gone through tonight and now my sin of laughter, you damn sure can't go back to bed without your sardine sandwich."

"It's okay. The cheese and onion are ruined, and you don't have anything else in your refrigerator. And I really have to have cheese and onions with sardines…"

"Trust me. There's more onions and cheese in Manhattan."

"It's late. I don't want to be a bother. I should let you go to bed."

"I'm making you a sardine sandwich, the sardine sandwich slathered in cheese and onions of your dreams… whether you agree to eat it or not."

She considered before she said yes. "I'm agreeing to this only because you are too obstinate to argue with. But—I'm taking the elevator down."

"You sure about that?" When he grinned, she nodded fervently. "It's only one floor. What could possibly go wrong?"

"Famous last words. So, do we go down together? Or one by one?" he asked, humoring her.

"One by one. That way if either of us gets trapped, the other can call for help."

"Right," he said. "Just for the record, there's a phone in my elevator, if you're ever caught in it alone."

"But the phone could malfunction."

"Are you always a worst-case-scenario thinker?"

"Always when it comes to elevators."

In the kitchen he cleaned up the mess, salvaging what he could, which was the can of sardines. The rest he threw in the garbage while she sat at his table and watched.

"Tell me exactly what you want on your sandwich, and I'll call my doorman."

"Can you do that? Will he do that? In the middle of the night?"

"Just tell me what you want."

"You must be impossibly spoiled."

"I pride myself on it."

When she told him the ingredients, he wrinkled his nose.

"Don't laugh at me again."

He smiled. "I believe you *are* pregnant."

He picked up his phone and made the call. When he hung up, he said, "One sardine sandwich will appear as if by magic in fifteen minutes."

Her opinion of his stuffy building and his uptight staff went up a notch.

"I've been thinking about your restaurant," he said while they waited for her sandwich. "I could help you turn it around."

She remembered he'd said that before—if she became his mistress.

"But why would you? I mean…" She frowned. "What would you want in return?"

"Nothing. You're my brother's widow. My brother sunk a quarter of a million dollars into it."

Her eyes widened. "That much? No wonder you're—"

"Didn't you know?" His voice was grim. "Really, you should know these things."

"You're right. I should have known. It was just that Z handled all that."

As he studied her, she would have given anything to be able to read his mind.

"Okay, then," she said, knowing she'd be a fool not to let him help her. "What exactly do you have in mind?"

"For starters, I'd send over an expert in the restaurant business to evaluate what's going on. Have you ever heard of Luke Coulter?"

"The genius with seafood on TV? Who hasn't?"

Not only was Luke Coulter a successful restaurateur, he was one of New York's most renowned celebrity chefs. Z had resented that she'd been hooked on one of Luke's cooking shows.

"Z considered him a fierce rival. Bijou knows how he felt about Luke."

"Well, you're not Z, and you're in serious trouble. From what I've read, Z was not only creative, he was practical. I'm sure he'd want you to do whatever it takes to succeed. Look, I recently helped Luke restructure the financing of his latest restaurant, which, as you know, is another big hit. So he owes me a favor or two. Why don't I ask him to come over? He'll take a look at your books and your costs, watch your staff, observe how you handle them, sample your food and then give you advice. You don't have to take it—if you don't think it applies to your bistro."

Had Will really invested a quarter of a million dollars in Chez Z? No wonder Michael thought she was out for all she could get. How much did she owe her other investors? He was right. She *should* know these things.

Fresh tension ate at her. The only thing she knew for sure was how much she didn't know.

Z had been in charge of the numbers. She had only a

vague idea about her food costs and the specifics of her financial situation. She felt a bit defensive at the thought of Michael sending in an expert who might humiliate her. But what was a little humiliation? The bistro was in trouble, and things were getting worse under her management, not better. If she kept on her same path, wouldn't she keep getting the same results?

In the end she decided she owed too much money to too many people to say no. What if Luke could give her a crash course that would help her turn things around?

"Okay," she whispered, her voice low and tight. "Thanks. I'd be happy to hear what he has to say."

Not that she was happy. No, she felt scared and nervy. Fortunately, the doorbell rang.

"Great! Your sardine sandwich is here, and it's right on time."

After Michael brought it to her, they sat down again at his kitchen table. She grew increasingly self-conscious when he smiled as she unwrapped her huge sandwich.

"Don't you want some? This really is much too big for me," she said.

He shook his head. "You're eating for two."

"I could cut it in two and share."

"That's very generous of you. But no."

"I'm absolutely ravenous."

"Enjoy."

When he didn't talk about business anymore, she began to relax. She studied her magnificent sandwich. Appetite and sensuality flooded her as she bit into the crusty bread and sardines.

"Careful," he whispered, handing her a napkin.

She munched happily, savoring the combination of tart mustard, cream cheese and fish.

A few minutes later she'd eaten all she could and was

feeling sick with pleasure when she set her huge sandwich aside.

He smiled. "Had enough? Okay, then. Run along to bed. I'll tidy up."

"Why are you being so nice to me all of a sudden?" she said, feeling suspicious again.

"Maybe because you were hurt in my home. Suddenly I've been thinking maybe we should call a truce. What are we accomplishing by being so rude to each other?"

She stared at him blankly. "You started it."

"I won't argue. So, will you let me end it? What do you think—can we have a truce?"

When she hesitated, his quick, easy grin made her blood heat, made her remember the kisses in the car and the wonderful sandwich he'd ordered for her.

"Come on," he coaxed. "You're always acting like you're the one who's all heart. Show me that you're a tolerant, liberal denizen of the West Side for real."

Knowing she shouldn't let her guard down, she nodded warily as she backed out of the kitchen.

Funny, she'd felt so much safer when he'd acted as though he was dead set against her than she felt when he was helpful and friendly. Was he trying to lower her defenses so he could move in for the kill?

With some effort she recalled his ruthless reputation in business and with women, and how ruthlessly he'd treated her to protect his brother.

His feelings for her hadn't changed. If she were smart, she wouldn't let her defenses down.

Seven

"Have you got those food costs for me yet?"

Luke Coulter smiled down at her as he stepped into her office.

"Not quite. But almost. Like you said, I haven't been keeping very good records, so it's taking me a while."

"It's essential that you know what they are. You can't be fuzzy about numbers or they'll kill you."

When she handed him her notebook, which bulged with dog-eared receipts, he took the jumble and sat down.

Bree couldn't believe how easy it was to work with Luke once Bijou and everybody had warmed up to him. With his shaggy blond hair and affable smile, he seemed like a huge blond bear, albeit a friendly one—most of the time. His quick temper could be formidable.

Michael had brought Luke to the bistro three days ago. After he'd gone over her books and sampled their menu, he'd been fairly brutal with his criticism about everybody, especially her. She and her staff had been doing their best to improve so they could please him.

He'd told her she had to take control of everything—the staff and every creative and financial detail. "You can't please everybody," he'd said. "This is a job—more than a job, it's your career. Your future."

And her baby's future. Who knew if the trust fund Will had so generously set up would be enough?

Besides, Bree didn't come from a family who sat around.

"You have to account for everything you buy and sell, and to know what everything costs so you can price your menu correctly. You can't keep advancing money to all your employees the way you've been doing. Marcie's in to you for five hundred dollars."

"Her little girl's been sick."

"You can't afford to be everybody's lifeboat when the mother ship is sinking. Will you let me talk to your staff about this and establish a new policy?"

"Yes."

He'd managed to squeeze in two more tables in their back dining room, he'd revised their menu and taught her cooks several new, delicious dishes that would be easier and less costly to serve.

"This place can make it," he said as he skimmed her receipts and slashed through several marks she'd made in her notebook with his red pencil. "You have a devoted staff and a loyal clientele. You were doing fine until you lost Z, who kept a firm rein on the finances. Nobody's stealing money. Things haven't slid that far. We don't have that much to tweak."

"You have been incredibly generous with your time. I can't believe you came over right after Michael called you."

Luke's intense blue eyes met hers. "Michael let me know just how important you are to him."

New hope sent hot blood rushing to her cheeks, but she was embarrassed that Luke might read her too accurately.

"It's not what you think. He was just trying to be helpful," she said.

"Michael is never helpful without some motive. I wouldn't underestimate his interest if I were you," Luke said. "Be careful. He's extremely focused, calculating and very, very dangerous. You're not exactly his type."

She looked away. "Right, he prefers models."

"That's not what I meant. Being a man, maybe I read him a little more clearly than you do."

"I'd rather not talk about Michael, if you don't mind."

Luke held up his hands. "Okay. We could go back and forth all day. Michael is not as fierce as he sometimes seems. He was different…before he married Anya. She made him feel as if he was worthless, made him believe no woman would want him for anything other than his wealth. Because of his past, when he felt he was nothing— he can't let those feelings go. Since he divorced her, he has concentrated single-mindedly on business and he's grown harder."

"I don't know why you're telling me this."

He laughed. "Don't you? Michael's unhappy, and you have a soft spot for people who are in trouble. Look at the way you've tolerated Mark's repeated absences even on nights when the bistro is packed or the way you've let Marcie take advantage of your generosity. Michael's like a wounded wild creature, and you want to heal him and tame him. If you aren't careful, he'll gobble you alive."

She felt her cheeks flame. He already had.

"I'm sorry." His voice was kind. "I've said too much. I've got you blushing and upset again. It's just so obvious that the two of you—"

"I'm not upset." But she was.

"Why don't we get back to these fascinating numbers before you are," he murmured drily. He pointed to
a number. "Did you know you were spending this much
on toothpicks?"

As Michael deftly whipped his silver Mercedes past
a honking cab, he parked at the curb just in time to see
Bree laughing as she walked out of Chez Z on Luke's arm.

She wore a brightly flowered pink blouse and a
flounced lavender skirt. Bright beaded necklaces dangled
from her neck, and her waist was sashed with a fringed orange scarf. He remembered how his doorman had smiled
and then refused to meet Michael's eyes when he'd left
the building with her this morning.

Michael had never seen her looking so lighthearted
and happy. He frowned. Yes, he had. She'd been like that
the first night he'd flirted with her at the fund-raiser, and
then again *that* night at the bistro when he'd seduced her...
before he'd told her the truth.

She had a beautiful smile, and he liked the way her
golden eyes sparkled and her bright curls tumbled. What
he didn't like was thinking that Luke had caused her special radiance.

Michael wanted Bree to look at him like that, to feel
that relaxed and happy around him.

When he called out to her, she blushed and gave Luke a
quick goodbye hug. Luke's broad, tanned face broke into
a grin, too, as he waved at Michael before lumbering off
down the crowded sidewalk.

Her eyes wary now, Bree came over to the Mercedes.
When Michael opened his passenger window, she leaned
down and he caught the fragrance of strawberries min-
gling with the rich aroma of onions a vendor was grill-
ing on a cart.

"Ready?" he growled.

"I'll just be a minute," she said, smiling. "I need to get my purse."

A few seconds later, purple clutch in hand, she slid breathlessly into his Mercedes.

"How did it go today?" he asked as he'd asked her every day after work. He liked the way it was beginning to feel like a pleasant habit.

"Better and better. Luke's wonderful, like you said."

He knew how things were going because he talked to Luke every night. Luke liked her.

"Great," Michael replied.

"Thanks so much for asking Luke to take a look at the bistro. He's made me see all sorts of things I never saw before."

"I'm glad it's working out." He was, but at the same time, he envied her easy friendship with his friend.

"Yes. But it's been a stressful three days."

"Change is never easy."

"I'm lousy with money, but I'm determined to improve."

When he pulled into the traffic she fell silent and stared out the window.

"How did it go at the doctor's?" he asked.

"Wonderful. He cleared me. The baby's doing great. I'll be fine on my own now."

"He released you a day early, did he?"

He was relieved she was out of danger. Even so, her bright smile and quick nod darkened his mood.

"What did he say about your foot?"

"That you missed your calling, that you would have given him a run for his money if you'd gone into medicine. If we go to your place now, I can pack and be out of your hair in no time. I'm sure you think that's wonderful because you won't have to explain me to your super or your board or come down to breakfast every morning and be bombarded by hard rock anymore."

"Right."

Funny, how little the thought of peace and quiet and indulgent luxury or the approval of a bunch of nosy, uptight neighbors mattered to him.

He wanted Bree with him in his penthouse. He enjoyed her. He wanted…

What he wanted was dangerous as hell.

"Hey," he said, "I've been making the arrangements for Will's memorial, so there are a few last-minute details we need to go over together."

"Sure. We'll talk while I pack."

That would mean she'd be gone in less than an hour.

He shook his head. "I worked through lunch. Since we both have to eat, why don't I take you somewhere nearby for a quick dinner?"

It annoyed him when she argued, but he easily overrode her complaints and drove them to one of his favorite restaurants with a magical view of Central Park.

"I thought you said a quick dinner," she said as he let her out at the five-star hotel.

"I know how you love really good food."

"But you shouldn't bring me here," she protested even as they followed the maître d' into an elegant dining room accented with soft, muted colors and the glow of warm candlelight.

"Why not?"

"You said we were going to discuss the memorial arrangements."

"All the more reason we should choose an enjoyable place, don't you think?"

"But I'm not dressed properly."

"Nonsense. You look lovely."

"Like a gypsy with too many scarves and bangles."

"A truly lovely gypsy," he replied in a husky tone that was meant to coax and seduce.

This time, he knew her vivid blush, which said *don't you dare try to seduce me over a meal again,* was meant for him instead of Luke.

The waiter seated them by a window with a magnificent view. As soft music tinkled in the background, he watched her as she admired the park and the city. Why did he feel so at home in her presence and so uneasy at the thought of her moving out?

The sky was dark, and the sommelier pointed out the lightning in the far distance.

"Looks like it's going to rain," Michael said. "It may get a little chilly."

"It's that time of year," she replied.

With a smile, Michael ordered the tasting menu and asked the sommelier to bring appropriate wines for each course.

"You know I can't drink right now," she said.

"Wine looks so nice on the table."

"It's extravagant to use wine to decorate."

"You've already told me I'm spoiled. Indulge me. After all, you did agree to that truce, and it is our last night together."

He made quick work of the memorial details and settled down to enjoy her, a pleasure that began even before the waiter brought them a tiny plate with a minuscule porcini tart and other delicacies, including slim slices of lamb tucked into crisp greenery.

"An amuse-bouche, mademoiselle," the waiter said in his perfectly accented French. "*Un petit* gift from the chef."

"This is too exquisite, Michael," she said as soon as the waiter vanished. "I can't believe what I'm tasting. Lamb sorrel, chickweed and dandelion. What an imaginative combination of flavors. So rich…and yet subtle. How do they do this? I feel like I'm in a romantic forest glade."

What the hell was chickweed? He didn't care. All that mattered was that his lovely gypsy was running her tongue over her lips and shutting her eyes in pure, sensual bliss and looking so aroused it was all he could do not to reach across the table and touch her. Too bad they were in a public restaurant instead of her imaginary forest glade.

He caught himself. He knew what she was, so why did he continue to want her in his life?

Next, they had soup. Again, she noted her surprise at its originality. She couldn't stop rhapsodizing about the sharp mint of the chives mingled with the sweetness of the garlic.

"I've never had such an elegant soup made from such basic ingredients," she said in pleasure and awe. "How does he get the flavors to run so deep?"

And so it went, her attitude toward him improving with each marvel that she tasted, each course delighting her more than the last. All around them the rich fragrances of roasted ducks being carved at nearby tables and caramel sauces being drizzled over poached foie gras swirled around them.

The festive and voluptuous richness of the food seemed to make her forget her fear of him. It definitely made him forget his doubts about her.

He was so mesmerized by her sparkling eyes and quick blushes, he scarcely noted the clinks of silverware or the sounds of the other diners' muted laughter. It was as if they were the only two people in the universe.

For dessert he ordered a chocolate napoleon and she ordered warm raspberries followed by vanilla cream, which she ate with the relish of a true gourmet.

"That was all so delicious," she said dreamily as she licked the last of the cream off her spoon with the pink tip of that tongue of hers that he knew could be so wickedly clever at other erotic things.

A hot frisson of desire shot through him. God, he wanted her—wanted her to continue living with him indefinitely, wanted to sleep with her again.

Not that he gave her any indication of his feelings or intentions as he caught the waiter's eye, held up his hand and signaled for their bill.

When it was time to leave, she arose reluctantly, as if she'd enjoyed dining with him as much as he'd enjoyed her.

"That was nice. Really, really nice," she gushed. "You shouldn't have done it, but thank you so much."

He nodded. "I assure you. It was my pleasure."

She was still blushing when the valet brought his car around and Michael helped her slide into the cocoon of the plush, black leather interior.

Her heart beat much too fast as they stepped outside into the damp coolness of the rainy night.

She shouldn't trust him. The meal, which had been too fantastic for words, combined with his attentive, amusing companionship, had her in a dangerously aroused mood. Had he remembered how their first shared meal had primed her senses in the same way? All night his gaze had been so dark and intense, she burned. Had he planned tonight's dinner tonight for some underhanded reason?

She, who never wanted to believe the worst of anyone—not even him—didn't want to think that. He'd been nicer since she'd injured her foot, treating her almost as if he was her friend. He was helping her with the bistro, wasn't he? Maybe he was beginning to like her a little. She felt a dangerous hunger to finish this night of sensual delights in his bed.

Stupid idea. She couldn't let him know.

He helped her into his sleek Mercedes and then slid behind the wheel. When she dared a glance at him, their eyes met and she felt the familiar sizzle. Then her gaze fell to his tight mouth and lingered as she remembered the erotic pleasures those lips were capable of giving her.

Realizing how desperately she longed for him to kiss her, she tore her gaze away and forced herself to focus on the pedestrians that streamed past them on the sidewalks in an endless, colorful flood.

Closing her eyes, she tried to settle down as the big silver car—its tires hissing, its windshield wipers slashing—raced through the rain.

Why had she told him the doctor had released her early? If she hadn't told him, she could have stayed another night. Then maybe she wouldn't feel this perverse urgency, this sense that it might be her last chance to be with him....

When she nervously began to chew on a fingernail, he seized her hand, brought it to his lips and blew a warm breath over her skin.

"Don't!" he admonished. "Your hands are too pretty to ruin."

She yanked the offending hand free and sat on it as stubbornly as a guilty child. All the while, savage, inexplicable desire for him pulsed inside her like a jungle drum. He didn't look at her or speak again, but she was afraid he read her mind because suddenly the air between them grew so tense it sparked.

She wanted him—this impossible, difficult man, who was the secret father of her precious, unborn child. Despite his critical opinion of her and all the other reasons she shouldn't want him, what she wanted, more than anything, was another taste of the forbidden in his bed.

She did *not* have to surrender to temptation.

She *would not* surrender to it. After spending the past

few days with him, her feelings now ran deeper. She was pregnant with his child. If he insulted her this time, the hurt would be even more unbearable than before.

What she *would* do was throw her belongings in her duffel bag and march out of his penthouse with her head held high.

Geography, if not willpower, would save her from herself and this much-too-sexy man.

But she'd forgotten about his elevator.

Eight

Even before the doors of the elevator trapped her inside a tiny box with Michael, her heart was drumming madly in her throat. Then the cage jerked, throwing her against him. She let out a shriek before they shot upward. Her heart spiked to rocket speed, and her wide eyes lifted beseechingly to his.

He put his lips softly against her ear. "Don't be so afraid. You're perfectly safe. This stuffy building, as you call it, is state of the art. I'm on a committee that oversees maintenance issues." His deep voice was a comforting rumble.

"You're right," she said. "I'm fine."

"Let's make sure, why don't we?"

When he caught her closer, her breath hitched.

"Oh, my God. You're as cold as ice and shaking. Don't tell me I'm going to have to give up my penthouse view and move to a lower floor."

She was too foolishly pleased that he'd said he'd move

just for her, too pleased he was holding her close. She pressed herself against his powerful body and gasped when she found him rock hard and fully aroused.

"See, you make me even crazier than this elevator makes you," he whispered. "I can't help myself where you're concerned. I don't care who you are or what you've done."

His words cut. "But I care what you think. If you don't see me as I really am, how can we ever have a real connection? I'm not the bad person you think I am. I'm not your ex-wife, you know," she murmured.

"Why did you bring her up?"

"Luke told me she married you for your money."

"Leave her out of this."

"Did you love her?"

"I don't want to talk about her."

"Well, FYI—*I'm not her.*"

His jaw tightened, but he didn't argue.

"I'm just a dull working girl."

"A very attractive one."

"You prefer glamorous."

"Maybe we should concentrate on the present," he muttered bitterly. "You have plenty of charm."

His hard arms tightened around her, and he drew her closer—so close she forgot to be afraid, so close she forgot to be logical or sensible. All that mattered was his fierce power and the raw desire she saw in his eyes.

Her hands wound into his silky black hair. In the restaurant, she'd barely been able to think because of his intense gaze and dominating presence. He'd been so nice for the past three days, and then tonight he'd swept her away with the meal and his sexiness.

He bestowed a soft kiss on her forehead. His gentleness and unexpected kindness lessened her doubts.

Maybe he'd loved his wife and had been hurt. Maybe

if he moved past that he would be able to see Bree more clearly.

"Hold me," she whispered. "Hold me forever."

Standing on her tiptoes, she pressed her lips gently to his chin, tempting him to kiss her for real.

"Now who's seducing who?" he teased in a triumphant tone.

"Don't be so impossibly conceited. As soon as we're off this elevator, I'll remember how terrible you've been to me because you're determined to think me a horrible person, and I'll want to avoid you all over again."

"In that case, I'd better seize the advantage while I still have it."

Pushing her back against the wall, his lips found hers. He kissed her hard and long, plunging his tongue into her mouth again and again. Glorious heat rushed through her veins as she kissed him back. Her heart still knocked, but no longer with fear. Reading her response, he lowered his mouth and kissed her nipple through her shirt.

He lifted his head. Dazed, her heart racing, her mouth open, her eyes met the wildness in his gaze. He was the father of her unborn baby. In spite of all the walls she'd tried to erect against him, she still felt connected to him.

What she really wanted was for him to love their child and maybe someday love her, too. And when he kissed her like this, some idiotic part of her believed that could happen, that he might change some day, that he might see her as she was and be capable of respecting her…of loving her.

When the doors opened, he took her hand and tugged her into his dimly lit hall. He pulled her to his door, which he unlocked. In the entry, he slammed his door and locked it. Then he scooped her into his arms and carried her to her bedroom behind his kitchen, all the while kissing her as if he'd been driven mad by forced abstinence.

"I've been a fool," he whispered, "to deny myself when

you make me feel like this. When no other woman, not ever, has come close to affecting me the way you do. The last few days with you have been hell because I've wanted you so much. I don't care how you manipulated my brother."

She wished he'd quit saying that. Will had demanded she marry him—for the baby's sake.

"I...didn't manipulate Will."

"Shh. I don't care."

"But you don't believe me—"

"I don't care."

But she did. Why couldn't Michael wrap his mind around that?

He was the one who had manipulated her and gotten her pregnant. Will had felt so horrible that his brother had abandoned her that he'd insisted she marry him.

Gently Michael laid her on the bed and then followed her down. She opened her eyes and met the heat of his gaze as he smoothed her hair from her fevered brow and kissed her lips, nose and throat.

"I don't believe in happily ever after," he whispered as his mouth moved lower.

"I know." He didn't listen to her or believe her or even *see* her. "Believe me—I get all the bad stuff about you."

"But I'll give you everything else...if only you'll live here and become my mistress."

"No."

"I want you. Never again will you have to worry about money or losing your bistro. I'll take care of you...and Will's baby. No matter what you say, I know those things matter to you."

Money, she thought but with only the faintest irritation. He wanted her, and he still thought she was so low that he could buy her. Their relationship was just another negotiation, a deal to him, terms to be established, services to be rendered for money that would be owed.

She got him, but he didn't get her. Did anything other than money and closing deals really matter to him?

Money wasn't the most important thing to her. Far from it. She was going to have his child. To her, *that* was all-important. Would that even matter to him if he knew? And if it did, what kind of deal would he propose?

She could not be with a man like him on a permanent basis.

But being with him tonight was a different matter. Tonight his passionate ardor had stirred her past caring that he was incapable of giving her what she really wanted for herself and their child—a lifetime of commitment and happiness, tenderness, trust and love.

Deliciously pinned beneath his massive body, knowing he would soon strip her and fill her, felt so pleasurable she didn't want to think about all the negatives. Dimly she remembered her plan to pack and run, to get herself as far away from him as possible. But she was much too weak to follow such a wise course that might protect her heart from a man who didn't seem to have one.

So she smiled up at him and kissed him on the lips.

Tonight she would enjoy him. Tomorrow, and all the dreary tomorrows after that one, would be soon enough to deny herself.

Tonight, she wanted him far too much to walk away.

She seemed so utterly sweet as she lay radiant beneath him.

His wallet lay facedown on her bedside table, the packet of condoms he always carried inside ripped open. They were naked, and he was buried to the hilt in her slick, satin heat. He inhaled her sweet strawberry scent. She was warm, silky, tight—perfect, just as he'd remembered. Better than he'd remembered. Knowing her better had somehow increased his craving for her.

His heart thudded violently. Primal urgency drove him to withdraw and plunge into her again and again, to rush, to finish, to make this an animal conquest instead of a spiritual connection. Instead, as if she was infinitely precious to him in ways he couldn't begin to understand, he held her close, savoring this first moment of being joined to her.

Relief that had nothing to do with sex flooded him.

He felt whole.

As a child he'd known the insecurity and the degradation of poverty, known too much about the things his mother had done for money.

His mother had loved him, he supposed, but he'd never felt loved. He'd seen other mothers fuss over their kids. They'd come to games, cheered at competitions, met with teachers or worked in the classrooms. Not his mother, and he'd felt the lack of her concern. She hadn't pushed him to succeed either or even believed that he could.

He, however, had believed that if he became wealthy, he'd have power, respect and happiness—he'd have everything he'd craved as a child, including love.

But it hadn't worked out like that. He'd made it big in the financial sector. Somehow his loneliness and sense of alienation had only increased, until finally he'd let down his guard and trusted Anya. She'd gutted him, making him feel as powerless as he'd felt as a neglected child. He'd vowed never to allow himself to feel that vulnerable again.

Irony of ironies: here he was again, wanting Bree so much he risked everything for her even though he knew she'd used his brother. The increasingly powerful need he felt for her terrified him.

Being with her felt so good, so immensely pleasurable. Nothing had ever come close to the intensity of his feelings for her. He liked sharing the penthouse with her. All day as he worked, he liked knowing she'd be waiting for him when he came home. He'd enjoyed grocery shopping because he'd known she'd revel in the cheeses and crackers and sweets he'd bought her.

He mustn't let himself feel so much, couldn't let himself want so much. Not with Bree, a woman who'd used his beloved brother.

Money and power were the sources of his strength, not this woman. Maybe money couldn't bring the happiness he'd once believed it could, but it bought some awfully nice substitutes. He had to be content with that.

Bree moved in his arms and whispered his name, bringing him back to the present as she begged him in husky tones to kiss her, to take her, to please, please take her.

His mouth found hers, and her instant response made him want her even more. Where would this end?

Something stronger than he was made a mockery of his best intentions not to yield to his feelings for her. In her thrall, his lips ground against hers; his tongue mated with hers. When she clutched him frantically, he lost all control. Her nails bit into his back as she gasped.

In that timeless moment when she melted and clung, he cried out her name. Shattered, he held her close, and all their differences fell away.

His arms tightened around her as she bathed his face with kisses. She was his, and he was hers, so completely that nothing could ever come between them. Never before had he known such pleasure. Despite his doubts, the experience felt so true and honest happiness filled him.

Slowly the moment of shared bliss ebbed. A few minutes later, when she idly stroked his nape, he tensed. As a small child he'd longed for such a simple caress.

He blinked, terrified that she might sense how much such thoughtless affection meant to him.

She couldn't matter this much. Whatever this was, it had to be controlled, managed, put away.

He could not lose himself completely to her. He would not.

Without a word, he slid away from her burning finger-tips and arose, knowing grimly that if he didn't, he would make love to her again and again. And every time they came together, she would increase her hold over him until she was everything to him while only his money would matter to her. He didn't want to feel craven, rejected and alone as he had as a child.

Feeling doomed and miserable at the thought of leaving her, and yet knowing it was a matter of survival to do so, he forced himself to climb the stairs to his own bed-room. He would boot up his computer and work tonight. Work would be his salvation. Surely with work he could drive her out of his heart and mind.

It wasn't her fault that he had not felt enough love as a child or that no woman could ever make him feel loved now that he was a man. But he didn't have to put himself under her power. He would lock this thing away, contain it, forget about it, admit nothing to her.

Though earlier this same evening he'd been looking for ways to keep her here, now he wanted her gone—out of his penthouse.

As for the rest of tonight, he couldn't allow himself to see her again before he had himself firmly mastered. It would take every ounce of discipline and willpower he had, but he was determined not to wreck his life a sec-ond time.

Bree felt acute heartache when Michael deliberately rolled away from her and got up, cutting their connection.

She wanted another night like their first. She wanted him to take her in his arms again. She wanted him to say he liked her, respected her. If he did, maybe she could trust him enough to confide the truth about her unborn child.

A compulsion to bare her soul, to reach for him, to seize his hand and pull him back, took possession of her. But instead of begging him to stay as she'd done that first night, she lay still and quiet and watched him walk away. Even when she saw him stop in the doorway and turn, his profile was so stern she refused to call out to him.

Then he walked out and closed the door, and she was left to toss restlessly in the dark, telling herself sorrowfully that his departure was really for the best. She should will herself to sleep. But she was too edgy, and she wanted so much more from him. Counting hundreds of imaginary sheep while she knotted and unknotted the corner of the sheet, she lay frozen in misery for at least an hour.

When he didn't come back to bed, she finally arose and pulled on his overlarge robe. Stealthily, she made her way out of her suite, down the hall and across his vast, opulent living area that was bathed in shadow and moonlight. Avoiding his elevator, she tiptoed up two flights of stairs. His bedroom door stood ajar, a stream of light spilling across the dark hall.

He didn't want her; he'd left her. She should go. But what if something was troubling him? Maybe no one had ever been there for him before. Maybe she could help him in some way.

When she pushed the door open, she saw him hunched over his computer. In the bright glare of the screen his face was haggard and fierce. He was working; he often worked so hard he forgot to eat.

"Michael," she whispered softly as she slid inside the room. "You shouldn't be working at this hour. Is anything wrong?"

He was shirtless, so she saw every muscle in his powerful back swell and harden when he whirled on her. His strong body was as tough and hard as his brilliant business mind. He clenched his fists, as if he felt the need to defend himself from her attack.

But she had no intention of attacking him.

"What are you doing here?" he demanded so harshly he froze her heart.

"I couldn't sleep," she murmured, seeking to soothe him rather than frighten or anger him. "I was too worried… about you."

"Worried? Right." He sounded edgy, dubious, angry.

Was he afraid? Of her? No, that couldn't be. Not when his black eyes were so hard. It was she who felt terrified that he would reject her or be cruel.

"Have I done something wrong?" she asked. "Tonight was wonderful for me. Even better than before. I hoped… I thought that maybe we could start over."

"I'm fine," he ground out. Then as if he couldn't bear the sight of her, he closed his eyes and turned his back on her. "Go back to bed. I have an important meeting tomorrow. I need to go over a few things as you can plainly see."

Hurt swamped her. Swaying a little, her nails dug into the doorframe. She didn't know how she summoned the nerve to hold her ground.

"You can't work all the time, darling, now can you?" she said gently. Before she lost her courage, she crossed the room and slid her arms around him.

He jumped as if her touch and nearness burned him.

"I'm sure your meeting will go better if you get some sleep," she persisted.

"As if I could sleep with you—downstairs."

"I could stay up here and maybe give you a massage."

"No!"

"Yes! You're much too tense. Your muscles are all knotted."

"Because I have work to do!"

Beneath her exploring fingertips his warm, bare skin was smooth as she kneaded the deep tissue of his muscles. When he slowly relaxed and then sighed as if in defeat, she sucked in a breath and laid her lips against his wide chest.

"I can't bear it down there without you, darling. Not when tonight's our last night together."

He hesitated briefly before slamming his laptop closed and folding his arms around her. "I left you because I thought it was best for both of us."

"You won't be sorry. I'm really very good at massages," she said. "I even took a course once…at night school during a short-lived self-improvement kick."

"Bree, oh, my darling," he murmured, the tension flowing out of his deep voice. "Like I said, I came up here with the best of intentions."

"Did you now?"

"You have no idea what you do to me."

"You have the rest of the night to tell me…or better yet, show me. Whichever you prefer, my love."

His mouth claimed hers in a long kiss that was the sweetest he'd ever given her. *He did feel something.* She was almost sure of it.

Maybe there was hope, she thought. Maybe…

For a long moment, as she pondered the possibility, she didn't dare breathe.

Pulling her closer, he opened her robe and stroked her body, knowing just where to touch to arouse her.

"Oh, God, I want you too much to say no to you." Frustrated by the thick fabric, he yanked it off and carried her to his bed where he made love to her again and again, each time as fervently and as passionately as she'd dreamed of him doing.

He did everything he could to please her, and he was

everything she had ever wanted or imagined a perfect lover would be.

If only he could be as good for her in other ways, she thought afterward as she lay in the dark beside him. She'd say yes to him, stay with him and tell him about the baby. Maybe their affair would turn into something meaningful.

With an effort she reminded herself that he cared about one thing only—money.

Funny that he should despise her because he thought she was the same.

It was hard to concentrate on packing with him standing over her, his black gaze watching her every movement. He sipped steaming black coffee she'd brewed for him from a porcelain mug.

"I know it's smart for both of us to end it, but I don't want you to go." His tone was that of a command. "I don't want it to be over. You know that."

When she looked up, his eyes were so hot her tummy turned over. The long night of sex had left her tender both physically and emotionally. She couldn't look at him without feeling too much.

As always he was devastatingly handsome in an impeccably tailored three-piece suit he'd put on for his important meeting this morning. He was dazzling. Would their child be equally so?

"I'll miss you, too." Her voice was choked.

Last night in his arms, she'd been so happy, felt so cherished.

She *would* miss him. Too much. More than was sensible. So what else was new? Angrily she threw a blouse toward her duffel bag.

She had to do this.

Had he ever once told her she could matter as a person to him? No. If she thought there was any hope—any hope at all—that he could ever see her for who she was or really care about her, maybe she would have agreed to the abysmal, degrading terms of his affair on the slight possibility she could make him so happy he would change his mind about her over time.

But he was absolutely incapable of being the kind of man she needed in her life, and he could never trust her to be the right woman for him. So why prolong a relationship that wouldn't work?

Because it works in bed, said a sneaky little voice inside her. *Be fair. Not just in bed. Remember how he was last night at dinner? He deliberately took you somewhere special. He was kind when he tended your foot, too, and protective when he slept all night in that awful chair watching over you.*

Remembering everything he'd done to her last night and how she'd reveled in the expertise of his mouth and tongue on all her intimate body parts, she colored.

They'd had last night. Nobody could ever take that away from her.

"Why won't you move in with me permanently?"

"I need my own place where I can be *me* and have *my* friends over."

"You can have whoever the hell you want here."

"Are you kidding? In this stuffy co-op on Fifth Avenue? Your doorman rolls his eyes every time I walk into the building. I value my independence. And you value yours."

"To hell with my independence. I want you."

"For sex."

"I don't deny it."

"That's not enough. If I stayed, I wouldn't respect myself."

"Why the hell not? This is the twenty-first century."

"Because to you, our relationship would just be another business arrangement. Everything is a deal to you. You pay—I continue to sleep over, only in your bed. It's as simple as that."

"No. That's not how it would be." But he spoke sheepishly.

"Isn't it? You don't want a real relationship with me based on respect and trust, and I don't want to be with a man who doesn't really *like* me."

He changed tack. "But you do admit that you enjoy me…as much as I enjoy you?"

Again she blushed. "That's hardly the point. You think all I've ever wanted from you and your family is money."

"Well, I know you like me in bed, so maybe not *all*."

"See!"

"What do you mean, *see?* Okay, I didn't want to mention this, but since you're forcing the issue, I know that you had my brother set up a million-dollar trust fund for you and your baby. And that you got him to sign it over to you on the day he married you."

"*I* got him to sign it over to me?"

"You heard me! Do you deny you signed documents to claim those monies on your wedding day?"

"Get out! Go to work! Go to your precious meeting! This is what you've been thinking about me all week… and last night when we were making love? A hibernating snake in a frozen hole in the dead of winter has a warmer heart than you do."

"I'd be a fool if I refused to face facts."

"I don't want to sleep with a man who always thinks the worst of me. What can't you understand about that? You'll never change. I'm glad you brought this up because now I can leave here without caring if I ever see you again!"

Tears stung her eyes, but she didn't want to cry. She couldn't give him the satisfaction of knowing how much he was hurting her. Why couldn't he have just asked her about the documents? Why did he always assume the worst?

"Did you or did you not sign them the day you married my brother?" he demanded.

"Yes! Yes! Yes!" Her voice dropped to a whisper. "You've got that part right. I signed them."

When a single tear tracked down her cheek she scrubbed at it furiously with her fist and turned away.

"But it didn't happen like you said, Michael!" she blurted out through strangled sobs. "Or for the reasons you think. I swear it didn't! But did you ask me for the truth? Ever? No!"

"I'm asking now, and you're telling me not to believe what I've seen with my own eyes—which is your damn signature on a dated document. On your wedding day!"

It had all been Will's idea. Not hers. He'd feared his brother wouldn't do the right thing for her or his child.

But would Michael believe that?

"I'm not what you think, but I'm past caring about your opinion of me. I'm through talking to you, through trying to explain myself. It's hopeless to try to change your mind because you *want* to believe the worst. I wish I'd never met you, wish I'd never slept with you. I don't want to ever see you again! Not for as long as I live! I don't want you in my baby's life either—because I want him to grow up with a trusting heart, which is something you'll never have!"

He went white, absolutely white.

"If you change your mind, call me," he said in a voice that was like ice. "Because I want you, no matter who you are, no matter what you've done."

Every time he said that, he carved out a little piece of her.

When he turned and strode out of the room, she lunged at her duffel on the bed and heaved it onto the floor, spilling her clothes everywhere.

Nine

Michael looked so lost, haunted and alone as he stood by his brother's urn. She couldn't take her eyes off him. It was all she could do not to rush to him and put her arms around him.

She was such a wuss. Was it only two days ago that she'd told Michael she never wanted to see him again?

For the past forty-eight hours she'd missed him horribly. The raw agony in his face when his eyes sought hers compelled her for an interminable second or two. He'd loved his brother deeply.

In that long moment when neither could tear their eyes from the other, she shared his all-consuming grief. Maybe that was all they could ever share.

Besides the baby she was too afraid to tell him about.

Whatever faults Michael had, he'd loved Will and was grieving now. She wanted to go to him, to thread her fingers through his, to pull him close and say comforting words in the hope that she could ease that pain.

What if she told him they were going to have a child, that Will had only married her to protect Michael's future child? Would that ease some of his conflict and grief? Or would it add fresh torment since he despised her and believed the baby to be a part of Will?

He was so alone. Maybe Michael had money, but he'd lacked love when he'd needed it most. And the lack had hardened him. Only Will had seen Michael's faults and loved him anyway. Now Michael had to say goodbye to the one person who'd loved him.

When the preacher introduced Michael, he stepped up to the podium and began to speak, his deep voice filling the sanctuary. The words he chose to celebrate his brother's life were so eloquent, they resonated inside her. Hot tears filled her eyes. Her heart ached for him. Soon everybody around her was sniffing and sobbing, too.

Funny that such a heartless man knew exactly what to say to touch so many. If he could speak like that and love that deeply, why couldn't he love her and their child?

When her tears threatened to fall, she brushed them away. Will was dead. Michael was who he was. She couldn't help him or change him. She had to say goodbye to both brothers, keep her secret and move on.

After the service, when the family stood beside the urn receiving mourners, a middle-aged woman with hard gray eyes and a thin, pursed mouth pointed her silver-handled cane at Bree.

"*You!* I've been wanting to have my say," the woman said. "Michael told me that you were pregnant and injured. But here you are—looking fit as a fiddle."

Suddenly Michael, his face grim, materialized beside Bree. Not that he greeted her by word or smile. He was just there, shielding her from the older woman like a protective force field.

When the woman's brows knitted, Michael's hand touched Bree's elbow

"I saw her watching you during the service, so don't think I don't see how it is between you two," the woman said. "She didn't love Will. If either of you think I believe for one minute she had a real marriage with my nephew or that her baby is his…"

Bree reeled.

"Not here, Alice," Michael warned in a voice of steel.

"You can't stop me, Michael. You're as greedy as she is. It wouldn't surprise me to learn you set some sort of trap for Will and used her for bait."

"Don't be absurd," Michael said. "Leave her alone."

"You can't tell me what to do, and I'll sue you again if you try."

His fingers tightened protectively on Bree's elbow. Drawing her closer, he gave Alice a warning look that was so fierce the woman squinted and backed away.

"Thank you," Bree said stiffly as Alice fled down the aisle.

"I told you…the family can be difficult," he murmured. "She was equally cruel to my mother."

Thankfully the next person to approach them was a lovely older woman with silver hair who was dressed in soft grays and blues.

She clasped Bree's hand. "I've wanted to call you and tell you how sorry I am about Will, but I just couldn't work up the strength…until now. I'm Mrs. Ferrar, Tony's mother."

"I'm so sorry for your loss, Mrs. Ferrar. So very sorry," Bree said.

"I know you are. Tony told me how much you and your child meant to Will." Her kind, sympathetic blue eyes shifted to Michael. "He told me how much you meant to

Will, too, Mr. North. I know you will take good care of Bree and her precious baby. Will would want that."

Mrs. Ferrar opened her arms, and Bree stepped into them. "There…there… That's right. Give me a big hug. Tony's service will be tomorrow. I sure hope you'll come. I don't know how I'll get through it if people like you, people who knew Tony, aren't with me."

"I will be there," Bree promised. "Again, I'm so sorry."

"I've been cleaning out their apartment, sorting through Tony's things. You two will have to do that for Will. The landlord told me he already has a new tenant, so he's willing to forgive their lease. So, the sooner, the better."

"We'll take care of it, Mrs. Ferrar," Michael said.

We'll…

"I'll miss them both," Mrs. Ferrar said, "and so will you. Some days are going to be hard for you…really, really hard. But when that happens, you think about your precious baby. I have young grandchildren. And they're so full of life, just their pictures on my fridge are enough to cheer me up. I'll do all right."

Despite the sorrowful occasion, Mrs. Ferrar's warmth cheered Bree. In the future, whenever she became sad or confused, she needed to focus on her baby.

"Mr. North, I want a hug from you, too. Such a shame you never got to meet my Tony. I told Will, and more than once, I was sure you'd like him."

"I'm sure of it, too," Michael said, but the new questions in his eyes when he regarded Bree made her swallow hard.

How long would it be before he figured out the truth? The whole truth?

Michael locked his Mercedes, crossed the street and strode to his brother's building. After an endless week of bleak days and nights grieving for Will without seeing or talking to Bree, he couldn't believe she'd actually taken a phone call from him and agreed to meet him at Will's apartment today. He had Bijou to thank for that, he supposed—Bijou, whom he'd bribed with flattery and with dozens of red roses.

Unsure about the reception he'd receive from her daughter, he felt on edge riding up to Will's floor in the tiny elevator.

If the past seven days without Bree had felt like an eternity, what would a lifetime without her be like?

He had it bad. He couldn't sleep, and food, no matter how expensive or how beautifully presented, tasted like cardboard. Even work failed to distract him.

He wanted her. And not just in his bed.

He wanted to talk to her, to look forward to her company at night when he came home. He wanted to make love to her. But he wanted more than all that—so much more. He wanted her companionship and affection, her adoration. She'd adored him that first night—before he'd come clean and ripped her heart open. He wanted her eyes to shine when she looked at him again.

Last week he'd screwed up a major deal because his mind had been on Bree. Since he hadn't pushed ruthlessly enough, he would have to look for new financing for the deal. He needed to go to Shanghai to sort out a mess over there, but he couldn't make himself get on a plane because he didn't want to leave New York with their relationship unresolved.

Why did he feel so lost and alienated with her out of his life?

Because of his illogical need for her, he felt resentment toward her. Had she suffered at all?

Probably not, he thought. Then his heart leaped when he unlocked his brother's door, stepped into the apartment and heard her singing an aria from *Carmen*. She was a little off-key maybe, but not too bad. Hell—off-key or not, the music was charming. She sounded happy.

She was probably thriving without him. And who could blame her?

"Hello!" he yelled, not wanting to follow that train of thought.

She continued to sing. No reply. Either she didn't hear him or she was deliberately ignoring him.

"Hello, damn it!"

The singing stopped, but she didn't call out to him. Annoyed, he stomped into Will's bedroom and found her kneeling over a box of thick wool sweaters.

"What's with the opera? I thought you were into rock music."

Her quick blush made his gut tighten and his body harden.

"Apparently, Mrs. Ferrar took Tony's player and speakers. So I was singing something Luke was humming earlier at the bistro."

"Luke? I thought he finished his assessment of Chez Z. Doesn't he have his own empire to run?"

"I'm sure he does, but he came by because he's so sweet."

Sweet, my ass.

"He took me to dinner at one of his restaurants last night to show me a few more tricks."

Dinner? *Sweet* had nothing to do with it. He was hitting on her.

"Sorry. I know I can't carry a tune. Luke has the most beautiful voice."

Luke, again. Damn. "You sounded okay. Not bad," he said, grumpily, his mind on Luke.

"What can I do to help around here?" Michael muttered.

She refused to look at him. "Just pack everything, I guess."

"Okay. I can do that."

"Maybe you could work in the living room, that way—"

"Right. That way you can avoid me."

"Did I say that?"

"I was rough on you last week, so you think maybe I should apologize."

"Why? You meant what you said. I'm glad I know what you think of me. Now I can move on."

Her cutting words made him feel bleak as hell. But she was right. He didn't trust her. Why should he? Unfortunately, he still wanted her in his life.

He let out a long, frustrated breath and shoved a hand through his hair. Not knowing what else to do, he grabbed a box off the floor and went into the living room where he began slinging books into it with a fury. Consumed with her, he worked, banging about in the living room for more than an hour. After he finished unloading the bookshelf, he started on the desk and then the computer.

The drawers were slower going because he couldn't pack papers and files without going through them in an effort to figure out if they were important. After an hour, he'd finished two drawers and filled two boxes. Then he opened the bottom drawer and found it stuffed with discs and flash drives that were labeled as photos and videos.

Curious, he loaded a disk that Will had titled *Our First Night Together and Honeymoon* into the computer, because Michael had to prove to himself once and for all that she'd been lying about her relationship.

But the pictures weren't of Will and Bree; they were of Will and Tony.

In the first series of shots, Will and Tony were holding hands. In the next, they were hugging. Then the pictures got racier.

In each shot, the two of them wore less. Hell, was this some kind of strip session? When they were down to their briefs, Michael decided he'd seen enough and tore the disc from the machine.

Will and Tony?

He stared into space blankly. Why hadn't he seen what had been right before his eyes? Will had always been so sensitive, so sweet and caring. So damned perfect in all the ways Michael wasn't. Michael remembered how Jacob used to beg Will to bring a girl home. *Any girl,* he'd say. Had he suspected?

I will, Dad. I just have to meet the right girl.

But just after Jacob's death, Will had moved here and become nearly impossible to reach.

Had Will been nervous about introducing Michael to Tony? Afraid Michael wouldn't accept their partnership?

But he would have. He did accept it. Realities were realities. People were what they were. He'd loved Will. Period.

The reason Bree hadn't displayed a single photograph of Will in her apartment was because they'd been friends, not lovers.

Just like she'd said.

She'd been telling the truth about that at least.

So why the hell had Will married her?

Michael remembered his brother's glazed eyes in the E.R. and his final words.

"She's a wonderful girl. Not what you think. In a way, what you did to her was all my fault. So, if you'll just promise me…you'll take care of her, that'll do this one thing for me, we'll be square."

What you did to her…

What had Will meant? What was Michael missing?

When Michael got up and walked into the bedroom again, Bree looked up absently from the growing mountain of packed boxes.

"What? What is it, Michael?"

"Will was gay."

She drew a breath and quickly averted her eyes. "Okay."

"You knew!"

She swallowed.

"So—apparently everybody knew but me...even Aunt Alice. This puts everything in a new light."

Her face was flushed and her lips trembled.

"Who got you pregnant? Why the hell did he marry you?"

"It's complicated."

Her answer drove him over some edge. "You've said that before. My work is complicated. I bet this is simple. If he was in love with Tony, if he lived here with Tony, if he was never your lover as you claimed all along, how the hell did you manipulate him into marrying you? Who's the father of your baby? Some other guy I don't know about? Tell me his name!"

"Damn you," she lashed out at him. "I was a virgin when I slept with you. You have to know that!"

On some rational level, maybe he did. But women had been tricking men about their virginity for centuries, and he was too angry for logic to work.

She stood up, her eyes aflame, her cheeks dark with rage. "This from you right now...is too much!"

She was angry, angrier than he'd ever seen her. Fighting for control, she shut her eyes. Not that she calmed down any. When she opened her eyes again they were so bright they shot sparks at him. "I don't want to talk about this with you. Not even now."

"Well, I do. You had some sordid affair and made my brother feel sorry for you—"

"Used him? Had a sordid affair? This is the final straw! I've had it with you! You always think I'm some cheap hustler! You always think everything is my fault! It's *my* fault we got married! It's *my* fault because I'm greedy and manipulative!"

Eyes aflame, she stared at him for a long moment.

"Well, it's not my fault! It's yours!"

"What are you saying?"

"When you slept with me to drive a wedge between me and Will, I *was* a virgin, and *you* got me pregnant!"

He'd gotten her pregnant? Her accusation jolted him like a blow. He reeled backward.

He'd taken every precaution; he always took every precaution.

"I couldn't have gotten you pregnant. That's not possible." Then why did his chest feel heavy as he stared into her eyes that blazed with outrage and hurt? It was as if her eyes were a fist she'd rammed inside him.

"Apparently it *is* possible because I *am* pregnant. This mess is your fault as much as it is mine! But unlike you, I take part of the blame because I was the simpleminded idiot who slept with you."

"You're claiming I'm the father, and that's *why* Will married you?" Michael's voice was hoarse.

"Yes! I didn't know who to turn to. Like a fool, I cried on his shoulder. He said you were so set against me, it was up to him to do the right thing. He felt someone in the family had to help me get on my feet. He said you'd had a grudge against all women ever since Anya lied about being pregnant and you married her. He said you wouldn't change your mind about me easily. And, oh boy, how right he was! Your brother had a sense of honor— which you don't."

Her words were sinking in, making sense. Horrible sense.

Pregnant. She was pregnant.

"You're sure it's mine?" he rasped.

"Damn you!"

"Sorry," he growled, hanging his head with genuine repentance.

"Look, I've never been with another man. How many times do I have to tell you that? Not that I'm proud of that fact. I wish I'd been with ten other men before you, men who had hearts. Maybe if I'd been the gold-digging slut you thought I was, I would have seen through you. I wish I was pregnant by somebody else!"

He was going to be a father.

Michael felt too shocked to say anything for what felt like an interminably long interval.

She was pregnant with his child and she'd been doing her damnedest to hide that fact from him. And he didn't blame her for that.

He felt sick with regret. What could he say to her now? What could he do? His thoughts were a painful jumble.

He'd gotten a virgin pregnant and had run off to Shanghai to try to forget her. He had a lot to answer for.

"I did my best to protect you—you have to know that. I did everything in my power to prevent this."

"I know. I remember. *Because I was the last person you wanted to have a baby with*. I'm sure there's a lot of collateral damage with every deal you close."

Her voice cut like an ice shard.

"So," she continued, "here we are. You and I are going to have a baby. What now? How are you going to spin it so I'm the evil one? Do you still think I'm trying to manipulate you the way Anya did?"

"No. You're not like her."

"Wow! I can't believe you said that."

What he couldn't believe was that he'd been so blind to the truth where she was concerned. But so many people lied to him, not only in his relationships but in the business world. Too often the men he negotiated with would say or do anything to make a deal.

Bree was not like Anya or the sharks in Shanghai.

The reality hit him hard as he considered how badly he'd behaved toward her.

She was so different from the women he usually dated that he hadn't understood that she might be genuine.

"Were you ever going to tell me about the baby?" he asked softly.

"Maybe…in time."

"You mean in a year or so? Or maybe in twenty years?"

"Maybe."

After the way he'd treated her, he knew he deserved that answer or worse. "Which was it going to be?"

"I don't know. Maybe I wasn't ever going to tell you."

He raked a hand through his hair. His heart was hammering violently.

God, what had he done? Had he thrown away the best thing that had ever happened to him?

"Damn it, Bree."

"You made your feelings for me very, very clear, Michael, on that first night. And on all the nights since."

His gut twisted. Yes, he'd sweet-talked her and made love to her until she'd become radiant every time he looked at her. He'd caressed her so seductively she'd trembled when he barely touched her. Her every nerve had leaped in response to him, but he'd thought she'd been faking.

She hadn't been. While she'd been sincere with him, he'd treated her as deceitfully as Anya had treated him. He was guilty of everything he'd accused Bree of. Afterward he'd told her he hadn't wanted her, that he'd been lying all along and had only pretended he'd cared about her. While she'd been sweet and authentic, he'd been a blind, brutal, rampaging fool. Now, as he remembered the despair in her eyes that night, he knew her virginal pain would haunt him for as long as he lived.

"Everything's different now," he said.

"Not for me, Michael," she said quietly. "You hurt me. You've expressed your poor opinion of me too many times for me not to believe that's how you really feel."

He couldn't blame her. "I know. I'm truly sorry."

"Michael—"

When she looked up at him, distress and confusion showing in her damp eyes, the suffering he'd caused her tore him apart.

"What I did to you that night was wrong. The things I accused you of, even after the accident, were wrong. I see that now. I did something I'd never do in a business deal. Because it involved Will, I rushed into the situation, thinking I had all the facts, but I was clueless. I'm sorry for what I did to you, what I said to you then, and ever since."

She lowered her eyes and bit her lip. Then she lifted her chin. Her eyes were cool, passionless. "I accept your apology. But none of this really matters anymore."

Because he didn't matter to her anymore.

He took a deep breath. "I want to make this right," he said, "but I don't know how."

"It's too late for us."

"We're going to have a baby," he said. "We need to do what's right for our child…maybe get married, maybe—"

"What? Maybe get married? You're willing to marry me because you feel guilty right now? Or because you want control of your precious North heir? Are you out of your mind? You haven't thought this through. You don't want to marry me, and I certainly don't want to marry you. We'd make each other miserable."

"Hear me out. You're going to have my son or daughter."

"Right. Like I said—your precious North heir."

"Listen to me—"

"No! You hear *me* out for a change! I want to marry a

man who loves me for me, who wants to conceive a child with me, who thinks well of me, and you're not capable of that. All you're good at is making money."

When he moved toward her, she went white and shrank against the wall to avoid his touch.

"It wouldn't be about your child being my heir."

"I don't believe you, Michael."

"I still want you," he muttered thickly. "I want you so much, and I don't want to hurt you ever again."

"But you would hurt me. Because you can't love me. You can't love anyone. Money is all you really care about because that's what saved you from poverty. I'm sorry for you, but I've accepted the fact that you are how you are…and that no amount of wishful thinking on my part can change you. I won't change my mind. We come from very different worlds and we are very different people."

The undiluted pain in her eyes pierced his heart. "I can change," he said. "We'll make it work. Somehow. I swear to you."

"I don't think so." She didn't fight him when he lifted her chin and tried to convince her with a kiss. She trembled when his mouth covered hers, but she didn't move into him or pull him close. Her taste intoxicated him even though she simply waited stiffly until he ended the kiss.

"I want you too much to let you go, Bree. The past few days have been hell for me."

"For me, too. But what we feel about each other doesn't really matter. We don't have the same values. You instantly accused me of sleeping around, and I'm not like that. You care only about money and deal-making…we're not right for each other."

"I lost Will. And now I'm losing you. And our child."

"You didn't lose us. You can't lose what you never had. At least, I keep telling myself that. I can't lose you for the same reason—because I never had you."

"Damn it, Bree—"

"Go back to the living room and pack. I don't want to talk to you any longer."

There was a roar in his ears, a fire in his blood as he caught her roughly to him again. "You're pregnant with my child, and I want to do what's right."

"Then stay out of my life!"

His mouth was hard when it met hers. He was determined to claim every part of her, to make her see that love wasn't necessary when two people belonged together. She was like the air he breathed, the water he drank, the food he ate and the earth he walked on. He couldn't live without such essentials. He didn't love the air or water or food, did he? He just had to have them, or he would cease to exist.

"Kiss me back, damn it." His command was crisp and impatient. "You know you want to."

Her heart pulsed erratically and her skin warmed with fiery need, but she didn't put her arms around him or lift her face to his or give him any indication that she was tempted.

"No—let me go," she whispered raggedly. "Please, just let me go."

The warmth of her breath against his cheek alone was enough to drive him crazy. "Why? You know the sex would be great."

"I told you," she whispered huskily. "I want to be valued as a person. Not bought. Or kept. This is just another deal to you. I'm the mother of your child. You enjoy me in bed. I'm not quite as bad as you thought. All in all, I'm a better deal than Anya. In order to get control of your heir, you're willing to marry me."

"Damn it, no." He lifted her dark golden hair and pushed it back from her neck. "I do value you. Or…or, damn it, I'll learn to value you."

"You're just saying that to get what you want. But I know what you really feel and think about me. You've always thought I'm greedy and unscrupulous and can be bought. That's simply your viewpoint."

He lowered his lips to the base of her throat where her pulse pounded. "Because before you, that's all I knew."

"Well, that's not who I am, and I don't want to be with a man who lusts after me but can't respect me. Nothing's different except now you know the baby I'm carrying is yours."

"That's a helluva big difference."

When his hand cupped her breast, and he kissed her again, she shuddered. But she didn't kiss him back.

"I can change. I can learn," he said. "I will try to see you as you are. I will."

"It's too late. Because now it's me who doesn't believe you, Michael. How can I believe anything you say? I'm through. Finished. The suspicions you feel toward others are ingrained so deeply into your character, you'll never rid yourself of them."

"I'm the father of your baby."

"If you insist, I'll inform you about anything that has to do with your child."

"I insist."

"Okay. I'll keep you informed. Other than that, we're through." She picked up her purse and slung it over her shoulder. "I can't even pack up Will's apartment with you. I thought I could, but I can't. You'll have to finish on your own. Or use your precious North money to hire movers. Frankly, I don't care how you handle it."

She turned on her heel and walked past him, out of the apartment, leaving him for good.

Feeling hollow at the core, he stared after her, the tomb-like silence of Will's apartment closing in around him.

He needed a drink, so he began to ransack the shelves and open the closets.

Where the hell was Tony and Will's liquor cabinet?

Ten

It was amazing what money could buy. And what it couldn't.

Not personal happiness. Not love.

Not the one woman he wanted in his life.

For two months, she'd avoided him.

Michael, who had jet lag from hell, was staying in one of the world's most opulent hotels while on business in Abu Dhabi. Gold glittered from the walls. The drapes and upholstery were decorated in an Arabian theme without restraint. Many floors beneath him, waves lapped gently at the building's foundation and caused a faint and constant hum no matter where one stood in the hotel.

And still he couldn't stop thinking about Bree.

"May I run your bath, sir?" The butler appointed to Michael's lavish hotel suite spoke politely in an upper-class British accent.

Rubbing his temple, Michael switched off the giant plasma-screen TV and went to the floor-to-ceiling windows that overlooked the sparkling blue waters of the Persian Gulf. "No. You can go. I'm expecting an important business call."

The hotel was otherworldly, over-the-top. Michael had a meeting with the sheikh who owned it. He aspired to build another that would be even more ostentatious, more luxurious and more expensive than this one. It was the deal of the decade.

Normally Michael would have been excited to be here, excited to be asked to be part of such an ambitious project.

But he missed Bree.

She'd sounded so cool over the phone when she'd told him they were having a little boy.

A little boy they'd agreed to name Will.

She'd refused to talk about anything other than her doctor's visit. When she'd finished, she'd hung up.

"I'll call you when I have something else to tell you about our child," she'd said right before she'd ended the call.

Michael missed her so much. More than anything. She didn't answer when he phoned her. She didn't reply when he texted. He sent her roses every day, and every day she sent them back to the florist.

Before he'd left for Abu Dhabi, he'd gone to Chez Z to check on her, but she'd made it plain she didn't like seeing him in person. She'd answered his questions in unenthusiastic, monosyllabic tones before she'd asked him to leave.

When he'd told her his agent had found her a two-bedroom, second-floor apartment in her neighborhood in a building that had an elevator, she'd shaken her head. "Leave me alone, Michael. I don't want to discuss anything other than our child."

"But this is about our child. It's about you avoiding stairs until he's safely born. I'll pay for it."

"This is about your money."

"No. It's about the baby. After he's born, I don't want you carrying him down five flights of stairs. What if you fell?"

"I'll figure something out on my own."

"You're carrying my son. Why won't you let me do this for you?"

"I know what apartments cost in this city," she'd whispered in a shattered tone that had cut him. "A favor like that would give you financial power over me. I don't want to be dependent on you for anything."

"No way will I let you stay in that apartment and risk our baby on those stairs," he'd said. "Why won't you let me help?"

"You know why. Because you use your money to get what you want. Because you think I'm out for anything I can get from you."

"I don't think that anymore!"

"This isn't a deal. I'm not for sale. Neither is our baby. You've used your money to control people for so long, you don't know any other way. Remember how you used to treat Will? Well, I'm determined never to take anything from you again."

"This isn't about money!"

"With you, everything's about money. I can't live that way, or think that way. It's too cold."

He'd once believed that if he became rich enough, he'd have everything he wanted. But he'd been wrong.

Too often his money had put him on the defensive. All he'd been able to see was who wanted what from him. Waiters wanted big tips. Women wanted jewels. Socialites wanted him to give to their causes. He'd been catered to by everybody because they'd all wanted his money. And on some level he'd loved it, because he'd felt strong and powerful and in control.

Michael didn't know what to do to win Bree back.

She'd been a virgin and grieving for her brother. Since Michael was her best friend's brother, she'd trusted him and had shyly opened herself to him body and soul. Then he'd deliberately crushed her.

To win her back, he had to become the kind of man she admired. But how?

What if she was right? What if he couldn't change?

Michael, who sat near Chez Z's cash register, looked up from smearing marmalade on a slice of warm, crusty bread and grinned. Bree was storming out of the kitchen toward him. Her cheeks brightened with indignation and that only made her look lovelier in her tight yellow dress and starched white apron that molded to her lush curves.

When he raked his eyes down her shapely body she reddened even more.

"You have to stop this," she said.

"Stop what?" Michael ignored the desperation he heard in her husky voice.

"Coming to Chez Z every single morning you're in town. Constantly embarrassing me like this. Looking at me like that."

His smile broadened. As always, he was so dazzled by her beauty and the immensity of his attraction to her, he felt momentary hope that she might feel a spark of warmth for him if he kept pushing her.

"Embarrassing you? How?" he asked with seeming innocence.

She yanked out a chair and sat down. Leaning across the table so that her staff couldn't hear her, she said, "You know perfectly well how. You send flowers every day."

"I'm the money guy, remember. They look good on the tables. I'm just protecting my investment."

"You drop by every morning on your way to work.

You eat breakfast here. You devour me with those black eyes of yours."

"Devour…" He let the word linger as his gaze traveled to her mouth. "Can I help it if you're the most talented cook in Manhattan as well as the most beautiful?"

"Don't you dare compliment me!"

"Sorry." He bit into his crispy hash browns.

"You call so frequently you've got Bijou feeling sorry for you. Everybody who works here is talking about us and taking sides."

"Who's winning?" he asked flirtatiously.

"Since my vote is the only one that counts—me! So stop! You're supposed to be a powerful CEO. Why can't you fly off to Abu Dhabi or Shanghai or at least hole up in your office and run your empire like a good boy?"

"A man has to eat breakfast."

When his gaze touched her as intimately as a caress, her hand darted to her throat. "We have a rule—I call you when I have something to tell you about the baby, otherwise we stay away from each other. Please, just go."

"That's your rule. I'm playing by my own."

"Which is still another reason we can't be together. Look, I need to get back to the kitchen and supervise the prep work."

"I thought maybe you'd like to see the papers for the foundation I'm setting up in Will's name."

Despite her obvious intention to dismiss him, her annoyance gave way to curiosity. "What foundation?"

"It will provide educational opportunities for disadvantaged boys in this city."

"What's in it for you?"

"Would you believe the pleasure of giving back?"

Her eyebrows lifted. "Your PR guy must have told you that a charitable foundation would improve your image. Am I right?"

Teeth gritted, he swore softly. "That's your unwavering opinion of me? You can't imagine that I might empathize with kids who have it as tough or tougher than I did and want to help them? Or that I might want to honor Will?"

"No. This is probably just camouflage. You're hoping to make yourself look less like the shark you are to your gullible prey."

"I want to take care of you and our baby. You probably don't believe that either."

"Michael, we're having a kid because we both made a huge mistake in judgment. Huge! We have no reason to be together other than the baby."

"That's reason enough for me."

"But not for me! Why can't you just go away and let me run my bistro?"

"Okay, I get it. You think I'm always motivated by greed—even when I try to do good things. We're going to have a baby. I want to take care of you. Why is that bad?"

She just looked at him. "I've told you."

"What if you're wrong?" he demanded. "What if I can change?"

"What if cows could fly over the moon?"

"What if we could get past our mistakes, huge as they are, and become...er...friends?"

"Friends? You and me?" She lifted her chin and stared at him. "Not possible."

"I'll bet our baby would disagree if he had a vote."

"Even for you, that's low."

"There's one more thing." He hesitated. "I found a building in your neighborhood that just happens to have a vacant first-floor apartment that I thought would be perfect for you."

"Please, please don't tell me you've bought it."

"No, but I want you to take a look at it and see what you think. I'm willing to buy the lease on your present apartment and make the owner a very good deal on the one in this building."

"How many times do I have to tell you that you can't buy me?" She pushed her chair back from his table. "You've finished your breakfast, and I've got a full day ahead of me."

"Right," he murmured. "But just so you know, I'm leaving the keys to the apartment with your mother—on the slim chance that she can talk you into looking at it."

"Leave my mother out of this." She whirled and left him.

He watched her until she disappeared. Then he arose and pulled out the envelope containing the photos and information about the building and the necessary keys. Documents in hand, he paid the bill and tracked down Bijou.

"The apartment *is* perfect! I love the garden. I'll try to talk some sense into her," she said after looking at the pictures. She tucked the keys into her purse. "But she's stubborn…especially when it comes to you. This may take a while…and a miracle. I think I'd better go to church tonight and pray. Yes. I think so, yes."

Bree raced ahead of Marcie on the cracked concrete sidewalk that edged the riverbank. She almost passed two joggers, so determined was she to get far enough ahead of Marcie that her friend would be forced to stop nagging Bree about Michael.

The afternoon was cold and sunny, perfect for a walk in the park if only Marcie would change the subject. The humid breeze that gusted off the silvery Hudson River smelled of the sea while gulls laughed and wheeled above them.

"I really think you should reconsider about Michael," Marcie was saying as she caught up to Bree after stooping to hand a dollar to a street musician playing a trumpet.

Bree, who had finally had enough, stopped abruptly, and a guy on Rollerblades nearly slammed into her.

"Hey!" he cried. "Watch where you're going!"

"I mean, if someone rich like Michael was interested in me and wanted to 'buy me' as you put it," Marcie continued, undeterred, "I'd let him."

"Look, Marcie, I love Riverside Park. I come here to exercise and relax and get away from my problems. Right now Michael is a big problem. So please stop talking about him or go home."

Marcie's brows knitted as she watched an immense white yacht pull up to the 79th Street Boat Basin. "But a foundation? How cool is that? How bad can he be if he gives a fortune away for a cause like that?"

"He told you about that to manipulate you. He's using his money to buy your good opinion. It's a trick."

"Well, if he created that foundation to win you over, I think it's sort of romantic...and sweet."

"Believe me, he is *not* sweet. He's a cunning manipulator who uses his money for insidious, calculating reasons that profit him."

"He thought badly about you not so long ago. And he was wrong about you, wasn't he? He sees that now."

"Do not compare me to him."

"I'm just saying he was wrong about you, so maybe you could be wrong about him."

Two bikers whizzed past them.

"Marcie, he seduced me just to make Will dislike me. That's bad. He's not to be trusted. Not ever."

"But he's so-o-o cute...and rich. And...and even if he did seduce you for the reasons you say he seems genuinely interested in you now. You should see the way he looks at you. He's got the major hots for you."

Bree's heart constricted. She knew he wanted the baby, and he wanted her in his bed, but she knew as well that he didn't love her. Her mother had married her father because he'd gotten her pregnant, then she'd complained about it so often, Bree had felt guilty for being the baby in question.

"And, God, all those flowers! I wish somebody half as handsome and half as rich would try to seduce me."

"Did he put you on his payroll or something?"

"Hey, I'm not the only one. Everybody else at the bistro thinks you should forgive and forget."

The only reason Michael wanted her was because she was pregnant with his child, and he wanted control over his heir. His attitude hadn't changed until he'd realized Will was gay and had proof that she'd been telling the truth about only being Will's friend.

"You want to know something—sometimes it's very hard to forgive."

A light must have gone out somewhere in the stairwell because the second-floor landing of Bree's steep Victorian staircase was as dark as a cave.

Bree, who was tired and weighted down by two bulging grocery sacks and her purse, grumbled as she readjusted her load before tackling the final, shadowy flight to her apartment. It was only four in the afternoon, but she'd left Chez Z earlier than usual because she'd been too tired to stay. She was looking forward to a cup of tea and a long, hot bath and maybe a nap when her cell phone buzzed inside her purse.

Don't answer it. Not now.

But after it stopped for a short interval it began ringing again. She set her bags on the dark stair above her and began to dig in her purse.

When she saw Michael's name, her heart beat a little faster. He'd been in Asia for the past five days, and so hadn't been by Chez Z to pester her while he ate his breakfast. Was he back? Was he okay?

Even though she knew she shouldn't take his call since she had no news about the baby, she couldn't resist picking up to find out where he was and to make sure he was okay. But just as she touched the phone and his husky voice wrapped around her, something in the bags on the stair shifted. The sack ripped open and shot a barrage of cascading apples and oranges straight at her.

"No!" she cried as she jumped to catch them before they rolled down the stairs.

"What is it?" Michael demanded. "What's wrong?"

Caught off-balance as she stupidly grabbed for an apple, she lurched to one side. Frantically, she reached for the balustrade and missed, falling backward, tumbling along with her fruit back down to the second-floor landing. At least, she had the presence of mind to throw out her hands defensively. Even so, she rammed the wall so hard a white-hot burning sensation shot through her abdomen.

"The baby," she whispered. "Please let him be okay."

For a long time she lay in a crumpled heap, too dazed and winded to move. As the unpleasant burning in her belly subsided, she thought she heard Michael shouting.

"Where are you? Tell me what happened? What's wrong? Bree? Bree! Are you there?"

The phone, she thought. Her phone had to be somewhere nearby. Michael had been talking to her before she'd fallen? Was he back? Oh, how she hoped he was in the city!

Where was her phone?

With a supreme effort, she sat up and discovered her phone blinking madly in a dark corner.

"I'm…on my staircase," she said shakily after she'd managed to inch her way to the phone. "I fell."

"Damn it, Bree. I told you those stairs were dangerous."

"I think I'm okay. I have to be okay."

"Stay where you are," he ordered. "I'm not far. I'm coming over. I'll be there in five minutes—max."

Good. He was nearby. She'd never felt more thankful about anything in her life.

"No hurry.... I'm fine," she whispered. But he couldn't have heard her feeble protests because her phone had dropped his call.

Realizing she was in one of the building's dead spots so there was no use calling him back, she forced herself to her knees. The last thing she wanted was for him to find her on the stairs and panic.

Pushing up to her feet, she stood. For a second or two, she swayed dizzily. When her head cleared, she grabbed the railing and began climbing, grateful that she hadn't sprained an ankle, or worse.

It was slow going, but once she was safely inside her apartment, she collapsed on her couch and willed the cramping in her belly to stop.

She had to be all right. The baby had to be all right.

Four minutes later she heard her buzzer in the foyer downstairs. Then Michael rang her on her intercom. "It's me."

"Michael!" Unabashed joy filled her as she hit the button and buzzed him inside.

She heard the thunder of his heavy footsteps as he ran up her stairs, taking them two at a time, never slowing even when he neared the top. He ran through the door that she'd left ajar and rushed to her side.

For the first time since their quarrel at Will's apartment, she didn't try to push him away when he pulled her close. She was much too thankful to be wrapped in his powerful arms while he quizzed her about her delicate condition.

He was breathing hard, and his heart was pounding.

He was as scared for her and the baby's safety as she was.

"How far did you fall?" His unsteady tone told her that he'd feared the worst, that he still feared it.

Did that mean he wanted their baby as much as she did? That maybe his interest in her wasn't just about controlling the North heir?

"Not so very far."

"How are you feeling now?"

"I was shaken at first. But I feel better now." Especially now that he was here. "And lucky. I feel very, very lucky." With a deep sigh, she laid her head against his heaving chest and listened to the violent thudding of his heart. "It's going to be okay. Don't worry so much."

"Your doctor's agreed to meet us at the emergency room just to make sure."

"Michael, that really isn't necessary."

"Shh," he whispered. His eyes met hers. "It is for me, so let me take care of you. Just this once…for the baby's sake."

Upon hearing the very real concern in his husky voice, the lump in her throat grew larger.

"I'm glad you're here," she admitted as she pulled him closer. "So glad."

His powerful arms tightened around her. "Well, that's a first."

She was so happy she didn't object, at least not very much, when the team of paramedics he'd summoned arrived, checked her vitals, strapped her to a stretcher and carried her back down the stairs.

Thankfully, her doctor, who beat them to the hospital, confirmed her opinion that although she'd been shaken up a bit, essentially she was fine. "I would suggest that you climb as few stairs as possible for a while. And as for resuming intimate relations, I advise you two to take a break for a couple of days. After that, just be careful."

"I like your doctor," Michael said after the man left.

"Because he agreed with you about the stair thing."

"No—because he said we can have sex in two days."

She felt her cheeks heat. She glanced around to make sure they were alone. "Michael! We don't have that kind of relationship anymore."

"I miss it. He just reminded me of how much I miss it." He leaned into her and cupped her chin with his fingers. "I want you all the time, and it's been too long. Way too long," he murmured right before he slanted his hard mouth over hers.

"Don't," she whispered, but when he didn't stop, she didn't push against his chest as she should have.

She was thinking about how frantic he'd been when he'd arrived at her apartment, how capable and truly caring. Maybe he wasn't so bad; maybe he truly was trying to change.

Or maybe her pregnancy had her feeling more vulnerable and, therefore, more forgiving. Whatever the reasons, she was glad he'd come over and so obviously wanted to take care of her.

When his arms wound around her waist, her pulse quickened. Then he pressed her against his muscular length and her hips arched against him.

At her response, he slid his hands over her bottom. "I missed you, missed this."

Desire licked through her like a hot tide. Unbidden came the realization that she still hoped he could care for her. She still hoped that maybe him wanting her in his life because of the baby could be a fresh beginning.

Suddenly all the emotions she'd been fighting exploded, and she rubbed herself against the bulge in his slacks.

"Too bad we have to hold off…for a couple of nights," he whispered grimly.

She pressed herself against him again and then smiled. "You're killing me. We've got to stop."

His expression was so tender and his eyes were so warm, they melted the ice around her heart.

Eleven

The city sparkled in the night like a million jewels.

Michael lay in his bed counting his blessings for the first time in a while. Thank God he'd been in town two days ago and had been able to get to her apartment so fast.

Two days! For two whole days, ever since her fall, she'd been nice to him. When he'd come into the bistro every morning for breakfast, she'd joined him willingly. She'd even laughed at some of his jokes. When he'd called to check up on her during the day, she sometimes answered her phone.

He was feeling lucky about sex tonight, too.

Her pregnancy was showing—just a little—but that only made her more beautiful to him. Her tummy, which had been a smooth, flat plane when they'd met, was slightly rounded. The bump fascinated him and made him feel protective.

She was carrying his son. He was going to be a father. Maybe after the baby came, he wouldn't feel so alone.

"This doesn't mean anything," she murmured as she lay down on his bed and eased out of her black lacy bra.

"Right." He attempted to suppress his excitement as his eyes feasted on the silky skin and voluptuously soft curves she revealed. "Of course not."

She was still wearing her pants and he his jeans.

They'd eaten Chinese earlier in the evening because he'd wanted Peking duck, and she'd indulged him by accompanying him to a favorite restaurant that wasn't far from his penthouse.

In a corner booth of a glossy black dining room accented with white marble monkeys dangling from the ceiling and golden dragons encircling the walls, she'd eaten jellyfish and oxtails with increasing rapture. He'd feasted on Peking duck presented with scallions, julienned cucumber, delicate crepes and amber-colored hoisin sauce.

Of course they'd shared, nibbling off each other's plates and feeding each other—although she'd been much fonder of his duck than he'd been of her jellyfish. His glass of plum wine had glittered on their table like an enormous jewel. On their walk home they'd stopped at a chocolate shop for plump, chocolate-covered strawberries. Now they lay in his penthouse bedroom lit with silver moonlight.

They'd talked for hours about themselves. He'd told her more than he'd ever told anyone. At one point, when he'd confessed how ashamed he'd felt of the homes he'd lived in with his mother, Bree had placed her hand on his.

"My mother was a little like Anya. She chose her men for what they could give her. I thought all women were like that."

The soft shining light in Bree's eyes had eased the tension caused by the memories and confessions. Normally he never told such stories because they made him feel weak and powerless, but sharing them with Bree had made him feel closer to her, and less alone.

It was a beautiful night. Not that he had the slightest interest in the sweeping panorama of gilded buildings or the immense park beneath them, all of which had been selling points before he'd signed a contract and applied to the board to purchase the apartment.

No, his body's terrible longings had taken him over; it was she alone who compelled him. But unlike the first night they'd been together, his feelings for her now were honest. He liked her as a human being, and he wanted her to like him, too. He knew it would take a while, but he intended to show her he would never again treat her with anything less than the respect she deserved.

Her breasts were fuller than they'd been that first night, their tips dark and tight. He wanted to pull her close, lick her nipples and revel in her fecundity. But he knew better than to rush her. What they had was still too fragile.

"It's just sex," she said.

Not to him, not anymore.

"Whatever you say…as long as you'll keep getting naked for me," he murmured.

She laughed.

Nothing like a good meal to ease her anxieties and turn her on, he thought.

Finding out that she was carrying his child had made him feel far more closely connected to her. She had never slept with another man. She'd chosen him.

Her justifiable fury and their separation combined with his fear for her and the baby after the fall had taught him that she meant even more to him than he'd imagined. Not that he was comfortable with the depth of his feelings for her.

After her fall, with the help of her mother, he'd convinced Bree to move into his penthouse for a few days. So once again, she was installed in his downstairs guest suite behind his kitchen. He was in the process of acquiring the first-floor apartment he'd mentioned to her earlier, but he hadn't told her yet because he didn't want to argue about it.

For the past two evenings they'd spent the early hours after work together, and in an effort to gain her trust he'd deliberately kept things light and friendly. He hadn't touched her.

After meeting her doctor at the E.R., he'd brought Bree straight home and put her to bed. When she'd said she was ravenously hungry, he'd ordered pizza and served it to her on a tray in her room. Afterward, he'd sat on her bed and they'd talked. He'd been pleased that she'd wanted to know everything he'd done while he'd been away. He'd loved telling her of his adventures and business problems. Then he'd caught up on her activities in New York. He, too, had been thrilled that the bistro was doing better.

He'd stayed in her room for a long time even after she'd shut her eyes and fallen asleep. He'd liked listening to her gentle breathing, liked knowing she was safe in his home…and that their baby was out of danger.

"Kiss me," she whispered now, bringing him back to the present. "I want you to undress me. Then I'll undress you."

A sizzle of heat shot straight through him. With a long sigh, he reached for her and pulled her close.

Coiled around him, with her breasts nestled against his chest, she fitted him perfectly, like the vital piece of a missing puzzle. Holding her, he felt good, safe, on fire. He would feel even better when he was inside her.

With deft expertise they began to undress. Then with a silent moan, she slid her fingers along his nape.

"Oh, how you turn me on," she said.

"You could have fooled me," he said with a smile.

"I'm probably being a fool again, but I can't help myself." Brushing her parted lips along his jawline, she kissed her way down to the base of his throat.

He made a silent, secret vow to be good to her, to believe in her, no matter what. Maybe in time, he would win her.

He threw his head back so that her mouth and tongue could have easier access. She was warm and soft, everything he needed and desired in a woman but hadn't known he had to have.

He'd missed her so much while he'd been away. Every night he'd lain in his lonely hotel bed thinking about her hair, craving her body and that oh-so-intoxicating scent of strawberries.

Now that she was in his arms, the time he'd spent without her in those lavish surroundings seemed drab and empty. If he'd never met her, he would have gone on seeing and being seen with the world's most beautiful women, but feeling restless and empty because he felt no emotional involvement. He would have gone on closing deal after deal all the while longing for something more. He would have had no idea what "more" he wanted, other than more of what left him feeling so empty.

"Kiss me back," she begged.

Their mouths met, open and equally needy. Once he started kissing her, he couldn't seem to stop.

The tips of their tongues flicked against each other and then mated. Heat flooded him, pulsing between his legs. He wanted her, all of her, especially her heart and soul.

For a long time they necked like teenagers, teasing each other mercilessly by remaining partially dressed until their need grew to such a fever pitch they tore each other's clothes off, their bodies contorting so their mouths wouldn't have to part.

When they were both naked, he gently eased her onto her back, spread her legs apart and positioned himself so that his sex touched hers. She gasped in breathless delight at the liberty.

He rubbed himself against her. "I want to be with you like this all the time. When I kiss you, I feel you here. Even on the first kiss, I felt you here." His voice was so raw and intimate she blushed.

"I feel the same way."

He stroked her hair and stared into her shining eyes that finally dared to meet his. He savored the shy warmth in her gaze as well as the heat of her body underneath him. Then slowly, oh-so-slowly, she arched upward, inviting him, and he slid inside her. Holding on to his wide shoulders, she let out a shudder and tugged him closer.

"Why do I want you so much?" she whispered as she began to writhe. "Why?"

"Just accept it like I have."

"So, I'm doomed…just like my mother before me."

"Don't say that," he muttered fiercely, hating that she felt that way. She'd become so important to him.

He withdrew and then pushed deeper. She cried out and pulled him back. Then he lost all control and carried her over the flaming edge.

Afterward as he lay sated in the moonlit dark with his arms looped around her perspiring body, she turned to him. "You've had a lot of women and I haven't had anyone else. Since there's a lot lacking in my sexual education, there's something I have to know—"

"Don't," he muttered in a low, hoarse tone, feeling awkward. "Don't ask me about other women. They don't matter to me—do you understand?"

She tensed. "I don't mind about them so very much."

He knew better than to believe that, but he said nothing.

"I mean…sometimes I do mind, just not so much at this moment. I'm the odd duck, you see, who never would…

maybe because I was too shy or too busy or maybe because my mother was always telling me that the minute I had sex with a guy, he would have all the power."

"What did she mean by that?"

"The reason she married my father was because she was already pregnant with me. She wanted to have this big career, but she felt she had no say in her life after she got pregnant with me."

He tensed, wondering where she was going with this. "Oh."

"You wouldn't believe how guilty she made me feel."

"What they did before you were born isn't your fault."

"Bijou is not a logical person. She said sex can ruin a woman's life if she lets it, that more good women have been brought down by bad men than she could count, that it's women who always pay the price for mistakes in love. And she paid dearly."

"It's not always just the women who pay," he muttered gloomily, thinking of Anya.

"Bijou didn't want me to ruin my life the way she did."

"Then why has she been okay to me?"

"That doesn't make sense. When I told her I'd made this huge mistake and had gotten myself pregnant with your child, she didn't have much to say at first. She's impressed with you, with who you are, with what you've achieved. I don't know. Maybe she just likes it that you're rich."

"Ouch."

"Well, you asked. She must approve of you for some reason."

He smiled, glad that her mother seemed more or less on his side, whatever the reason.

"So, about those other women," she persisted. "Is the sex always this good?"

"No," he muttered fiercely. "How can you ask that?"

"Curiosity." She ran her fingertip down his nose. "You see, I researched you. I saw who you dated. They're all so beautiful. So much more beautiful than I am."

"Bree, baby, you have to understand—they were just going out with me to get things they wanted. Models are into enhancing their image, their brand. I was sort of using them, too. Sex like that, when it's between two people who are out for what they can get, is like…well, it's like a sport or a commodity that you both enjoy but neither of you feel all that deeply about. I was a single man, in need of an escort to parties and feminine companionship. Don't worry about those women because they don't matter at all."

"I don't matter either," she murmured. "Not really. You're only with me because of the baby."

Was she right? Then why did he enjoy doing things with her so much, like eating dinner, talking and laughing? He'd liked her in bed from the first. From the beginning he'd felt connected to her—even when he'd thought she was after the North money, even *then,* he'd liked her.

She was beginning to matter to him so much it scared him.

Instead of reassuring her, he kissed her.

Spiked high heels clicked impatiently on the wooden floor as the Realtor pointed out the many charms of the truly lovely apartment Michael wanted her to move into.

"Original, wide-plank floors!" Lisa Morris gushed. "Can you believe it? Well, what do you think?"

"I don't know."

"You already live in the neighborhood, so you know how wonderful the Upper West Side is. The people in this building are all young, hardworking professionals like yourself. Michael wants you to have the apartment so badly he's willing to meet the seller's first price. Believe

me, sweetie, Michael never goes to contract without negotiating. You have no idea how utterly ruthless he can be."

"Oh, I have an idea." A very good idea. That's why she
still felt wary about their relationship even though he'd
been so nice of late.

"For a lower floor, the apartment is amazingly sunny."
Lisa's voice was as rapid as gunfire. She walked to a window and impatiently snapped open the blinds.

If Michael's high-powered Realtor was small in stat-
ure, she made up for it in presence. She was in her forties,
fit and sexy in her own brash way. She had big orange
hair and bright red lipstick. Nail polish of the same color
matched her bright stilettos and the huge leather designer
bag. Her short black skirt showed off great legs.

"It's modern," she said. "And cheerful. And totally updated. The garden makes it so special."

If only the woman would stop pressuring her, maybe
Bree could think.

"You wouldn't have to spend a dime. Not that Michael
would be against remodeling it for you—if that's what
you want. He's made it clear he's willing to do *anything*
to please you."

"I already owe him a lot because of an investment his
brother made in my business, so I don't want be obligated
to him for this, too."

"I'm beginning to see why he's so taken with you. Unlike the women I've seen him with before, you have principles. But trust me, principles will only carry a girl so far.
If I were you, I'd snap this place up in a heartbeat. Then
I'd snap him up, too. He's a prize catch, sweetie. Nail the
deal and the man before they slip through your fingers
and you spend the rest of your life regretting it. This is
New York. Beautiful women are throwing themselves at
him all the time."

"He's just trying to buy me."

"So, let him. He's gorgeous and he can give you the kind of fairy-tale life girls dream of."

"He doesn't care about anything but money."

"So? Sweetie, what do you think drives this city and everybody who lives here? What do you think buys all the goodies…like this apartment with its lovely garden and historic floors? Money. Always has. Trust me, you're lucky if a chance like Michael North comes once in a lifetime."

"Okay, I'll think about it," Bree said.

"You have my card," Lisa said. Her phone rang as she headed for the door. "We'll be in touch." She smiled, lifted her phone to her ear and was gone.

Giving the apartment a final look, Bree couldn't shake the feeling that Michael was trying to buy her by offering what he'd offered every other woman in his life.

Why say no to the apartment when you no longer say no to the flowers he sends, when you're sleeping with him?

Because I don't want to give in to all his demands until I am sure of what I really want. I don't like being pressured.

Michael was nothing if not relentless.

He could take care of her financially. She understood that. But could he love her?

Bree's heart knocked as she followed Michael's beautiful secretary down the marble hall to his office. She felt tense and defensive about her reason for visiting him on such short notice. The girl, a gorgeous brunette who had introduced herself as Eden, had told Bree in pleasant, hushed tones that Michael had canceled an important conference call to make time to see her.

"I'm sorry to interrupt you without giving you more warning," Bree said to him as soon as Michael opened the door and dismissed Eden. "I understand you postponed an important call."

"It'll wait." He looked deeply into her eyes. "You look upset. Are you okay?"

When she nodded, he pulled her to him and kissed her gently. Then he let her go. "What is it? What's wrong?"

Putting his hand against her waist, he led her to a guest chair and then sat down across from her.

She felt nervous, so she stared at his office. Compared to the glamorous marble lobby of his building and the waiting rooms and secretary's office outside, Michael's office was Spartan. Other than his sunny corner view of the city, no luxuries adorned his personal working space.

His immense, sleekly modern desk was flanked by equally minimalistic tables with monitors. Floor-to-ceiling bookshelves and cabinets were stacked with documents and file folders. Here, there were no photographs, no evidence he had a personal life at all.

"You have a nice view," she said, feeling the need to say something.

"Do I?" he replied, turning to look at it absently. Then he swiveled so that he faced her again. "I prefer this view," he said, his intense gaze causing her to blush. She'd put on a black dress, dangly silver earrings and a red pashmina just to please him. "So—why the visit?"

Feeling a mixture of pride and anxiety, she pulled an envelope out of her purse and pushed it across his desk.

Watching her, he grabbed it, tore it open with his bare hands, pulled out her check and then whistled. "What is this?" he demanded almost angrily.

"I made out a schedule," she said in her most business-like tone. "I intend to start repaying you on Will's investment in Chez Z."

"That is not necessary."

"You're saying that because I'm pregnant with your child, and you feel obligated to me now."

His black eyes narrowed. "I am obligated."

"I know how everything's a deal to you…." Her cheeks turned red and her voice faltered.

He flushed darkly. "Our relationship is not a deal."

"I'm pregnant, and you feel you have to take care of me. I want you to understand that even though I am pregnant, I can take care of myself. And from now on, I'm going to do so."

"We're sleeping together. Did it occur to you I might want to be generous to you?"

"I don't want our relationship to revolve around money."

"Then why are you here with this check?"

"It's a matter of principle. A time or two, you proposed that if I slept with you, you'd keep Chez Z afloat. Well, I refused that deal then, didn't I? So, I don't want you to think that because we're sleeping together I don't owe you that money."

"Damn it, Bree. You're having my child. Everything's different now."

"I don't want you to think I'm greedy or that I'm only involved with you because of your money. That's not the case."

"I don't think that. The money's a dead issue to me. So, can we not do this?"

"But I don't quite believe you. You've always bought your women, paid them off—"

"You're not like them, okay? How many times do I have to tell you that I was wrong about you before you'll believe me?"

"I…I don't know."

Sometimes she did believe him. Other times she remembered how he'd crushed her.

He must have seen her face fall because he said, "I guess I deserve that. I know I hurt you badly."

"Let's just say the way you made me feel is burned into me like a brand. I'm having a hard time letting it go."

He cursed softly. "I want to make that up to you. I don't want to hurt you like that ever again. As you know, I had a rough start and got knocked around a lot as a kid, so I'm not always an easy guy—and that's when I'm not deliberately being a jerk. Not that my history is an excuse, but I was prejudiced against your sex after Anya. Now, though…everything's different. I only hope that someday I'll be able to prove to you I've changed my attitude."

"For now—just take the money," she whispered. "It's important to me…in ways I can't explain. I'm going to start repaying you in two-week intervals."

"Okay. Whatever you want. However you want." His cynical tone was low and biting.

When she stood up, he led her to the door.

"One more thing," he said. "Since we're discussing finances maybe now would be a good time to inform you that I signed a contract on that building in your neighborhood."

"Oh, no. I wish you hadn't."

"I know, more proof you're nothing but a financial obligation to me, but hey, why don't you look at this a different way? My purchasing the building gives you choices. You can continue to stay with me at the penthouse. I told you last night how much I look forward to coming home to you. Or if you need more independence you can move into the apartment and be on your own."

"I would not be on my own, if you own the apartment."

"Then you can pay rent."

"I have a lease where I am."

"I'm sure I could work out a deal with your landlord.

I don't want to force you to be with me. I just want you and the baby to be safe."

"Okay," she said. "I'll think about it."

"So—do we have any more finances to discuss?"

She shook her head.

"Good." His gaze warmed as he took her hand and drew her to him. Realizing that he wanted her to kiss him goodbye in spite of their disagreement, she softened, too.

Standing on her tiptoes, she closed her eyes and slid her arms around his neck. Against all logic, her resistance melted when his lips claimed hers. Why did she always feel that something was very right in her world when he held her like this?

"See you tonight?" he whispered, sweeping the back of his hand across her cheek.

She nodded. "I'll cook. What are you in the mood for?"

"Not food." His hot glance and quick grin made her knees go weak.

"We were discussing supper," she whispered primly.

"We were?" He arched his dark brows.

She nodded.

"How about steak and potatoes?"

"Okay, then," she said, her eyes aglow as she envisioned juicy slabs of beef topped with mushroom sauce, baked potatoes oozing with crunchy bits of bacon, chives and sour cream. She would buy a deep red wine for him, a burgundy maybe, and crisp garden-grown greens to make a salad for herself.

"Followed by you for dessert," he whispered with a sexy smile right before he kissed her again.

Twelve

Four weeks had passed, and in that time Michael had grown relaxed in his relationship with Bree. She'd allowed him to help her get out of her old lease and move into the apartment he'd bought for her. She'd agreed to pay him the same rent she'd paid her previous landlord.

Tonight, Michael felt heavy and sated after an hour or so of deeply satisfying sex that had followed the lamb dinner she'd cooked for him. Funny how the more times he had her, the more his need for her grew.

Utterly content, he pulled her closer.

The doors to her garden were open. City sounds and moonlight crept over the walls and filled her bedroom. He was glad she'd relented about the apartment. Before she could change her mind, he'd sent a team of movers and packers to her old place.

Maybe it was time he pushed on a much more important issue.

"I want to marry you. I want you in my life forever,"

he said, speaking softly as his hand caressed her arm. "We've had a month together. I think we work."

He felt her tense, but she stayed where she was.

"We've been over this," she said tightly.

"Not lately."

"You only want to marry me because of the baby— *your heir.*"

Damn it, he thought. Ever since her fall, he'd spent as much time as he could with her because he cared about her. Why couldn't she see that?

He'd taken her to the theater, to movies and out shopping. He'd joined her on her afternoon walks in Riverside Park. They'd picnicked in Central Park, enjoyed dozens of fabulous dinners in New York's top restaurants. Then there were the countless rounds of mutually satisfying sex.

They got along. More than got along. He looked forward to every moment he had with her. They enjoyed friendship as well as sex. Weren't those things they could build on?

"As soon as I found out you were carrying my child I wanted to take care of you. I asked you to marry me then, remember?"

"Because you felt obligated."

"You said no, and because you felt that way, I've worked hard to develop a relationship with you."

"Because you just see this as the best solution, the best deal. Or you feel you *have* to do this, maybe for the baby—"

"What if I said that maybe I do feel obligated because of the baby, but I want *you* in my life, and that maybe I do…love you."

Hissing in a breath, she pushed away from him, plumped her pillows and sat up straighter. "Well, I wouldn't believe you, Michael." She crossed her arms over her breasts. "So don't do this."

"Why the hell not?"

"Because loving me has never been part of your agenda. You'll say or promise anything to close this deal."

"I admire you. I like hanging out with you. I can't keep my hands off you. I miss you when we're not together. I miss you so much it consumes me. If what I feel isn't love, it'll do until love comes along."

"Marriage demands a total commitment. For me, it demands love. Even then, there's a fifty percent divorce rate."

"Love is just a four-letter word for a complex emotion that means different things to different people."

"Look, Michael, Will told me you would say anything to get what you want. Look at this apartment. Look at the way you've been sending flowers to the bistro for months. You got my mother and everybody who works for me to badger me until I agreed to move in here. They're all on your side. You've totally won them over."

"So, I've been vetted. Maybe you should take that as a sign we belong together."

"No, I take that as a sign you'll do anything to close the deal. I can't believe that even you would stoop so low as to try to trick me into letting myself believe you could love me. Do you think I'm such an illogical romantic that I'll do what you want if you just toss out the word *love?*"

"You think that my reasons for proposing to you have to do solely with a pragmatic concern for gaining more control over my heir?"

"I didn't at first. In the beginning I was starry-eyed about you. But the way you treated me that first night and right after Will died burned away my romantic illusions. I can't help it if I see you plainly now. I don't dislike you, Michael. Far from it. You have to know I'm crazy stupid about you in bed. And you're fun to hang out with. But this is an affair. Nothing more. An affair I think I'm stupid to engage in because I'm not sophisticated enough to keep my emotions guarded all the time."

"Guarded?"

"Yes. Guarded. I can't let myself care too much again. You have affairs all the time with women like Natalia."

"What I have with you isn't like that."

"I may be naive, but I know that an affair between people like us, who have different values about life, will end. I don't want ours to end now…so let's not discuss this. And let's not talk about marriage, either. Let's just enjoy each other while we can. Later, we'll part, and when we do, we'll work out a way to raise our son, okay?"

"Not okay!" He threw off his sheet, stood up, scooped his clothes off the floor and began to throw them on.

"Oh, so now you're mad at me? This is so unfair, Michael. You're the one who seduced me and got us into this mess. No matter what you say, I know the only reason you'd ever want to marry me is because I'm pregnant with your heir!"

"Well, I don't deny I've been a damned fool when I stupidly thought you were using my brother. If I was prejudiced then it was because I couldn't see who you were. But now you're the one who can't see who I am. For the past month I've tried to show you that I'll be good to you. Maybe I deserve this. I thought we were happy together."

"It has been fun," she agreed.

"It's been way more than fun. But if you don't want this to go any further, then I won't push myself on you any longer. If you think this relationship is all about closing a deal, well, the deal's off."

"Michael, stop this. You've got to see that we could never have a real marriage. My mother married my father because she was pregnant with me and she was miserable. The only thing you and I have in common is the baby. You do international deals. I'm the owner of a bistro. I'd hold you back."

"The hell you would."

"You'd resent me just like she resented him. Why don't we just enjoy our affair until its natural conclusion…and then we'll figure out a way to raise our baby together?"

He felt raw and sick to the core at that prospect—devastated. Bitter pride made him mask the deep wound she'd inflicted.

"If that's the way you really feel, maybe you're right." His voice was cool. "Maybe you are better off without me. I've given it my best shot. I'm through."

"Michael!"

He tore his key to her apartment off his key ring and flung it on her bedside table. "Consider our affair concluded. No deal."

His heart wasn't in what he was saying as he shoved his shirt into his slacks and picked up his cell phone. Why couldn't she see who he was now? Why couldn't she accept that he truly wanted to be with her? That he could come to love her? That he didn't want this half-assed deal she was proposing?

As he strode out of her bedroom blind to any emotion other than his own hurt, he willed her to come after him.

But she didn't see who he was, didn't feel the pain that was choking off his breath and she didn't follow him. When he left the building, he prayed that she would call him on his cell and agree that what he felt for her was enough. Love grew day by day, like a flower, didn't it, if it was real? Hell—what did he know about love?

When his cell phone buzzed, his heart raced. Thinking it was Bree, he grabbed for it, but it was Natalia, of all people, so he declined the call.

As he looked up from the sidewalk, he saw Bree standing in her window wrapped in a tangled bedsheet.

She was as pale as a ghost. Did he only imagine the shimmer of brightness on her cheeks? His heart constricted. Had he made her cry?

He wouldn't let himself care. She'd rejected him.

When she let go of the curtain, and it fell back into place, he tore his gaze from her window and hurried down the sidewalk.

When Natalia called him again a few minutes later, he picked up. Why the hell shouldn't he?

Bree stared up at her bedroom ceiling. Feeling lost and uncertain, she'd been staring at it for hours.

With shocking, devastating suddenness their affair was over.

Bree had known she'd be hurt when he left her, but the pain that pulsed in the center of her being cut like a blade. It was as if all hope for happiness was draining out of her like blood seeping from a fatal wound.

Hours later, when the sun turned the rooftops in her neighborhood bloodred, she got up, dressed and walked out of her apartment, feeling heavy from her long, sleepless night.

Hoping to clear her head, she made her way toward the park. She wanted to be around noisy cars on their way to offices and schools, around people rushing to catch buses or subway trains. Near the park, she bought herself a bagel and coffee from a street vendor and kept walking.

Michael had said he cared about her, that he knew he craved her, missed her.... And because she'd been a fool to believe him before, she'd refused to let herself believe him now.

But what if he'd been telling the truth? She remembered how tenderly he'd treated her when she'd fallen on her stairs. He'd said he'd been happy with her this past month. She'd certainly been happy with him.

What if he *had* come to care for her? What if he *could* love her? What if this relationship wasn't just a deal to him?

What if she was wrong? What if he'd been telling her the truth? What if he didn't feel trapped into marrying her? What if he really was beginning to fall in love with her, and instead of giving him a chance, she'd driven him away? What if she'd hurt him with her rejection exactly as he'd hurt her?

Oh, God. Thinking herself a naive fool, she pulled her phone out of her pocket and called him.

"What do you want?" he said, his tone so harsh he terrified her. "I'm on another line."

"Michael…"

The line went dead.

She wanted to hold on to his voice, but he was already gone.

She caught a slow, agonized breath. Had he deliberately hung up on her?

Motion on the street seemed to stop as she clasped the phone against the violent pounding of her heart. The horns and sirens around her grew silent. The hawker's voice died away. The pedestrians passing her seemed to walk in slow motion. All she could feel was the pain in her heart.

She felt like screaming, like crying out, but of course she did not. Instead, she stumbled back to her apartment where she waited in her living room for over an hour for him to call her back. When he didn't, she set her phone on an end table and picked up her purse.

She took the key to his penthouse off her own key ring. She dug an envelope out of her desk, addressed it and put his key inside. Leaving the package on the table, she walked outside to water the ivy that climbed her garden wall.

While she watched water from her hose rain down on the bricks, she tried to imagine how she would live the rest of her life without him.

"Aren't you sleeping?" Bijou demanded.

"I'm fine," Bree said, annoyed by her mother's constant hovering of late.

"Why the dark glasses then? Afraid I'll see the shadows under your eyes? Why aren't you sleeping?"

Bree yanked off the offending glasses and tossed them into her purse. "I am sleeping!" she lied. "Why wouldn't I be sleeping?"

She hated it when her mother poked her long nose where it didn't belong and kept poking it—which had been happening way too often lately.

"No more flowers?" Bijou persisted.

It was now day two after Michael had walked out on her, day two since he'd stopped sending flowers.

Bijou lifted a vase from a table in the main dining room and removed two withered roses. "Did you have a quarrel? Or is this more serious?"

Bree wasn't ready to talk about Michael. "Why don't you go check on the prep work? Or maybe sweep outside?"

"Why hasn't he been coming by for breakfast anymore? I miss him."

"Bijou! Please!"

"Should I maybe call him, yes? And tell him we miss him, very much, yes?"

"No!"

"So—you did quarrel. Then you foolish, sad girl, you must call him and make up!"

She'd tried, hadn't she? And he hadn't called her back.

"You don't know anything." When Bree's eyes began to sting she went to her purse, grabbed her sunglasses and slammed them back on her face. "Please. Don't ask me about him right now."

"You two are so romantic," Marcie whispered from a table in the back. "Such passion. Such fire."

Not anymore.

Her life felt empty, colorless.

Feeling hollow despair, Bree shut her eyes.

"You're just as unhappy as he is," Luke said as he set his fork down. "I came by because I thought that would be the case."

"It's just an off night," Bree countered defensively as she stood over his table.

"Yes. Everything about this place is off...*you,* the service, the pastries, the soup, even the omelets, which were always perfect, but especially you. Since I know what you're capable of and what your staff is capable of, you can't fool me. A month ago, you were doing so well. This place was fun. Hot."

Since Michael had walked out two weeks ago, she'd had to force herself to go through the motions of living. She knew she hadn't been concentrating at work.

"I'm sorry if your dining experience has been such a disappointment."

"Bull! What's going on between you and Michael?"

"Nothing."

"Funny, he said the same thing when I went to check on him."

"You've seen him?" She tried to keep her face blank but her heart had begun to race.

"Yesterday. Did you know that he's all but withdrawn from the world?"

"We haven't been in contact lately, so—no."

"Really? Well, he's taken the week off—hell, he never takes a week off—he's a ruthless workaholic for God's sake! Right now he's just sitting around his penthouse reading. Or watching his cleaning lady do her tasks. *Watching his cleaning lady!* He's not shaving or showering. She took me aside when I was leaving. She told me she's worried sick about him. He won't answer the phone—especially if it's Eden, his secretary, calling about work.

"I asked him about you. I said if you love her, for God's sake, man, tell her. He looked up at me with eyes that were as dark and dead as death. You know what he said?"

She shook her head.

"He said, 'I tried, Luke. But I guess I don't know what love is. Or at least she doesn't think I do. Or I'm not the man she wants. Do you really think I didn't try?'"

Bree sank into the chair across from Luke. Had Michael really said all that?

"Thank you for caring about him. And thank you for coming by to check on me. It was sweet, really. Thank you."

"So—are you going to call him?"

"I don't know. He broke up with me."

"Call him. He loves you, woman."

Did he? Did she dare believe that she was really more than an obligation or another deal he had to close?

She thought about the way he'd grown up…without ever getting enough love. Maybe he did love her. Maybe love was such a new experience for him, he wasn't sure what it was or how to express it.

She remembered how sweet he'd been after her fall, how committed and determined he'd been to have her in his life ever since.

He could have any woman he wanted, and he'd chosen her.

Maybe he *did* love her. Maybe she'd been wrong.

Whether he truly cared or not, she was worried about

him. Should she go to him? Check on him? After all, he was the father of her child. They would have to talk at some point. Why not now?

But what if he wouldn't let her in?

Her key. Since she'd procrastinated as usual, the envelope with his key was still in her purse, waiting to be mailed.

When the intercom buzzed for the fifth time, Michael got to his feet, swaying slightly. How many shots of scotch had he had? Who cared? He'd lost count.

On unsteady feet he crossed the room that was littered with newspapers and business magazines and answered his intercom.

"It's me, Natalia."

Surrounded by media, she looked gorgeous on his video screen.

"Go the hell away," he said.

"Carlo, I told you about Carlo, he jilted me. He thinks he's this big important producer. But nobody jilts Natalia publicly and gets away with it. I was so wrong about you, wrong to blame you for anything. Carlo—he is the real bastard."

"Well, I'm sorry about Carlo, but I can't talk right now."

"Can I please come up?"

"I said this is a bad time, Natalia. Look, you're a beautiful girl. Sooner or later your luck with men will change."

Platitudes, he thought. Who was he to give advice to the lovelorn when he was in a lot worse shape than Natalia?

He cut the connection and poured himself another scotch. Then he slumped onto his couch again and tortured himself with more memories of Bree—Bree with her cute baby bump climbing on top of him, Bree taking him into her mouth, Bree kissing him everywhere with those little flicks of her tongue that drove him wild.

What the hell was he doing, dreaming of a woman who didn't want him? Luke was right. He couldn't go on like this.

Michael had brought this on himself. She saw him as deal-maker, not as a husband. He'd offered her all he had to give and she'd rejected him.

She was the mother of his child, and he had to establish a workable, familial, brotherly relationship with her so they could raise that child together. That was all that was left, their bond as parents.

With Michael's key clutched tightly in one hand and her purse in the other, Bree walked up to his building just as Natalia emerged with a smile meant to dazzle the paparazzi lying in wait for her.

"Yes, I'm dating Michael North again," she said to a reporter when he thrust a microphone to her lips. "He invited me here." When flashes blazed, she laughed triumphantly and raced for her limo.

An inner voice cried inside Bree. *See how easily he replaced you with someone more beautiful. You were just an obligation, a deal he wanted to close. Go home. Forget him.*

On the walk through the park from her place to his, visions of married life had flooded her mind. She'd imagined Michael beside her when the baby came, Michael beside her at their son's first birthday, Michael beside her at the holidays and dining at home with friends. And all the while that she'd been imagining a shared life with him, he'd been entertaining Natalia.

She flung the key into the bottom of her purse. Lacking the strength to walk home, she went to the curb and asked the doorman to hail a taxi for her.

* * *

Somewhere a bolt turned in a lock. Michael blinked, annoyed at the sound. Dimly he grew aware that someone was outside his front door fumbling with a key. Who the hell could it be?

Natalia? Hadn't he sent her away? Despite the liquor that fogged his brain he was almost sure he had sent her away. He hadn't given her a key, had he?

When his door gave way, he shot to a sitting position in time to see a woman glide gracefully inside.

"Natalia?"

The great room was filled with gloom and long shadows and his vision was blurry from drink, so he couldn't make out her features. Still, something didn't seem right. Natalia was several inches taller, wasn't she?

"Not Natalia. It's me, Michael," said the soft feminine voice he'd dreamed of for days.

A pulse in his gut beat savagely.

"Bree?"

"Yes."

When she turned on the lights, he blinked at the glare and sat up straighter, pushing back his tangled hair. When was the last time he'd showered or shaved? Why did he give a damn? She'd turned him out, hadn't she? She saw him as nothing more than a crass deal-maker.

"Why are you here?" he demanded coldly.

She shut the door and moved cautiously around the newspapers that littered his floor. She moved as if she was approaching a dangerous wild animal.

Aware suddenly that he wore the same T-shirt and pair of jeans he'd put on yesterday, the same ones he'd slept in, he flushed. His eyes burned as he studied her, and his head ached.

Damn it. He didn't want her pity or her tenderness.

"Tell me what you want and go," he growled fiercely.

"Luke came to the bistro and told me…you weren't well."

"The two of you should mind your own damn business. As you can see, there's nothing wrong with me. I'm fine. Having the time of my life! Go home."

She picked up his empty scotch bottle. "Looks like we've got one dead soldier. Why don't I make you some coffee?"

"Because I don't want coffee," he snarled.

"Well, maybe I do. Why don't you freshen up so you can play host while I putter around in the kitchen?"

"What gives you the right to barge into my house and boss me around? We broke up—remember?"

"I'll be happy to tell you why I'm here after you take a shower and make yourself presentable. You really don't look very civilized, darling." Again her voice was maddeningly light and cheery as she disappeared into his kitchen.

He considered going after her, but when he took a step in pursuit, he stumbled. Feeling unsure, he thought better of following her.

One glance in his bathroom mirror had him shuddering in disgust. Who was that man with the narrowed, bloodshot eyes and the greasy, tangled hair?

Ashamed at how low he'd sunk, he stripped and stepped into an icy shower.

The cold water was hellish, but it revived him. Five minutes later, when he returned to the great room, he'd shaved, brushed his teeth and slicked back his damp hair.

She smiled. "You look like a new man."

Except for his headache, he felt a lot better. Not that he was about to admit it.

"Why the hell are you here? If you've come because you pity me, so help me…"

"I don't pity you. I love you. I've missed you. Picnics in

the park. Dinners out. And the passionate things you did
to me in bed. I think I'm okay with you thinking maybe
you love me."

He looked down at her, unable to comprehend her
words.

"What?"

"Drink your coffee," she whispered as she handed him
a steaming cup.

His hand shook slightly, but he took a long sip and then
another. It was strong and black, just what he needed.

"What are you saying?" he demanded.

"Luke came to see me."

"Oh."

"I was worried about you, so I came over. Then I was
so scared when I saw Natalia downstairs in your lobby.
She was all but holding a press conference and telling everybody you two were back together."

"We're not back together," he said.

"I know. The doorman told me you hadn't let her up. If
he hadn't told me that while he was helping me hail a cab,
I would have lost my courage and gone home."

"We haven't been together since I called it off months
ago. Her new boyfriend broke up with her and she has
such low self-esteem she goes crazy when that happens.
She can't stand to feel abandoned or rejected, so she came
over here. But I was in no shape to deal with her."

"It's a very difficult feeling…abandonment," Bree
whispered.

"Yes, it is," he said.

"That's how I felt that first night when you told me
you'd lied and didn't care about me."

"I'm so sorry." He sucked in a breath. Without Bree
these past few weeks, he'd felt as if he was a dead man.
Now that she was here, he felt alive again. "I missed you,"
he whispered. "I missed you so much."

She sat down and put her arms around him. "I love you, too. I love you enough for both of us. I'm going to hope that what you feel for me will grow...as you said it would."

"Bree. I do love you. Now. And forever. If I didn't know it before, I know it now. You don't know what I've been through...without you. I couldn't work or think. I was utterly worthless without you. I want you and our baby... more than anything."

He set his coffee cup down as she circled his neck with her arms. Her hands moved gently through his hair, which was still damp from his shower.

"You really love me?" she said.

Their eyes met. "Yes, these past few days I haven't been able to forgive myself for how I treated you. You don't know how I despised myself. You were so sweet and wonderful that first night. And I never gave you a chance. I tried to crush you. And I nearly did. I couldn't blame you for not trusting me."

"We both must forget about that night."

"Never. It's the night I first began to love you...I just didn't know it or couldn't admit it. Forgive me...please."

"I do. Oh, I do."

He took her face between his hands, his thumbs lightly brushing her lips. "I thought I'd lost you, and I didn't know how I'd live without you."

"I felt the same way. Isn't it wonderful we don't have to live without each other?"

It was too wonderful for words.

He kissed her long and hard. He pulled her closer and kissed her again and again, drinking of her deeply, tasting her, reveling in her nearness, her sweetness, until they were both breathless. "I will never get enough of you."

"I love you," she said again.

"Yesterday, I dreaded all the tomorrows of my life," he murmured. "Now I'm looking forward to them. You, dear, sweet Bree, have freed me from myself, from Anya, from all the dark emotions that hardened me."

"If I've helped you even a little I'm very glad."

"You've given me such happiness, a whole new life."

His lips claimed hers, and he didn't let her go for a very long time.

Epilogue

Never had Bree felt so content, so proud of herself, nor so filled with love and affection as she did right now. Lying in her hospital bed she watched Michael pace proudly, his voice soft as he tried to soothe their darling, newborn son.

Michael was such a good husband. Every morning she woke up loving him a little more, and she knew he felt the same. Not only had he stayed with her during labor and stood beside her during the delivery, he'd gone with her to every doctor's visit and to every childbirth class she'd taken.

Baby Will's eyes and hair were as black as ebony. The instant the nurses had laid him in her arms she'd fallen in love. She'd uncurled his fingers and he'd wrapped them around hers and hung on. Maybe she loved him so much because he was a tiny replica of his handsome dad.

Michael walked over to the bed and leaned down to show her their son was sleeping. As she lifted back the blue blanket to stare at her son's wrinkled, red face, a great rush of tenderness swept her.

She was the luckiest woman in the world.

"Michael," she whispered. "Isn't he wonderful?"

"He is, and so are you. I love you," he said in a low tone that shook her to the depths of her soul. "I love you more than anything in the world."

His words shook her because she was sure, so very sure, he meant them. Deep down, he'd always been a family man. Even though he'd been wrong about her in the beginning, love of his younger brother and his fierce desire to protect him was what had brought them together. He'd wanted his brother to experience the kind of love he'd never had himself, but had craved.

She was so glad she saw who he really was now—a man who had found the love he must have been looking for his whole life.

He was a fighter. He would always be there for her; he would always love and protect her.

Yes, she was the luckiest woman in the world to have this man and be loved by him.

* * * * *

"Our marriage will be companionable with a progression toward intimacy when it seems appropriate."

Daniella's tone wavered, just a touch, and was coupled with a glint in her eyes he couldn't interpret. "Like we discussed."

His exact words. And suddenly Leo wished he could take it all back.

"We'll have separate bedrooms for now. Take things slowly," he said.

That had been his intent from the beginning and seemed even more necessary given the unexpected chemistry between them. It should solve everything.

So why did the back of his throat burn with inexplicable disappointment?.

* * *

Matched to a Billionaire
is part of the Happily Ever After, Inc. trilogy:
Their business is makeovers and matchmaking,
but love doesn't always go according to plan!

MATCHED TO
A BILLIONAIRE

BY
KAT CANTRELL

MILLS &
BOON

Published in Great Britain 2014
by Mills & Boon, an imprint of Harlequin (UK) Limited,
Eton House, 18-24 Paradise Road, Richmond, Surrey, TW9 1SR

© 2014 Katrina Williams

ISBN: 978-0-263-91471-9

51-0714

Harlequin (UK) Limited's policy is to use papers that are natural, renewable and recyclable products and made from wood grown in sustainable forests. The logging and manufacturing processes conform to the legal environmental regulations of the country of origin.

Printed and bound in Spain
by Blackprint CPI, Barcelona

Kat Cantrell read her first Mills & Boon® novel in third grade and has been scribbling in notebooks since she learned to spell. What else would she write but romance? She majored in literature, officially with the intent to teach, but somehow ended up buried in middle management in corporate America, until she became a stay-at-home mom and full-time writer.

Kat, her husband and their two boys live in north Texas. When she's not writing about characters on the journey to happily-ever-after, she can be found at a soccer game, watching the TV show *Friends* or listening to '80s music.

Kat was the 2011 Harlequin So You Think You Can Write winner and a 2012 RWA Golden Heart finalist for best unpublished series contemporary manuscript.

To Jennifer Hayward,
because you're always there for me.
And because you liked Leo from the beginning.

One

Leo Reynolds wished he could marry his admin. It would make life so much simpler.

Unfortunately, she was already married and nearly twice his age. Plus, women didn't stick around once they figured out he worked a hundred hours a week on a consistent basis. Loneliness was the price of catapulting Reynolds Capital Management into the big leagues of the venture capital game.

"You're a life saver, Mrs. Gordon." Leo shot her a grateful smile and leaned back in his chair.

His laptop was refusing to speak to the printer and a critical document had gotten caught in the middle of the dispute. The signed hard copy now in his hand was due to Garrett Engineering on the other side of Dallas in less than an hour.

"I'd hardly call printing a proposal saving your life." Mrs. Gordon glanced at her watch in a deliberate gesture designed to point out the time. "It's late and it's Friday. Take Jenna to that new restaurant in Victory Park and let me handle the proposal. Relax for once. It'll be good for you."

Leo grimaced as a ping of remorse bloomed and faded. "Jenna and I split up. She's already seeing someone else."

Hopefully, the new relationship would make her happy. She deserved a man who could shower her with attention and affection. He regretted not being able to give her what she wanted, but it would be patently unfair to let Jenna keep hoping he'd ever become a man capable of focusing on a relationship. As a result, he'd lost a comfortable companion.

"Of course she is. It's not like she ever saw *you*." Mrs. Gordon crossed her arms and looked down her nose at Leo with a tsk. "Now who are you going to take to the museum dedication?"

Leo groaned. He'd conveniently forgotten about that, but it wasn't as if he could skip the dedication. The new children's museum in the Dallas Arts District bore his name, after all, since he'd donated the money to build it. "You're free next Saturday, aren't you?"

Mrs. Gordon cackled as though Leo had been joking. "One of these days, I'm going to say yes when you ask me out and really mess with you. If Jenna's not in the picture, find another woman. They seem to be pretty thick on the ground."

Yeah, he tripped over women on a regular basis who would like to go out with him. Or at least they thought they did, right up until they realized they wouldn't be satisfied with what little time and attention he could give. It never took very long to reach that point.

A vague hollow feeling invaded his gut, one he'd experienced more and more lately. He'd written it off as an increased urgency to hit that elusive, unachieved mark of success. But now that it had happened during a discussion about his personal life, he wasn't so convinced.

"I hate dating." *And small talk.* That getting-to-know-you period took time and energy he didn't care to expend. Reynolds Capital Management came first. Always.

"That's because you don't do it often enough."

Here they went, off on her favorite subject. She never got tired of scolding him about the lack of a permanent female in his life.

"Have you been talking to my mother again?"

"We went to lunch Tuesday, as a matter of fact. She says hi." Mrs. Gordon raised her eyebrows and planted guilt simultaneously, as Leo was sure she intended. He got it. He should call his mother. And date eligible women.

Problem was, he not only hated dating, he also hated constantly standing up dates and disappointing women who deserved better. But he liked companionship and, well, he *was* a guy—sex was nice, too. Why couldn't the perfect woman fall in his lap so he could focus on work?

"It is late," Leo said in what was no doubt a transparent attempt to change the subject. "Why don't *you* go home and I'll take the proposal to Garrett?"

He had until five o'clock to get it to Garrett Engineering, formally expressing his interest in doing business with them.

What Steve Jobs was to cell phones, Tommy Garrett was to internal combustion engines. Or would be, as soon as funding was in place. Garrett had invented a revolutionary modification to increase the gas mileage of a standard car engine and Leo intended to be Garrett's venture capital firm of choice. The partnership would net a sizable, long-term profit for both men, and Leo could do what he did best—pull strings behind the scenes.

If Leo won the deal.

No, not *if. When.*

Leo would never rest until his company hit that sweet spot of security, where longevity was a given, not a question mark. His first million hadn't done it. Neither had the first eight figures, because his profits went straight back into leveraged investments that wouldn't pay off until some point in the future. So he didn't rest.

"Since you've scared off yet another female with your dogged determination to work yourself into an early grave, be my guest." Mrs. Gordon waved her approval for Leo to deliver the proposal. "I filled up your car with gas this morning. It wouldn't kill you to glance at the gauge once in a while."

"Thanks. You're too good to me. By the way," Leo threw in as Mrs. Gordon pulled her handbag from a desk drawer,

"I was thinking of having a gathering at my house to wine and dine Tommy Garrett. If I ask very nicely, would you plan it?"

"It's not my job to be your stand-in wife." Mrs. Gordon firmed her mouth, which meant she had a lot more to say but didn't know how to do so tactfully. In the eight years she'd been keeping him sane, he'd seen that look a lot.

With a half laugh, Leo said, "Of course not. That's not part of your job description."

Except it had the ring of uncomfortable truth. When his hair grew too long, Mrs. Gordon scheduled a haircut. His mother's birthday—Mrs. Gordon picked out the gift. The wine-and-dine request had been a bit of a blurred line, but based on the set of Mrs. Gordon's mouth, he'd pretty well turned the line into a trapezoid.

Mrs. Gordon shut down her computer for the night. "Well, it should be part of someone's job description."

"What, like a party planner?" Maybe he should hire a professional in some capacity, which wouldn't cover all his social obligations. But it was better than nothing.

"Like a girlfriend. Or someone who might actually still be around in six weeks. Hire a wife," she said with a nod. "You need a good woman to take care of you out-side of the office. Ask *her* to glance at your gas gauge. She can schmooze Garrett and make sure your life is running smoothly. Keep you warm at night."

Her eyebrows waggled but Leo barely noticed.

Hire a wife.

Could you even do such a thing? It seemed too perfect a solution.

He had no time—or the desire—to sift through women until he found one he liked but who also wouldn't expect him to be available. Reynolds Capital Management did not manage itself. His employees and partners depended on him.

A wife couldn't leave him with no notice. It was the ultimate security.

Leo would have a permanent companion to help fill that occasional hollow feeling, one with no hidden agenda involving his assets and connections. They'd both know from the get-go what to expect—stability. There'd be no hard feelings when she realized he hadn't been kidding about giving 100 percent to his company, leaving nothing left over for her.

All or nothing. Commitment was Leo's kryptonite. Once he latched on to something, he gave it everything and then some. Early on, he'd realized that trait was inherited and tried not to make the same mistakes as his father.

Then he'd met Carmen, who taught him the true depths of his weaknesses, and how easily one obsession could become the center of his existence. He practiced putting everything but the goal aside until it was second nature.

Love or success. His personality didn't allow for both and after clawing his way out of the ghetto, he refused to gamble his future.

If he had an understanding wife, work and his personal life would remain completely separate. And best of all, Leo would never have to engage in small talk with a new woman or experience that sharp pang of guilt over canceling on one ever again.

Leo tugged on his suit jacket and hand delivered the proposal to Garrett's people in their tiny downtown office. It wouldn't be tiny for long. Investors far and wide were clamoring to get in on the ground floor with Garrett's technology. Once the company went public, its worth would shoot to legendary status.

Leo had to land the deal with Tommy Garrett, and the wine-and-dine thing would be a fantastic opportunity to solidify his chances. A wife could handle the logistics, leaving Leo to engage in uninterrupted dialogue with Garrett about what Reynolds Capital could do for him that no one else could. His offer to Garrett didn't expire for several weeks. He had plenty of time to get a wife in place.

When Leo returned to his darkened office, he sat at his

laptop. Within fifteen minutes, Google provided a potential answer to the question of how to hire a wife. He'd had to wade through all the cleaning services and concierge services, then a few distasteful escort services, to find the definitive solution.

A matchmaking service.

Yes. Of course. It was not what he'd had in mind when he started the quest. Actually, he hadn't been sure *what* he'd intended to find. But this was an intriguing answer. Leo had always thought he'd get married one day, when he could afford to transfer his energy to a relationship. Yet here he was on the downside of thirty-five and Reynolds Capital Management still took all of his focus. All of his time.

He stared at the logo for EA International. The website was professional and tasteful, with earth tones and a classic font. Most importantly, this particular matchmaker catered to exclusive clients, promising discretion and a money-back guarantee. Guarantees warmed Leo's heart.

The tagline said it all—*Let us help you find "the one."*

Presumably, "the one" for Leo would fit all his qualifications. EA International would do the screening, the interviewing, the background checks, and ultimately filter out candidates who were looking for some mystical connection. Love didn't pay the bills, and Leo would never allow the power to be turned off on his family, the way his own father had.

It was brilliant. The matchmaker would do everything required to find Leo a wife. One he could never disappoint. All he had to do was make a phone call.

Then, with that settled, he could get back to work.

Daniella White had dreamed of her wedding since the first time she'd created crayon invitations to a ceremony starring Mr. Fourpaws as the tattered velveteen groom and herself as the fairy-tale bride wrapped in dingy sheets. Someday she'd wear a beautiful dress of delicate lace and silver heels. The guests would receive heavy card-stock in-vitations with a vellum overlay and eat a three-tiered French vanilla cake with fondant flowers.

Best of all, a handsome husband-to-be would wait for her at the end of a church aisle, wearing a tender smile. Later that night, the love of her life would sweep her away to a romantic honeymoon somewhere exotic and breath-taking. Theirs would be a marriage of grand passion and enduring love.

When her real wedding day finally arrived, Dannie could never have envisioned it would involve a groom she'd never met in person. Or that in a few minutes, she'd be marrying Leo Reynolds in the living room of a matchmaker's house in North Dallas, with only a handful of guests in attendance.

"What do you think, Mom?" Dannie beamed at her mother in the cheval mirror and straightened a three-quarter-length sleeve. A dress of any sort usually appealed to Dannie, but this unadorned ecru one would be her wed-ding dress and she wanted to love it. She didn't. But she'd make the best of it, like always.

EA International's sophisticated computer program had matched her with businessman Leo Reynolds and he ex-pected a wife with a certain refinement—one who dressed the part, acted the part, lived the part. Dannie had spent the past month under the matchmaker's intensive tutelage to become exactly right for that part.

Dannie's mother coughed profusely, hand to her chest as if she'd clear the scar tissue from her lungs through sheer will alone. "You're beautiful, baby," she said when she'd recovered. "Every bit a proper wife. I'm so proud of what you've accomplished."

Yeah, it was really hard to put my name in a database. Dannie bit back the comment. She wasn't a smart aleck anymore. No one ever got her jokes anyway.

Two sharp raps at the door shoved Dannie's heart into her throat. Elise Arundel, Dannie's fairy godmother–slash–

matchmaker, popped into the room, her sleek, dark pageboy swinging. "Oh, Dannie. You look lovely."

Dannie smiled demurely. She needed a lot of practice at being demure.

"Thanks to you."

"I didn't pick out that dress." Elise nodded once. "You did. It's perfect for your willowy frame. I've never had anyone who glommed on to cut and style with such natural talent."

"I made up for it by being hopeless with cosmetics." Dannie frowned. Did that seem too outspoken? Ungrateful? That was the problem with changing your personality to become a society wife—nothing came naturally.

Elise's critical eye swept over Dannie's face and she dismissed the comment with a flick of her manicured hand. "You're flawless. Leo's socks will be knocked off."

And there went her pulse again.

The figure in the mirror stared back at her, almost a stranger, but with her dark brown hair and almond-colored eyes. Would Leo be happy with her sophisticated chignon? The erect posture? The scared-to-death woman in the ecru dress? What if he didn't like brunettes?

She was being silly. He'd seen her picture, of course, as she'd seen his. They'd spoken on the phone twice. Their conversations had been pleasant and they'd worked through several important marital issues: they'd allow the intimate side of their relationship to evolve over time, a clarification that had clinched it since he didn't believe he was buying an "exchange of services," and he was open to eventually having children.

Neither of them had any illusions about the purpose of this marriage—a permanent means to an end.

Why was she so nervous about what was essentially an arranged marriage?

Her mother smoothed a hand over Dannie's hair. "Soon you'll be Mrs. Leo Reynolds and all your dreams will come true. For the rest of your life, you'll have the security and companionship I never had." Racking coughs punctuated the sentiment and the ticking clock in Dannie's mind sped up. Pulmonary fibrosis was killing her mother.

Dannie was marrying Leo to save her.

And she'd never forget what she owed him. What she owed Elise.

Her mom was right. Dannie had always dreamed of being a wife and mother and now she was getting that chance. Marriage based on compatibility would provide security for her and her mom. She had no business being sad that security couldn't be based on love.

Maybe love could grow over time, along with intimacy. She'd hang on to that hope.

With a misty smile, Elise opened the door wider. "Leo's waiting for you in front of the fireplace. Here's your bouquet. Simple and tasteful, with orchids and roses, like you requested."

The clutch of flowers nearly wrenched the tears loose from Dannie's eyes. "It's beautiful. Everything is beautiful. I can't thank you enough."

She still couldn't believe Elise had selected *her* for the EA International matchmaking program. When she'd applied, it had all seemed like such a long shot, but what choice did she have? Her mother needed expensive long-term care, which neither of them could afford, so Dannie gladly did whatever her mother needed—doctor's appointments, cooking, cleaning. Her father had left before she'd been born, so it had been the two of them against the world since the beginning.

Unfortunately, employers rarely forgave the amount of time off Dannie required. After being fired from the third job in a row, her situation felt pretty dire. She'd searched in vain for a work-from-home job or one with a flexible schedule. After hours at the library's computer, she'd been about to give up when the ad for EA International caught her eye.

Have you ever dreamed of a different sort of career?
Coupled with a picture of a bride, how could she not click
on it?

EA International invited women with superior adminis-
trative skills, a desire to better themselves and the drive to
become "the woman behind the man" to apply for a bold,
innovative training program.

Who had better admin skills than someone managing
the care of a perpetually ill mother? Without much to lose,
Dannie sent her information into the ether and shock of all
shocks, got the call.

It was fate that EA International was based in Dallas,
where Dannie lived.

Elise polished Dannie until she shone and then matched
her with a man who needed an elegant society wife. In exchange for organizing Leo's household and hosting parties,
Dannie could take care of her mother without any more financial worries.

A marriage that was little more than a contract seemed
a small price to pay.

"You're one of my most successful graduates." Elise
handed Dannie the bouquet and shifted a couple of flowers to face the outside. "I predict you'll be one of my most
successful matches, as well. You and Leo couldn't be better suited."

Dannie's stomach lurched. She wanted to like him. To
enjoy being married. Would she be attracted to him? What
if she wasn't? Would the intimate side of their marriage
never happen? Maybe she should have insisted they meet
first in spite of their mutual agreement not to.

It hardly mattered. Attraction wasn't a factor here, but
surely they'd eventually hold a great deal of affection for
each other, regardless of what he looked like.

Nose to the bouquet, Dannie inhaled the sweet scent of
her wedding flowers. "We have similar goals and both rec-

ognize the practicality of this union. I expect we'll be very happy together."

Leo had gobs of money. She'd have been happy with half a gob. That level of wealth intimidated her, but Elise insisted she could handle it. After all, Dannie would have a valued place in his life and she might eventually be the mother of his children. Her training had made it very clear the woman behind the man worked as hard as women in other careers.

"Happy is exactly what you'll be." Elise pinched the clasp of Dannie's necklace, dragging it to the nape of her neck. The open-heart lavaliere hanging from the chain had been a gift from the matchmaker when Dannie agreed to marry Leo. "My computer program is never wrong."

Dannie's mother chimed in. "This is the best kind of match, one that will last forever, because it's based on compatibility, not feelings. It's everything Dannie wants in a marriage."

Dannie forced a nod, though she wished she could disagree, and spared only a passing thought to Rob. She'd been so gaga over him.

Look where that had gotten her—brokenhearted and determined to make over her temperament so no man could call her opinionated and blunt again. She'd screwed up that relationship but good.

She wasn't going to screw up this one. Her mother couldn't afford it.

"Yes," she agreed. "Security and companionship. What else could I possibly ask for?"

Fairy tales were stories about magical solutions to problems and full of people who fell in love, but whose relationships couldn't possibly stand the test of time. In real life, women had to make sacrifices and Dannie was making hers.

Without any further melancholy and ridiculousness, she marched out the door of the room she'd stayed in during her transformation and went to meet her fate on a prayer that she and Leo would at least grow to care for each other. If there was more, great. She'd consider it a bonus.

Her mother and Elise followed. Dannie paused at the top of the sweeping staircase and took in the scene below.

With cheerful optimism, Elise had placed flower arrangements on the mantel and on each side of the fireplace. Dannie's heart fluttered at the thoughtfulness of the woman who had become her friend. A photographer stood at the back of the room, poised to snap memories at a moment's notice, and the gray-haired minister Elise had recommended waited in front of the fireplace.

To his right was Leo Reynolds. Her husband-to-be.

He looked up and met her gaze.

A shock of…something zapped across her shoulders. He looked exactly like his picture, but in person—*hello*. Dark, straight hair brushed his collar and an expensive, well-designed suit encased a masculine body Leo clearly kept in great shape. Classic, smooth features formed a face handsome enough to sell out an entire print run of *GQ* magazine. More Ashley than Rhett, which was appropriate since she'd banished her inner Scarlett O'Hara to a place where the sun didn't shine.

Leo also looked kind, as though he wouldn't hesitate to carry an elderly lady's groceries to the car. Dannie almost snorted. If Leo Reynolds had ever seen the inside of a grocery store, she'd eat her bouquet. He was a busy man and it was a good thing for her that he was, or he wouldn't need a wife.

Not for the first time, she wondered why he'd resorted to a matchmaker. He was good-looking, rich and well-spoken. By all rights, the eligible-woman line should be wrapped around the block.

Eyes on Leo, she descended the stairs with practiced ease—she'd done it in four-inch heels dozens of times and didn't falter today despite the severity of the occasion. In far too few steps, she reached Leo. In her bone-colored pumps, she and Leo were nearly the same height.

She searched his expression as he did the same to her. What did you say to a man you were about to marry but whom you were seeing for the first time in the flesh? *Hey, fancy meeting you here.*

A hysterical giggle nearly slipped out. Not an auspicious start.

"Hello." Well, that should be reasonably safe.

"Hello," Leo returned and smiled, setting off a nice, warm flutter in her chest.

Up close, he was solid and powerful, capable of carrying a baby in one arm and taking out a carjacker with the other. The flutter that thought set off was a little warmer and little more south than the first one. In theory, she'd known Leo equated to safety. But reality was far more… real. And affecting.

They faced front. Nerves locked Dannie's knees and she tried to loosen them without drawing attention. If she pitched over in the middle of her wedding ceremony, Elise would never forgive her.

"Let's begin." The minister raised a Bible in his wrinkled hands and began reciting the vows Leo had insisted Dannie select.

The words flowed from the minister's mouth, sounding completely different aloud than she would have imagined. For better or worse, richer or poorer. None of that really applied, not in the way it did for most couples. Those vows were a call to remember the reasons you fell in love in the first place when marriage got tough.

From her peripheral vision, she tried to catch a glimpse of Leo to see how all this was registering. Suddenly she wished they'd had a few more conversations so she'd know better what he might be thinking.

It had just seemed so unnecessary. Elise wouldn't have allowed her to marry someone awful. Her screening process was diligent and faultless, matching her with Leo on all forty-seven points of the personality profile. So long as he wasn't a criminal or a wife beater, what did it matter if he had a good sense of humor or liked sweeping historical dramas?

"Do you take Leo as your lawfully wedded husband?" the minister intoned.

Dannie cleared her throat. "I do."

With a trembling hand, she slipped a plain platinum band on Leo's finger. Or tried to. She couldn't get it over the knuckle and when he covered her hand with his to assist, she glanced up to meet his blue eyes.

That same odd shock she'd experienced on the stairs rocked her shoulders. It wasn't awareness, but deeper, as if she'd just seen someone she knew but couldn't place.

She shook it off. Nerves. That's all.

Leo repeated, "I do," his voice even and strong. Because he wasn't nervous. Why would he be, with all that masculine confidence?

The platinum band he slid on her finger matched his and winked in the living room's overhead lighting. She stared at it, transfixed by the sheer weight such a simple band added to her hand.

Divorce wasn't an option.

Both she and Leo had indicated a strong belief in honoring commitments in their profiles and it had been the first thing addressed in their phone conversation. Leo had been far too generous in the original prenuptial agreement and she'd refused to marry him without serious alterations, namely that any future children would be provided for but she'd get nothing. In her mind, that was the best way to demonstrate the seriousness of her word.

Leo represented security, not free money. And in exchange for that security, she'd be the wife he needed.

This marriage was a permanent solution to their problems, not a love match. Which was fine by her. Leo would never leave her the way her father had and she'd never have to worry about whether he'd stop loving her if she screwed up.

The minister signaled the end of the short ceremony with the traditional, "You may kiss the bride."

Oh, why had she asked for that part? It was going to be so weird. But it was her *wedding.* Shouldn't she get a kiss from her husband? A kiss to seal their bargain.

Leo turned to her, his expression unreadable. As his lips descended, she closed her eyes. Their mouths touched.

And held for a shimmering moment, launching a typhoon of flutters in her abdomen. Maybe the possibility of having a whole lot more than just affection between them wasn't as remote as she'd thought.

Then he recoiled as if he'd licked a lemon wedge and stepped away.

Their first kiss. How…disappointingly brief, with a hint of possible sparks she'd had no time to enjoy. Hadn't he felt it? Obviously not.

Her mother and Elise clapped, gathering around her and Leo to gush with congratulations.

Dannie swallowed. What had she expected—Leo would magically transform from a venture capitalist into Prince Charming? Elise's computer program had matched her with the perfect husband, one who would take care of her and her mother and treat Dannie well. She should be happy they'd have a fulfilling partnership.

She should *not* be thinking about how Leo might kiss her if they'd met under different circumstances. If they were getting married because they'd fallen in love, and during the ceremony he'd slid her a sizzling glance that said he couldn't wait for the honeymoon.

She shouldn't be dwelling on it, but the thought wouldn't fade—what would his calm blue eyes look like when they were hot with passion?

Two

Daniella stood by the door with her hands clasped and chin down. Leo's new wife was refined and unassuming, exactly as he had specified. What he had not expected was to find her picture had lied. And it was a monstrous lie of epic proportions.

She wasn't girl-next-door attractive, as he'd believed. This woman he'd married radiated sensuous energy, as if her spirit was leashed behind a barrier of skin that could barely contain it. If that leash ever broke—look out.

She wasn't merely gorgeous; in person, Daniella defied description.

The stuff of poetry and Michael Bublé songs. If one was inclined toward that sort of thing.

Even her name was exotic and unusual. He couldn't stop looking at her. He couldn't stop thinking about the way-too-short kiss he'd broken off because it felt like the beginning of something that would take a very long time to finish. His entire body buzzed in response to that concentrated energy it badly wanted to explore.

What was he going to do with a woman like *that*?

"I'm ready to leave whenever you are, Leo." Her voice, soft but self-assured, carried across the foyer of Ms. Arundel's house.

He was going to take her home. Regardless of having *distraction* written all over her, they were married.

His recon skills clearly needed help. Why hadn't he met

her first? Because he'd dotted as many *i*'s and crossed as many *t*'s as possible before fully committing to this idea. Or so he'd thought. Leo had spoken with other satisfied clients of EA International and then personally met with Elise Arundel several times. He had confidence in her ability to find the right match, and the thorough background check Ms. Arundel had supplied confirmed her choice.

Daniella White was the perfect woman to be his wife.

Their phone calls had sealed the deal. He'd recognized her suitability immediately and everything fell into place. Why wait to marry when they were like-minded and neither cared if there was any attraction between them? It was better to get on with it.

If he had it to do over, he'd add one more criteria— *doesn't make the roof of my mouth tingle*. It was Carmen all over again, but worse, because he was no longer a lovesick seventeen-year-old and Daniella was his wife. No woman could be allowed to set him on the same catastrophic path as his father, not when Leo knew how hard it was to repurpose himself. What painful test of his inherent all-in personality had he inadvertently set himself up for now?

His marriage was supposed to be about compatibility and convenience, not a headlong sprint into the depths of craziness. It was important to start it off on the right foot.

"Did my driver get all of your belongings?" he asked her and winced.

That wasn't the right foot. *My driver*. As if he regularly employed servants to do his bidding. Was he *really* going to act that pretentious around his new bride? He usually drove himself, for crying out loud. He'd only hired a car because he thought Daniella might enjoy it.

She nodded, taking it in stride. "Yes, thank you."

"Have you said your goodbyes to everyone?"

"Yes. I'm ready."

The conversation was almost painful. This was why he'd rather have a root canal than take a woman to dinner, why he'd opted to skip dating entirely. They were married, well matched and should be able to shoot right past small talk.

Leo waited until they were seated in the town car before speaking again. She crossed her long legs, arranging them gracefully, skin sliding against skin, heels to one side. And he was openly watching her as if it was his own private movie.

Before he started drooling, he peeled his gaze from the smooth expanse of leg below her skirt. "If you don't mind, I'd like to invite my parents over tonight to meet you."

"I would be very happy to meet your parents." She clasped her hands together, resting them in her lap serenely. "You could have invited them to the ceremony. I recall from your profile how important family is to you."

He shrugged, mystified why it pleased him so much that she remembered. "They're less than thrilled about this marriage. My mother would have preferred I marry someone I was in love with."

"I'm sorry." Her hand rested on his sleeve for a brief, reassuring moment, then was gone. "You have to live your life according to what makes sense for you, not your mother."

Everything about her was gracious. Her speech, her mannerisms. Class and style delineated her from the masses and it was hard to believe she'd come from the same type of downtrodden, poverty-stricken neighborhood as he had. She had strength and compassion to spare, and he admired her pledge to care for her mother.

So she possessed a compelling sensuality and he couldn't take his eyes off of her. This was all new. By tomorrow, the edge would surely have worn off.

He relaxed. Slightly.

This marriage was going to work, allowing him to focus on his company guilt-free, while his wife handled wifely things and required none of his attention. He'd paid Ms. Arundel a sizable chunk of change to ensure it.

"Daniella, I realize we barely know each other, but I'd

like to change that. First and foremost, you can always talk to me. Tell me if you need something or have problems. Any problem at all."

"Thank you. That's very kind."

Gratitude beamed from her expression and it made him vaguely uncomfortable, as if he was the lord of the manor, bestowing favors upon the adoring masses. They were equals in this marriage. "As I told you on the phone, I have a lot of social obligations. I'll depend on you to handle them, but you can come to me if you need help or have questions."

"Yes, I understand." She started to say something else and appeared to change her mind, as if afraid to say too much. Probably nervous and unsure.

"Daniella." Leo paused, weighing the best approach to ease the tautness between them. She gazed at him expectantly, her almond-colored eyes bright, with a hint of vulnerability. That nearly undid him. "We're married. I want you to trust me, to feel relaxed around me."

A building was only as good as its foundation.

"I do." She nodded, her expression so serious, he almost told her a joke to see if she'd smile. "You're everything I expected. I'm very happy with Elise's choice."

She was clutching her hands together so tightly, her knuckles had gone white. The art of small talk was not his forte, but surely he could do better than this.

"I'm pleased, as well." Pleased, not happy. This marriage had never been about being happy, but being sensible. "But now we have to live together and it should be comfortable for us both. You can talk to me about anything. Finances. Religion. Politics."

Sex.

His mind had *not* jumped straight to that…but it had, and unashamedly so, with vivid mental images of what her legs looked like under that prim skirt. She glanced at him, held his gaze. A spark flared between them and again, he sensed her energy, coiled and ready to whip out—and his body strained to catch it.

Stop, he commanded his active imagination. He and Daniella had an agreement. A civilized, rational agreement, which did not include sliding a hand over her thigh. His fingers curled and he shoved them under his leg.

She looked down and shifted, angling slightly away. One finger drummed nervously against her skirt. "Thank you. I appreciate that."

His very carnal reaction to a mere glance had obviously upset her.

He cleared his throat. "Are you still okay with letting the intimate side of our relationship unfold naturally?"

Her eyes widened and he almost groaned.

What a fantastic way to set her at ease. He needed to dunk his head in a bucket of cold water or something before he scared her into complete silence. Though that might be better than her constantly starting sentences with *yes,* as if she thought he expected a trained parrot.

"Yes." She met his gaze squarely and earned a couple of points for courage. "Why wouldn't I be?"

Because you feel this draw between us and it's making your palms sweat, too.

Chemistry had been far down the priority list, for both of them.

He just hadn't anticipated having so much of it right out of the gate. Or that it would pose a very real danger of becoming such a distraction, the exact opposite of his intent in hiring a matchmaker.

His focus should be on work. Not on getting his wife naked. Indulgent pleasures weren't on the menu, particularly not for someone with his inability to stop indulging.

"I want to be sure we're on the same page," he said.

"We are. Our marriage will be companionable with a progression toward intimacy when it seems appropriate." Her tone wavered, just a touch, and was coupled with a glint in her eyes he couldn't interpret. "Like we discussed."

His exact words. And suddenly he wished he could take it all back. Wished he could put a glint of happiness in her eyes instead of the look currently drilling a hole through his chest. The unsettling feeling bothered him more than the chemistry, because he had no clue what to do with it.

"We'll have separate bedrooms, for now." That had been his intent from the beginning and seemed even more necessary given her nervousness. It should solve everything. The back of his throat burned with inexplicable disappointment. "Take things slowly."

Separate bedrooms would serve to put some distance between them. Ease the tension, give them both time to acclimate. Give the chemistry time to cool. And definitely allow him to refocus.

Then they'd settle into what he'd envisioned: a marriage where they had fulfilling lives outside of each other and enjoyed a pleasant relationship both in the bedroom and out. No one with his intense personality could have any other kind of marriage.

His phone beeped and he glanced at it. He'd taken a half day to attend his wedding and given his employees the rest of the day off as well, but he was never "out of the office."

The email was a brief courtesy notice from Tommy Garrett's people to let him know Garrett Engineering had narrowed the field to Leo and another firm, Moreno Partners. Excellent. The timing couldn't be better. His new wife could organize the wine and dine for Garrett as soon as she was settled.

"Do you need to make a call?" Daniella asked politely. "I don't mind. Pretend I'm not here."

That wasn't even possible. "Thanks, but it was an email. No response needed."

A different strategy was in order. In light of the wife he'd ended up with, thinking of her as an employee might work best to stave off the urge to spend the weekend in bed, making his wife laugh and then making her gasp with pleasure. And then hitting *repeat* a hundred times.

If he fit Daniella into a predefined box, she'd slide into his life with little disruption and that was exactly what he wanted. What he needed.

Success guaranteed security. It was the only thing that could and no price was too high to ensure he kept his focus on Reynolds Capital Management—even continued solitude.

Dannie kept her mouth shut for the rest of the ride to her new life.

Where she would not share a bedroom with her husband.

She was alternately very glad for the space and very confused. The flash of awareness between them must be one-sided. Or she'd imagined it. Leo could not have been more clear about his lack of interest in her.

Maybe he'd seen right through Elise's makeover.

And now her fantasy about the way he'd kiss if he really meant it had shattered. Such a shame. Her husband was attractive in that unattainable way of movie stars, but in her imagination, he kissed like a pirate on shore leave, and no one could take that away.

She stole a peek at this hard-to-read man she'd married for life.

Her lungs froze. What if Leo decided he didn't like her after all? Just because he claimed to have a strong sense of commitment didn't mean he'd tolerate screwups. And screwups were her specialty.

Her mother was counting on her. She was counting on herself, too. If Leo divorced her, she'd have nothing. One of his first acts upon learning she'd accepted his proposal was to hire a full-time caregiver for her mother who specialized in pulmonary rehabilitation. The nurse was slated to start today.

Without Leo, her mother would surely die a very slow and painful death. And Dannie would be forced to watch helplessly.

Her nails bit into her palm and she nearly yelped. Long nails. Yet another thing she had to get used to, along with all the other things Elise had done to make her over into Leo's perfect wife. Organization and conversation skills came naturally, but the polish—that had taken a while to achieve.

She had to remember her job here was to become the behind-the-scenes support for a successful man. Not to be swept away in a haze of passion for her new husband.

"We're here," Leo said in his smooth voice.

Dannie glanced out the window and tried not to gape. Leo's house practically needed its own zip code.

They'd discussed her comfort level with managing a large house. During the conversation, she'd pictured a two-story, four-bedroom house with a big backyard, located in a quiet suburban neighborhood. That would have been her idea of large after the small two-bedroom apartment she'd shared with her mother.

She'd known the house was in Preston Hollow, one of the most elite neighborhoods of Dallas. But *this* she could never have anticipated.

Wrought-iron gates caught between two large brick-and-stone posts swung open as if by magic and the driver turned the car onto the cobblestone drive leading up to the house. Colossal trees lined the drive, partially blocking the sun and lending a hushed, otherworldly feel to the grounds. And *grounds* was the only fitting term. Neatly manicured grass stretched away on both sides of the car all the way to the high stone wall surrounding Leo's house.

Her house. *Their* house.

The car halted in a semicircular crushed-stone driveway, and the hulking residence immediately cast it in shadow. The manor sprawled across the property, pointy rooflines dominating the brick-and-stone structure. Four—no, five—chimneys stabbed toward the sky.

She should have asked for a picture before agreeing to handle a property this size. What was she *doing* here?

"What do you think?" Leo asked, but it was hardly a question she could answer honestly.

"It's very…" *Gothic.* "Nice."

She bit the inside of her lip. All of Elise's hard work would go up in smoke if Dannie couldn't keep her smart-aleck gene under control. The thought of Elise calmed her. They'd done exhaustive work together to prep Dannie for this, with endless days of learning to set a table, to make proper tea. Practicing how to sit, how to walk, how to introduce people. In between, Elise had transformed Dannie's appearance into something worthy of a magazine cover.

This was it—the test of whether the makeover would stick or Dannie would fail.

With a deep breath, Dannie smiled. "It's beautiful, Leo. I'm very eager to learn my way around."

"Let me show you." He placed a hand at the small of her back as she exited the car and kept it there, guiding and supporting, as they ascended the stone steps to the front door. "Please think of this as your home. Anything you want to change is open for discussion."

Anything. Except the arranged-marriage part.

It was ridiculous to even think that. But her wedding day felt so anticlimactic. And disappointing. She shouldn't be wishing Leo would sweep her up in his arms and carry her over the threshold, Rhett-style. Or wishing they had a timeless romance.

The palm at her back signaled security. Not passion. A partnership based on mutual affection was enough. Dannie was Leo's wife, not the love of his life, and she didn't have the luxury of entertaining daydreams of eventually being both.

Leo led her into the foyer. The interior of the house

opened before her, with soaring ceilings, twenty-foot windows and grand arches leading to long hallways. It reminded her of a cathedral, beautiful and opulent.

The tour of her new home took close to thirty minutes. By the time Leo concluded it in the kitchen, she was out of breath and ready to get started on the first thing she wanted to change—her shoes. The house had *four* flights of stairs.

Leo leaned a hip against the granite island in the center of the kitchen and picked up a cell phone from the counter. "For you. The number is written here, along with the alarm system security codes and the code for wireless internet access."

She took the phone with numb fingers and stared at the glossy screen. Her current cell phone was of the make-a-call-only variety. It would take hours to figure out how this one worked. "Thank you. Is your phone number written down, too?"

"I programmed it into your phone. Here's the user manual." He slid it across the counter and stuck a hand in his pocket, casually, as though they were a normal married couple chatting in the kitchen. "This model has great planning features. Feel free to add things to my schedule as needed. My admin's phone number is programmed in, as well. Mrs. Gordon. She's eager to meet you."

He had an admin, one who knew him far better than Dannie did, like how to make his coffee and whether he paced while on the phone or sat at his desk.

Suddenly, she felt completely out of her depth. "Oh. All right. I'll contact her right away."

"The car and driver will be on call for as long as you like," he continued, and his mellow voice soothed her nerves as he ticked off the items on his mental list. His confidence and self-assurance were potent. "But please, take some time to visit a dealership and buy yourself a car. Whatever kind you like. You'll want the independence."

A *car.* Any car she wanted. She'd been hopping public

transportation for so long, she nearly swooned at the idea. Was there anything he hadn't thought of? "That's very nice. Thank you."

But he wasn't finished waving his benevolence around. "I opened a bank account for you. It will be replenished regularly, but if you find yourself low, let me know. Spend it like it's your money, not mine." From his pocket, he produced a shiny black credit card and handed it to her. "No limit."

"Leo." He'd spun her around so many times now, she could hardly keep her balance. The phone and credit card in her hands blurred as she blinked back overwhelmed, appreciative tears. "This is all very generous. I'm sorry if this is too forward, but I have to ask. Why would you do all this and expect nothing in return?"

His dark eyebrows drew together in confusion. "I expect quite a bit in return, actually."

"I meant in the bedroom."

Leo went still.

Yeah, far too forward. But jeez, really? A no-limit credit card and he didn't even want one conjugal visit a month? There was a punch line here she didn't get and she'd prefer not to have it smack her in the face later.

"Daniella..." Leo swallowed and she realized he was at a loss for words.

Why couldn't she keep her big mouth closed? She should have stuck to *yes* and *thank you*.

"I'm sorry," she said in a rush. "Forgive me. You've been nothing but kind and I have no right to question your motives."

The lines of his handsome face smoothed out and he held up a hand. "No apology needed. I want to have a good relationship, where you feel like we're equals. The best way to achieve that is to give you your own money and the power to do as you like with it."

She stared at him. *Power.* He'd been granting her power with these gestures. The man she'd married was thought-

ful, generous and very insightful. This whole experience
could have gone very differently. Gratitude welled in her
chest. "I don't know what to say."

"You don't have to say anything." He smiled and it was
as powerful as it was comforting. "Remember, I'm going to
be at the office a lot. You should find a hobby or volunteer
work to keep you busy. A car will come in handy."

Implausibly, he was giving her the ability to entertain
herself, when her sole focus should be on him and his needs.
"Won't I be busy with all your social obligations?"

He waved it off. "That won't take one hundred percent
of your time. You're building a life here and when our paths
cross, we should enjoy each other's company. You can regale
me with stories of the things you're involved in."

Elise had coached her on this extensively. It was part of
her role to provide stimulating conversation for Leo's business associates. Who better to practice with than her husband? After all, they *were* a married couple having a chat
in the kitchen. "That makes sense."

"Good." His eyes warmed, transforming him from
movie-star handsome into something else entirely. Her
breath caught.

If that's what happened to his eyes when he was pleased,
she *really* wanted to see them stormy with desire.

She shook her head. They were talking about *hobbies*.

Leo took her hand, casually, as if he'd done it a thousand
times. "I don't want you to be disappointed by our marriage.
In the past, it's been a struggle to balance work and a relationship because the expectations weren't clear from the
beginning. Women in my circles tend to demand attention I
can't give them and I'm grateful we won't have that issue."

The feel of her hand in his sparked all the way up her
arm, unsettling her. It was the only plausible excuse for why
she blurted out, "You couldn't find one woman besides me
who was willing to forgive your absence in exchange for a
life of luxury?"

Her mother would have a coronary if she could hear Dannie being so outspoken. But he'd said in the car they could discuss anything. She hoped he meant it.

"Sure. But I wanted the right woman."

All at once, the reason he'd gone to a matchmaker seemed painfully obvious. He'd tried to buy his way out of putting any effort into a relationship and his previous girlfriends had told him to take a hike. So to avoid a repetition, he bought a wife.

Her.

No wonder he'd been so adamant about honoring commitments. He didn't want her to bail when she figured out she'd be all alone in this big house from now on.

Gothic indeed.

"I see."

"Daniella." His gaze bored into hers, pleading with her to believe…something. But what? "Neither of us have any illusions about this marriage, and that's why it will work. I understand the drive for security. I'm happy to provide it for you because it's a drive we share."

She nodded and excused herself to unpack—and get some breathing room. Security *was* important and she'd married a good, solid man who'd never leave her like her father had. She just hadn't expected gratefulness for that security to blossom into unexpected warmth toward the husband who'd provided it. And who promised to never be around.

As she climbed the stairs to her room, she realized what his unspoken plea had been meant to communicate.

He needed her as much as she needed him.

Three

The scraps of silk had definitely not been in Dannie's suitcase when she packed it.

She fingered the baby-doll lingerie set and noticed the note: "For a red-hot wedding night. —Elise."

Dannie held up the top. Such as it was. Black lace cups overlaid red silk triangles, which tied around the neck halterstyle. Red silk draped from the bust, allowing a flirty peek at the tiny G-string panties beneath. Or it would if she was insane enough to actually wear something so blatantly sexy for her husband.

This lingerie was definitely the ticket to a red-hot wedding night. For some other woman, not Daniella Reynolds. Dannie had married a workaholic. With her eyes wide-open.

She tucked the sexy lingerie into the very back of the drawer she'd designated for sleepwear. Ha. There'd be no sleeping going on if she wore *that* outfit. She sighed. Well, it would be the case if her husband pried his eyes off his bottom line. And was attracted to her. And they shared a bedroom.

And what exactly had she expected? That Leo would take one look at his new wife and fall madly in love? She needed to get over herself and stop acting as though Leo had taken away something that she'd never planned on having in the first place.

Elise, the eternal optimist despite being perfectly aware Dannie and Leo had only met that same day, couldn't have known how things would shake out. It was still depressing to be so soundly rejected. How would there be a possibility of children if they didn't share a bedroom?

Dannie slammed the drawer a little harder than an adult probably should have and stomped to the bed to finish unpacking her meager wardrobe.

If she was going to be alone, this was certainly the place to do it. Her bedroom rivaled the finest luxury suite she'd ever seen featured in a movie. She didn't have to leave. Ever. There was a minibar with a small refrigerator, fully stocked. An electronic tablet lay on the bedside table and she suspected Leo had already downloaded hundreds of books since her profile had said she liked to read.

The entertainment center came equipped with a fifty-inch flat-screen TV, cable, a DVD player, a sound system worthy of a nightclub and a fancy touch-screen remote. The owners' manuals lay on the raw silk comforter. Of course. Leo never missed a trick.

She wondered where he kept the owner's manual for Leo Reynolds. That was something she'd gladly read from cover to cover. A forty-seven-point profile only went so far into understanding the man.

There had to be more to Leo than met the eye, because no one voluntarily cut themselves off from people without a reason.

By the time she folded the last pair of socks, the hour had grown late. Leo's parents were due in thirty minutes. She called her mother to see how she was getting along with the nurse and smiled at the effusive recounting of how her mother's new caregiver played a serious game of gin rummy. Her mother sounded happy.

Relieved, Dannie went into the bathroom, where she had left half a cosmetic counter's inventory strewn across the marble vanity. She took a few minutes to organize it in the drawers, which had built-in compartments of different sizes. The bathroom alone was bigger than her entire apartment.

Dannie agonized over what to wear and finally selected a simple pale lavender skirt and dove-gray button-up shirt. Her small wardrobe of coordinated pieces had been another gift from Elise. She was between sizes so everything had to be altered, adding yet more cost to the already expensive clothes. Shoes, however, posed no problems whatsoever. She stepped into a pair of calfskin sling backs that fit as if they'd been custom-made for her foot, then redid her chignon and makeup.

Who *was* that woman in the mirror?

"Daniella Reynolds," she whispered to her reflection, then said it louder to get used to the sound of it. Only telemarketers and her grandmother called her Daniella. She liked the way Leo said it, though.

Since it was far past time to assume her duties as hostess to Leo's parents, she navigated downstairs with only one wrong turn.

Leo was not in the lavishly appointed living room. Or the kitchen, or any of the other maze of rooms on the first floor. Finally she spied his dark head bent over the desk in his study, where he was clearly engrossed in the dollar signs marching across his laptop screen.

Leo was working. Gee. What a shock. Why hadn't she thought to check his study first? Wishful thinking?

For a moment, she watched him, curious to see her husband unguarded. Towering bookshelves lined the room and should have dwarfed the man in it. They didn't. Leo's persona dominated the room. He'd shed his suit jacket and rolled up his shirtsleeves to midforearm. With his hair slightly rumpled, he was kind of adorable.

He glanced up with a distracted, lopsided half smile and her stomach flipped with a long, feminine pull. Okay, he was more than adorable. He was quite delicious and thoroughly untouchable, a combination she suddenly found irresistible. Her inner Scarlett conjured up a naughty mental scenario involving that red-hot lingerie and Leo's desk. *Hey, here's a bottom line you can check out.*

"Busy?" she croaked and cleared her throat. Duh. Of course he was.

"I'm, uh, just finishing up." He shot a furtive glance at his laptop as if the screen contained something shamefully un-work-related.

"What are you doing? Watching YouTube videos?" *Shut up, Scarlett.* It was none of her business whether he was monitoring stock prices or carousing in a role-playing-game forum. "I mean…"

Well, there was really no recovery for that slip.

"No." He shut the lid and she thought that would be the end of it. But then his mouth twitched. "I mentor college students online. I was walking through a business plan with one. Via chat."

"That's wonderful." What in the world was shameful about that? "They must really pay close attention when they see your name pop up. That's like winning the mentor lottery."

Her new husband was so generous and kind. Of course he was. Elise wouldn't have matched her with this man otherwise.

"I mentor anonymously."

"Oh. Why?"

"The business world is—" Flustered, he threaded fingers through his already slightly rumpled hair and she itched to smooth it back for him. "Let's just say my competitors won't hesitate to pounce on weakness. I don't present them with any."

Mentoring the next generation of businessmen could be perceived as a weakness? "Richard Branson mentors young kids. I don't see why he can do it, but you can't."

"He's considered successful." The unspoken *I'm not* hung in the air, but Leo stood and rolled his sleeves down, then rounded the desk, clearly signaling the end of the conversation. "Shall we?"

Her mouth fell open and she clamped it closed, swallowing the dozens of questions that sprang to her lips. His expression had closed off and even she could read the tread-with-caution sign. "Of course."

The doorbell rang and she trailed Leo to the foyer to meet Mr. and Mrs. Reynolds. Leo introduced his parents and Dannie shook hands with smiling, silver-haired Mr. Reynolds.

The spritely woman with Leo's dark hair bounded into the house and swept Dannie up in a fierce hug. "I'm so happy to meet you!"

"I'm happy to meet you, too, Mrs. Reynolds." Dannie breathed in her new mother-in-law's perfume, which reminded her of vanilla cookies.

"Oh, please. I'm Susan."

"I'm sorry, but I was expecting someone…" *Cold. Unforgiving. Judgmental.* "…older."

Susan laughed. "Aren't you sweet? Come with me to the kitchen and let Leo talk to his father while we fetch drinks."

After a glance at Leo to gauge the appropriateness, Dannie followed Susan into the kitchen and proceeded to watch while Leo's mother bustled around gathering glasses and chattering as if they were old friends. Obviously Susan felt comfortable in her son's house. Unlike her son's wife. Dannie wouldn't have known which cabinet contained glasses.

"I apologize for missing the ceremony, Daniella." Susan handed her a glass of tea and touched her shoulder. "It was a stupid, useless protest. But I'm mad at Leo, not you."

"Oh." She had to find a new response. That one was wearing thin. But it had been so appropriate. All day.

"He's just so…*Leo.* You know?" Susan sighed dramatically and Dannie nodded, though she didn't know. But she'd like to. "Too focused. Too intense. Too everything but what matters."

No way was she letting that pass. "What matters?"

"Life. Love. Grandchildren." With narrow eyes, Susan peered at Dannie. "Did he tell you that he draws?"

The tea she'd just sipped almost went down the wrong pipe. "Draws what?"

Susan snorted. "That's what I thought. Leo would rather die than let anyone know he does something frivolous. He can draw anything. Animals. Landscapes. Bridges and buildings. He's very talented. Like his namesake."

"Leo was named after someone who draws?" She envisioned a stooped grandfather doodling cartoon characters on the back of a grocery list.

"Leonardo da Vinci."

Dannie nearly dropped her tea. Leo's full name was Leonardo? Not Leonard? She'd noticed the little extra squiggle at the end of his name on the marriage license but had been so fixated on signing her own name she hadn't thought anything of it.

It shouldn't matter. But it did.

She'd married a man with a romantic name who created art from nothing more than pen and paper. She wanted to see something he'd drawn. Better yet, she wanted him to voluntarily show it to her. To share a deep-seated piece of himself. To connect with his wife.

Leo's mother had torn open a tiny corner of her son's personality and it whipped up a fervor to tear away more. They'd been *matched* and Dannie hungered to learn what they might share beyond a love of books, family and commitment.

"Daniella." Susan crooked her finger and Dannie leaned in. "I get that your marriage to my son is some kind of arrangement and presumably, that's all right with you. I won't pry. But Leo needs someone to love him, someone he can love in return, and neither will come easy. If it's not going to be you, please step aside."

Her pulse hammered in her throat. This marriage was

nothing more than a means to an end. An arrangement between two people based on compatibility, not love—exactly
what she'd signed up for. But nothing close to what she
wanted, what she dreamed could be possible.

Leo had asked for a wife to run his household, organize
his parties and charm his business associates. Most important, his wife should give him what he needed, which wasn't
necessarily the same as what he *professed* to need.

The woman behind the man had to be smart about how
best to do her job.

Her inner Scarlett snickered and said *new plan*.

"What if it *is* going to be me?"

Leo had such a generous heart, but he cut himself off
from people. He needed Dannie's help to understand why.
If she could figure him out, it could lead to so much more
than an arrangement. It could lead to the enduring love story
she'd dreamed of.

Susan's smile could have powered every light in Paris.
"Then I say welcome to the family."

Leo shut the door behind his parents and paused a moment before turning. For fortification. It did nothing to ease
the screaming awareness of his vibrant wife. Sure enough,
when he spun, there she was. Watching him with those keen
eyes, chest rising and falling slightly, straining against her
soft gray shirt.

He was noticing the way she *breathed*.

Clearly, he needed to go bury himself in a spreadsheet
for a couple of hours.

His parents had liked Daniella, fortunately, because their
lively discussion covered the fact that Leo hadn't contributed much. He'd been too busy pretending not to be preoccupied by his wife. But she'd been so amazing. A good
conversationalist. A good hostess. Warm, friendly. Sexy.

It was just the two of them now. Talking was unavoidable.

"Thank you for entertaining my parents."

She shot him a perplexed look. "You're welcome. That's what I'm here for. Right?"

Since she was gazing at him expectantly, he answered her, though the question should have been rhetorical. "Yes, and I appreciate it."

"I enjoyed meeting your parents. Your mother is very interesting."

That sounded like a lead-up if he'd ever heard one. "What did she say to you in the kitchen?"

"Nothing of consequence." The smile on his wife's face was gracious and innocent. Too much so.

"Don't listen to anything my mother says, Daniella. She suffers from a terrible affliction with no cure—overt romanticism."

"Dannie."

"What?"

She'd inched forward until they were breathing the same air. And her chest nearly touched his with each small inhalation. "Daniella is too formal and stuck-up, don't you think? Call me Dannie."

He shook his head. The more formality the better for his peace of mind. "There's nothing wrong with the name *Daniella*. It's unusual. Beautiful. It suits you."

Her eyes lit up and suddenly, she was the only one breathing because all the organs in his chest stopped functioning. Nothing to the south suffered from the same problem. Everything there hummed on high alert.

"You think I'm beautiful?"

Had he said that? His brain was not refreshing fast enough. "Your name. I said your name is beautiful." Her expression fell and he cursed. If only he could converse with his wife exclusively by email, then maybe he could avoid hurting her feelings. "Of course you are, too. Very lovely."

Nice save, he thought sarcastically. *Lovely.* That described a winter snowscape. From the perspective of an eighty-year-old woman. This was the point where he usually escaped to go do something where he possessed proficiency—work.

Without looking at her again, he muttered, "Good night."

"Leo." A firm hand on his arm stopped him before he'd taken two steps past her. "I asked you to call me Dannie because that's what my friends call me. We're friends, aren't we?"

The warmth in her voice washed over him, settling inside with a slow burn. He didn't turn, didn't dare face her.

Something fundamental had changed in her demeanor—the leash she'd kept on her energy had snapped and yeah, he needed to look out. It leached into the air, electrifying it. She certainly wasn't afraid to speak to him any longer. "I… Yes. Of course."

She brushed against his arm as she rounded it, apparently not content to talk to his back. Her shirt gaped slightly, revealing a tantalizing peek at her cleavage. The slow burn blazed faster. They were talking about being friends, not lovers. What was wrong with him?

Dannie. No, too intimate. *Daniella* was too intriguing. What was he supposed to call her, *hey, you?*

He couldn't compartmentalize his wife. That was bad.

"Friends," he rasped because he had to say something.

Okay, good. Daniella could go into the friends box. It could work. He'd envisioned having a companion to fill a hole in his life. Now he had one.

"Friends." Without breaking eye contact, she reached up and loosened his tie, leaning into it, fingers lingering far too long for the simple task. "Who help each other relax."

Relax? Every nerve in his body skated along a razor's edge, desperately seeking release from the power of his wife's touch. The faint scent of strawberries wafted from her glossy lips and he wanted to taste it. "What makes you think I need to relax?"

"I can feel the tension from here, Leo."

Was that what they were calling it these days? Felt like a good, old-fashioned hard-on to him.

As if pulled by imperceptible threads, his body circled closer to hers and the promise of heat turned into a reality as their lower halves brushed once, twice. His hand flew to the small of her back to clamp her tight against him.

Fingers still tangled in his loosened tie, she tugged slightly. Her face tipped up, lips primed to be taken in another kiss, but this time nothing prevented him from finishing it. From dragging his lips down the length of his wife's torso, straight to…

He cursed—they'd agreed to be platonic only a few hours ago and they were in the middle of an innocuous conversation about being *friends*. Yet he was salivating at the thought of kissing her, of laughing together over a joke, of being so much more than a convenience to each other.

He took a deliberate step backward and her hand dropped from his tie.

If she had this strong an effect on him, he was in hotter water than he'd realized. He did *not* want to be so obsessed with his wife.

"I'm tense because I have a lot of work to do." He willed his body and his bothersome loneliness back into submission. Or tried to. Seemed as though it was destined to be a losing battle. Since she was clearly no longer too scared to talk, he'd have to put space between them another way. "We'll spend time together, but this will not be a conventional relationship. If that's not going to work for you, we should get an annulment."

A hint of hurt crept into her expression. His chest panged. She'd just asked to be friends and loosened his tie. Why was he turning it into a cardinal offense? Wasn't this part of letting their relationship grow more intimate naturally?

"What happened to make you so jaded?" she asked quietly, not the slightest bit cowed by his speech. He liked it better when she said nothing more than *yes* and *thank you*.

"I'm not jaded. I don't have anything against relationships or love in general. Without it, I wouldn't be here. My parents still make googly eyes at each other across the table. Didn't you notice?"

"Of course. They're a very happy couple. Why don't you want the same?"

There was the reason he'd nipped the tie loosening in the bud. They were married and might even become friends, but they were never going to be anything more, and it was a disservice to Daniella to let her have the smallest hope otherwise.

He was already doing himself a disservice by even contemplating "otherwise."

"Oh, they're happy, all right." He rolled his eyes. "At the expense of everything else. My parents have no money. No savings."

And they refused to accept what they called handouts from Leo. He'd like nothing more than to take care of them, had offered a house, cars, even vacations, to no avail. Apparently, they enjoyed the gangs and graffiti spray-painted on the front sidewalk. Their memories appeared to be short, but Leo could never forget the gun-wielding thief who'd broken into their house when he was six. The terror had fueled his drive to escape and kept him on the straight and narrow.

"You fault your parents for being happy over making money?"

"No, I don't blame my father for working a low-paying job so he could be home with my mom and me. I choose to live my life differently. I'll never force my child to be grateful for one gift under the Christmas tree. To stay home from school on the days when the rest of the class goes on field trips to the zoo because I can't afford for my kid to go."

"Oh, Leo."

The compassion shining in her eyes unearthed something poignant inside. That had to go. This wasn't about feeling sorry for poor, little Leo Reynolds from the section of east

Dallas where even the churches had bars on the windows. It was about making a point.

"See all this?" He cut a hand through the air to indicate the house at large. "I worked for every dime. I held three jobs in college so I could graduate with no debt and then put my nose to the grindstone for years to get ahead. I'm still not there. If I take my eye off the prize for even a moment, poof. It all vanishes."

His wife gazed at him without speaking, lips pursed in a plump bow. Firm breasts strained against her blouse, inviting him to spread the fabric wide and—maybe he needed to internalize which prize he wasn't supposed to take his eyes off of.

Other venture capital companies were unearthing the next Google or staking start-ups that sold to competitors for billions of dollars. Reynolds Capital would be there soon if he kept on course. All he had to do was resist temptation. He'd married a woman who would help him avoid the dangers of giving in.

If she'd just stay in her box, that is.

He breathed in the scent of strawberries and the sizzling energy of his wife. "I work, Daniella. All the time. I can't invest in a relationship. It wouldn't be fair if I let you believe in that possibility."

He couldn't let himself dwell on the possibilities, either. No weakness. Indulgence led to immersion and immersion led to ruin. Carmen had proved that, nearly derailing his entire senior year and subsequently, his life. It was easier to never start down that path and the last thing he wanted was to hurt Daniella.

Four

Dannie slept poorly that night. The bed was comfortable, but she wasn't. Leo had her tied up in knots.

Now that she knew how truly earthshaking his eyes looked when they were hot with passion, she didn't know if she'd ever be comfortable again. The spike of awareness inside—deep, *deep* inside—had peaked the second he touched her and then died a miserable death during the "I'm a workaholic, deal with it" conversation.

He was definitely attracted to her. And perfectly willing to ignore it in favor of his bottom line. How exactly did he envision them moving past being polite strangers?

Her new plan might need some refining. Just because she and Leo's mother thought he might benefit from a woman's tender affections didn't mean Leo thought that. And if Dannie irritated him any further with unwanted advances, he might seek that annulment on his own. At which point she'd get nothing and she'd let her mother and Elise down. Plus herself.

But as far she was concerned, they were married for life, and she wanted to eventually be friends *and* lovers. Despite Leo's impassioned speech, she really didn't understand why he didn't want that, too.

Hence the sleepless night.

She woke in the morning, groggy but determined to be a better wife to Leo Reynolds than he could ever dream. Rob had wanted a fade-into-the-background woman and she'd messed up. Elise's training had taught her how to beat back that strong-willed inner Scarlett.

Leo was going to get what he'd asked for.

If she addressed his needs—especially the unrealized ones—maybe *that* would lead them into a deeper relationship.

After she dressed and arrived downstairs, one of the maids informed her Leo had already left for the day. Instead of wallowing in disappointment she had no business feeling, she familiarized herself with the kitchen as she toasted bread and scrambled eggs. Tomorrow morning, she'd set an alarm and be up early to make Leo coffee or breakfast or whatever he preferred, which she needed to learn pronto if she hoped to see him in the morning.

Dannie spent the rest of the morning in an endless parade of tasks: learning the ins and outs of a difficult phone that she refused to believe was smarter than she was, memorizing the brands of Leo's clothes, determining how he preferred his closet to be organized, researching the recommended care of all the fabrics. As mistress of the household, it was her responsibility to ensure the servants did their jobs well and correct poor performance as necessary. By lunch, her brain hurt.

And she hadn't even started on Leo's social calendar.

Once she tapped into the wealth of information named Mrs. Gordon, Dannie breathed a little easier. Leo's admin talked for a solid hour and then sent a dozen emails full of links and instructions about the care and feeding of a venture capitalist.

Dannie read everything twice as she absently shoved a sandwich in her mouth.

Mrs. Gordon wrapped up the exchange with a tip about an invitation to an alumni event from Leo's college, which was that very night. She kindly agreed to delete the reminder entry she'd already set up so Dannie could practice scheduling.

Perfect. Dannie plunked the stupid phone into her palm and eyed it. "I'm the boss. You better cooperate," she told it, and proceeded to manhandle the appointment onto Leo's calendar.

When his acceptance appeared, she nearly broke into an impromptu dance. Until she noticed she'd scheduled it for tomorrow night. Grimly, she rescheduled and got it right the second time. Leo was probably sitting in his office shaking his head as he accepted the updated request.

Enough of that job. Dannie went to agonize over her meager wardrobe in anticipation of her first social appearance as Mrs. Leo Reynolds. This she'd have to get right on the first shot. She couldn't carry a second outfit in her clutch in case of dress remorse.

Leo walked through the door at precisely six o'clock. Dannie was ready and waiting for him in the kitchen, the closest room to the detached garage. The salmon-colored dress she wore accentuated her figure but had tasteful, elegant lines. Elise had taught her to pick flattering clothes and it looked fantastic on her, especially coupled with strappy Jimmy Choos heels. Would Leo notice?

"How was your day?" she asked politely while taking in the stress lines and shadows around his eyes that said he'd slept poorly, as well.

Something unfolded in her chest, urging her to smooth back the dark hair from his forehead and lightly massage his temples. Or whatever would soothe him. She wanted to know what to do for him, what he'd appreciate.

He set a brown leather messenger bag on the island in the kitchen. "Fine. And yours?"

"Wonderful." Except for the part where he hadn't kissed her goodbye. Or hello. *Shut up, Scarlett.* "The alumni gala is at the Renaissance Hotel. My driver will take us as soon as we're ready."

He hadn't said a word about her dress. Perhaps she'd take that as a sign he wouldn't be ashamed to be seen with her and not dwell on whether it got a response or not. Compliments weren't the reason she'd married Leo.

"That's fine. Let me change and we'll go." Leo set off for the stairs, fingers already working on his tie, which she'd have gladly taken off for him, if he'd let her. "They're giving an award to a friend of mine, and we should take him to dinner afterward."

Reservations. Where? For how many? But Leo was gone before she could ask.

Totally winging it, she called the most expensive restaurant she'd heard of and booked a table for four in Leo's name. If nothing else, the restaurant might be willing to add a few more to the party for a distinguished guest like Leo Reynolds.

Leo returned to the kitchen a short time later and she forgot all about a little thing like reservations. In black tie, Leo simply stole her breath.

"Ready?" he asked with raised eyebrows, likely because her fish-mouth impersonation amused him.

He was so delicious with his dark hair and dark suit, all crisp and masculine with a slight sensuous edge that set off something sharp and hot inside her. Last night, she'd felt just enough of the body he carried under that suit and the memory reintroduced itself as she let her eyes travel the entire length of her husband.

He cleared his throat and her gaze snapped to his. He was still waiting on her response.

"Ready," she squeaked and grabbed her clutch.

Leo kept up the conversation as they rode to the hotel with his confident, steady presence. She suspected—and appreciated—it was a ploy to dispel her nervousness, but it didn't work.

Leo escorted her through the lobby of the hotel with a hand at the small of her back. She liked the way his hand fit there. It served a dual purpose of providing support and showing everyone they were together.

And boy, did people notice. Heads swiveled as they entered the crush in the Renaissance ballroom. A string quartet played Strauss on a small platform in the corner, but the music couldn't cover the rush of whispers that surely were about the woman with Leo.

One flawless society wife in progress. Who hadn't gone to college but was going to be brilliant or die trying. Dannie squared her shoulders.

The neckline of her dress slipped, revealing a healthy slice of breast. Surreptitiously, she fingered it back into place. The deep vee over her cleavage wasn't terribly daring, but it was low-cut and the spaghetti straps were too long for her torso. Since the svelte salmon-colored dress had cost Elise seven hundred dollars, paying to have it altered felt like a sin.

It slipped down again as Leo steered her toward the far corner. As she walked, she lowered one shoulder, Quasimodo-style, hoping to nudge the neckline back where it belonged through a combination of shifting her balance and sheer will.

"Are you okay?" Leo whispered.

She should have worn the dress all day and practiced walking in it. Hindsight. Double-sided tape could have fixed the problem in a jiffy.

"Of course." She pasted on a serene smile as they halted before a group of men and women Leo clearly knew. Nodding, she greeted people and used all her tricks to remember names. Constantly being fired from a variety of jobs had an upside—few situations or people intimidated her.

"And this is Jenna Crisp," Leo concluded, indicating a gorgeous redhead on the arm of Leo's friend Dax Wakefield, who was receiving the alumni award that evening. "Jenna, this is my wife, Daniella Reynolds."

Dannie shook the woman's hand but Jenna wasn't looking at her. The redhead's attention was on Leo. Hmm. Dannie glanced at him. He didn't notice Jenna's scrutiny. Too busy discussing a patent infringement case with Dax. "I'm happy to meet you, Jenna. Have you known Leo long?"

Jenna focused on Dannie, and her expression noticeably cooled. "Long enough. How did you two meet, again?"

The redhead's tone oozed with challenge, as if there might be something tawdry to the story.

That was one area they'd definitely not covered. Did his friends know he'd gone to a matchmaker? She'd have to settle for a half-truth lest she embarrass Leo. "A mutual acquaintance introduced us."

"Interesting." The other woman nodded, sweeping long locks over her bare shoulders. She curled her lips in a semblance of a smile, which didn't fool Dannie for a second. Jenna did not like her.

"That's how Dax and I met, too. Leo introduced us."

"Oh?" Leo—a matchmaker himself? That *was* interesting. "I'm sure he was happy to help his friends find each other."

"You think so? Considering the fact that Leo and I were dating at the time, I wasn't sure what to make of it."

Oh, dear. No wonder the daggers in Jenna's eyes were so sharp. Dannie groaned inwardly. The dinner reservations had just gotten a whole lot more complicated than whether the table would be big enough.

"I'm sorry. I can't speak for Leo. If you're curious about his motives, you'd best ask him. Champagne?" she offered brightly, intending to put some distance between herself and Leo's ex-girlfriend. At least until she figured out how to navigate the bloody water full of sharks her husband had dropped her into.

"That would be lovely," Jenna said just as brightly and took Leo's arm to join in his conversation with Dax, physically blocking Dannie from the group.

In historical novels, they called that the cut direct. In real life, Dannie called it something else entirely, and if she said that many four-letter words out loud, Leo would have a heart attack.

Instead, she went to get Jenna and Leo a glass of champagne.

Really, she understood Jenna's animosity. She'd be confused, too, if Leo had shuffled her off on a friend and then promptly married someone else. Dannie also had the superior position between them, a point Jenna likely hadn't missed. At the end of the day, Dannie's last name was Reynolds and Jenna's wasn't.

Now she wondered what had really happened between Jenna and Leo. It was a little uncivilized of Leo not to have warned her. Men. Didn't he realize what he'd dragged Dannie into?

In reality, he probably hadn't considered it a problem. And it wasn't. Their marriage was an arrangement and her emotions weren't Leo's primary concern. That put a little steel in her spine. She had a job to do.

When she rejoined the group, Leo shot her a sidelong smile in gratitude for the glass of champagne. The flutters his very private grin set off were enough to forgive him. Almost.

A good wife might choose to forget the whole conversation. She bit her lip.

Then again, a good wife who paid attention to unspoken nuances might also ensure she didn't mistakenly cause her husband embarrassment. Forewarned was forearmed, and if Leo expected her to chat up his associates, she should know exactly what that association was. Right?

"You used to date Jenna?" she murmured in his ear as Dax engaged his date in their own conversation.

"Briefly." Leo's gaze sought out the woman in question, his eyes narrowing and growing a tad frigid. "She told you? I'm surprised she'd be so tactless. And I apologize if I put you in an uncomfortable position."

He'd leaned in, breath teasing along her cheek as he

spoke, and she caught a whiff of something fresh and maybe a little wintry but definitely all male. His hip brushed hers. Heat pooled at the contact and spread, giving a whole new meaning to an uncomfortable position.

She waved off his apology. "Nothing I can't handle. I'm sure you didn't do it on purpose."

He'd apologized instead of calling her out for sticking her nose in his business. That was a relief. Walking that line between being a complement to Leo and fading into the background was harder than she'd anticipated. Regardless, she was going to be a star wife. No compromise.

Leo frowned. "We only went out for a little while and obviously it didn't work out, or I wouldn't have introduced her to a friend. Jenna wanted more than I could give and Dax pays attention to her. It seemed perfect."

Oh. Of course. Jenna was the reason Leo needed a wife who wouldn't expect him to be around—she'd presumed to spend time with a man she liked and grew weary of the "I'm a workaholic, deal with it" speech.

The longing glances Jenna kept throwing Leo's way made a heck of a lot more sense now. Despite most likely being told in no uncertain terms not to get emotionally involved, Jenna had done it anyway. Only to be cast aside.

It was a sobering reminder. Dannie had a lot to lose if she made the same mistake.

Sobering. But ineffective.

As her husband's hand came to rest against the small of her back, she couldn't help but be tremendously encouraged that Leo had cared enough about Jenna to help her find happiness with someone better suited for her. In the kitchen yesterday, he'd expressed genuine interest in ensuring Dannie wasn't disappointed with their marriage.

Small gestures, but in Dannie's mind, they added up to something much larger. He had a good heart underneath all that business acumen. And despite his determination to keep her at arm's length, he needed her to break through the shell he kept around himself.

But how?

The champagne left a bitter taste in Leo's mouth.

If he'd known Jenna would deliberately upset Daniella, he'd never have brought his wife within a mile of her.

He should be having a conversation with Miles Bennett, who was about to launch a software product with some good buzz around it. John Hu was on his radar to speak to as well, and there John was by the bar, talking to Gene Ross's ancient wife. That conversation couldn't be about anything other than Mrs. Ross's show poodle or Miami this time of year, and Leo had no qualms about interrupting either.

Several recent investments hadn't panned out the way he'd hoped. He needed new blood now. Yesterday would have been better.

Instead of the dozen other things he should be doing, he was watching his wife. Out of the corner of his eye, no less, while he pretended to talk to Dax, who pretended he didn't notice Leo's fixation.

Daniella dazzled everyone, despite Jenna's mean-spirited disclosure.

The mechanics of marriage were still new and he hadn't fully considered the potential ramifications of introducing the two women. A wife was supposed to be *less* complicated than regular females, not more. Was Daniella uncomfortable being in the same room with Jenna? Or was she taking it in stride like everything else?

Daniella didn't *look* upset. She looked like a gift-wrapped present he'd put on his list a month ago and Christmas was still a week away.

That dress. It dipped against her breasts, revealing just enough to be interesting but not enough to be labeled indecent. The zipper in the back called his name. One tug and the wrapping would peel away, revealing a very nice gift indeed. The delicate shoes she wore emphasized her shapely legs and he liked that far more than he wanted to.

Daniella was the most gorgeous woman in the room. And the most interesting, the most poised and the most vivacious. Bar none. And he wasn't the only one who thought so, instilling in him a quiet sense of pride with every appreciative glance she earned.

In case she was more upset about Jenna than she let on, he kept a close eye on her as she talked to a couple of Reynolds Capital's partners. No hardship on his part to watch her graceful hands gesture and her pink-stained lips form words. Then she laughed and the dress slipped a tantalizing inch farther down her breasts. And then another inch.

A flash of heat tensed his entire body and tightened his pants uncomfortably.

He swore and Dax stared at him as if he'd lost his mind. Which didn't appear to be as far out of the realm of possibility as it should.

"I need a refill," Leo explained and waved his empty champagne flute at a passing waiter.

When the waiter returned, he downed the glass in two gulps. It didn't cool him down. Something needed to change, very quickly.

He glanced at Daniella. She didn't turn her head, but her eyes swiveled and she met his gaze with a secret smile, as if to say, *later*.

Or maybe that was his lower half projecting her meaning. The upper half refused to entertain even one little fantasy about later. Intimacy was supposed to be a progression, and abandoning that idea on day two didn't bode well for Leo's state of mind.

They hadn't developed a *friendship* yet and he was fantasizing about skipping right over that.

The music swelled, signaling the start of the awards ceremony. Daniella moved toward him at the same moment he stepped forward to grasp her arm. They bumped hips and somehow, the button on his jacket caught her dress.

One of Daniella's nipples popped free of the fabric, searing his vision and sending a surge straight to his groin. She gasped with a feminine squeal of humiliation, hands flying to her chest.

Instantly, Leo whirled her into a snug embrace, hiding her from view. And oh, dear God. His wife's body aligned with his like flowing honey, clinging sweetly to every groove.

"No one saw," he murmured into her hair and prayed she wouldn't take offense to the obvious erection pushing into her abdomen. It wasn't as though he could step away and compose himself.

The sight of that bare, rosy nipple was emblazoned on his brain and worse, both of her nipples pressed against his chest, raising the temperature in the stuffy ballroom about a hundred degrees.

"Are you all…arranged?" he asked hoarsely.

She was shaking. Or was that him?

"I can't," she whispered and her hand worked between their bodies, brushing his erection an ungodly number of times. "The button won't come loose."

He nearly groaned. "We'll have to get to the hall. Somehow. Can you turn?"

"Yes. If you keep your arm around me."

They did a fair impression of Siamese twins, shuffling as one toward the back of the ballroom, Daniella clutching Leo with one hand and her dress with the other. Which meant her hands were nowhere near his erection—and that was good. One more brush of those manicured nails against him would have produced fireworks better left unlit in public.

Miraculously, the crowd had thinned. The awards presenter droned from the next room. Leo was missing the ceremony but Dax would have to understand.

An eternity later, they reached the hall and Leo hustled

Daniella into a deep alcove housing a giant sculpture of a mermaid.

"We're totally hidden from view. It's okay," he said.

She took a half step backward, as far as their tangled clothes would allow.

"My definition of okay and yours must be different." Head bent, she studiously fingered the threads holding his button hostage until they finally came apart. "I'm sorry, Leo. You must be mortified."

Her head was still down, as if she didn't want to look at him.

"Me?" He tipped her chin up with a loosely fisted hand. Her cheeks were on fire. "You're the one who has a reason to be mortified. I can't imagine how you must feel. First I force you to make nice to Jenna and then almost rip off your dress. I'm the one who's sorry."

"It's not *your* fault," she countered fiercely. "This dress doesn't fit quite right. I shouldn't have worn it."

Five minutes ago, he'd have agreed. If she'd dressed a little more matronly, he might be having that conversation with John Hu right now. Except the alternative—being wedged into a secluded alcove with his wife—suddenly didn't seem so terrible. "That dress fits you perfectly."

She shook her head as she twisted the waistline back into place. "All my clothes have to be altered. I know that. But I didn't have this one done. Stupid. I should have thought about the consequences. My job is to make you look good, not embarrass you in public. I'm sorry. I'm not making a very good first impression."

That's what she was worried about? That she'd messed up and displeased him? A weight settled onto his chest. Did she think he was that concerned about their agreement?

Obviously so.

"On the contrary, you've made a great impression. Exactly as I expected. I watched you with my business associates. They liked you." She'd charmed them easily and he could already envision her doing the same at future events. Daniella was amazing, through and through.

"Really?" The disbelief in her voice settled that weight a little deeper. She seemed so disheartened by what was such a small blip in the evening.

Daniella was his wife, not a casual date he might or might not see again. The very act of making her his wife changed everything. He wanted her to be happy, which he hadn't planned, could never have predicted. Not only did he want her to be happy, he'd discovered a healthy drive to care for her and ensure her security. He wanted her to know she could depend on him, always.

Problem being, of course, that his experience with serious relationships started and ended with the woman in front of him.

He nodded, scouting for a way to put a smile back on her face. "If nothing else, you can take solace in the fact that your wardrobe malfunction didn't take place on national TV."

She laughed, as he'd intended. The resurrection of his hard-on, he hadn't. But who could blame him? Her laugh curled through him like fine wine and came coupled with the distinct memory of her beautiful breast.

The secluded alcove grew close and heavy with awareness as she locked on to his gaze. Her irises warmed. "Thank you for rescuing me. It was very chivalrous."

The back of his neck heated at the adoration in her eyes. He felt like a fake. There wasn't a romantic bone in his body. "I wouldn't have abandoned you."

"Your button." Without breaking eye contact, she touched it with her fingertips. "It's loose."

"No problem." He swallowed and his throat was on fire. Everything was on fire. "I have another one."

Slim eyebrows arched as she cocked her head. Loose tendrils of dark brown hair fell against her cheeks and he barely resisted an urge to tuck them back for her. And as a treat for himself. The shiny, slightly wavy locks would be soft against his fingers.

"Should we rejoin the party?" she asked in an incredible show of courage. Not many people would walk back into a room where they'd performed a free peep show. His admiration for her swelled. "As long as I don't move around too much, I should stay tucked away."

His gaze dropped to her cleavage automatically. She was quite tucked away, but the promise of what he knew lay beneath the fabric teased him. How easily he could thumb down that dress and run the pads across those taut nipples. No effort required at all. No one could see them back here behind the sculpture.

He sucked in a hot breath.

"Leo," she murmured and slid lithe fingers along his lapels, straightening them as she traveled south.

"Hmm?" She was so close he could see golden flecks in her eyes. Raw energy radiated from her, wrapping around him in a heated veil.

"The party?" Her lips met on the last syllable and he recalled how they'd sparked against his when he'd kissed her at their wedding ceremony.

This was like a first date, wasn't it? He'd kissed women on dates, lots of times. It might even be considered expected. A major disappointment if he didn't do it.

Would kissing her be as hot the second time? Hotter?

His curiosity would only be satisfied one way.

"We should go back. Shouldn't we?" she asked. But she stood there, frozen, peeking up from beneath her lashes coyly, as if she could read the intent in his eyes.

Yes. They should go back. His body strained toward her, desperate to be closer.

The scent of strawberries wafted to him on a sensuous cloud as she swayed into his space. Or maybe he was the one who moved.

Like honey, he thought as their bodies met. Their lips

touched hesitantly, then firmly, deliberately, and his mind pushed out everything except the sizzle of flesh on flesh.

His wife's mouth opened under his and he swept her deep into his embrace as he kissed her. His back hit the wall but he scarcely noticed as Daniella came alive, hands in his hair, her mouth strong and ferocious against his.

Hunger thundered through his veins. His hips circled against hers involuntarily, uncontrollably as he sought to ease the ache she'd inflamed. With one hand, he enveloped her neck and pushed, tipping her head back so he could open her wider, then tentatively stroked her tongue with his.

She stroked him back, deeper, harder. Leo groaned against her mouth. She kissed like a horny teenager's fantasy. Deep. Wet. Carnal.

Those perfect breasts haunted him. *Touch them,* his libido begged. The temptation was almost too much to bear, but he feared if he gave in to it, he might never surface.

Home. They could go home. Right now. They lived together, after all.

If he took her home, he could strip that dress away to taste every peak and valley of his wife's body. Especially the parts he hadn't yet seen but could feel easily through the silky drape of cloth over her luscious skin.

The kiss deepened, heating further, enflaming his skin. Desire screamed through his body. He'd never kissed a woman on a date quite like this. Hell, he'd never kissed a woman like this *ever,* not even in bed.

She was luring him into a dark pit of need and surfacing suddenly wasn't so appealing.

He trailed openmouthed kisses along her throat and palmed her sexy rear again. Unbelievably, this incredible, stimulating woman was *his.* She moaned under his touch and her head fell back.

"Leo," she murmured as he slipped a pin from her fancy done-up hair. "Don't you need to go back?"

As if she'd thrown a bucket of water over him, his lust-hazed bubble burst. They were in the hallway of a hotel and his wife was reminding *him* of the importance of circulating at the alumni ceremony.

He pulled back to breathe the cool air of sanity. "I do."

Her face remained composed, but a storm of desire brewed in her gaze, one he suspected would easily explode again with his touch. She'd been just as turned on as he had.

"Till later, then?" she asked.

Oh, no. That wouldn't do at all. *Focus, Reynolds.*

At least four people he must speak with mingled in the ballroom less than a hundred yards away and his wife's mussed hair and plump, kiss-stung lips alone threatened to steal his composure. If he had to suffer through the rest of the night while anticipating *later,* nothing of consequence would be accomplished.

You're weak, the nasty voice of his conscience whispered. And that was the real reason he couldn't lose his single-mindedness.

If he let himself indulge—in drawing, in a woman, in *anything* other than the goal—he'd be lost. Look what had just happened with a simple kiss.

He released her and his body cooled a degree or two. It wasn't enough to erase the imprint of her in his senses. "I apologize. That was inappropriate. Please, take a few moments in the ladies' room and meet me back in the ballroom. We'll act as if that never happened."

Disappointment replaced the desire in her expression and made him feel like a world-class jerk.

"If that's what you want."

It was absolutely not what he wanted. But distance was what he needed in order to get a measure of control.

This marriage should be the perfect blend of necessity and convenience. *Should be.* But the possibility of being friends was already out the window due to the curse of his weaknesses, and it would only get worse the further under his skin she dug.

"This is a business event and I haven't been treating it like one."

"Of course." Her tone had become professional, as it should. Even in this, she remained poised, doing her duty as expected, because *she* wasn't weak. She was thoroughly brilliant.

He hated putting up a barrier, but she'd become exactly what he'd suspected she would—a disturbance he couldn't afford.

But she was also proving to be exactly what he'd hoped. The perfect complement of a wife. She deserved happiness and he'd provide no assurance of security—for either of them—if he took his eye off the success of Reynolds Capital Management for even a moment. His wife would not be forced into the poorhouse because of him, like his father had done to Leo's mother.

No more digressions. It was too dangerous to kiss her. Or think about her as a friend.

Daniella was back in the employee box. She had to stay there.

How in the world was he going to forget what those strawberry-scented lips could do?

Five

Leo was already gone by the time Dannie emerged from her bedroom the next morning. Even though she'd set an alarm, he still beat her.

She'd screwed up at the alumni gala. Leo had been kissing her—*oh, my God,* had he been kissing her—and then he hit the brakes. Of course work came first, and the woman behind the man should never forget that. But to pretend *that kiss* hadn't happened? It was impossible. She wasn't naive enough to believe she'd break through his shell in one evening, but she thought she'd lifted it a little at least.

At home, his obsession with work shouldn't be a factor, especially before he left for the office. Tomorrow morning, she'd shove the alarm back thirty minutes. If she beat him to the kitchen, they'd have a chance to talk and maybe share a laugh. Then think about each other fondly over the course of the day.

All good elements of both friendship and marriage.

The next morning she missed him again, and continued to miss him for a week.

Four declined event appointments should have clued her in, but it wasn't until she caught the startled look on his face when he came out of his bedroom one morning that she realized he'd been avoiding her.

"Good morning." She smiled despite his wary expression and the fact that she'd been awake since five hoping to catch him.

"Morning." He nodded and brushed past without another word.

Stung, she watched him retreat down the stairs and vowed not to think about Leo Reynolds the rest of the day. She had a job to do here.

Dannie spent an hour with the staff going over weekly household accounts, then interviewed a prospective maid to replace one who had given notice. She enjoyed organizing Leo's life. At the alumni gala, she'd navigated Leo's social circles, recovered from a humiliating dress fail and smiled through dinner with her husband's ex-girlfriend.

What more could Leo possibly want in a wife?

At four o'clock, Leo texted her with a short message she'd come to expect: I'll be home late. Make dinner plans on your own.

As she'd been doing for a week. Leo clearly planned to keep her at arm's length, despite *that kiss*.

Fuming, she called her mother and invited her over for dinner. Might as well take advantage of the cook Leo kept on staff. She and her mother ate prime rib and lobster bisque, both wonderfully prepared, but neither could keep her attention. Her mother raved about the food, about Dannie's marriage, about how much she liked her new nurse. Dannie smiled but nothing penetrated the cloud of frustration cloaking what should have been a nice evening with her mom.

As far back as Dannie could remember, her mother had constantly passed on relationship advice: *Men don't stick around. Don't listen to their pretty words and promises.* And variations aplenty espousing the evils of falling in love. The whole point of this arranged marriage was so Dannie wouldn't end up alone and miserable like her mother. And despite her mother's best attempts to squash Dannie's romanticism, it was still there, buried underneath reality.

All men couldn't be like her father. Leo didn't flatter her with slick charm, and he'd been nothing but honest with her. Furthermore, her husband had kissed her passionately, madly, more completely than Dannie had ever been kissed in her life. She couldn't pretend it hadn't happened or that she didn't want more than an occasional text message out of her marriage.

They'd never get past being virtual strangers at this rate. Maybe it was for the best, if Jenna's fate bore any credence to what might become Dannie's story. But she couldn't accept that she and Leo would *never* see each other. Surely they could spend a little time together. An hour. Thirty minutes.

How was she supposed to handle his social commitments and take care of his every need if he kept avoiding her?

After she saw her mother off in the chauffeured car that Dannie couldn't quite give up yet, she parked on the couch nearest the stairs, determined to wait for Leo until the cows came home, if necessary. They needed to talk.

An hour later, Dannie started to wonder if Leo intended to sleep at the office. He wouldn't. Would he? Had she screwed up so badly that he couldn't even stand to be in the same house with her?

She flung her head back on a cushion and stared at the ceiling. He certainly hadn't lied to her. He did work all the time and she had done nothing to find her own amusements. Because she didn't want to. She wanted to be Leo's wife in every sense of the word, or at least she thought she did, despite being given little opportunity to find out.

Another hour passed. This was ridiculous. Not only was he hindering her ability to take care of him, but he'd agreed they could be friends. How did he think friendship developed?

New tactics were in order. Before she could remind herself of all the reasons she shouldn't, she sent Leo a text message: I heard a noise. I think someone is in the house. Can you come home?

Immediately, he responded: Call the police and hit the intruder alarm.

She rolled her eyes and texted him back: I'm scared. I'd like you to come home.

Leo: Be there as soon as I can.

Bingo. She huffed out a relieved breath. It had been a gamble, but only a small one. Leo had a good heart, which wouldn't have allowed him to do anything else but come home to his wife.

Twenty minutes later, Leo pulled into the drive at the front of the house. Dannie flicked on the enormous carriage lights flanking the entrance arch, illuminating the wide porch, and met him on the steps.

"Are you okay?" he asked, his hard gaze sweeping the shadows behind her.

His frame bristled with tension, saying in no uncertain terms he'd protect her from any threat imaginable, and it pulled a long, liquid flash from her core that sizzled. An intruder wouldn't stand a chance against so much coiled intensity.

"I'm fine." In a manner of speaking.

Leo's dark suit looked as superb on him as a tuxedo did. More so, because he was at full alert inside it, his body all hard and masculine. Warrior Leo made her mouth water. She might have to fan herself.

"Did you call the police?" He ushered her inside quickly, one hand steady at her back.

"No. I didn't hear the noise again and I didn't want to waste anyone's time." Especially since the noise was entirely fictional. Hopefully, once she hashed things out with Leo, an excuse wouldn't be necessary to get his attention.

He shot off a series of questions and she answered until he was satisfied there was no imminent danger. "Next time, push the panic button. That's what the security alarm is for."

"Did I interrupt something important at work?"

Lines deepened around his eyes as his carriage relaxed and he smiled. "It's all important. But it's okay. It'll still be there in the morning."

Relaxed Leo was nice, too. So much more approachable. She returned his smile and tugged on his arm. "Then sit down for a minute. Tell me about your day."

He didn't budge from his statue impression in the foyer. "Not much to tell. Why don't you go on up to bed? I'll hang out downstairs and make sure there's really nothing to worry about."

Oh, no, you don't. "I'm not tired. You're here. I'm here. Come talk to me for a minute."

He hefted the messenger bag in his hand a little higher in emphasis with an apologetic shrug. "I have some work to finish up."

"That'll be there in the morning, too." Gently, she took the bag from him and laid it on the Hepplewhite table against the wall, a little surprised he'd let her. "We haven't talked since the alumni gala."

The mere mention of it laced the atmosphere with a heaviness that prickled her skin. Leo's gaze fell on hers and silence stretched between them. Was he remembering the kiss? Or was he still determined to forget about it? If so, she'd like to learn that trick.

"There's a reason for that," he finally said.

Her stomach tumbled at his frank admission that he'd been avoiding her. She nodded. "I suspected as much. That's why I want to talk."

His gaze swept over her face. "I thought you wanted me to tell you about my day."

"I do." She started to reach out but stopped as she took in the firm line of his mouth. "But we need to talk regardless. I was hoping to be a little more civil about it, though."

"Maybe we can catch up tomorrow." He picked up the messenger bag from the table, but before he could stride from the foyer, she stepped in front of him, blocking his path.

Arms crossed, she stared him down. "Be straight with

me. I can handle it. Are you regretting your choice in wives? Maybe you're wishing you'd picked Jenna after all?"

The bag slipped from Leo's hand and thunked to the floor. "Not now, Daniella."

"You mean *not now,* and by the way, *not ever?* When will we have this conversation if not now?" Too annoyed to check her action, she poked a finger in his chest. Being demure had gotten her exactly nowhere. "You've been avoiding me. I want to know why. Am I not performing up to your expectations?"

"I'm not avoiding you." Guilt flitted through his expression, contradicting the statement. "I've got three proposals out, the shareholder value on one of my major investments took a forty percent loss over the last week and a start-up I staked declared bankruptcy today. Is that enough truth for you? The reason we haven't talked is because I'm extremely busy keeping my company afloat."

The Monet on the wall opposite her swirled into a mess of colors as she shared some of that guilt. "I'm sorry. I shouldn't have bothered you about the noise. I just wanted to…" *See you. Talk to you. Find out if you've been thinking of me.* "Not be scared."

Leo's expression softened and he reached out to grip her shoulder protectively. "You shouldn't have been. I had the security system installed as soon as you agreed to marry me and it's top-of-the-line. It would take a SWAT team to breach it. You're safe here. Do you not feel like you are?"

She stared up into his worried blue eyes and her insides liquefied. He genuinely cared about the answer. "I do."

It dawned on her then that Leo did a lot behind the scenes—far more than she'd realized. Almost as if he preferred for no one to know about all the wonderful gestures he made or that he was such a kind person underneath. Was he afraid she'd figure out he cared about her more than he let on?

"Good." The worry slipped from his expression and was

replaced with something that looked an awful lot like affection. "The last thing I want is for you to feel anxious or insecure."

Perfect segue. They shared a drive for security. Surely he'd understand her need to settle things. "You know what would make me feel a lot less anxious? If I knew what was going on between us." Emboldened by the fact that Leo had cared enough to rush home for her, she went on. "We're supposed to enjoy each other's company when we cross paths, but we never cross paths."

"We just went out a week ago," he protested with a glint in his eye that warned her to tread carefully.

She wasn't going to. If Leo pulled another disappearing act, this might be her only chance to make her case. Besides, he said they could talk about anything.

"Exactly. A whole week ago and we haven't spoken since then, other than a terse 'Good morning.' I can't handle your life if I'm not in it. Besides, our relationship won't ever develop without deliberate interaction. On both our parts."

"Daniella." He put a thumb to his temple. Great, now she was giving him a headache. "What are you asking of me?"

He said it as if she hoped he'd blow through the door and ravish her, when all she really wanted was a conversation over a nice glass of wine. "For starters, call me Dannie. I want to be friends. Don't you?"

Wariness sprang into his stance. "Depends on your definition of friends. The last time you brought that up, I got the distinct impression it was a euphemism for something else."

"You mean sex?" Oh, Scarlett had just been chomping at the bit to get in the middle of this conversation, hadn't she?

Leo gave a short nod. "Well, to be blunt."

Oh, no. There was that word again. Her last fight with Rob flashed through her mind and she swallowed. Was she trying to ruin everything?

But Leo wasn't a spineless, insecure guy like Rob who

couldn't handle a woman's honest opinion. Besides, this was her marriage and she was prepared to go to the mat for it.

"Our marriage apparently calls for blunt. Since I might not get another opportunity to speak to you this century, here it is, spelled out for you. My offer of friendship is not a veiled invitation to jump me."

His brows rose. "Then what is it?"

Laughter bubbled from her mouth. "Guess I don't spell as well as I think I do. Didn't we decide our relationship would eventually be intimate?" *Not blunt enough.* "Sorry, I mean, that we'd eventually have sex?"

To Leo's credit, he didn't flinch. "We did decide that. I envision it happening very far in the future."

Gee, that made her feel all warm and fuzzy. "Great. Except intimacy is about so much more than shedding clothes, Leo. Did you think we'd wake up one day and just hop into bed? It doesn't work like that. There's an intellectual side to intimacy that evolves through spending time together. By becoming *friends.* I want to know you. Your thoughts. Dreams. Sex starts in here." She tapped her forehead. "At least it does for me."

"You want to be romanced," he said flatly.

"I'm female. The math shouldn't be that hard to do."

"Math is one of my best skills."

What was that supposed to mean? That he'd done the math and knew that's what she wanted—but didn't care? She stumbled back a step.

With her new distance, the colors of the Monet swirled again, turning from a picture of a girl back into a jumble of blotches.

She and Leo needed to get on the same page. She took a deep breath. "How did *you* think we were going to get from point A to point B?"

"I never seemed to have any trouble getting a woman interested before," he grumbled without any real heat. "Usually it's getting them uninterested that's the problem."

Ah, so she'd guessed correctly from the very beginning. "You've never had to invest any energy in a relationship before, have you?"

Gorgeous, well-spoken, rich men probably never did as often as women surely threw themselves at them. He'd probably gone through a series of meaningless encounters with interchangeable women.

"I don't have time for a relationship, Daniella," he said quietly, which only emphasized his deliberate use of her full name all the more. "That's why I married you."

Blunt. And devastating. She nearly reeled from it.

This was what he'd been telling her since the beginning, but she'd been determined to connect the dots in a whole new way, creating a mess of an Impressionist painting that looked like *nothing* when she stepped back to view the whole. The spectacular kiss, the security system, the gentle concern—none of it had signaled anything special.

He'd meant what he said. He didn't *want* to invest energy in a relationship. That's why he cut himself off from people. Too much effort. Too much trouble. Too much fill-in-the-blank.

There was no friendship on the horizon, no tenderness, no progression toward intimacy. He expected her to get naked, get pleasure and get out. Eventually.

She nodded. "I see. We'll enjoy each other's company when we cross paths and then go our separate ways." *He'd* been the one euphemizing sex and she'd missed it.

Her heart twisted painfully. But this wasn't news. She just hadn't realized that being in a marriage that wasn't a marriage was worse than being alone.

How could Elise's computer have matched her with Leo? Oh, sure, neither of them had professed an interest in a love match, which was more of a tiny white lie in her case, but to not even be *friends?* It was depressing.

Leo looked relieved. "I'm glad we talked, then. To answer

your earlier question, you're everything I'd hoped. I'm very happy with my choice of wife. Jenna wasn't right at all."

Because she'd inadvisably bucked the rule: don't ask Leo for more than he chooses to give.

"Speaking of which," he continued, "I'd like you to plan a dinner party for twenty guests in about two weeks. Does that give you enough time?"

"Of course."

Two weeks?

Panic flipped her stomach inside out. How would she organize an entire party in two weeks? Well, she'd just have to.

This was why Elise matched her with Leo, and running his personal life was what she'd signed up for. She couldn't lose sight of that. "I'd be happy to handle that for you. Can you email me the guest list?"

He nodded. "Tommy Garrett is the guest of honor. Make sure you pick a date he's available. No point in having the party if he can't be there. Any questions?"

A million and five. "Not right now. I'll start on it immediately."

That was the key to enduring a marriage that wasn't a marriage. Jump into her job with both feet and keep so busy she didn't have time to castigate herself. After all, if she'd begun to believe this marriage might become more than an arrangement because of a few sparks, it was her fault. Not Leo's.

Her mother was being taken care of. Dannie was, too. Furthermore, she'd spoken her mind with as much blunt opinion as she could muster and Leo hadn't kicked her out. What else could she possibly want? This was real life, not a fairy tale, and she had work to do.

She bid Leo good-night, her head full of party plans. It wasn't until her cheek hit the pillow that she remembered the total discomfort on Leo's face when he thought friendship had been code for sex.

If he expected her to get naked, get pleasured and get out, why wouldn't he take immediate advantage of what he assumed she was offering?

Leo's forehead thunked onto his desk, right in the middle of the clause outlining the expiration date for his proposal to finance Miles Bennett's software company.

That woke him up in a hurry.

Why didn't he go upstairs to bed? It was 3:00 a.m. Normal people slept at this time of night, but not him. No—Leo Reynolds had superpowers, granting him the ability to go days without sleep, because otherwise he'd get behind. John Hu had slipped through his fingers at the alumni gala and was even now working with another backer. It should have been Leo. Could have been Leo, if he'd been on his game.

And not spending a good portion of his energy recalling his wife's soft and gorgeous smile. Or how much he enjoyed seeing her on the porch waiting for him, the way she had been tonight.

Sleep was for weaker men.

Younger men.

He banished that thought. Thirty-five—thirty-six in two months—wasn't old. But lately he felt every day of his age. Ten years ago he could have read contracts and proposals until dawn and then inhaled a couple of espressos to face the day with enthusiasm.

Now? Not so much. And it would only get worse as he approached forty. He had to make every day count while he could. No distractions. No seductive, tantalizing friendships that would certainly turn into more than he could allow.

Maybe he should up his workout regimen from forty-five minutes a day to an hour. Eat a little better instead of shoveling takeout into his mouth while he hunched over his desk at the office.

Gentle hands on his shoulders woke him.

"Leo," Daniella murmured as she pressed against his arm. "You fell asleep at your desk."

He bolted upright. Blearily, he glanced up at Daniella and then at his watch. Six-thirty. Normally he was already at work by now.

"Thanks for waking me up," he croaked and cleared his throat. "I don't know how that happened."

She lifted a brow. "Because you were tired?"

Her stylish dress was flowery and flirty, but clearly altered to fit perfectly, and her hair hung loose down her back. Flawlessly applied makeup accentuated her face and plumped her lips and he tore his gaze away from them.

"Besides that." He shuffled the Miles Bennett proposal back into some semblance of order without another glance at his wife. Though he wanted to soak in the sight of her. How did she look so amazing this early in the morning?

"Let me make you a cup of coffee," she offered and perched a hip on his desk as if she planned to stay awhile.

"I have to go. I'm late."

She stopped him with a warm hand on his bare forearm, below his rolled-up sleeve. "It's Saturday. Take ten minutes for coffee. I'd like to make it for you. Indulge me."

The plea in her eyes unhitched something inside. After he'd thrown up barrier upon barrier, she still wanted to make him coffee. How could he gracefully refuse? "Thanks. Let me take a quick a shower and I'll meet you in the kitchen."

The shower cleared the mist of sleep from his mind. He dressed in freshly pressed khakis and a button-down shirt instead of a suit since it was Saturday. A concession he couldn't recall making before. What had possessed him to do it today?

When he walked into the kitchen, the rich, roasted smell of coffee greeted him only a moment before his wife did.

She smiled and handed him a steaming mug. "Perfect timing."

He took a seat at the inlaid bistro table off the kitchen

and sipped. Liquid heaven slid down his throat. He wasn't surprised she'd somehow mastered brewing a cup of coffee to his tastes. "You even got the half-and-half right."

"Practice makes perfect." She slid into the opposite seat and folded her hands into her lap serenely.

Something in her tone piqued his interest. "How long have you been practicing?"

"Since the wedding." She shrugged, and her smile made light of the admission. "I've been trying to get up before you every morning so I could make you coffee. Today's the first day I succeeded."

The coffee didn't go down as smoothly on the next sip. Why had she put so much effort into something so meaningless? "That wasn't part of our agreement. You should sleep as late as you want."

"Our agreement includes making sure your life runs fluidly, especially at home. If you want coffee in the morning, it's my job to ensure you get it."

My job.

Daniella was in the employee box in his head, but he'd never expected her to view herself that way. Of course, why would she view herself any differently when all he talked about was their arrangement?

The cup of coffee—and the ironed clothes, ready at a moment's notice—took on implications of vast proportions. Everything EA International promised, he'd received. Daniella had slipped into her role as if she'd always been his wife. The staff liked her and already deferred to her judgment, which freed him from having to deal with the cook's grocery account or the gardener's questions about seasonal plants.

She was incredible.

If only he'd gotten the wife he really meant for EA International to match him with—one he could ignore—his life would be perfect.

It wasn't Daniella's fault he suffered from all-or-nothing syndrome. Intensity was the major backbone of his temperament. That's why he didn't draw anymore. Once he started, he could fill an entire notebook with landscapes, people's faces—Carmen's beautiful form—and then scout around for a blank book to begin filling that one, too.

If it hadn't been for his calculus teacher's timely intervention, Leo would probably be a starving artist right now, doodling in the margins of take-out menus and cursing the woman who'd been his first model. And his first lover. He'd been infatuated with capturing her shape on the paper, infatuated with her. His teacher had opened his eyes to his slipping grades, the upcoming SATs and a potentially bleak future mirroring his parents' if he didn't stop skipping school to draw Carmen. Fortunately, he'd listened and turned his intensity toward his education, then Reynolds Capital Management, vowing to never again let his obsessive personality loose on anything other than success.

He knew it the way he knew the sky was blue: the second he let himself taste Daniella again, that would be it. He wouldn't stop until he'd filled them both. And once wouldn't be enough. He'd be too weak to focus on anything except her.

"Thanks for the coffee. I should go." Leo shoved away from the table.

Her warm almond-colored eyes sought his. "Before you do, I have a couple of questions about the party for Tommy Garrett."

He settled back into the uncomfortable wrought-iron chair. "Sure."

It was the only subject that could have gotten him to stay. The party was critically important since Garrett had narrowed down the field to two firms. Leo didn't intend to lose out to the other guy.

She leaned forward on her forearms with all the attentiveness of someone about to leap into a negotiation. "What does Garrett Engineering make?"

Not *What china should I use?* or *What hors d'oeuvres should I serve?* "Why does that matter?"

"I'm curious. But also because I'd like to know more about the guest of honor. From you. I'll call his admin but I want your opinion. It will help me plan the menu and the decorations."

There was something hypnotic about Daniella's voice that pulled at him. He could listen to her recite the phone book. "I wouldn't have thought of that."

Her mouth tipped up in a smile that was so sweet, it pulled one from him. "That's why I'm here. Tell me."

"Tommy's a bit of a whiz kid." Leo pursed his lips as he contemplated the most relevant facets of the man—and he used the term *man* in the loosest sense—he wanted to do business with. "One of those geniuses who wears Converse sneakers and hoodies to work. He's just as likely to spout Xbox stats as engineering principles and no one cares because he graduated summa cum laude from Yale. He designed a modification to the way gasoline is consumed in a car that will increase gas mileage by almost double. It's revolutionary."

"You like him."

"Yes." The admission surprised him.

He hadn't thought one way or another about whether he *liked* Tommy Garrett. Leo liked the instant profitability of Garrett's design. He liked the idea of orchestrating the financing and letting Tommy be the face of the venture. Tommy had a lot of spirit, a quick wit and, despite the hoodies, he also had a work ethic Leo respected. It wasn't unusual to have a conversation at eleven o'clock on a Saturday night to brainstorm ideas.

Impressed, he cocked his head at his wife. "How did you ferret that out from what I said?"

"Because I listened with my eyes." Her smile widened as he snorted. "I could see it in your expression."

Leo tried to scowl but he was enjoying the back-and-forth just as much as the sound of Daniella's voice.

"It doesn't matter whether I like him. We stand to make a lot of money together and that's the key to our association. The party is paramount. He's got another potential partner on the hook and I need to convince him to go with Reynolds."

"What percentage stake in his company did you offer in the proposal?" He did a double take and she laughed. "I read up on how venture capital works. How can I help you land the deal if I don't know what I'm talking about?"

Perhaps he should have had a cup of coffee with his wife long before now. "I guess I thought you'd handle the party details and I'd handle Garrett. But I'm reconsidering that plan."

If he unleashed the formidable force of Daniella on Tommy Garrett, the poor guy probably wouldn't even know what hit him.

"You do that. Tell me more."

Her smile relaxed him. She had the best smile, easily given, genuine. He liked seeing it on her, but liked being the one to put it there even more. Making women smile wasn't a skill he felt particular proficient at, though. Maybe he should take a cue from his wife and practice.

"Not only will his design fit new engines, it retrofits to existing engines so it can be sold to both consumers and automobile manufacturers. It's almost miraculous. He might as well have designed a way to print money."

"Sounds like you really believe in the product. I can't imagine why Mr. Garrett would choose another venture capital firm."

"Because it's business. Not personal. And actually, I couldn't care less what the product is as long as the entrepreneur comes to me with a solid business plan and proven commitment."

"All business is personal, Leo," she said quietly. "If you

didn't spend so much time behind the scenes, you might discover that for yourself."

"Behind the scenes is where I function best." Ensuring the players never had to worry about money as they took center stage—that was his comfort zone. He couldn't afford to get truly involved or he'd bury himself.

Her expression softened, drawing him in. "But in the middle of things is where the best experiences are."

He had the distinct impression they weren't talking about Tommy Garrett anymore and had moved on to something he did not want to acknowledge in any way, shape or form.

"Thanks for the coffee. I'm going to head in to the office." He glanced at his watch. Almost seven-thirty, but there was no rush hour on Saturday, so he hadn't lost too much time. "If you have any more questions about the party, don't hesitate to call me."

"Have a good day." She covered his hand with hers and squeezed. "Don't look now, Leo, but I think we just had a friendly conversation. Are you shocked it didn't kill you?"

No, the shock happened when he laughed.

Her return smile stayed with him as he climbed into his car. The gas gauge needle pointed to full. When was the last time he'd even glanced at it? He drove to the office and instead of thinking about whatever else should be on his mind, he thought about Daniella.

Dannie. Maybe she could be Dannie and that wouldn't kill him, either.

No way. He couldn't imagine allowing it to roll from his tongue.

As much as he wished he could ignore his wife, he was painfully aware she conversely wished he wouldn't. They had an agreement, but it didn't seem to be sticking and she was flesh and blood, not a piece of paper. Or an employee.

And agreements could be terminated.

He was getting what he hoped from this marriage. She wasn't, not fully. If he wanted her to be happy, he had to give a little. Otherwise she might walk. A sick worm of insecurity wiggled into his stomach at the idea of losing a woman who fit into his life so well. And who, against all odds, he liked.

Friends. It didn't sound so terrible. Surely he could handle a friendship with his wife.

Six

Dannie hummed as she drew up proposed menus. She hummed as she perused the guest list Leo emailed her and savored the little thrill she got from the short message at the bottom.

You make a great cup of coffee.

She hummed as she waited on hold to speak with Tommy Garrett's admin and later as she checked off several more things on her to-do list. The tune was aimless. Happy. Half of it was due to finally connecting with Leo on some small level, especially after he'd made it clear he wasn't interested in developing their relationship.

The other half had to do with finding her niche. Growing up, her chief source of entertainment had been old movies and TV shows on the free channels, and she'd always wanted to have her own household like the glamorous women of the '50s. It was everything she'd expected. Being in charge of her domain gave her a heady sense of accomplishment and purpose, which popped out of her mouth in song.

When Leo strode through the door at six o'clock that evening with a small, lopsided grin, her throat seized up and quit working entirely.

"I thought we'd have dinner together," he said as she stared at him, wordless. "If you don't have other plans."

Dinner? *Together?* Why?

"Oh," she squeaked and sucked in a couple of lungfuls

of oxygen in hopes it might jar everything else into functioning. "No plans. I'll let the cook know."

Clothes, she thought as she flew to alert the staff Leo
would be dining in. She should change clothes. And open a
bottle of wine. Her foot tangled on the edge of the Persian
runner lining the stairs to the second floor. *And slow down.*
A broken leg wouldn't do her any favors.

This was the first time she'd dine alone with Leo since
they'd gotten married. It was practically like a date. Better than a date, because it had been his idea and totally a
surprise. She wanted it to be flawless and so enjoyable he
couldn't wait to do it again.

In spite of a triple-digit pulse and feeling as though her
tongue was too big for her mouth, she could get used to that
kind of surprise.

Dannie opened her closet and surveyed her small but
lovely wardrobe. She'd never owned such amazing clothes
and shoes before and never got tired of dressing up. She
slipped into a casual black cocktail dress that veed over
her breasts, buckled her feet into the sexiest Louboutins she
owned and curled her lip at the state of her hair. Quickly
she brushed it out and twisted it up into a sleek chignon.

Done. That was as close as she could get to looking like
the kind of wife a man would enjoy coming home to. She
took her time descending the stairs in her five-inch heels
and spent a few minutes in the wine cellar glancing at labels
until she put her hand on a sauvignon blanc *Wine Spectator*
had talked up. A perfect date-night wine.

She stuck the bottle in a bucket of ice and left it on the
formal dining room sideboard to chill until dinner, which
the cook informed her would be a few minutes yet. At loose
ends, she tormented the place settings until the silverware
was either perfectly placed or exactly where it'd been when
she started. She couldn't tell, which meant *stop obsessing.*

The cook announced dinner at last. She went to fetch
Leo and found him in his study, of course, attention deci-

sively on his laptop. His suit jacket hung on the back of the leather chair. His shirtsleeves were rolled up on his forearms and he'd already removed his tie. Rumpled Leo might be her favorite.

Leaning on the doorjamb, she watched him type in efficient strokes, pause and type again. Mentoring anonymously via chat again, most likely. She hated to interrupt. But not really.

"Dinner's ready."

He glanced up without lifting his head and the way he peeked out from under his lashes was so sexy, it sent a spiral of heat through her tummy.

"Right now?" he asked.

"Um, yeah." She cleared the multitude of frogs camping out on her vocal cords. "We don't want it to get cold."

He typed for another couple of seconds and then closed the laptop's lid with a snick as he stood. "That would be a shame."

Boldly, she watched him approach, aware her body blocked the doorway and curious what he'd do about it. "I'm a believer in hot food, myself."

He stopped a healthy distance away when he apparently realized she wasn't budging. "I'm looking forward to a home-cooked meal. Thought I should start eating better. I've had too much takeout lately."

Whose fault is that? "Just the food, then? The company wasn't a draw?"

"Of course the company was a factor." Something flickered in the depths of his blue eyes and heat climbed all over her.

Oh, that had all sorts of interesting possibilities locked inside. They gazed at each other for a long, delicious moment, and he didn't look away. Or back up.

Then he gestured to the hall. "Shall we, Mrs. Reynolds?"

And somehow, that was far more intimate than calling her Dannie. Deliberate? Oh, goodness, she hoped so.

Leo's capable palm settled into the small of her back as they walked and she felt the contact all the way to the soles of her feet. Something had changed. Hadn't it? Was her coffee *that* good?

In the dining room, Leo drew back the heavy chair and allowed her to sit on the brocade cushion before pushing it in for her. Then he expertly poured the wine to exactly the same level in both glasses on the first try—impressive evidence of how good Leo was with both detail and his hands.

Not that she'd needed additional clues the man hid amazing things under his workaholic shell. Were they at a point where she could admit how outrageously attracted to Leo she was? Or was that going past blunt into another realm entirely?

Placing her glass on the table before her, he took the seat catercorner to hers instead of across the table. "So we can talk without shouting," he said when she raised her eyebrows.

All small, small gestures, but so huge to her romance-starved soul. Flutters spread from her stomach to every organ in her body. Especially her heart.

For whatever reason, he was trying, really *trying,* to give her some of his time. But what was his intent? The friendship she'd hoped for or merely a small gesture toward crossing her path?

She'd keep her wits about her and under no circumstances would she read anything into what was essentially just dinner. As they dug into Greek salads served with crusty bread, she stuck to discussing her progress on the party. The more the wine flowed, the more relaxed they both became.

About halfway through her swordfish, she brought up the one thing she'd been dying to ask since the night of their marriage. "Do you still draw?"

Leo's fork froze over a piece of grilled zucchini. "How did you know about that?"

"Your mother told me."

He grimaced. "I should have guessed. She still has every piece of paper I've ever touched with a pencil."

Which was no answer at all. "Is it a sensitive subject?"

"No." Carefully, he cut a hunk of fish and chewed it in a spectacular stall tactic she recognized a mile away. He didn't want to discuss his art, that much was clear.

"So, never mind then. It's not important," she lied. His reaction said there was more to the story and it was very important, but she didn't want to alienate him. "Tell me something else instead. Why venture capital?"

His expression warmed. "If you're good, you can make a lot of money. You just have to recognize the right opportunities."

"Are you good?"

She already knew the answer but was curious what he thought about the empire he'd built. Most of her research into the complexities of venture capital had been conducted by reading articles about her husband's successful company before she'd even spoken to him on the phone for the first time.

"I'm competent. But I've made my share of mistakes."

As if that was something to be ashamed of. He seemed determined to downplay all his positives. "Everyone makes mistakes. You've recovered from yours quite well. The reputation of Reynolds Capital Management is unparalleled."

He inclined his head with a pleased smile. "It's a work in progress."

Fascinated with the way his eyes turned deeper blue when he engaged, she drained her wineglass and propped her chin on a curled hand. This was exactly what she'd envisioned their friendship would look like. "So how do you recognize the right opportunity?"

The cook bustled in and cleared their empty dinner plates, replacing them with bananas Foster for dessert. She lit the rum and blew it out in an impressive culinary display, then efficiently disappeared.

Leo spooned the dessert into his mouth and murmured appreciatively before answering Dannie's question. "Experience. Gut instinct. A large percentage of success is simply showing up. I create the remaining percentage by getting there first and staying until everyone else has gone home."

"Do you see your job as creative?" Dannie took a small bite of banana, gratified Leo liked the dessert as much as she did, but determined to keep him engaged in conversation. A full mouth wouldn't lend itself well to that.

He pursed his lips. "In a way, I suppose. Without backing, a lot of entrepreneurs' ideas would never see the light of day. I provide the platform for other people to tap into their creativity."

Which was what he'd done for her—given her the opportunity and the means to be exactly what she wanted to be. A wife. If tonight was any indication, Leo had changed his mind about spending time getting to know each other. Maybe she'd get the relationship—in some form or fashion—she craved out of it, too.

"You're the puppet master, then," she said.

"Not at all. I never stick my fingers in the pie. Micromanagement is not the most effective way to do business. I'm the money, not the talent."

"But you have talent," she protested.

His expression dimmed. "You've never seen one of my drawings."

"I meant you have a talent for recognizing the right opportunity." She smiled in hopes of keeping things friendly. "But I have a feeling you've got artistic talent, too. Draw me something and I'll let you know."

She was pushing him, she knew she was. But she wanted to know him, and his mysterious artistic side intrigued her.

"I don't draw anymore," he said, the syllables so clipped they nearly drew blood.

Message received. They hadn't connected nearly as deeply as she'd hoped, but they'd only just begun. One day, maybe he'd open up that part to her. "You've moved on to bigger and better canvases. Now you're creating your art with completely different tools."

Leo pushed his chair back. "Maybe. I've got some work to finish up. Thanks for dinner."

He escaped, leaving her to contemplate whether to open another bottle of wine in celebration of a successful dinner or to drown her disappointment since Leo had abandoned her once again.

Drown her disappointment. Definitely.

She located a bottle of pinot that went better with her mood than white wine and filled her glass almost to the rim. Then she called her mother to talk to someone uncomplicated and who she knew loved her always and forever, no matter what.

"Dannie," her mother cried when she answered. "Louise just told me. Thank you!"

Dannie grinned. Her mother's caregiver had turned into a friend almost instantly, and the two were constantly chattering. "Thanks for what?"

"The cruise, silly. The Bahamas! I'm so excited, I can hardly stand it." Her mother clucked. "I can't believe you kept this a secret, you bad girl."

The wineglass was somehow already half-empty again, but she didn't think she'd drunk enough to be *that* confused. "I didn't know. What cruise?"

"Oh. You don't? Louise said Leo booked us on a seven-day cruise, leaving out of Galveston. Next week. I thought for sure you suggested it. Well, thank him for us. For me, especially."

A steamroller flattened her heart. Her husband was a startling, deeply nuanced man underneath it all.

Dannie listened to her mother gush for several more minutes and managed to get a couple of sentences in sideways in spite of the question marks shooting from her brain. Were Leo's nice gestures indicative of deeper feelings he didn't want to admit for some reason? No man did a complete about-face without a motive. Had he come home for dinner in hopes of developing a friendship—or more?

Regardless, *something* had changed, all right, and her husband owed her a straight answer about what.

Sometimes talking to Leo was worse than pulling teeth, like their conversation after her text about the fake noise. Her marriage didn't just call for blunt—if she wanted to get answers, it apparently called for Scarlett, as well. And Scarlett had been squashed up inside for a really long time.

Three glasses of wine put a good dose of liquid courage in Dannie's blood. She ended the call and cornered Mr. Behind the Scenes in his office.

She barged into the study. Leo glanced up, clearly startled. She rounded the desk to pierce him with the evil eye, not the slightest bit concerned about the scattered paperwork under his fingers.

"About this cruise." Bumping a hip against the back of his chair, she swiveled it so he faced her, swinging his knees to either side of hers.

Not the slightest bit intimidated, he locked gazes with her. "What about it?"

Good gravy, when he was this close to her, the man practically dripped some sort of special brand of masculinity that tightened her thighs and put a tingle between them.

"Are you going to deny you did something nice for my mother?"

"No?" He lifted his brows. "Or yes, depending on whether *you* thought it was nice, I suppose."

His voice hitched so slightly, she almost didn't notice it until she registered the rising heat in his expression. *Oh, my.* That was lovely. Her proximity was putting a tingle in his parts, too.

"It was nice. She's very excited. Thank you."

He sat back in his chair, as if trying to distance himself

from the sizzling electricity. "Why do you seem a little, ah, agitated?"

"Agitated." She inched forward, not about to give up any ground, and her knees grazed the insides of his thighs. "I *am* agitated. Because I don't get why you won't ever acknowledge the wonderful things you do."

His gaze flicked down the length of her body and back up again slowly. "What would be the point of that?"

Her husband was nuanced all right…and also incredibly frustrating. He likely refused to take credit for his actions because that would require too much of an *investment* from him. Someone might want to reciprocate and make him feel good, too, and then there'd be a whole cycle of emotions. *That* would never do.

She huffed out a noise of disgust and poked him in the chest, leaning into it as her temper rose. "You do these things and it's almost like you'd prefer I didn't find out you've got a kind streak. Jig's up, Leo."

He removed her finger from his rib cage, curling it between his and holding it away from his body instead of releasing it. Probably so she wouldn't wound him, but his skin sparked against hers and nearly buckled her knees.

The memory of *that kiss* exploded in her mind and heightened the gathering heat at her core.

But she still didn't know what was happening between them—friends, lovers, more? Maybe it was actually none of the above. If she gave in to the passion licking through her, would he disappear afterward until the next time he wanted sex? Or could this be the start of something special?

"You have an active imagination," he said.

She rolled her eyes to hide the yearning he'd surely see in them. "Yeah, I get it. You're a ruthless, cold-blooded businessman who'd rather be caught dead than disclosing your real name to a couple of students. What's it going to take to get you off the sidelines and into the middle of your own life?"

That was the key to unlocking his no-emotional-investment stance on marriage. It had to be. If he'd only wade into the thick of things and stop cutting himself off, he'd see how wonderful a real relationship could be. How satisfying. Fulfilling. Surely their marriage could be more than an occasional crossing of paths. He needed her to help him see that.

Leo's frame tensed and slowly he rose from the chair, pushing into her space. "I like the sidelines."

Toe-to-toe, they eyed each other, the impasse almost as palpable in the atmosphere as the swirl of awareness. "Why did you book my mother on a cruise?"

He shrugged, lashes low, shuttering his thoughts from her. "I thought she would like it."

"That's only half the truth. You did it for me." A huge leap. But she didn't think she was wrong.

Their gazes locked and the intensity shafted through her. "What if I did?"

Her pulse stuttered. Coffee, then dinner. Now this. What was he trying to accomplish? "Well, I'm shocked you'd admit that. Before you know it, we'll be buying each other birthday cards and taking vacations together. Like real couples."

Like the marriage of her dreams. Just because neither of them had expressed an interest in a love match didn't mean it was completely impossible to have found one. What better security was there between two people than that of knowing someone would love you forever?

He threw up a palm. "Let's don't get out of hand now."

She advanced, pushing his palm into her cleavage, burning her skin with his touch and backing him against the desk. She wanted to bond with her husband in the most elemental way possible. To complete the journey from A to B and see what they really could have together.

"I like getting out of hand."

"Do you have a response for everything?" His fingertips curled, nipping into her skin.

"If you don't like what I have to say, then shut me up."

His expression turned carnal. He watched her as he slid an index finger down the valley between her breasts and hooked the neckline of her dress. In a flash, he hauled her forward, capturing her lips in a searing kiss.

On legs turned to jelly, she melted into it, into him as he wrapped his arms around her, finally giving her what she'd been after since she walked in. Maybe since before that.

Greedy for all of him, she settled for the small, hot taste of Leo against her mouth. With a moan, she tilted her head and parted his lips with hers. She plunged into the heat, seeking his tongue with hers, and he obliged her with strong, heated licks.

His arms tightened, crushing her against his torso, aligning their hips. Need soaked her senses as his hard ridge nudged her. She cupped the back of his neck as his hand snaked under her dress to caress the back of her thigh.

Yes. As seduction techniques went, he could teach a class.

Soft cotton skimmed under her fingers as she explored the angles and muscles of his back. Delicious. Her husband's body was hard and strong, exactly as she liked, exactly perfect to keep her safe and satisfied at the same time.

The kiss deepened and the hand on her thigh inched higher, trailing sparkling warmth along with it. She tilted her hips in silent invitation, begging him to take those fingers wherever he so desired.

But then he pulled away, chest heaving, and spun her to face the wall, his torso hot against her spine.

"Daniella," he murmured in her ear, and his fingertip traced the line of her dress where it met the flesh of her back, toying with the zipper. "I'm about to pull this down and taste every inch of you until we're both mindless. Is that what you want?"

Damp heat flooded her and she shuddered. "Only if you call me Dannie while you do it."

He strangled over a groan and moved her forward a confusing foot, then two. "I can't do this."

"Don't say you don't want me." *So close. Don't back off now.* She whirled and tilted her chin at the bulge in his pants she'd felt branding her bottom. "I already know that's not true. You don't kiss someone like that unless you mean it."

"That's the problem." Breath rattled in his throat on a raw exhale. "You want me to mean it in a very different way than I do mean it. I'd rather not disappoint you and that's where this is headed. Making love will not change the fact that tomorrow I'm still going to work a sixteen-hour day, leaving little time for you. Until both of us can live with that, I need you to *walk away*."

He was blocking himself off from her again, but for a very good reason. The rejection didn't even bother her. How could it? He was telling her he didn't want to treat her like a one-night stand.

That set off a whole different sort of flutter.

"I'm walking." *For now.* She needed a cooler head—among other parts—to navigate this unexpected twist to their marriage.

She skirted the desk, putting much-needed distance between them.

Raking a hand through his hair, he sank into the chair with a pained grimace. "Good night."

"This was the best date I've ever been on."

With that parting shot, she left him to his paperwork, already plotting how to crack that shell open a little wider and find the strong, amazing heart she knew beat beneath. He thought they were holding off until she was okay with no-emotional-investment sex, but he was already so emotionally invested, he was afraid of hurting her.

That's what had changed. Somehow, she had to help him see what he truly needed from her.

If a large percentage of success happened by showing up and then outwaiting the competition, she could do that. Yes, her competition was an intangible, unfathomable challenge called *work,* but the reward compensated for the effort.

Time for a little relocation project.

Seven

The silky feel of Daniella's thigh haunted Leo for days. And if he managed to block it from his mind, her fiery responses when he kissed her replaced that memory immediately.

It didn't seem to matter how many spreadsheets he opened on his laptop. Or how many proposals for new ventures he heard. Or whether he slept at the office because he lacked the strength to be in the same house with Daniella. Sleeping as a whole didn't work so well when his wife invaded his unconscious state to star in erotic dreams.

There was no neat, predefined box for her. For any of this. It was messing him up.

He hadn't seen Daniella in four days and the scent of strawberries still lingered in his nose.

Fingers snapped before his eyes and Leo blinked. Mrs. Gordon was at his desk, peering at him over her reading glasses. "I called your name four times."

"Sorry. Long night."

Mrs. Gordon's gaze flicked to the other end of Leo's office, where a sitting area overlooked downtown Dallas. "Because that couch is too short for a big, strapping young man like you."

He grinned in spite of being caught daydreaming, a mortifying situation if it had been anyone other than his admin. "Are you flirting with me?"

"Depends. How much trouble are you in at home?" Her

raised eyebrows wiped the smile off his face. "Enough that an old woman looks pretty good right about now?"

"I'm not in trouble at home. What does that even mean? You think I got kicked out?" He frowned.

It bothered him because deep down, he knew he'd taken the coward's way out. Being friends with his wife hadn't worked out so well. She was too sexy, too insightful.

"Au contraire. You're in trouble. It's all over your face."

"That's ridiculous." Leo scrubbed his jaw, not that he believed for a second he could erase whatever she thought she saw there, and fingered a spot he'd missed shaving that morning. The executive bathroom off his office left nothing to be desired, but two hours of sleep had affected his razor hand, apparently.

"Forget her birthday, did you?" Mrs. Gordon nodded sagely.

Soon we'll be buying each other birthday cards, Daniella had said, but he didn't even know when her birthday was. "Our marriage isn't like that."

Mrs. Gordon's mouth flattened. Her favorite way to remind him she had his number. "Why do I get the feeling you and your wife have differing opinions about that?"

He sighed and the hollow feeling in his stomach grew worse because she was right. "Did you hear from Tommy Garrett's people yet?"

"Don't change the subject. I'd have told you if I heard from Garrett and you know it. Just like you know you've got a problem at home that you better address sooner rather than later. I've been married for thirty years. I know things." She clucked. "Take my advice. Buy her flowers and sleep in your own bed tonight."

He had the distinct impression Mrs. Gordon believed his wife would be in the bed, as well. He didn't correct her.

After all, what sort of weakness did *that* reveal?

He couldn't have sex with his own wife because he'd backed himself into an impossible corner. She wanted some kind of intimacy, which he couldn't give her, and he didn't want to hurt her. He'd thought friendship might be enough, but friends apparently talked about aspects of themselves that he just couldn't share. Especially not drawing. It was tied to his obsessive side, which he kept under wraps.

How long would Dannie remain patient before finding someone who *would* give her what she wanted? Women in his life usually lasted about two months before bailing.

He'd never cared before. Never dreamed he'd experience moments of pure panic at the thought of Daniella going the way of previous companions. They had a convenient marriage, but that meant it would be easy to dissolve when it was no longer convenient for her.

By 9:00 p.m., Leo couldn't argue with his admin's logic any longer. His body screamed to collapse in a dead sleep, but he couldn't physically make himself lie down on that couch.

What was he really accomplishing by avoiding his wife? When he'd told her to walk after nearly stripping her bare right there in his study, she had. No questions, no hysterics, no accusations. She was fine with holding off on advancing their relationship.

Daniella wasn't the problem. He was.

He was a weak daydreamer who'd rather scratch a pencil over pieces of paper all day and then spend several hours exploring his wife's naked body that night. And do it again the next day, abandoning all his goals with Reynolds Capital Management in a heartbeat for incredible sex and a few pictures. He'd done exactly that before, and he feared the consequences would be far worse if he did it with Daniella.

If he could resist the lure of drawing, he could resist the Helen of Troy he'd married. As long as he didn't kiss her again, he had a good shot at controlling himself. Of course, the real problem was that deep down, he was pretty sure he didn't want to.

He drove to the house he'd bought with his own money,

where he'd created a safe, secure home that no one could take away. The lights always shone brightly and the boiler always heated water. And Leo would die before allowing that to change.

Daniella wasn't downstairs. Good. Hopefully she was already asleep in her room. If so, he could get all the way to his bedroom without running into her.

As he passed the study, his neck heated as the dream from last night roared into his mind—the one where he finished that kiss from the other night by spinning Daniella facedown onto the desk, pushing up that sexy dress and plunging into her wet heat again and again until she convulsed around him with a cry.

That room was off-limits from now on. He'd buy a new desk and have it moved into his bedroom.

So exhausted he could hardly breathe, he climbed the stairs and stumbled to his bedroom. No lights. Too bright for his weary eyes.

His shin cracked against something heavy and knocked him off balance. He cursed as his hand shot out to break his fall and scraped across…whatever he'd tripped over.

Snick. Light flooded the dark room via the lamp on his bedside table.

"Are you okay?" Daniella asked.

His head snapped up in shock. "What are you doing here? Why are you in my bed?"

His wife, hair swept back in a ponytail and heavy lidded with sleep, regarded him calmly from beneath the covers of *his bed.* "It's my bed, too, now. I moved into your room. If you'd come home occasionally, you might have known I rearranged the furniture."

The throb in his shin rivaled the sudden throb in his temples. "I didn't… You ca—" He sucked in a fortifying breath. "You had no right to do that."

She studied him for a moment, her face contemplative and breathtakingly beautiful in its devoid-of-makeup state.

"You said I should think of this as my home. Anything I wanted to change, you'd be willing to discuss."

"Exactly. *Discuss.*"

The firm cross of her arms said she'd gladly have done so, if he hadn't been hiding out at the office.

"You're bleeding." She threw the covers back, slipped out of bed and crossed the room to take his hand, murmuring over the shallow cut.

As she was wearing a pair of plaid pants cinched low on her slim hips and a skintight tank top that left her midriff bare, a little blood was the least of his problems.

"And you're cold," he muttered and tore his gaze from the hard peaks beneath the tank top, which scarcely contained dark, delicious-looking nipples.

Too late. Heat shuddered through his groin, tightening his pants uncomfortably. Couldn't she find some clothes that she wasn't in danger of bursting out of? Like a suit of armor, perhaps?

"I'll be fine." She tugged on his hand, flipping the long ponytail over her shoulder. "Come into the bathroom. Let me put a bandage on this cut."

"It's not that bad. Go back to bed. I'll sleep somewhere else." As if he had a prayer of sleep tonight.

Adrenaline coursed through his veins. Muscles strained to reach for her, to yank on the bow under her navel and let those plaid pants pool around her ankles. One tiny step and he could have her in his arms.

He tried to pull away but she clamped down on his hand, surprisingly strong for someone so sensuously built.

"Leo." Her breasts rose on a long sigh and under her breath she muttered something about him that sounded suspiciously uncomplimentary. "Please let me help you. It's my fault you're hurt."

It was her fault he had a hard-on the size of Dallas. But it was not her fault that he'd been avoiding her and thus didn't know the layout of his own bedroom any longer. "Fine."

He followed her into the bathroom, noting the addition of a multitude of mysterious girly accoutrements, and decided he preferred remaining ignorant of their purposes.

Daniella fussed over him, washing his cut and patting it dry. In bare feet, she was shorter than he was used to. Normally she had no trouble looking him in the eye when she wore her architecturally impossible and undeniably sexy heels. He hadn't realized how much he liked that.

Or how much he'd also like this slighter, attentive Daniella who took care of him. Fatigue washed over him, muddling his thoughts, and he forgot for a second why it wasn't a good idea to share a bed with her.

"All better." She patted his hand and bent to put the box of bandages under the sink, pulling her pajama pants tight across her rear, four inches from his blistering erection. He closed his eyes.

"About the room sharing," he began.

She brushed his sensitive flesh and his lids flew up. He'd swayed toward her, inadvertently. She glanced up to meet his gaze in the mirror. The incongruity between her state of undress and his buttoned-up suit shouldn't have been so erotic. But it was.

"Are you going to read me the riot act?" she asked, her eyes enormous and guileless and soft. "Or consider the possibilities?"

"Which are?" The second it was out of his mouth, he wished he could take it back. Foggy brain and half-dressed wife did not make for good conversation elements.

"You work a hundred hours a week. Our paths will never cross unless we do it here." She gestured toward the bedroom. "This way, we'll both get what we want."

In the bright bathroom light, the semitransparent tank top left nothing to the imagination. Of course, he already knew what her bare breast looked like and the longer she stood there with the dark circles of her nipples straining against the fabric, the more he wanted to see them both, but this time with no interruptions.

"What do you think I want?"

"You want me." She turned to face him. "All the benefits without the effort, or so you say. I don't believe you. If you wanted that, my dress wouldn't have stayed zipped for longer than five seconds after dinner. Sharing a bedroom offers you a chance to figure out why you let me walk away. It won't infringe on your work hours and it gives me a chance to forge the friendship I want. Before we become physically involved."

That cleared the fog in a hurry. "What are you saying, that you'll be like a *roommate?*"

"You sound disappointed." Her eyebrows rose in challenge. "Would you like to make me a better offer?"

Oh, dear God. She should be negotiating his contracts, not his lawyer.

"You're driving me bananas. No. Worse than that." He squeezed the top of his head but his brain still felt as though she'd twirled it with a spaghetti fork. "What's worse than bananas?"

"Pomegranates," she said decisively. "They're harder to eat and don't taste as good."

He bit back a laugh. Yes, exactly. His incredibly perceptive wife drove him pomegranates. "That about covers it."

"Will you try it my way? Give it a week. Then if you still think sex will complicate our marriage too much, I'll move back to my bedroom. I promise I'll keep my hands to myself." To demonstrate, she laced her fingers over her sexy rear and he swore. She'd done that exact thing in one of his dreams. "If you'll promise the same."

His shin didn't hurt nearly as badly as his aching groin. "Are you seriously suggesting we share a bed platonically?"

"Seriously. Show me you think our marriage is worth it. Sharing a room is the only way we'll figure this out, unless you plan to work less. It's unorthodox, but being married to a workaholic has forced my creative hand, so to speak."

It was definitely creative, he'd give her that, and hit him where it hurt—right where all the guilt lived. If he wanted her to be happy in this marriage and stick with him, he had to prove it.

Her logic left him no good reason not to say yes. Except for the fact that it was insane.

Her seductive brown eyes sucked him in. "What are you going to do, Leo?"

Somehow, she made it sound as if he held all the cards. As if all he had to do was whisper a few romantic phrases in her ear and she'd be putty in his hands. If only it was that easy.

And then she shoved the knife in a little further. "Try it. What's the worst that can happen?"

He groaned as several sleepless nights in a row hit him like a freight train. "I'm certain we're about to find out."

Fatigue and a strong desire to avoid his wife's backup plan if he said no—that was his excuse for stripping down to a T-shirt and boxer shorts and getting into bed next to a woman who blinded him with lust by simply breathing. Whom he'd agreed not to touch.

Just to make her happy. Just for a few days. Just to prove he wasn't weak.

He fell into instant sleep.

Dannie woke in the morning quite pleased but quite uncomfortable from a night of clinging to the edge of the bed so she didn't accidentally roll over into Leo's half. Or into Leo.

She'd probably tortured him enough.

But her will wasn't as strong as she thought, not when her husband lay mere feet away, within touching distance, breathing deeply in sleep. The alarm on his phone had beeped, like, an hour ago, but hadn't produced so much as a twitch out of Leo. Who was she to wake him when he obviously needed to sleep? A good wife ensured her husband was well rested.

The view factored pretty high in the decision, too.

Goodness. He was so gorgeous, dark lashes frozen above his cheekbones, hair tousled against the pillow.

How in the world had she convinced him to sleep in the same bed with her *and* agree to hold off on intimacy? She'd thought for sure they'd have a knock-down-drag-out and then he'd toss her out—bound and determined to ignore his own needs, needs he likely didn't even recognize. But instead of cutting himself off from her again, he'd waded right into the middle of things like she'd asked, bless him.

Because his actions spoke louder than words, and his wife was an ace at interpreting what lay beneath.

If this bedroom sharing worked out the way she hoped, they'd actually talk. Laugh over a sitcom. Wake up together. Then maybe he'd figure out he was lying to himself about what he really wanted from this marriage and realize just how deeply involved he already was.

They'd have intimacy—physically and mentally. She couldn't wait.

She eased from the bed and took a long shower, where she fantasized about all the delicious things Leo would do when he finally seduced her. It was coming. She could feel it.

And no matter how much she wanted it, anticipated it, she sensed she could never fully prepare for how earthshaking their ultimate union would truly be.

When she emerged from the bathroom, Leo was sitting up, rubbing the back of his neck, and her mouth went dry. Even in a T-shirt, he radiated masculinity.

"Good morning," she called cheerfully.

"What happened to my alarm?" He did not look pleased.

"I turned it off after listening to it chirp for ten minutes."

"Why didn't you wake me up?"

"I tried," she lied and fluttered her lashes. "Next time would you like me to be a little more inventive?"

"No." He scowled, clearly interpreting her question to mean she'd do it in the dirtiest, sexiest way she could envision.

"I meant with a glass of water in your face. What did you think I meant?"

He rolled his eyes. "So this is what roommates do?"

"Yes. Until you want to be something else."

With that, she flounced out the door to check off the last few items on the list for Tommy Garrett's party. It was tomorrow night and it was going to be spectacular if she had to sacrifice her Louboutins to the gods of party planning to ensure it.

Leo came downstairs a short while later, actually said goodbye and went to work.

When he strolled into the bedroom that evening, the hooded, watchful gaze he shot her said he'd bided his time all day, primed for the showdown about to play out.

"Busy?" he asked nonchalantly.

Dannie carefully placed the e-reader in her hand on the bedside table and crossed her arms over her tank top. What was it about that look on his face that made her feel as if she'd put on Elise's red-hot wedding night set? "Not at all. By the way, I picked up your dry cl—"

"Good." He threw his messenger bag onto the Victorian settee in the corner and raked piercing blue eyes over her, all the way to her toes tucked beneath a layer of Egyptian cotton. They heated, despite the flimsy barrier, and the flush spread upward at an alarming rate to spark at her core.

What had she been talking about?

He shed his gray pin-striped suit jacket and then his tie. "You caught me at a disadvantage last night. I had a few other things on my mind, so I missed a couple of really important points about this new sleeping arrangement."

Her relocation project had just blown up in her face. He was good and worked up over it.

"Oh? Which ones?" The last syllable squeaked out more like a dolphin mating call than English as he dropped his pants, then slowly unbuttoned his crisp white shirt. What had she done to earn her very own male stripper? Because she'd gladly do it fourteen more times in a row.

"For starters, what happens if I don't keep my hands to myself?"

The shirt hit the floor and her jaw almost followed. Her husband had quite the physique hidden under his workaholic shell.

So maybe he wasn't mad. But what was he?

Clad in only a pair of briefs, Leo yanked the covers back and slid into his side of the bed. She peeled her gaze from his well-defined chest and refixed it on his face, which was drawn up in a slight smirk, as if he'd guessed the direction of her thoughts. Her cheeks flamed.

"I'll scold you?" She swallowed as he casually lounged on his pillow, head propped on his hand as if settling in for a nice, long chat instead of using those hands to do something far more...intimate. "I mean, it wouldn't be very sporting of you."

"Noted." He stretched a little and the covers slipped down his torso. "What happens if *you* don't keep your hands to yourself?"

He was toying with her, seeing if he could get her to break her own vow of chastity. In his thoroughly male mind, he'd be in the clear if *she* made the move. His eyelids dropped to a very sexy half-mast and sizzled her to the core.

"And Daniella? Be sure you spell really well so it's all very clear for those of us who didn't barge into someone else's bed and start slinging rules around."

Actually, the relocation project might be working better than she'd assumed. At least they were talking. Now to get him to understand this wasn't a contest. Their relationship was at a crossroads and he had to choose which fork he wanted to take.

"There are no rules," she corrected. "I don't have a list of punishments drawn up if you decide you're not on board with being roommates, whether you want to go back to separate bedrooms or strip me naked right now. You're calling the shots. You're the one who shut it down after dinner the other night. *Walk away,* you said, and I did, but that's not what either of us wanted."

"Yeah?" Lazily, he traced the outline of her shoulder against the propped-up pillow at her back, carefully not touching her skin but skating so close the heat from his finger raised every hair on her body. "What would you rather I have told you to do?"

"No games, Leo." She met his gaze squarely. "I'm giving us an opportunity to develop a friendship. But I also readily admit I want you. I want your mouth on me. Here." Just as lazily, she traced a line over her breast and circled the nipple, arching a little. "I want it so badly, I can hardly stand it."

She watched him, and went liquid as his expression darkened sinfully.

"No games?" he asked and cleared the rasp from his throat. "Then what is this?"

"A spelling lesson." And she obviously had to really lay it out for him. She dropped her hand. "You want me, then come and get me. Be as emotionally naked as you are physically. Strip yourself as bare as your body and let's see how fantastic it can be between us."

Stiffening, he closed off, his expression shuttering and his body angling away. "That's all? You don't ask for much."

"Then forget I mentioned it. We don't have to hold out for a connection that may not ever happen. If either of us becomes uninterested in the hands-to-yourself proposition I laid out, it's off." She flung herself back against the pillow, arms splayed wide. "Take me now. I won't complain. We'll have sex, it'll be great and then we'll go to sleep."

He didn't move.

"What's the matter?" she taunted, glancing at him sideways. "It's just sex. Surely you've had just sex before. No brain required. I have no doubt a man with your obvious, um...*talent* can make me come in no time at all. In fact, I'm looking forward to it. I'm hot for you, Leo. Don't make me wait a second longer."

"That's not funny. Stop being ridiculous." Translation: he didn't like being thoroughly trounced at his own game.

She widened her eyes. "Did you think I was joking? I'm not. We're married. We're consenting adults. Both of us have demonstrated a healthy interest in getting the other naked. We'll eventually go all the way. It's your choice what sort of experience that will be."

This had never been about withholding sex. She'd be naked in a heartbeat as soon as he made a move. All the power was in his hands and when that move came, it would be monumental. And he'd be so very, very aware of exactly what it meant.

He shoved both hands through his hair. "Why is it my choice?"

Poor, poor man. If he was too clueless to know she didn't have a choice, far be it from her to fill him in. This was something he had to figure out on his own. Besides, he was the one with the crisis of conscience that prevented him from making love to her until something he probably couldn't even articulate happened.

But she knew exactly what he needed—to let himself go. She'd exploit this situation gladly in order to get the marriage she desperately wanted and help him find the affection and affinity he so clearly yearned for.

She smiled. "Because. I'm—" *Already emotionally invested.* "—generous that way."

She was going to drag Leo off the sidelines kicking and screaming if that's what it took to have the love match she sensed in her soul Elise had actually orchestrated.

Eight

By nine o'clock, the party hummed along in full swing, a success by anyone's account. Except perhaps Leo's. In the past hour, he'd said no more than two words to Dannie.

She tried not to let it bother her as she flitted from group to group, ensuring everyone had a full glass of champagne and plenty to talk about. The final guest list had topped out at twenty-five and no one sent their regrets. Chinese box kites hung from the ceiling, artfully strung by the crew she'd hired. Their interesting geometric shapes and whimsical tails provided a splash of color in the otherwise severe living room. A papier-mâché dragon lounged on the buffet table, breathing fire under the fondue pot in carefully timed intervals.

Tommy's admin had mentioned his love of the Orient and the decorations sprang easily from that. More than one guest had commented how unusual and eye-catching the theme was, but Tommy's signature on the dotted line was the only praise she needed.

Well, she'd have taken a "You look nice" from Leo. The ankle-length black sequined dress had taken three shopping trips to find and a white-knuckle twenty-four hours to alter. She'd only gotten it back this morning and it looked great on her.

Not that anyone else had noticed.

She threw her shoulders back and smiled at the knot of

guests surrounding her, determined to be the hostess Leo expected.

Hyperawareness burned her back on more than one occasion, and she always turned to see Leo's piercing blue eyes on her and his expression laced with something dangerous.

The bedroom-sharing plan was a disaster. He hated it. That had to be his problem—not that she'd know for sure, because he'd clammed up. Was he waiting until the party was over to give her her walking papers?

Turning her back on Leo and the cryptic bug up his butt, she came face-to-face with Leo's friend Dax Wakefield. "Enjoying the party?" she asked him brightly.

Not one person in this room was going to guess she had a mess of uncertainty swirling in her stomach.

"Yes, thank you." Unfailingly polite, Dax nodded, but his tone carried a hint of frost. "The buffet is wonderful."

Her radar blipped as she took note of the distinct lack of a female on Dax's arm. A good-looking guy like Dax—if you liked your men slick and polished—was obviously alone by choice. Was he no longer dating Jenna? Or had Leo asked him not to bring her in some misguided protective notion?

"I'm so glad." She curved her lips graciously and got nothing in response. Maybe he was aloof with everyone. "Congratulations again on the distinguished alumni award. Leo assures me it was well deserved."

"Thank you." Not one hair on his perfectly coiffed head moved when he granted her a small nod. "Took me a little longer to achieve than Leo. But our industries are so different."

What did that mean? There was an undercurrent here she couldn't put her finger on, but Dax definitely wasn't warming up to her. *Problem alert.* Dax and Leo were old friends and a wife was a second-class citizen next to that. Was Dax the genesis of Leo's silent treatment?

"Well, your media empire is impressive nonetheless. We watch your news channel regularly." It wasn't a total lie—

Leo had scrutinized stock prices as they scrolled across the bottom of the screen last night as she pretended to sleep after the spelling lesson.

Dax smiled and a chill rocked her shoulders. If Leo wanted people to believe he was a ruthless, cold-blooded businessman, he should take lessons from his friend. That guy exuded *take no prisoners*.

One of the servers discreetly signaled to get her attention and she pounced on the opportunity to escape. "Will you excuse me? Duty calls."

"Of course." Dax immediately turned to one of Leo's new partners, Miles Bennett, and launched into an impassioned speech about the Cowboys roster and whether they could make it to the Super Bowl this time around.

The server detailed a problem in the kitchen with several broken champagne bottles, which Dannie solved by pulling out Leo's reserve stash of Meunier & Cie. It was a rosé, but very good and would have to do in a pinch. Most of the guests were men and such a girly drink had definite potential to go over like a lead balloon.

Mental note—next time, buy extra champagne in case of nervous, butterfingered staff.

She poured two glasses of the pink champagne and sought out Tommy Garrett. Something told her he'd take to both an out-of-the-norm drink and being roped into a coconspiracy.

Maybe because of the purple canvas high-tops he'd worn with his tuxedo.

"Tommy." Grateful she'd caught him alone by the stairs, she handed him a champagne flute. When Leo had introduced them earlier, they'd chatted for a while and she'd immediately seen why her husband liked him. "You look thirsty. Humor me and drink this. Pretend it's beer."

A brewery in the Czech Republic exported Tommy's vice of choice, which she'd gleaned from his admin. But he'd already had two pints and hopefully wouldn't balk at her plea.

The young man flipped chin-length hair, bleached almost white by the sun, out of his face. "You read my mind. Talking to all these suits has parched me fiercely."

Half the champagne disappeared into Tommy's mouth in one round and he didn't gag. A glance around the room showed her that others weren't tossing the rosé into the potted plants. Crisis averted.

"Thanks, Mrs. Reynolds." She shot him a withering glare and he winked. "I mean Dannie. Sorry, I forgot. Beautiful women get me all tongue-tied."

She laughed. "Does that geek approach actually work?"

"More often than I would have ever imagined. Yet I find myself devoid of promising action this evening." Tommy sighed dramatically and waggled his brows, leaning in to murmur in her ear. "Wanna see my set of protractors sometime?"

Her grin widened. She really liked him, too, and was almost disappointed he hadn't worn a hoodie to her fancy party. "Why, Thomas Garrett, you should be ashamed of yourself. Hitting on a married lady."

"I should be, but I'm totally not. Anyway, I couldn't pry you away from Leo with a crowbar and my own private island. Could I?" he asked hopefully with a practiced once-over she suspected the coeds fell for hook, line and sinker.

"Not a chance," she assured him. "I like my men all grown-up. But feel free to keep trying your moves on me. Eventually you'll become passable at flirting with a woman."

Tommy clutched his heart in mock pain. "Harsh. I think there might be blood."

That prickly, hot flash traveled down her back an instant before Leo materialized at her elbow. His palm settled with familiarity into the groove at her waist and she clamped down on the shiver before it tipped him off that such a simple touch could be so affecting. *Why* had she worn a backless dress?

"Hey, Leo." Tommy lifted his nearly empty glass in a toast. "Great party. Dannie was telling me how much she likes protractors."

"Was she, now?" Leo said easily, his voice mellower than the scotch in his highball.

Uh-oh. She'd never heard him speak like that.

Swiping at Tommy with a flustered hand, she glanced up at Leo and nearly flinched at the lethal glint in her husband's eyes. Directed at her or Tommy? "Protractors. Yes. They get the job done, don't they? Just like Leo. Think of him as a protractor and Reynolds's competitor, Moreno Partners, as a ruler. Why not use the right tool for the job from the very beginning?"

Tommy eyed her. "Moreno is pretty straight and narrow in their approach. Maybe that's what I need."

Good, he'd picked up on her desperate subject change.

"Oh, no." Dannie shook her head and prayed Leo's stiff carriage wasn't because he didn't like the way she was sticking her nose in his business with Tommy. This was absolutely what she was here for and she absolutely didn't want to blow it, especially with Leo in such a strange, unpredictable mood. "Reynolds can help you. Leo's been doing this far longer than Moreno. He has connections. Expertise. You know Leo has a degree in engineering, too, right?"

Leo's hand drifted a little lower. His pinky dipped inside her dress and grazed the top edge of her panties. Her brain liquefied into the soles of her sparkly Manolos and she forgot to mention he'd actually double majored in engineering and business.

"Daniella," Leo murmured. "Perhaps you'd see to Mrs. Ross? She's wandering around by the double glass doors and I'm afraid she might end up in the pool."

"Of course." She smiled at Tommy, then at Leo and went on the trumped-up errand Leo had devised, likely to avoid saying outright in front of a prospective partner that he could handle his own public relations. Which she appreciated.

As she guided Mrs. Ross toward the buffet, she laughed at the sweet old lady's jokes, but kept an eye on Leo and Tommy. They were still talking near the stairs and Leo's expression had finally lost that edge she so desperately wanted to understand.

If she'd gone too far with the bedroom-sharing idea, why didn't he just tell her?

This party was a measure of how effectively she could do her job as Leo's wife and how well she contributed to his success. Coupled with the high-level tension constantly pulsing between them, her nerves had stretched about as tight as they could without snapping.

Dannie showed the last guest to the door and spent a long thirty minutes with the auxiliary staff wrapping up postparty details.

Leo was nowhere to be seen.

Around midnight, she finally stumbled to their bedroom with the last bottle of champagne, uncorked, intending to split it with him in celebration of a successful party. Surely Leo shared that opinion. If he didn't, she really should be told why.

Darkness shrouded the bedroom.

She set the champagne bottle and two glasses on the dresser and crossed to the freestanding Tiffany torchiere lamp in the corner. She snapped it on and bracing against the wall, fingered apart the buckle on one shoe.

"Oh, you should leave those on." Leo tsked, his voice silky as scotch again.

She whirled. He was lounging on the settee, tie loose and shirt unbuttoned three down. Not that she was counting. "What are you doing sitting here in the dark?"

"Seemed appropriate for my mood."

That sounded like a warning. She thumbed off the other shoe in case she had to make a run for the door. "Would you like me to turn off the light?"

He contemplated her for a long moment. "Would darkness make it easier for you to pretend I was Tommy Garrett?"

She couldn't help it. The laugh bubbled out.

It was a straight-from-the-bottle kind of night. Retrieving the champagne from the dresser, she gulped a healthy dose before wiping her mouth with the back of one hand. "Jealousy? That's so…" *Cliché.* Well, it seemed like a tell-it-like-it-is night, too. "…cliché, Leo."

His gaze scraped her from head to toe, darkening as he lingered at the vee of her cleavage. "What should I feel while watching my wife flirt with another man?"

"Gratitude?" she offered. "I was working him for you."

Leo barked out a laugh. "Shall I call him back, then? See if he's up for a threesome?"

This was going downhill fast. Not only was he not thrilled with her party, he'd transformed into a possessive husband. "Are you drunk?"

Maybe she should catch up. If she downed the entire bottle of champagne, her husband might make a lot more sense. Or it would dull the coming rejection—which this time would no doubt include an annulment. Alcohol had the potential to make either one more bearable.

"Not nearly drunk enough," he muttered. Louder, he said, "Since you're so free with your favors this evening, perhaps you'd do me another one."

Her eyes narrowed. "Like what?"

"Show me what's under that dress."

Okay, *not* the direction she'd anticipated him going.

More champagne, STAT. She swigged another heady gulp and set the bottle on the dresser. "Why? So you can stake your claim? Jealousy is not a good enough reason to strip for you."

His mouth quirked. "What would be?"

"Diamonds. A trip to Bora-Bora. A Jaguar." She ticked

them off on her fingers airily. If he was going to be cliché, she could, too. "The typical kept woman baubles."

"What if I called you...Dannie?" He drew it out and in that silky voice, it swept down her spine and coalesced in her core with heat. "It's the key to intimacy, isn't it? You let Tommy call you that. The two of you were very cozy."

She cursed under her breath. How dare he turn her on while accusing her of dallying with Tommy? "He's twenty-four, Leo. I'm old enough to be his...older sister. Stop being such a Neanderthal."

"So that's your objection to Tommy? His age?" Leo slid off the settee and advanced on her, slowly enough to trip her pulse. "What about Dax? He's my age. Maybe you'd like him better."

"What's this really about?" Boldly, she stared him down as he approached, determined to get past this barrier she sensed he'd thrown up to avoid the real issue—she'd failed at being the wife he needed, on all levels. Somehow. "You're not threatened by Tommy. Or Dax. You've been weird all evening. If you've got a problem with me, lay it out. No more smoke and mirrors."

Only a breath away, he halted, towering over her. Without heels, she wasn't that much shorter than he was, but his presence—and his dark, intense mood—overwhelmed her.

"You know, I do have a problem with you." His gaze traveled over her and that's when she saw the vulnerability he'd hidden behind a mask of false allegations. "You're still dressed."

Baffled, she cocked her head and studied him. Hints of what he was so carefully not telling her filtered through. All at once, she realized. He *was* threatened by other men and conversely paralyzed by his conscience, which had dictated that he wouldn't touch her until she was okay with what he could give.

His body language was equally conflicted. His fingers

curled and uncurled repeatedly, as if he wanted to reach for her but couldn't.

She was his wife. But not his wife, in the truest sense.

Her heart softened. He wanted something he had no experience with, no vocabulary to define. And she'd been trying to force him into admitting his needs by sharing his bed and denying him the only outlet for his emotions that he understood, assuming her way was best.

Well, this was all new to her, too, but she wasn't above changing course to give him what he needed.

Their connection was already there. Instead of waiting on some murky criteria she doubted either of them could verbalize, she'd just show him.

That was a good enough reason to strip for him.

Dannie locked her gaze on his and reached up to her nape to unclasp her dress.

Leo was acting like an ass.

Knowing it didn't give him any better ability to control it, or to eliminate the constant spike of lust when he caught sight of his wife. Seeing her laugh with another man had generated something ugly and primal inside.

He didn't like it.

He didn't like how he'd focused so much energy and attention on this deal with Tommy Garrett and then spent the night sulking in the corner instead of using the opportunity to do his job. His wife had picked up the slack. *His wife.* Once again, she'd kept the importance of the evening front and center while he wallowed in jealousy.

How dare she be so perfect and imperfect at the same time?

A few more fingers of scotch might have dulled the scent of strawberries. But he doubted it. When he was this close to his wife, nothing could dilute the crushing awareness.

Daniella's fingers danced across the back of her neck. His gut clenched as he realized what she was doing, but the protest died in his throat as her glittery dress waterfalled off her body, catching at the tips of her breasts for one breathless second. Then it puddled on the floor, baring her to his greedy gaze.

A beautiful, half-nude vision stood before him. Daniella, in all her glory. Fire raged south, ravaging everything in its path to his center, numbing his extremities and nearly bringing him to his knees.

It would be fitting to kneel before a goddess.

"Daniella." His raw voice scraped at his throat and he cleared it. "What are you doing?"

He knew. She was doing what he'd been pushing her to do. But she was supposed to slap him. Or storm out. Or push him in kind, the way she always did. As long as she punished him for being an ass, any response would have been fine.

Except this. And it was a far more suitable penance to get exactly what he asked for.

"I'm eliminating the problems," she said, head held high. "*All* the problems."

That was impossible, let alone this way. "Put your clothes back on. I'm—"

Actually, he had no clue what he was. Nothing could have prepared him to feel so…ill equipped to be in the same room with a woman who radiated power and sensual energy.

He shut his eyes.

Strip yourself as bare as your body, she'd suggested. But his wife's simple act of disrobing, of making herself vulnerable, had accomplished that for him, even while he was still fully dressed.

Everything about her touched him in places no one had ever dared tread.

This night was not going to end well. She wanted something he couldn't allow himself to give her. Once that bottle was uncorked, he'd focus on nothing but Daniella and lose his drive to succeed. Then he'd fail her—and himself—on a whole different level, which he could not accept.

"Leo." The softness in her voice nearly shattered him. "Open your eyes. Look at me."

He did. God help him, but he couldn't resist. His gaze sought hers, not the gorgeous bare breasts there for his viewing pleasure. His eyes burned with effort to keep them trained straight ahead.

"I would never—" she emphasized the word with a slash of her hand "—dishonor you with anyone else, let alone a friend or a business partner. I respect you too much. I'm sorry if I behaved in a way that made you question that."

Her words, sweetly issued and completely sincere, wrenched that hollow place inside. He'd been treating her horribly all night for who knew what reason and she was apologizing. "You didn't. You were just being a good hostess."

A very poor depiction of how absolutely stellar a party she'd thrown. She deserved far more than degradation at the hands of her husband. Far more than the absent, unavailable man she'd cleaved to.

"I really hope you think so." Her expression warmed. "You're the only man I want. Forever. That's why I married you."

The sentiment flowed like warm honey through his chest. This was the kind of romantic nonsense he'd gone to EA International to avoid. But then, wasn't she describing exactly what he'd asked for? Fidelity and commitment? It just sounded like so much *more* than that from her mouth, so deep and profound.

What was he supposed to do with that? With her?

"Don't you want me, too?" she asked, her voice dropping into a seductive whisper that funneled straight to his erection.

"So much more than I should," he muttered and regretted saying it out loud.

"Then come over here and show me."

His feet were rooted to the carpet. It wasn't going to be just sex. Maybe just sex wasn't possible with someone he'd made his wife.

Regardless, he'd married Daniella, and consummating their relationship meant they were embarking on forever at this very moment.

Part of him strained to dash for the door, to down the rest of the scotch until the unquenchable thirst for Daniella faded from memory. Then he wouldn't have to deal with the other part that compelled him to accept everything she was offering him, even the alarming nebulous nonphysical things.

"So the touching moratorium is lifted?" he asked. "Or is this the precursor to another round of rules?"

Apparently he wasn't finished lashing out at her. If he infuriated her enough to leave, they could go back to circling each other and he'd put off finding out exactly how weak he was.

He didn't want her to leave.

"This is about nothing more than being together. Do whatever feels right to you." She spread her arms, jutting out her perfectly mounded breasts. His mouth tingled and he imagined he could taste one. "Standing here in nothing other than a tiny thong is turning me into Jell-O. I'd really like it if you'd kiss me now."

"A thong?" He'd been so focused on her front, the back hadn't even registered. The feel of silk beneath his pinky when he'd pushed past the fabric at her waist during the party rushed back and he groaned.

Slowly, she half turned and cocked a hip, bare cheek thrust out. "I wore it for you. Hoping you'd pick tonight to make me your wife in more than name only."

He was so hard he couldn't breathe. Let alone walk. Or kiss. Neither was he ready to cross that line, to find out how far she'd suck him down the rabbit hole if he gave in to the maelstrom of need.

Her lips curved up in a secret, naughty smile. Palms flat against her waist, she smoothed them downward over the curve of her rear, down her thighs. "If you're not going to touch me, I'll just do it myself."

Provocatively, she teased one of her nipples with an index finger. Her eyes fluttered halfway closed in apparent pleasure and he swore. Enough was enough.

She was serious. No more choices, rules, games or guidelines. She wanted him.

It was too late to address all the lingering questions about the status of their relationship or how this would change it. It was too late to imagine he'd escape, and far too late to pretend he wanted to.

Daniella was going in the lover box. Now.

In one stride, he crossed the space between them and swept her up in his arms. He swallowed her gasp a moment before his lips captured hers. Crushing her against him, he leaped into the carnal desire she'd incited all night. Actually, since that first glimpse of her on the stairs at their wedding. Every moment in between.

Their mouths aligned, opened, fed. Eagerly, she slid her tongue along his, inviting him deeper. He delved willingly, exploring leisurely because this time there'd be no interruptions.

He was going to make Daniella his, once and for all. Then he'd recover his singular concentration and no more deals would slip away as he daydreamed.

The taste of her sang through his veins and instead of weakening him, she gave him strength. Enough strength to pleasure this woman until she cried out with it. Enough to grant her what she'd been begging for. Enough to make love to her all night long.

He'd hold on to that strength, because he'd need it to walk away again in the morning. It was the only outcome he'd allow, to delve into the physical realm without losing himself in it. Just tonight, just once.

Leo broke the kiss long enough to pick her up in his arms. Carefully, he laid her out on the bed and spent a long moment drinking in the panorama of his wife's gorgeous body. All that divine skin pleaded for his touch, so he indulged himself, running fingertips down her arms, over the peaks and valleys of her torso and all the way down to her siren-red toenails.

He glanced at her face. She was so sensuously lost in pleasure, his pulse nearly doubled instantly.

She shivered.

"Cold?" he asked.

Shaking her head, she got up on her knees and pulled his tie free. "Hot. For you."

Then she slid off his jacket and went to work on the buttons of his shirt, watching him as she slipped them free.

Finally, she'd completely undressed him. Taking her in his arms, he rolled with her to the middle of the bed and picked up the kiss where they'd left off.

Her lips molded to his and his mind drained as her warm body snugged up against him. They were naked together, finally. Physically, at least.

Almost naked. He skimmed a hand down her spine and fingered the thong. Silky. Sexy. She'd worn it for him. If he'd known that, the party would have been over at about seven-thirty.

Her palm raced across his skin in kind and her touch ignited an urgency he couldn't allow. He'd take as little pleasure from this as possible. Otherwise he'd never leave the bed. It was a delicate balance, made more complicated by the fact that no matter what she'd said, she still wished for something cataclysmic out of this.

He'd make it as physically cataclysmic as he could. That was the best he could do.

Still deep in her mouth, he yanked off the thong and then explored her torso with tiny openmouthed kisses until he reached her core. There, he licked her with the very tip of his tongue.

"Leo," she gasped, which only drove his urgency higher.

"You taste like heaven." He wanted more and took her nub in his mouth to nibble it gently, then harder, laving his tongue against it until she writhed beneath his onslaught.

Mewls deep in her throat attested to her mindless pleasure and then she cried, "More. I'm about to come," which was so hot it shoved him to the brink.

His erection pulsed and he clamped down, aching with the effort to keep from exploding. He drove a finger into her wet core, then two, and tongued her and she arched up as she clinched around him, shattering into a beautiful climax.

He rose up and tilted her chin to soak up the sated, satisfied glint in her eyes as he gave her a minute to recover. But not too long. When her breathing slowed a bit, he guided her hands upward and curled them around the top edge of the headboard.

If she touched him, he'd lose all his hard-won control.

"Hold on," he murmured, and she did, so trusting, so eager.

He parted her thighs and slowly pushed into her. Rapture stole across her face, thrilling him. She enveloped him like a vise, squeezing tight. She was amazing, open, wet.

His vision flickered as Daniella swamped his senses.

More. He thrust into her. *Again.*

Desire built, heavy and thick, and he thumbed her nub, circling it. Heat broke over him and he ached to come but needed her to come first. To prove he wasn't weak, and that he could still resist her.

"Daniella," he ground out hoarsely, and she captured his gaze.

He couldn't break free.

Everything shrank down to this one suspended moment and her bottomless, tender irises ensnared him, encouraging him to just feel. And he did feel it, against his will, but heaviness spread alarmingly fast through his chest, displacing what should be there. Against all odds, she'd wrenched something foreign and indefinable and magnificent from his very depths.

Only one thing could encapsulate it, one word. "Dannie."

It left his mouth on a broken plea and she answered with a cry, convulsing around him, triggering his release. He poured all his desire, all his confusion—and what he feared might be part of his soul—into her, groaning with sensual gratification he'd never meant to experience.

Daniella had taken his name, taken his body. Taken something primal and physical and turned it into poetry. The awe of it engulfed him, washing through his chest. He wanted to mark every page of her again and again and never stop. And let her do the same to him.

Intellectually, he'd realized long ago that one small taste of her would never be enough. But the actual experience had burst from its neat little box, crushing the sides, eclipsing even his wildest fantasies.

He couldn't allow himself to indulge like that again. Otherwise his wife would swallow him whole and take every bit of his ambition with her.

Nine

Dannie awoke at dawn tangled with Leo. Her husband, in every sense.

Muscles ached and begged to be stretched so beautifully again. Above all, her heart longed to hear him say "Dannie" with such raw yearning as they joined. Like he had last night, in that smoking-hot voice.

The bedroom-sharing plan deserved an award.

Leo was still asleep, but holding her tightly against him with his strong forearms, her back against his firm front. The position seemed incongruous for someone so determined to remain distanced. But in sleep, his body told her what he couldn't say with his mouth.

He craved a relationship with her, too. The yearning bled from him in waves every moment she spent in his company. It was all over the good deeds he did behind the scenes, which she no longer believed were designed to avoid emotional investment.

He just didn't know how to reach out. And she'd gladly taken on the job of teaching him.

As he guided her toward her full potential as his wife, she'd done the same, pushing him to keep opening up, giving him what he needed. She'd keep on doing it until he embraced everything this marriage could be. The rewards of being the woman behind the man were priceless.

She hated to disturb him, but his front was growing

firmer by the moment and it pressed hot and hard against her suddenly sensitized flesh.

Heat gathered at the center of her universe and her breath caught.

Involuntarily, her back arched, pushing her sex against his erection. She rubbed back and forth experimentally. Hunger shafted through her. Oh, *yes*.

Then his whole body stiffened and his hands curled against her hips, forcing her to be still. Awake, and obviously not on board with a round of morning love.

Wiggling backward, she deliberately teased him without words.

"Daniella," he murmured thickly. "Stop. I forgot to set my alarm. I have to go to work."

"Yes, you do." She wiggled again, harder, and he sucked in a ragged breath. "Ten minutes. I'm so turned on, I'm almost there already."

Cool air rushed against her back as he rolled away and left the bed without another word.

Her heart crashed against her ribs as he disappeared into the bathroom. The shower hummed through the walls.

Nothing had changed between them.

Last night had meant everything to her. But she'd vastly overplayed her hand. Instead of viewing it as a precious stepping-stone toward a fulfilling marriage, Leo seemed perfectly content to sleep with her at night and ignore her the rest of the day.

Exactly what he'd warned her would happen.

She had no call to be disappointed. She'd given him what he needed and hoped it would be the beginning of their grand, sweeping love affair. It obviously wasn't. She'd dropped her dress, pushed him into making that final move and, for her effort, got a round of admittedly earth-shattering sex. She'd even given him permission to do whatever felt right.

At what point had she asked for anything more?

Since the *I do*s, she'd put considerable effort into preventing screwups, convinced each successful event or household task solidified her role as Mrs. Reynolds.

It never occurred to her the real screwup would happen when she invented a fictional future where Leo became the husband of her dreams.

Flinging the covers up over her shoulder, she buried herself in the bed, dry-eyed, until Leo left the bedroom without saying goodbye.

Then she let her eyes burn for an eternity, refusing to let the tears fall.

Her stupid phone's musical ringtone split the air. *Leo.*

Bolting upright, she bobbled the phone into her hands. He was calling to apologize. Tell her good morning. That it had been a great party. Something.

A bitter taste rose at the back of her throat when she saw *Mom* on the caller ID. She swallowed and answered.

"Hi," she said and her voice broke in half.

"What's wrong, baby?"

Great, now her mother was concerned. Worrying her mother was the last thing Dannie wanted.

"Nothing," she lied brightly. "I'm still in bed. Haven't woken up yet. How are you?"

"Fine." A round of coughing negated that. "Do you want to have lunch today?"

Oh, that would never do. Her mother would instantly see the hurt in her heart blossoming on Dannie's face. She had to get over the disenchantment first. "I've got a few things to do. Maybe tomorrow?"

"I'm leaving on the cruise tomorrow. Did you forget? I wanted to see you before I go."

Yes, she had forgotten and it was a brutal reminder about what was important—her mother. Not Dannie's bruised feelings.

Suck it up, honey. "I can rearrange my appointments. I'll pick you up around eleven, okay?"

"Yes! I'll see you then."

Dannie hung up, heaved a deep shuddery breath and hit the shower to wash away every trace of Leo from her body. If only she could wipe him from her mind as easily, but his invisible presence stained the atmosphere of the entire house.

She fought tears for twenty excruciating minutes as the car sped toward her mother's.

The driver paused at the curb outside her mother's apartment and Dannie frowned. Paint peeled from the wood siding and weeds choked the grass surrounding the front walk. The shabbiness had never bothered her before. How was it fair that Dannie got to live in the lap of luxury but her mother suffered both pulmonary fibrosis and near poverty?

But what could Dannie do about it? She didn't have any money of her own—everything was Leo's. A nasty voice inside suggested he could pony up alternative living space for her mother in reciprocation for last night.

She hushed up that thought immediately. Leo hadn't treated her like that. He'd told her what would happen on more than one occasion and she'd chosen to create a fairy tale in her head where love conquered all.

Her mom slid into the car and beamed at Dannie. The nurse had done wonders to improve her mother's quality of life with daily pulmonary therapy and equally important emotional support.

"I'm so glad to see you, baby," her mom gushed.

The driver raised the glass panel between the front seat and the back, then pulled out into the flow of traffic to ferry them to the restaurant. Dannie leaned into her mother's cheek buss and smiled. "Glad to see you, too."

What ills could she possibly have that Mom couldn't make all better? The pricking at her eyelids grew worse.

Her mother's hands on her jaw firmed. "Uh, oh. What happened?"

She should have known better—sonar had nothing on a

mom's ability to see beneath the surface. Dannie pulled her face from her mother's grasp and looked out the window in the opposite direction. "Nothing. Leo and I had a little... misunderstanding. I'll get over it."

Probing silence settled on her chest and she risked a glance at her mother. She was watching her with an unreadable expression. "Nothing serious, I hope."

Dannie half laughed. "Not in his opinion."

With a sigh of relief, her mother settled back against the seat. "That's good."

"Well, I don't think he's planning to divorce me, if that's what you're worried about."

At least not yet. By all rights, her desperate mental reorganization of their arrangement should have resulted in a firm boot to the backside long before now. Yet, he hadn't breathed a word about divorce, so apparently he still needed her for reasons of his own.

"Of course that's a concern." Her mother's warm hand found Dannie's elbow. "Fortunately, you married a solid, respectable man who believes in commitment. A very wise choice. You'll never end up brokenhearted and alone like I did."

Yes. That was the purpose of this marriage. Not grand, sweeping passion and a timeless love. This was a job. Wife was her career. Hardening her heart against the tiny tendrils of feelings she'd allowed to bloom last night in Leo's arms, Dannie nodded. "You're right. Leo is a good man."

The muted sound of sirens filtered through the car's interior a moment before an ambulance whizzed by in the opposite direction. She'd ridden in an ambulance for the first time not too long ago, on the way to the hospital, with her mother strapped to a gurney and fighting to breathe. When the bill came, she'd gone to the library that same day seeking a way to pay it.

And now she was riding in the modern-day equivalent

of a horse-drawn carriage, but better because it had air-conditioning and leather seats.

Leo had saved them both, providing security for her and for her mother. She couldn't lose sight of that again. He'd held up his end of the bargain honestly. It was time for her to do the same and stop wallowing in the mire of lost romance that she'd never been promised in the first place.

Love didn't work out for other people. Why would it be any different for her?

"The misunderstanding wasn't over the possibility of children, was it?" her mother asked.

Hesitantly, Dannie shook her head.

They hadn't used protection. Actually, she could be pregnant right now. Warmth soaked through her chilled soul. If Leo gave her a child, his absence would be notably less difficult. Her mother had raised her single-handedly. Dannie could do that, too.

Funny how she hadn't thought about procreation once last night. Yet children had been foremost on her mind when she'd agreed to marry Leo. Back when she assumed there was no possibility of more between them than an arrangement. Now she knew for a fact there was no possibility.

Suck it up. She pasted on a smile for her mother. "Tell me more about the cruise."

Her mother chatted all through lunch and Dannie responded, but couldn't have repeated the content of their discussion for a million dollars. Fortunately, Leo didn't come up again. That she would have remembered.

Leo didn't call and didn't join her for dinner. She got ready for bed, resigned to sleeping alone.

At ten o'clock, he strolled into the bedroom.

Her gaze flicked over him hungrily, searching for small clues to the state of mind of the man who'd put his lips on her body in very inventive ways not twenty-four hours ago.

"Hi," she said politely and flicked off the TV she'd been

staring at for who knew how long with no idea what was on. "How was your day?"

"Fine," he said. "I got you something."

Her eyebrows rose. "Like a present?"

Lifting the small silver gift bag clutched in his fingers, he nodded and crossed to the bed to hand it to her. She spilled out the contents and opened the square box. Diamond earrings sparkled against royal-blue velvet.

The box burned her hand and she threw it on the bedside table. "Thank Mrs. Gordon for me. She has lovely taste."

His face instantly turned into a brick wall. "I spent an hour picking them out myself. To thank you for the party. You were amazing. I should have told you before now."

"I'm sorry." Remorse clogged her throat. What had happened to the quiet, demure girl Elise created? Lately, Dannie rarely thought twice about what came out of her mouth. "That was obnoxious."

"And well earned." He cleared his throat and sought her gaze, his blue eyes liquid. "I'm sorry I left the way I did this morning. That was *far* more obnoxious. And undeserved."

"Oh." He'd robbed her of speech. Which was probably fortunate, since the question on the tip of her tongue was, *Why* did *you leave that way, then?* She didn't ask. If he'd intended for her to know, he'd have told her.

Regardless, he'd apologized. *Apologized.* And bought her a present.

Leo retrieved the box and handed it to her. "Will you wear the earrings? I'll take them back if you don't like them."

A touch of the vulnerability she'd witnessed last night darted across his expression. The earrings represented both a thank-you and an apology and he wanted her to like them. Just when she thought she had the dynamic between them straight in her head, he flipped it upside down.

"I love them." She unscrewed the backs and stuck them in her ears, then struck a pose. "How do they look?"

"Beautiful." His gaze skittered down her body and back up again. He wasn't even looking at her ears.

A wealth of undisclosed desire crackled below the surface. Some of it was physical. But not all. He'd picked out the earrings himself. What did that mean? She'd lay odds *he* didn't even know what the significance of that was.

Last night, she'd learned one surefire way to communicate with him.

She flung back the covers and crawled to him. He watched her, his body poised to flee, but she snagged his lapels before he could. Without speaking, she peeled his jacket from his shoulders and teased his lips with hers as she unknotted his tie.

"Daniella." He groaned against her lips and pulled back a fraction. "The earrings weren't... I'm not—"

"Shh. It's okay." The tie came apart in her hands and she leaned into him, rubbing his chest in small circles with her pebbled nipples.

Almost imperceptibly, he shook his head. "I don't expect sex in exchange for jewelry."

How could such a simple statement sink hooks so deeply into her heart? He was trying so hard to be honorable, so hard to keep from hurting her at great expense to himself. "And I don't expect jewelry in exchange for sex. Now that's out of the way. Shut up and put your hands on me."

His eyelids flew closed and he swallowed. That was close enough to a yes for her. She bridged the gap and claimed his lips with hers.

Winding the ends of his tie around her hands, she pulled him closer and deepened the kiss. A firestorm swept outward from their joined lips, incinerating her control.

Urgently, wordlessly, she undressed him, desperate to bare Leo in the only way he'd allow. He ripped off her pajamas and they fell to the bed already intertwined.

Leo kissed her and it was long and thorough. *This* was the man who'd held her in his sleep. The man who'd whispered her name with gut-wrenching openness. As she'd known beyond a shadow of a doubt, this joining of bodies spoke volumes beyond the scope of mere words. And it said Leo had far more going on beneath the surface than he dared let on.

As she cradled her husband's beautiful body and stared into the depths of his hot-with-passion blue eyes, something blossomed inside. Something huge and reckless, and she tamped it down with no small effort. But it rose up again, laced with images of Leo's child growing in her womb. She imagined the tenderness of his gaze as he looked down on their newborn child and the back of her throat heated.

Suddenly, the fear of Leo tiring of her romantic foolishness wasn't her only problem anymore.

She'd traded it for the painful, diametrically opposite problem of what was going to happen if she fell in love with him and doomed herself to a lifetime of marriage to a man who would forever keep his kind heart buried beneath a workaholic shell.

Tap. Tap. Tap.

Leo blinked and glanced up. Dax tapped his pen a few more times, his face expressionless as he nodded to the laptop screen filled with verbiage regarding the proposed joint venture to finance a start-up company called Mastermind Media.

"Clause two?" Dax prompted and lowered a brow. "They agreed to extend the deadline to midnight. We don't have long. You were supposed to be telling me why you don't like it."

I don't like it because it's standing between me and a bed with my wife in it.

Theoretically, that applied to the entire proposal he and Dax had been tearing apart since four-thirty with only a short break for General Tso's chicken in bad sauce from Jade Dragon.

Leo stole a peek at his watch. Nine o'clock on a Friday night.

If he left the office now, he could be home in twenty minutes. Sixteen if he ignored the speed limit. He might even text Daniella as he drove to let her know he'd be there soon. Maybe she'd greet him wearing nothing but the diamonds he'd given her.

What started as a simple thank-you gift had somehow transformed into something else. Hell if he knew what. He hadn't intended to make love to her again. At least not this soon, not while he was still struggling to maintain some semblance of control around her.

But one minute Daniella was threading the diamonds through her ears, and the next...

The memory of last night and his sexy wife invaded his mind. Again. The way she'd been doing all day.

"The clause is fine." *No.* It wasn't. Leo shook his head and tried to focus. "It will be fine. With a minor tweak to the marketing expectations."

More tapping. Then Dax tossed down his pen with a sense of finality.

"Leo." Dax shrank down in the high-backed chair and laced his hands over one knee, contemplating the ebony conference table. Lines appeared across his forehead. "I'm starting to get the impression you don't think we should do this deal."

"What?" Leo flinched. *No more daydreaming.* What was wrong with him? "I've put in sixty hours on this. It's a solid proposal."

"Then what's up?" His friend eyed him, concern evident in his expression. "We've been looking at Mastermind Media for months. If you're worried about you and me doing business together, you should have spoken up long before now."

Hesitating, Leo rolled his neck. They'd known each other

more than fifteen years—since college. Dax was the one person who'd call him on it if Leo zoned out. "That's not it."

"Is the financing sticky?" Dax frowned, wrinkling his pretty-boy face. "You're not using your own money on this because of our relationship, are you?"

"Of course not." Venture capital relied on other people's money. Leo never risked anything he didn't have to.

"I've run out of teeth to pull. Spill. Or I'm walking."

Walking. As in, he'd purposefully let the deal expire because Leo wanted to go home and sleep with his wife. He sighed. Apparently losing John Hu hadn't been enough of a wake-up call.

"I'm distracted. Sorry. It's not the proposal. Something else."

Something that needed to stop. Leo's will was ironclad and had been since he was seventeen. How had Daniella destroyed it so easily?

Dax smirked. "I should have known. You've been different since you married that woman."

He wasn't the slightest bit different. Was he?

"Watch your tone."

Friendship or not, Dax had no call to refer to Daniella as "that woman," as if Leo had hooked up with a chain-smoker in a tube top, straight from the trailer park. He'd deliberately chosen a classy, elegant woman. Not one who mirrored his childhood neighbors in the near ghetto.

Throwing up his hands dramatically, Dax flipped his gaze heavenward. "It begins. We've been through a lot of women together, my friend. What's so special about this one?"

The answer should be nothing. But it wasn't.

"I married her."

And now he was lying to his best friend. Not only was that just part of the answer, it was the tip of the iceberg. He couldn't stop thinking about her. About how beautifully she'd handled the party. Her laugh. The way she took care of things, especially him, with some kind of extrasensory perception.

When he was inside her, his world shifted. He'd never realized his world *could* be shifted. Or that he'd like its new tilt so much. That he'd willingly slide down Daniella's slippery incline.

Snorting, Dax glanced at the laptop screen positioned between their chairs and tapped on the keyboard. "So? It's not like you have feelings for her. She's a means to an end."

A vehement protest almost left his mouth unchecked. But Dax was right. Why would he protest? Daniella *was* a means to an end, like Leo had told him. It just sounded so cold from his friend's perspective. "Feelings aside, she's my wife. Not a casual date. It's important for her to be happy."

"Why? Because she might leave you? Think again. Gold diggers don't bite the hand that feeds them."

Quick-burning anger sliced through Leo's gut. "She's not a gold digger. Our marriage is beneficial to us both. You know that. Surely you don't believe it's acceptable for me to treat my wife like a dog and expect her to put up with it because I have money."

Dax quirked one eyebrow. "Like I said. This one is special."

Leo rolled his eyes. Dax saw meaning where there was none. Except they knew each other well. The Chinese food churned through Leo's stomach greasily. Or maybe that was a smear of guilt.

His track record with women spoke for itself—he wouldn't win any awards for tenderness, attentiveness or commitment. And maybe he did buy expensive presents to apologize for all of the above.

"Let's have this conversation again when *you* get married."

"Ha. That's a good one. There's no *when* in that statement. There's hardly an *if.* Women are good for one thing." Dax flashed his teeth. "They give you a reason to drink."

Perfect subject-change material. "Things not going well with Jenna?"

Too bad. Dax obviously needed someone in his life who could knock down all his commitment and trust issues. Jenna wasn't the right woman for that anyway.

"What are you talking about? She's great. The sex is fantastic." Waggling his brows, Dax leaned back in his chair. "Well, you know."

Leo's already unsettled stomach turned inside out at Dax's smarmy reference to the fact that she'd been Leo's lover first. Had Leo always treated women so casually, blowing it off as a necessary evil of success?

No. Not always. Daniella *was* special, but not the way Dax implied. Leo had treated her differently from the beginning, demonstrating a healthy respect for the institution of marriage. That's all. He was making an iceberg out of an ice cube.

Dax sat up to type out a few more corrections to the proposal. "Judging by the way you couldn't keep your eyes off Daniella at the party the other night, she must be a wildcat. Let me know if you get tired of her."

The chair's wheels squealed as Leo launched to his feet. Staring down at Dax, he crossed his arms so he didn't punch his oldest friend. "I strongly suggest you close your trap before I do it for you."

"Jeez, Leo. Calm down. She's just a woman."

"And you're just a friend." When Dax glanced up, surprise evident, Leo skewered him with a glare that couldn't possibly be misinterpreted. "Things change. Get over it."

Slowly, Dax rose to his feet. Eye to eye, they faced off and Leo didn't like the glint flashing in his friend's gaze as Dax gave Leo's stiff carriage a once-over.

"I can't believe you'd let a chick come between us. Especially not one you found through a matchmaker." Dax nearly spat the word. "Let the deal with Mastermind expire. When you come back from la-la land and realize you've lost your edge over an admittedly nice pair of boobs, I'll be around to help you pick up the pieces. We've been friends too long."

Dax stepped back and Leo let him, though his fingers were still curled into a nice, fat fist that ached to rearrange that pretty-boy face. "I agree. It's best not to go into business together right now."

"Go home to your wife," Dax called over his shoulder as he gathered his bag, phone and travel coffee mug. "I hope she's good enough in bed to help you forget how much money we just lost."

He strode out the door of Leo's conference room without a backward glance.

Sinking into the nearest chair, Leo stared out the window at the green argon lights lining the Bank of America Plaza skyscraper. Since the building housed the headquarters of Dax's far-flung media empire, the familiar outline drove the barb further into Leo's gut.

Yeah, they'd lost a lot of money. And a friendship.

He didn't imagine for a second this rift would be easily repaired. Not because of the sense of betrayal Leo felt, and not because Dax had said reprehensible things about Leo's wife.

But because Dax was right. Leo had changed since marrying Daniella. No longer could he stomach being that guy Dax described, who treated women horribly but rationalized it away and bought them shiny presents to make up for it. Or that guy who wasn't bothered by introducing an ex-girlfriend to Dax because she hadn't meant anything to him.

Dax didn't see a problem with either. Leo couldn't continue to be friends with someone who held such a low opinion of women. Why hadn't he seen that long before now? And what would it take to get Dax to recognize the problem? Maybe Dax should visit a matchmaker himself. If Elise could find the perfect woman for Leo, she could do it for anyone.

Losing the friendship hurt. Letting the deadline expire

for their proposal to Mastermind Media hurt worse. In his entire professional career, he'd never willfully given up. And one thing hadn't changed, would never change—Leo also didn't want to be that guy who lost deals or worse, lost his edge. For any reason. Let alone over a woman who drove him to distraction.

He'd lost John Hu. Now this deal. Was Tommy Garrett next?

He refused to allow that to happen. Daniella's invisible, ill-defined hold on him had to end. Immediately. He'd tried ignoring her. He'd tried sleeping at the office. He'd even tried going in the opposite direction and allowing himself small tastes of her. None of that had worked to exorcise his wife from his consciousness.

So he'd have to try the only thing left. He was going to spend the weekend in bed with Daniella in full-on immersion. By Monday, she would be out of his system and he'd have his focus back. He could share a house with her at night and forget about her during the day, like he'd planned all along.

It had to work. He'd toiled so hard to build a secure company and he owed it to everyone to maintain it. Especially Daniella. He'd vowed to care for her and he'd scrub floors at a state prison before he'd allow his wife to live next door to a meth lab like his own father had.

Ten

The book Dannie was reading held her interest about as well as the last one. Which was to say not at all. She'd parked on the settee to wait in hopes that Leo might come home soon, but it was already almost ten o'clock.

One more page. The story had to get better at some point. If it didn't, she'd get ready for bed. Leo's alarm went off before dawn and she was still adjusting to his routine.

The atmosphere shifted and she glanced up from her e-reader. Leo stood in the open doorway, one hand on the frame and the other clutching a bouquet of red roses. And he was watching her with undisguised, delicious hunger.

Heat erupted at her center and radiated outward, flushing her whole body. The e-reader fell to the carpet with a thunk, released by her suddenly nerveless fingers.

"Roses? For me?" Her voice trembled, and he didn't miss it. Her temperature rose as his expression darkened.

"In a manner of speaking." Striding to the settee, he held out his free hand and when she took it, he pulled her to her feet. His torso brushed hers and her nipples hardened. "Follow me."

Anywhere.

Mystified, she trailed him into the bathroom, where he flicked on the lights to one-quarter brightness and began filling the bathtub. Over his shoulder, he called, "It probably hasn't escaped your notice that I work a lot. I have very little opportunity to indulge in simple pleasures. So I'm correcting that oversight right now. I have this fantasy involving you, me and rose petals. This time of night, I had to buy them still attached."

He gathered the petals in one hand and wrenched them from the stalks, then released them into the water.

As the red circles floated down to rest on the surface, her heart tumbled along with them. "You have fantasies about me?"

The look on his face shot her temperature up another four thousand notches.

"Constantly."

"What am I doing in these fantasies?" she asked, her tongue nearly tripping over the words.

"Driving me pomegranates, mostly." He grinned and it was so un-Leo-like she did a double take. "By the way, I'm taking the weekend off. If you don't have other plans, I'd like to spend it with you. Maybe we could consider it a delayed honeymoon."

Honeymoon? *Weekend off?* She jammed her hands down on her hips and stared at him. "Who are you and what have you done with Leonardo Reynolds?"

His expression turned sheepish and he shrugged. "Let's say I had a revelation. We're married. I have to do things differently than I've done in the past. I *want* to do things differently," he stressed. "For you. Because you deserve it. You're a great wife."

A hard, painful lump slammed into her throat. He wanted to spend time with her. Romance her, as she'd asked. The roses were reciprocation—one great husband, coming up.

Little stabs at the corners of her eyes warned of an imminent deluge. What was he trying to do to her? She'd just become good and convinced their marriage was enough as it was. Now this.

I will not cry. I will not cry.

"You ain't seen nothing yet."

"Yeah?" He twisted the faucet handle and shut off the water. "You've been holding out on me?"

"Maybe. Talk to me about these fantasies." A good, strong dose of Leo's potent masculinity—that was what she needed to keep the emotion where it belonged. Inside. At least until she figured out where all this was coming from. Her husband had done so many about-faces she couldn't help but be slightly wary. "Have you really had a lot about me? Like what?"

"Oh, I've been so remiss, haven't I?" He tsked and sat on the edge of the garden tub, feet on the lowest step leading up to the rim. "Come here."

Her toes curled against the cold travertine as she approached and then she forgot all about a small thing like bare feet as Leo drew her between his split legs, his gaze heavy lidded with sensuous promise.

"I've been a very bad husband," he told her. "You clearly have no idea how wickedly sexy I find you. Let's correct that oversight, too, while we're at it."

Her insides disintegrated and she had no idea how she was still standing with no bones.

Slowly, he loosened each button on her blouse, widening the vee over her bra until he'd bared it entirely. The shirt slipped from her shoulders and Leo reeled in the fabric, pulling her forward.

"My fantasies are no match for the real thing." His open mouth settled onto the curve of her breast where the edge of her bra met skin. His tongue darted inside, circling her nipple. Pure, unaltered desire flared from her center, engulfing her senses.

Clutching at his shoulders, she moaned his name as he unzipped her skirt, still suckling her, wetting her bra with his ministrations. Impatiently, he peeled the cup from her breast and sucked the nipple between his teeth to scrape it lightly.

She pushed farther into his mouth and drowned in sensation as he lit her up expertly with a combination of hard teeth and magic hands against her bottom.

"Daniella," he murmured against her flesh, abrading it with slight five-o'clock shadow, which felt so amazing she shuddered.

Leo lifted his mouth and she nearly sobbed as it left her skin. He licked his lips in a slow, achingly obvious gesture designed to communicate how delicious he found her. Drinking in the sight of her pale pink bra-and-panty set, he reached around to unhook her bra, letting her breasts fall free.

He cursed, almost reverently. "Beautiful. You're the most beautiful woman I've ever seen. And you're all mine."

Her knees went numb, but his sure hands held her upright as he leaned down to kiss her waist, openmouthed, drawing her panties down simultaneously. His fingers trailed between her legs up the backside, wandering unchecked in some unknown pattern and thoroughly driving her insane.

"Leo," she choked out.

"Right here," he murmured and captured her hand. "In you go."

He led her up the stairs and into the tub, helping her lie back against the incline of the oval. She peeked up at him as he snagged a rose petal, swishing it through the water, through the valley of her breasts, around her already sensitized nipples. The motion shafted biting desire through her flesh.

When he rubbed the petal between her legs, a moan rumbled in her throat.

"Playtime is over." She yanked on his tie. "I want you in here with me."

His irises flared with dark heat.

Clothes began hitting the floor and she shamelessly watched as he revealed his taut body inch by maddeningly slow inch. A smattering of dark hair covered his chest, screaming his masculinity, and hard thighs perfectly showcased the prominent erection she wanted inside her with every shuddering breath.

He splashed into the water. The giant garden tub shrank as gorgeous, vibrant male filled it.

Leo grasped her arms and settled her into place against his chest spoon-style and immediately covered her breasts with his hands, kneading them. She gasped as his thick flesh ground hard against her rear.

Rose petals floated in the water, catching on wet skin, filling the air with their warm floral scent. He murmured wicked things in her ear as he touched her, and in combination with the warm water, his hands felt like silk against her skin, in her core, against her sensitive nub.

She reached behind her to grasp his erection. It filled her palm, hard and hot, and she caressed the slick tip. A groan ripped from deep in his chest.

He tore her hand away and clasped her hips, repositioned her and drove home in one swift stroke.

"Dannie," he whispered, his voice guttural, raw. Beautiful. It crawled inside her, filling her as surely as he filled her body. Clasping her close, he held her, torso heaving against her back as they lay joined in the water. Completed perfectly by the other.

After an eternity, he lifted her hips high enough to yank a long slice of heat from her center and eased her down again. They shuddered in pleasure together.

This *was* different. Leo was different. More focused. Drawing it out, allowing her to revel in the sensations, to feel so much more than the physical. It was a slow ride with plenty of mental scenery along the way.

Intense Leo was her new favorite and his brand of romance stole her breath.

"Dannie," he said again and increased the rhythm, hypnotically, sensuously.

He repeated her name over and over as he completed her. A dense torrent of heat gathered at the source and she split apart with a sob, not the slightest bit surprised he'd made her cry after all. She'd given him what he needed and it had been returned, tenfold.

What he'd started with the diamonds, he ended with the rose petals. She wasn't in the process of falling in love with him. It was done. Irrevocably. Wholly.

Her heart belonged to her husband.

"Leo, I..." What would he say if she told him? Surely he was in the throes, too. That's what this was all about, wasn't it? Their marriage looked different than what they'd originally thought. He wanted it to be different.

"Speechless? You?" He chuckled. "I'm incredibly flattered."

It took every ounce of Elise's personality-makeover training to bite back the words as he drained the tub and helped her out, then dried her with slow, tender swipes of a soft towel. This was too important to let Scarlett off the leash. Too important to screw up.

He'd never said he loved her. Only that he wanted to do things differently. Maybe this pseudohoneymoon was simply about sex. Goodness knew she'd given him permission to make it so often enough.

But honestly. If he didn't want her to fall in love with him, he should stop being so wonderful.

Leo threw on a robe and returned with flutes and a bottle of champagne. They drank it in bed while they talked about nothing and everything.

She kept looking for the right opening to blurt it all out. Shouldn't he know that he'd made her wildly happy? That their marriage was everything she'd ever dreamed of? Her feelings for Leo far eclipsed anything she'd ever felt for Rob. She'd found purpose and meaning in being a wife; she'd married a man who made her body and soul sing in perfect harmony and her mother was being taken care of. Leo was a sexy genie in a bottle, granting all her wishes effortlessly. She wanted to tell him.

The right moment never came.

He didn't shoot her long, lingering glances with his gaze full of love. When he took her glass and set it on the bedside table, then thoroughly ravished her, he didn't whisper the things in his heart while holding her.

Instead, he fell into a dead sleep. She lay awake, but he didn't murmur secret confessions into the darkness. Though he did seek her out while unconscious, sliding his solid thigh between hers and wrapping her up in a cloak of Leo. That part she had no difficulty understanding. He enjoyed having her in his bed. Enjoyed the closeness without the requirement of having to expose himself emotionally.

The feelings, the rush of love and tenderness, were strictly one-sided. For now.

Her marriage was *almost* everything she'd yearned for since she was a little girl. She had forty-eight hours to entice Leo that last few feet to the finish line.

When the early light of dawn through the triple bay window of the bedroom woke Leo, he didn't hesitate to indulge in another fantasy—the one he'd denied himself thus far.

He gripped Daniella's hips and wedged that sweet rear against his instant erection. His fingers trailed over her breasts and she sighed and it was sleepy. Erotic.

"Leo. It's—" One of her eyes popped open and immediately shut. "Six twenty-three. In the *morning*."

"I know." He nuzzled her neck and she arched sensuously against him. "I slept sinfully late. It's refreshing."

"Thought you were taking the weekend off," she muttered and rolled her hips expertly. The cleft between her bare cheeks sandwiched his raging erection. His eyes crossed.

"Taking the weekend off to—" She did it again. Deliberately.

"Talk a lot?" she suggested sweetly and choked on the words as he skimmed a finger through the swollen folds of her center.

Closing his eyes, he breathed in the scent of crushed roses and the musk of Daniella's arousal. "Not hardly."

He sank into her and it was amazing. There was something about spooning with her that just killed him. They fit together this way, moving in perfect cadence as they had last night, and he savored it.

All her beauty was within easy reach and he made full use of the access, tweaking her gorgeous breasts and circling her nub as he sheathed himself from behind again and again. Hot friction sparked, driving them both faster.

She climaxed with a sexy moan and he followed in a brilliant chain reaction of sensation that didn't quit.

Playing hooky from work had a lot going for it. He was slightly ashamed at how much he was enjoying his weekend off, especially given that it had essentially just started. There was a lot more indulgence to be had. A lot more fantasies to enact. A lot more dread at the imminent reel back Monday morning.

How was he going to forget Daniella and concentrate on work? It was like ordering your heart not to beat so your lungs could function.

Eventually, they rolled out of bed and he let his wife make him pancakes. It beat an energy bar by quadruple. Her coffee, as always, was amazing. He hadn't enjoyed it with her since the first time she'd made it after he fell asleep at his desk. But he never left the house without a full travel mug. Somehow it had become part of his routine to drink it on the way to work. The empty mug sat on his desk all day and the sight of it made him smile.

"What should we do with all this borrowed time?" he asked her and forked another bite into his mouth as they sat at the bistro table in the breakfast nook.

Daniella peered at him over her coffee mug. "Is that what it is? Borrowed?"

"Well...yeah." Something in her frozen posture tipped him off that he might have stumbled into quicksand. "The initiatives I have going on at the office didn't magically disappear. I'm putting them off until Monday."

"I see."

"You sound disappointed." The next bite didn't go down so well. He could stand a lot of things, but Daniella's disappointment was not one of them.

She shook her head, long brown hair rippling the way it had this morning over his shoulder. "Just trying to interpret your phrasing. *Borrowed* implies you'll have to pay it back at some point. I don't want you to have to do that."

"I made the decision to spend the weekend with you. I wanted to. Don't feel guilty."

Her eyebrows lifted. "I don't. I mean I wish you didn't have to choose. Like you've got a lot of balls to juggle and I'm the one you happened to grab."

"What other choice do I have, Daniella?" Suddenly frustrated, he dropped his fork into the middle of his half-eaten pancakes. "I have a company to run. But I'm here with you now, aren't I? I'm juggling the best I can."

It was the voice of his worst fears—that he would drop a ball. Or all of them. He was horrible at juggling.

She laughed. "Yes, you're here, but it doesn't seem like either of us are fond of the juggling. Isn't there a way to whittle down the number of balls until you can hold them all in your hand? Maybe you can hire some additional staff members or change your focus."

"You're telling me to scale back my involvement in Reynolds Capital. Take on fewer partners."

His gut clenched at the mere thought of how quickly the company would dissolve if he did what she suggested. Venture capital was a carefully constructed illusion of leveraged moving parts. Like a Jenga puzzle. Move one piece the wrong way and the whole thing crashed into an ugly pile.

"I don't know what would work best. But you do." Casually, she sipped her coffee. "Why don't you try it? Then you don't have to borrow time from work to spend it with you."

Really? She'd morphed into the opposite of an understanding wife who forgave her workaholic husband's schedule. He'd married her specifically to avoid this issue. Now she'd joined the ranks of every other woman he'd ever dated.

"*I'm* the Reynolds in Reynolds Capital. I spent a decade building the company from nothing and—" Quickly, he squashed his temper. *Give a woman an inch and forget a mile—she'll take the circumference of the Earth instead.*

"Forgive me if I overstepped. You were the one who said you wanted to do things differently and I was offering a solution. Less juggling would be different." She had the grace to smile as she covered his hand with her more delicate one. But he wasn't fooled. She had more strength in one pinky than most men did in their whole bodies. "I only meant to point out we all have choices and you make yours every day. That's all."

"Uh…" His temper fizzled. She'd only been trying to solve a problem *he'd* expressed. "Fair enough."

"Let's forget this conversation and enjoy our weekend."

Somehow, he had a feeling it wasn't going to be that simple. The die had been cast and she'd made a point with logic and style. Much to his discomfort.

True to his word, Leo didn't so much as glance at his phone or boot up his laptop once. He kept waiting for jitters to set in, like an addict deprived of his fix. The absence of being plugged in should be taking a toll. It wasn't.

He wrote it off as a keen awareness that he owed Daniella his attention until Monday morning. And then there was her gift for distraction. By midafternoon, they were naked in the warmed spa adjacent to the pool. He easily forgot about the blinking message light on his phone as they christened the spa.

He'd immersed himself in his wife's deep water and surfacing was the last thing on his mind.

So it was a bit of a shock to join Daniella in the media

room for a late movie and have her announce with no fan-
fare, "You need to call Tommy Garrett."

"Tommy? Why? How do you know?" Leo set down the
bottle of wine and stemware he'd gone to the cellar to re-
trieve and pulled the corkscrew from his pocket.

"He's been trying to reach you all day. He called my cell
phone, wondering if you'd been rushed to the hospital."

About a hundred things careened through his head, but
first things first. "How does Tommy have your cell phone
number?"

Anger flared from his gut, as shocking as it was powerful.

"Don't wave all that testosterone in my face. How do
you imagine he RSVP'd for your party if he didn't have my
cell phone number?" She arched a brow. "Pony Express?"

His stomach settled. Slightly. He eased the cork from
the bottle and poured two glasses. Wine scraped down his
throat, burning against the shame already coating it. "I'm
sorry. I don't know where that comes from."

"It's okay. It makes me all gushy inside to know you
care." She giggled at his expression. "The movie can wait.
Call Tommy. It seemed rather urgent."

Grumbling, he went in search of his phone and found it
on the counter in the kitchen. Yeah, Tommy had called a
time or twelve. Four text messages, one in all caps.

He hit Callback and shook his head. Kids.

"Leo. Finally," Tommy exclaimed when the call connected. "My lawyers got all their crap straightened out.
I'm going with you, man. Let's get started taking the world
by storm."

Leo blindly searched for a seat. His hand hit a bar stool
at the kitchen island. Good enough. "You're accepting my
proposal?"

"That's what I said, isn't it? Why didn't you answer
your phone, by the way?" Munching sounds filled a sudden pause. Tommy lived on Doritos and Red Bull, which

Leo always kept on hand at the office in case of impromptu meetings. Thankfully, there'd be a lot more of those in the future. "Took me forever to find Dannie's number again. I didn't save it to my contacts."

"I'm taking some…" Leo's mouth dried up and he had to force the rest. "Time off."

This was it—the Holy Grail of everything he'd worked for. Now Leo would find out if he was as good as he thought he was at selecting a winner. But not today. He'd have to sit on his hands for the rest of the weekend.

"That's cool. We can talk mañana."

It was physically painful for Leo to open his mouth and say, "It'll have to be Monday."

"Seriously?" Tommy huffed out a noise of disgust that crawled up Leo's spine. "Well, I gotta say. I'd tell you to piss off, too, if I had a woman at home like Dannie. They sure don't make many of 'em like that. I'll be by on Monday."

Leo bit his tongue. Hard. Because what could he say to refute that? Daniella *was* the reason Leo couldn't talk shop on a Sunday when normally no hour of the day or night was too sacred to pour more cement in the foundation of Reynolds Capital Management's success.

But dear God, it was difficult to swallow.

Even harder was the task of sitting next to his wife on the plush couch in the media room and *not* asking her for leeway on his promise to spend the weekend with her. He did it. Barely. And insisted Tommy's call was unimportant when she asked.

Why had he told her he was taking the whole weekend off? She would have been happy with just Saturday. It was too late now. After her speech about choices, he couldn't imagine coming right out and saying he was picking work over her.

While the movie played, Daniella emptied almost an entire bottle of wine by herself and then expressed her appreciation for the rose-petal bath the night before with a great deal of creativity. By the time the credits rolled, Leo couldn't have stated his own name under oath.

The whirlpool of Daniella had well and truly sucked him under and he could no longer pretend he was taking the weekend off for any other reason than because he physically ached when he wasn't with her.

He didn't want to pick work over her. Or vice versa. If there was a more difficult place to be than between a woman and ambition, Leo didn't want to know about it. Not just any woman, but one who tilted his world and righted it in the same breath. And not just ambition, but the culmination of banishing childhood fears and achieving adult aspirations.

Sunday, after the last round of sleepy morning indulgence Leo would permit himself to experience for a long, long time, Daniella kissed him soundly and retrieved a flat package from under the bed.

"For me?" An odd ping of pleasure pierced his chest as she nodded, handing it to him.

He tore off the plain brown wrapping to reveal a framed sepia-toned drawing.

"It's one of da Vinci's," Daniella explained quietly. "You probably know that."

He did. Reverently, he tilted the frame away from the light to reduce the glare. It was one of his favorites, a reproduction of da Vinci's earliest drawing of the Arno Valley. "The original hangs in the Uffizi. Thank you. What made you think of this?"

"Da Vinci was more than a painter. He invented. He drew. He was a sculptor and a mathematician. And, like, four other things I've forgotten." With a small laugh, she tugged the frame from his grasp and laid it on the bed, then took his hand. "He was so much more than the *Mona Lisa*. Like you're more than Reynolds Capital Management. I wanted you to know I see that."

The gift suddenly took on meaning of exponential proportions. And he wasn't sure he liked it. "Are you angling for me to show you something I drew?"

The exposure of such a thing was inconceivable. Drawing was for him alone. No one else. It would be like slicing open his brain and allowing his deepest secrets to flow out, then trying to stitch the gray matter back together. It would never heal quite right. There'd always be a scar and the secrets would be out there in the world, unprotected.

"I would have asked if that's what I was after."

"What are you after, then?"

Her expression softened. "No nefarious motives. All my motives are right here." Crossing her heart with an index finger, she sought his gaze, her irises as deep and rich as melted chocolate.

"What does that mean?"

"What do you think it means, Leo?" She smiled. "I gave you the picture because I love you and want to express that in tangible ways."

His insides shuddered to an icy halt.

I love you.

It echoed in his head, pounding at the base of his skull. Where had that *come* from? No one had ever said that to him before. Well, except his mom.

Oh, dear God. His overtly romantic mother would have a field day with this. Leo's arranged marriage had just blown up in his face. His wife had *fallen in love with him.*

What was he supposed to say in response?

"You can't drop something like that on me out of the blue."

"I can't?" She sat up, covers—and her state of undress—forgotten. "How should I have led up to it, then?"

He unstuck his tongue from the desert the roof of his mouth had turned into. "I mean, you didn't have to say it at all. That's... We're not—" He pinched the bridge of his nose and tried to corral his spooked wits before he told her the truth. That he'd liked the sound of those words far more than he would have expected. "That's not the kind of marriage we agreed to."

She recoiled and quickly composed her expression, but not before he saw the flicker of hurt. "I know that. It doesn't erase my feelings. You're a kind, generous man who makes me happy. We spent a romantic weekend together and you kind of pushed me over the edge after Tommy called and you blew him off. Wouldn't you rather I be honest with you?"

Not really, no. Not when it involved sticky emotions he couldn't fathom. Dangerous emotions. Wonderful, terrible emotions that quaked through him. Love was a hell of an indulgence and he could hardly comprehend the ramifications of her blithe announcement.

But it was out there and he couldn't ignore it. Like he couldn't ignore the corkscrew through his gut over what he had to do next. "Since you're such an advocate of honesty, I lost a couple of deals over those fantasies I couldn't get out of my head. I spent the weekend with you so I could go back to work on Monday and finally concentrate."

The pain radiating from her gaze sliced through his chest like a meat cleaver.

Get some distance before you hurt her even worse.

He couldn't reach for her. He wanted to. Wanted to tell her it was all a big lie and *I love you* was the sweetest phrase in the English language. It almost made the Tommy-free weekend worth it and that scared him the most. Because he might do it again.

Curling his fingers under, he said the most horrible thing he could think of.

"The rose petals weren't intended to seduce you into falling in love. It was an exorcism."

One that had just failed miserably. His wife had fallen in love with him. It was all over her face, in her touch. Had been for some time and he'd only just realized how much he liked it on her.

Worse, he had to pretend that her words hadn't lodged in his heart. That his soul wasn't turning them over, examining them from all angles and contemplating grabbing on with all its might. Whispering seductive ideas.

It could be like it was this weekend forever. Forget about work, not your wife. You don't have to surface. Not really.

Said Satan about the apple.

Love was the decisive destroyer of security, the ultimate quicksand that led to the ghetto, and he would not fall prey to the temptations of his weaknesses. He would not become his father. No matter how hard it was to force out the words.

"We have a marriage of convenience, Daniella. That's all."

"I understand," she whispered, and nodded once without looking up from her folded hands.

She wasn't going to slap him and storm out. The relief he'd expected to feel didn't materialize. Instead, the juggling act had grown exponentially harder. Now he had the Herculean task of continuing to push her away so she didn't utter *I love you* in his presence again. He couldn't take that raw devastation on her face, knowing that he was hurting her, knowing that he'd hurt her even more later if he slipped and said it back.

And neither would Leo allow Dax to be right. He still had his edge and that wasn't ever changing.

Eleven

The pill was so tiny. How could such small packaging prevent such a huge thing like pregnancy?

Dannie stuck the birth control pill in her mouth and swallowed, the action serving the dual purpose of getting it down her throat and keeping the tears at bay. The pill was both functional and symbolic. Not only was she preventing pregnancy, but she was giving up on grand, sweeping passion and love. Forever.

Her heart was too bruised to imagine having a baby with Leo. Not now. Maybe at some point in the future she'd get those images of him smiling tenderly at their child out of her head. Leo didn't have an ounce of tenderness in him.

Okay, that wasn't true. He had it, he just used a great deal of judiciousness in how and when he allowed it to surface. She couldn't willingly give birth to a child who would one day want his or her daddy's attention. No child deserved to be fathered by a man who refused to participate in his own life.

Scratch a baby off the list. Yet another sacrifice she'd make. She understood people didn't always get their heart's desire. But she'd about run out of dreams for her non-fairytale real life to strip away.

She'd had an entire weekend to show Leo how wonderful their marriage could be. And she'd failed. He didn't find the idea of opening his heart to her the least bit appealing. In her most spectacular screwup to date, she'd assumed they'd grow to care for each other. Maybe not at the same rate, but they'd eventually catch up, right? It had never occurred to her he'd refuse to show even a tiny bit of affection for his wife.

She was simply a convenience. Exactly as he'd always said. Reading unmet needs into his actions and pushing him into intimacy hadn't gotten her anywhere but brokenhearted.

Wife was her identity, her essence. Work was his. Cliché indeed.

So he went back to his sixteen-hour days and she made a doctor's appointment. After three days of falling asleep before Leo came home, the pills were unnecessary insurance thus far. Apparently telling her husband she loved him was birth control in and of itself.

The music of her stupid phone's ringtone cut the silence in the bathroom.

She glanced at it. Elise's name flashed from the screen. What in the world?

"Hello?"

"It's Elise. I'm sorry to bother you, but I'm in a bind and I need your help."

"Of course. Whatever you need, it's yours."

There was very little Dannie wouldn't do for the woman who had changed her life, broken heart notwithstanding. Elise had helped her find a secure marriage. This was the "for worse" part—so much worse than she'd predicted, and she'd expected it to *suck* if she fell in love with Leo and he didn't return her feelings.

"Thank you. So much. I've got a new applicant for the program and I'm totally booked. But I can't turn her away. Will you go through the preliminary stages with her?"

"You want *me* to teach someone else how to do her hair and makeup?"

Elise chuckled. "Don't sound so surprised. You're highly qualified."

That was only because her fairy godmother had no idea

how solidly catastrophic Dannie's match had become. "As long as it's just preliminaries. I couldn't do any of the rest."

"Oh, I'll pay you."

"I wasn't talking about that." But now she was thinking about how it was almost like a short part-time job. Good timing. That might get her mind off the empty house. "I'd do it for free."

"I insist. Can you help me out or am I imposing on your new marriage?"

Dannie bit back maniacal laughter. "I can do it. Be there in thirty minutes."

She ended the call and finished getting ready for the day. She'd stopped rolling out of bed before dawn and making Leo's coffee. What would be the point? He probably hadn't even noticed.

Elise's elegant two-story town house in uptown brought back bittersweet memories. Inside these walls, Dannie had transformed from an outspoken, penniless—and hopeless—woman into a demure, suitable wife for the man Elise's computer had matched her with.

Well, not so demure. Scarlett sometimes took over, especially when Dannie's clothes came off. And when Leo made her mad, or smiled at her or—okay, Scarlett was here to stay. Dannie sighed. The suitable part was still true. She'd orchestrated a heck of a party and Tommy had signed with Reynolds Capital. Clearly, *some* of Elise's training had taken root.

Elise answered the door and threw her arms around Dannie in an exuberant hug that knocked her off balance, despite the fact that Dannie had six inches on Elise in height. But what she lacked vertically, Elise more than made up for in personality and heart.

"Look at you," Elise gushed. "So gorgeous and sophisticated. Thanks, by the way. Come meet Juliet."

Dannie followed Elise into the living room where she'd married Leo. It seemed like aeons ago that she'd stood at that fireplace, so nervous about entering an arranged marriage she could barely speak. Never had she imagined as she slipped that ring on Leo's finger that she'd fall in love and when she told him, he'd so thoroughly reject it.

Not just reject it. He'd *exorcised* her. As if she'd been haunting Leo and he hoped to banish the grim specter of his wife from the attic in his head.

If she had known, would she have still married him? Her mother's face swam into her mind. Yeah. She would have. Her mother was too important to balk at a little thing like a broken heart.

Dannie turned her back on the fireplace.

The woman huddled on the couch unfolded and stood to greet her.

"Juliet Villere," she said and held out a hand.

Even without the slight accent, her European descent was obvious. She had that quality inherent in people from another country—it was in the style of her shoes, the foreign cut of her clothing and light brown hair, and in the set of her aquiline features.

Dannie introduced herself and smiled at the other woman. Curiosity was killing her. As Dannie did, surely Juliet had a story behind why she'd answered Elise's ad. "You're here to let Elise sprinkle some magic dust over you?"

"Magic would help."

She returned Dannie's smile, but it didn't reach her eyes and Dannie was sold. No wonder Elise hadn't turned her away. The woman radiated a forlorn aura that made Dannie want to cover her with a warm quilt and ply her with hot chocolate. And it was eighty-five degrees outside.

Elise nodded. "Juliet is a self-described tomboy. I couldn't think of anyone more ladylike than Dannie and I've already taken on more candidates than I can handle. It's a perfect match."

Heat climbed into Dannie's cheeks. She *was* ladylike when it counted. What had happened between her and Leo in the media room after he ignored Tommy's call was nobody's business but hers. Besides, he liked it when she put on her brazen side.

At least she excelled in that area of her marriage.

"Thank you for helping me, Ms. Arundel. I had nowhere else to turn." Juliet bobbed her head first at Elise and then at Dannie. "I would be grateful to find an American husband."

"Did your computer already spit out some possibles?" Dannie asked Elise.

Elise shook her head. "She's not entered yet. Makeover first, then I do the match. The computer doesn't care what you look like, but I find that the makeover gives women the confidence to answer the profile questions from the heart instead of their head. Then the algorithm matches based on personality."

"Wait." Dannie went a little faint. "External characteristics aren't part of the profile process?"

"Of course not. Love isn't based on looks."

"But…" Dannie sank onto the couch. "You matched me with Leo because he was looking for certain qualities in a wife. Organized. Sophisticated. Able to host parties and mingle with the upper crust."

Which had everything to do with external qualities. Not internal.

"Yes. That covers about four of the profile points. The rest are all related to your views on relationships. Love. Family. How you feel about sex. Conflict. You and Leo fit on all forty-seven."

"That's impossible," she countered flatly.

"Name one area where that's not true and I'll refund Leo's money right now."

"Love. I believe in it. He doesn't." Saying it out loud made it real all of a sudden and a breakdown threatened Dannie's immediate future.

"That's totally false." Elise's brow puckered as she paused. "Unless he lied on his profile. Which I suppose is possible but highly improbable."

"It can't be that foolproof."

Why was she arguing about this? The computer had matched her with Leo because they'd both agreed a marriage based on mutual goals made sense. Neither of them had expressed an interest in love from the outset and Elise was absolutely correct—Dannie had answered the profile questions from her heart. She loved her mother and marrying Leo had saved her. End of story.

"It's not. But I am." The flash of Elise's smile did not temper her self-assurance. "I administer the profile test myself and I wrote it."

Juliet watched the exchange as though it was a tennis match, eyelids shielding her thoughts. "But something is amiss or you would not be having this discussion, right?" she suggested.

Something as in Dannie had created this mess by forgetting love didn't create security, but honoring your word did. Her mother's stance on relationships had never steered her wrong before, and if she'd tried a little harder to embrace the idea of a loveless marriage, she could have avoided all this.

Elise deflated a little. "Yes, of course you're right. I'm sorry. I have to shut down my analytical side or it takes over."

Yeah, Dannie knew all about shutting down inappropriate emotional outbursts. "I'm just disappointed and mad at myself for thinking I could entice him away from his dollar signs with promises of fulfillment. It's not your fault."

Elise put a comforting hand on Dannie's arm. "My point is that you totally can. I'm sorry he's being difficult about accepting all that you have to offer beyond the ability to schedule personal appointments. But you've got what he needs emotionally, too."

Did she?

And did she have what he really needed or only what he thought he needed? For a long time, she'd smugly believed she knew the difference and her job was to guide him into understanding how to express his true desires. But really, her own pent-up needs had messed that up. And how.

Dannie took Juliet upstairs to Elise's war room, complete with a long lighted mirror and counter, racks of clothing and more hairstyling and makeup tools than a Vegas showgirl dressing room.

"All this is necessary?" Juliet's gaze darted around the room, her nostrils flaring. "What is *that?* Will it hurt?"

The panicked questions lightened Dannie's mood. "It's a straightening iron. For your hair. We don't stick your fingers between the plates unless you fail at balancing a book on your head." The other woman's cheeks blanched and Dannie laughed. "I'm kidding. Sit down in that chair and let's get started. Drink?"

Dannie crossed to the small refrigerator stocked with water, lemons, cucumbers and ice packs, the best beauty accoutrements on the planet behind a good night's sleep.

"Thank you. I'm not thirsty."

"You need to drink plenty of water. It's good for your skin and helps you stay full so you don't feel as hungry." Elise's lessons rolled out of Dannie's brain effortlessly. "Lemon gives a little bit of taste, if you prefer."

"I prefer to be sailing or swimming." The frown had no trouble reaching Juliet's eyes, unlike her smile. "I miss the water."

"Where are you from?" Dannie asked as she plugged in the hair dryer, straightening iron, curling iron and hot rollers. She hadn't decided yet how Juliet's long hair would best be styled, though it would surely benefit from a more elegant cut. And she'd definitely need a facial. Dannie mentally ticked off a few more details and realized she was humming.

It was the happiest she'd felt all week.

"South of France. Delamer." Juliet spat out the country's name as if it had the reputation of being a leper's colony instead of a Mediterranean playground for the rich and beautiful.

"That's a lovely place. And you've got those two gorgeous princes. I read that Prince Alain is getting married soon. I hope they televise it." Dannie sighed a little in what she assumed would be mutual appreciation for a dreamy, out-of-reach public figure and his royal romance.

Juliet instead burst into tears.

Dannie gathered the other woman into a wet embrace and patted her back. "Oh, honey. What's wrong?"

Juliet snuffled against her shoulder. "Matters of the heart. They can undo us like no other."

She had that right. "Is that why you left Delamer? Someone broke your heart at home?"

With one last sniff, Juliet pulled out of Dannie's arms and dragged the back of a hand under both newly steeled eyes. "I want to forget that man exists. In Delamer, it's impossible. They splash his picture on everything. If I marry an American husband, I don't have to return and watch him with his perfect princess."

Dannie finally caught up and sank into the second director's chair. "Prince Alain broke your heart?"

This story called for chocolate and lots of red wine. Unfortunately, it wasn't even lunchtime and Elise kept neither in the house.

With a nod, Juliet twirled a brush absently, her thoughts clearly thousands of miles away. "There was a scandal. It's history. I can't change it and now I have to move on. What should we do first to transform me into a woman who will attract an American husband?"

Dannie let her change the subject and spent the next two hours teaching Juliet the basics of makeup and hair. It was a challenge, as the woman had never learned an iota about either.

"If you line only the bottom lip with a pencil that's a shade darker than your lipstick, it'll create an illusion of fuller lips." Dannie demonstrated on Juliet's mouth.

"Why would I want to do that? I can't sleep in lipstick. In

the morning, my husband will realize I'm not pouty lipped, won't he?" Juliet pursed her newly painted lips and scowled at her reflection in the mirror.

"Well, figure out a way to distract him before he notices," Dannie suggested and moved on to eye-shadow techniques. There was no polite way to say Juliet needed some style.

Tomboy she was, down to her bitten-off fingernails, Mediterranean sailor's tan and split ends. The tears had unlocked something in Juliet and she talked endlessly with Dannie about her life in Delamer, minus any details about the prince.

Dannie bit back her questions, but she'd love to know how such a down-to-earth woman without an ounce of polish had gotten within five feet of royalty, let alone long enough to develop a relationship with a prince. Then there was the briefly mentioned scandal.

She didn't ask. The internet would give up the rest of the tale soon enough.

Elise checked in and offered to have lunch delivered. Since Dannie had nowhere else to be, she stayed the rest of the day. She took Juliet shopping at the Galleria in North Dallas and by the time they returned to Elise's house, Dannie had made a friend. Which, she suspected, they both desperately needed.

Before Dannie left to go back to her empty house, Elise pulled her aside. "You did a fantastic job with Juliet. If you're in the market for a permanent job, I would hire you in a second."

Dannie stared at the matchmaker. "Are you serious?"

"Totally." Elise flipped her pageboy-cut hair back. "It takes time to groom these women, and I've got more men in the computer than I ever thought possible. Successful men don't have a lot of patience for sorting out good women from bad and I provide a valuable service to them. Business is booming, in short. If you've got spare time, it would be a huge help to me."

Elise named a salary that nearly popped Dannie's eyes from their sockets. "Let me think about it."

Her job was Leo Reynolds's Wife. But suddenly, it didn't have to be. She could make money working for Elise and take care of her mother.

Leo was married to his company, first and foremost. He made that choice every day. And now, Dannie had choices, too.

She didn't want a divorce. She wanted to be Leo's wife and have the marriage of her dreams, but Leo was half of that equation. Before she made a final decision about how she'd spend the next fifty years, he should have the opportunity to fully understand what her choices were. And how they'd affect him. He might give her the final piece she needed to make up her mind.

Maybe she'd get an exorcism of her own out of it.

The exorcism was not only a colossal failure, but Leo had also learned the very uncomfortable lesson that he couldn't find a method to erase the scent of strawberries from his skin.

He'd tried four different kinds of soap. Then something called a loofah. In one of his less sane moments, sandpaper started looking very attractive. It was totally irrational. The scent couldn't actually still be there after so many days, but he sniffed and there it was. Essence of Daniella.

Leo clenched the pencil in his hand and pulled his gaze from the Dallas skyline outside his office window. The garbage can by his desk overflowed with crumpled paper. He balled the sheet on his desk and threw the latest in another round of useless brainstorming on top. It bounced out to roll under his chair. Of course. Nothing was happening as it should. Normally, paper and pencil was his go-to method when he needed to unblock.

Surprise. It wasn't working.

Tommy Garrett was very shortly going to be furious that

he'd signed with Leo instead of Moreno Partners. This deal represented the pinnacle of venture capital success and Leo's brain was fried. He had nothing to show for his half of the partnership. He was supposed to provide business expertise. Connections in manufacturing. Marketing. Ideas.

Instead he'd spent the past few days mentally embroiled in about a million more fantasies starring his wife, whom he'd deliberately driven away. For all the good it had done.

His pencil trailed across the paper and in seconds, graphite lines appeared in the form of a woman. He groaned and shut his eyes. Then opened them. What the hell. Nothing else was coming out of his brain.

As his long-suppressed muse whispered halting, undisciplined inspiration, his hand captured it, transforming the vision into the concrete. Details of Daniella's shape flowed onto the paper. Glorious. Ethereal. So beautiful his chest ached. The ache spread, squeezing his lungs and biting through muscle painfully.

Sweat broke out across the back of his neck and his hand cramped but he didn't stop. He yanked more minutiae, more emotion, from a place deep inside until he was nearly spent.

Another. More paper. Draw.

As if the drawing conjured the woman, Leo glanced up to see his wife standing in the doorway of his office. In the flesh. Dear God, Daniella was luminous in a blue dress and sky-high heels that emphasized the delicate arch to her feet.

Heart pounding, he slipped a blank sheet over the drawing and shoved everything he'd just freed back into its box. He glanced at the clock. It was eight-thirty. And dark. When had that happened?

"What are you doing here?" he asked her and stood. *Nice greeting for your wife, moron.*

"I came to see you. Do you have a few minutes?" She waltzed in as if he'd said yes.

He hadn't seen her awake since Sunday, but his body reacted as if she'd slid up against him into that niche where she fit like clinging honey instead of taking a seat on the couch in his sitting area.

"Would you like to sit down?" she offered politely, every bit the queen of the manor despite the fact that his business acumen paid the rent on this office space. Or it used to. He was this close to selling caricatures on the street if something didn't change ASAP.

He sat on the other couch. Good. Distance was good. Kept their interaction impersonal. "How are you?"

"Fine. Elise offered me a job today."

She smoothed her skirt and crossed her legs, which he watched from the corner of his eye. It was so much more powerful a blow to witness those legs sliding together when he knew what they felt like against his. What he felt like when she was near him, even when they weren't touching.

"A job? As a matchmaker?"

"As a tutor. She asked me to help her polish the women she accepts into her program. Hair, makeup. That sort of thing."

"You'd be a natural. Are you here to ask my permission? I certainly don't mind if you—"

"I'm here to ask if there's the smallest possibility you could ever love me."

A knot the size of a Buick hardened in his chest. All his carefully constructed arguments regarding the status of their relationship had ended up forming a bridge to nowhere. Probably because he could hardly convince her of it when he'd failed to convince himself.

"Daniella, we've been over this."

"No, we haven't." She clasped her hands together so tightly one of her knuckles cracked. "I told you I loved you and you freaked."

That was a pretty accurate assessment. "Well, I don't want to rehash it. We have an arranged marriage with a useful design. Let's stick with it."

"Sorry. We're rehashing it right now. Extenuating circumstances caused me to give up what I really want in a marriage. And extenuating circumstances have caused me to reevaluate. I love you and want you to love me. I need to know if we can have a marriage based on that."

I love you. Why did that settle into so many tender places inside all at once?

"You make it sound simple. It's not," he said, his voice inexplicably gruff. All the emotions drawing had dredged up weren't so easily controlled as they would have been if he'd resisted the temptation in the first place.

"Explain to me what's complicated about it."

Everything.

"You want me to choose you over my company and that's an impossible place to be."

"I'm not asking you to do that. I would never presume to take away something so important to you. Why can't you have both?"

It was the juggling-act conversation all over again. As if it was simple to just choose to have both. This would always be a problem—he saw that now. And now was the time to get her crystal clear on the subject. Get them both clear.

"I'm not built that way. I don't do anything halfway, something you might better appreciate after this past weekend. Surely you recall how thoroughly I threw myself into pleasuring you." He raked his gaze over her deliberately to make the point and a gorgeous blush rose up in her cheeks. Which made him feel worse for God knew what reason. "I went to a matchmaker to find a wife who would be happy with what I could provide financially and overlook the number of hours I put into my company. Because I don't do that halfway, either. One side is going to suffer."

All or nothing. And when it came to Daniella, he was so far away from nothing, he couldn't even *see* nothing.

Her keen gaze flitted over his expression and it wasn't difficult to pinpoint the exact instant she gleaned more than he'd intended. "But that doesn't mean you don't have feelings for me, just that you're too afraid to admit something unexpected happened between us."

"What do you want me to say, Daniella?" His voice dipped uncontrollably as he fought to keep those feelings under wraps. "That you're right? That of all the things I expected to happen in our marriage, this conversation was so far down the list it was nearly invisible?"

Her bottom lip trembled. "I want you to say what's in your heart. Or are you too afraid?"

She didn't get it. He wasn't afraid of what was in his heart; he just couldn't give in to it. The cost of loving her was too high.

"My heart is not up for discussion."

Nodding, she stood up. "Security is vitally important to me and I married you to get it. It was the only way I could guarantee my mother would be taken care of. Elise changed that today. I can support my mother on the salary she'll pay me."

An arctic chill bit into his skin, creeping through the pores to flash freeze his whole body. "Are you asking me for a divorce?"

Please, God, no.

If he lost her, it was what he deserved.

She shook her head. "I'm telling you I have a choice. And I'm making it. I took lifetime vows I plan to honor. Now I'm giving you a chance to make a choice as well as to how that marriage will look. Get off the sidelines, love me and live happily ever after. Or we'll remain married, I'll manage your personal life but I'll move back into my own room. Separate hearts, separate bedrooms. What are you going to do?"

Panic clawed at his insides, a living thing desperate to get out and not particular about how many internal organs it destroyed in its quest. She wanted something worse than a divorce. The one thing money couldn't buy—him. His time. His attention. His love.

"That's ridiculous," he burst out and clamped his mouth closed until he could control what came out of it. "I told you what I need, which is for you to be happy with what I can give. Like I've told you from the very beginning. You're throwing that back at me, drawing a line. You or Reynolds Capital Management."

A tear tracked down her cheek. "Don't you see, Leo? *You* drew that line. Not me."

"My mistake. The line you drew is the one where you said I can't sleep with you anymore unless I'm in love with you."

"Yes. That is my fault." Her head dropped and it took an enormous amount of will to keep from enfolding her in his arms. But he was the source of her pain, not the solution. "My mother...she's an amazing woman, but she has a very jaded view of marriage and I let it fool me into believing I could be happy with a loveless arrangement. And I probably would have been if you were someone different. Someone I couldn't love. Be the husband I need, Leo."

She raised her head and what he saw in the depths of her shiny eyes nearly put him on his knees, prostrate before her in desperate apology, babbling, "Yes, I will be that husband," or worse, telling her he'd do anything as long as she'd look at him like that forever: as though he was worthy of being loved, even though he'd rejected her over and over again.

The overflowing trash can taunted him.

Lack of focus is what happens when you let your wife swallow you. Other venture capital firms have fewer dominoes, more liquid assets, less leveraged cash. One push and it'll all vanish.

He could never do what she was asking.

Once and for all, he could resolve it. Right here, right now, give her that final push away before he gave in to the emotions and forgot all the reasons he couldn't have his company *and* love Daniella.

"I stay on the sidelines for a reason. It's how I balance my obsessive personality." His heart thumped painfully. This was the right thing, for him and Reynolds Capital. Why didn't it feel like it? "I need you to be the wife I thought I was getting from EA International."

Which was impossible. Daniella could never be the out-of-sight, out-of-mind wife he'd envisioned. He'd given up on categorizing her and forcing her into a box when she insisted on being in all the boxes simultaneously. His multitalented wife was the only woman alive who could do that.

Her expression went as stiff as her spine. "Then that's what you'll get. I'll schedule your appointments and host your parties and make you look good to your associates. I won't be in your bed at night, but I'll give you a hundred percent during the day and never mention how many hours you work."

It was everything he'd asked for. And the polar opposite of what he wanted. He vised his throbbing temples between his middle finger and his thumb but his brain still felt as though it was about to explode. How had she managed to twist this around so that they were back to their original agreement but it felt as if she'd kicked him in the stomach?

"I wish…" She crossed her arms as if holding herself in. "Love creates security, too. I wish you could see that. But if it's your choice for me to be nothing more than a glorified personal assistant, I hope it makes you happy. Just keep in mind that your company *and* your wife bear your name. You will always be a part of both."

And then she walked out, heels clicking on the stained concrete in perfect rhythm to the sound of his soul splitting in two.

Twelve

"Dorito?" Tommy offered and stuck out the bag.

Leo shook his head. Doritos didn't sit well on an empty stomach. Nothing sat well on an empty stomach, especially not the dreck in his coffee cup. Mrs. Gordon had remade it four times already and the look on her face said he'd better be happy with this round.

He shoved the half-full mug to the far end of the conference table, wished it was a travel mug filled by his wife and scrubbed his jaw. Rough stubble stabbed his fingers. *Forgot to shave. Again.*

"So, amigo." Tommy crunched absently and nodded to the TV on the wall, where Leo's laptop screen was displayed. "I've redone this schematic twice. The prototype passed the CAD analysis. What's it going to take to get you happy with it?"

Hell would probably freeze over before Leo was happy about anything. He'd officially labeled this funk Daniella's Curse, because until she'd said she hoped his choice made him happy, he'd never given a thought to whether he was or not. And this funk was the opposite of happy.

He missed his wife. Her invisible presence invaded every last area of his life, including his car, which never dipped below half a tank of gas. And smelled like strawberries.

"The schematic is still wrong. That's why I keep telling you to redo it." Leo flipped the drawing vertically inside the CAD program and glanced up at the TV. "Look, you can't take this to manufacturing as is. We have to shave another two cubic centimeters somewhere to meet the price point. Otherwise the markup will be too high and the distribution deals will fall through."

Leo's phone beeped. Daniella's picture flashed and he snatched it up. Text message. He frowned at the concisely worded reminder of his appointment for a haircut that afternoon. Of course she hadn't called to talk to him.

"Why does this have to be so complicated?" Tommy complained. "I designed the thing. That should be enough. Why don't *you* figure out where to shave off whatever you think makes sense?"

Leo fiddled with the pencil in his fingers, weaving it through them like a baton, and counted all the way to fifteen for good measure. It did not calm him. "You're the designer. You have to redesign when it's not ready." His fingers sought the leather portfolio on the table. The picture he'd drawn of Daniella was inside. It equaled serenity in the midst of turmoil. Oddly enough. "I help you on the back end. We've been over this."

Shades of the last real conversation he'd had with Daniella filtered through his mind. Why did he have to constantly remind people of things they should already know? Leo had a specific role to fill—in the background. Always. Nobody remembered that he stayed out of the middle, except him.

"I don't know how to get it to your specifications!" Tommy burst out in recalcitrant five-year-old fashion, complete with a scowl and crossed arms. "I've tried. I need help. That's why I signed with you."

"I'm your financial backer. I'm only talking to you about the schematic now because we're behind schedule and I need a good design today." With a short laugh, Leo shook his head. "Why would you assume I could do anything to help?"

Tommy flipped hair out of his face. "Dannie. She believes in you. She totally convinced me you walk on water daily and in your spare time you invest in people's potential. As far as she's concerned, you're the messiah of everything."

His gut spasmed. What exactly had his wife told Tommy to give him such a ridiculous picture of Leo? "That's entirely too fanciful for what I do."

Entirely too fanciful for a mortal man who'd made plenty of mistakes. But it didn't stop the low hum of pleasure behind his rib cage. Did Daniella really think of him like that, as someone heroic and unfailing? Or had she said those things for Tommy's benefit, playing her part as a dutiful wife?

Leo had the distinct, uncomfortable realization it was probably both. And he didn't deserve either.

Eyebrows raised, Tommy crossed his feet casually. "Yeah? If you tell me you don't know exactly what needs to happen with that schematic, I'll call you a dirty liar. You've been trying to lead me to it for an hour and I can't see it."

Leo sighed and thought seriously about driving the pencil through the table, but it would only break the wood, not solve his mounting frustration. Before he could count the reasons why it was a stupid, ridiculous path, he centered a piece of paper under the graphite and drew the first line.

Tommy's purple high-tops hit the floor as he leaned forward to peer over Leo's shoulder. The fuel-converter schematic took shape on the paper. With each new line, he explained to Tommy where he varied from the original design, why the modification was necessary, what the downstream manufacturing effect would be.

Occasionally Tommy interjected questions, objections and once, a really heartfelt "Dude. That's righteous."

One of Tommy's objections was sound and Leo reconsidered his stance on it. He erased that part of the drawing and incorporated Tommy's suggestion. Mrs. Gordon left for the day, shaking her head and mumbling about creative minds. After several hours, many heated exchanges and a few moments of near-poetic collaboration, they had a design they could both live with.

The last time Leo could honestly say he'd had that much fun was during the weekend he'd spent with Daniella. Before that—never.

Once Leo had scanned the finished product into his laptop and displayed it on the TV, Tommy whistled. "A work of art. I have to use every tool known to designers to put something that beautiful together. I can't believe you freehanded that. With a pencil, no less."

"A pencil gets the shading right," Leo muttered with a shrug. "I guess you could say it's a talent."

"I knew you had it in you," Tommy said smugly. "If I'd gone with Moreno Partners, I'd be screwed right now. Kiss your wife for me. She knows her stuff."

If only. Ironically, his current interaction with Daniella wasn't too different from how their marriage had started out, before they'd begun sharing a bedroom. If she hadn't barged in and demanded he start sleeping with her, would they still be exchanging text messages with no clue how much more there could be between them?

"She does have some kind of extrasensory perception," Leo said. "I'm afraid she's the one who walks on water."

No, *he'd* be clueless. She wouldn't. From the beginning, she'd seen possibilities, pushing their relationship into realms deeper and stronger than he'd ever imagined could be between any two people, let alone when one of them was Leo Reynolds.

How had that happened when he wasn't looking? And why did the loss of something he'd never asked for haunt him?

He'd done everything he could to drive her away so she wouldn't be hurt and instead of leaving him, his wife had stayed. Why didn't she get the message already?

With a grin, Tommy nodded vigorously. "Dannie's awesome."

His wife's nickname lodged in his gut, spreading nasty poison.

Leo liked Tommy. He was enthusiastic, tireless, brilliant. So what was it about Tommy simply saying his wife's name that burned Leo up? It was more than jealousy, more than a fear either Tommy or Daniella had less than pure intentions toward each other.

It was because Tommy held up a mirror and Leo hated his reflection.

This Dorito-crunching, Red Bull–slurping wonder kid was a younger, unrestricted, better version of Leo. Tommy could call a woman Dannie and think nothing of it, whereas Leo couldn't descend into that kind of intimacy unless he was drunk on Daniella's powerful chemistry.

And he wished he could be more like Tommy.

Tommy polished off the bag of Doritos. "You're awesome, too. I'm over here soaking it all up like SpongeBob."

A cleansing laugh burst out of Leo's mouth, unchecked. "Thanks. It's nice to have an appreciative audience."

"Dude, you talk and I'll listen, no matter what you say. I'm in awe of you right now. I think I learned more today than I did in four years at Yale. What else can you teach me?"

Oh, no. That was beyond the realm of his role. He and Tommy were financial partners, with a carefully constructed agreement separating their interests into neat boxes. That should be the extent of their relationship.

Should be. Everything should fit into a neat box. And nothing did, despite all of Leo's efforts.

"What do you want to know?"

With a lusty sigh, Tommy grinned. "Everything. Lay it on me."

And that was it. For the first time in his life, Leo had become an in-the-flesh mentor and for whatever reason, it felt right. It was a connection with his profit margin, one he'd never explored but suddenly wanted to.

All business is personal.

His wife had pointed that out long ago and he'd brushed it off as foolish sentiment. But it suddenly made brilliant sense. He hadn't lost the deal for Mastermind Media because he'd lost his edge, but because he'd willfully chosen not to enter into a partnership with Dax, for whom he'd lost a great deal of respect. His relationship with Daniella merely highlighted it, but hadn't caused it.

Leo's relationship with Daniella shone into all of his corners and scared away the excuses, the fears. She hadn't left him because she'd already figured out what Leo should have seen long ago.

Their arrangement was dead. Now they had an opportunity to make their marriage something else.

Instead of being like Tommy, maybe Leo should be a better version of himself. One that could be worthy of a woman like Daniella Reynolds.

Leo's morose mood lightened. After setting aside two afternoons a week for Tommy to bring his best SpongeBob absorption skills, Leo kicked his new disciple out of his office so he could leave.

When he got home, Leo paused outside Daniella's closed bedroom door and placed his palm flat against it, as he did every night. Sometimes he imagined he could feel her breathing through the door. The scent of strawberries lingered in the hall, wrapping around him.

He'd built this home as a fortress, a place that represented all the stability he'd never had as a child. Daniella had become an inseparable part of that. How could he ever have lived here without her? How could he explain to her what value she'd brought to his life?

Guilt gnawed a new hole in his gut. She deserved so much more than what he'd given her.

She should have left him.

The main goal of marriage was security. Odd how he

felt as though the ground was disappearing beneath him at an alarming pace the longer he had a wife in name only.

Instead of standing there like a stalker, he knocked and shifted the bulky package in his hand before him like a peace offering. He prayed it might change things but he had no clue how, or what that change might look like.

He just knew he couldn't do marriage like this anymore. The ball was in his court. Had been the entire time. Hopefully he'd picked up the proper racket.

Daniella opened the door, shiny hair down around her face and clad in a skintight tank top and loose pajama bottoms with her flat midriff peeking through. The swift, hard punch to his solar plexus nearly rendered him speechless.

Somehow he managed to choke out, "Hi."

Her luminous brown eyes sought his and a wealth of unexpressed things poured from them. "Hi."

"A gift. For you." He handed her the wrapped package and laced his fingers behind his back before he pulled her into an embrace she probably wouldn't welcome. But oh, dear God, did he want to touch her. "You gave me one. I'm returning the favor."

She ripped it open and his thudding heart deafened him as he waited.

Silently, she evaluated the basket of pomegranates. "What does this mean?"

She tilted the basket as if to show him, which was unnecessary. He'd placed each one in the basket himself, positioning it just so to interlock with the others. "You're still driving me pomegranates. Sleeping in separate bedrooms hasn't changed that."

The tension spiraled between them, squeezing his lungs, and he smiled in hopes of loosening it.

"I got that part. *Why* are you giving them to me?" Her gaze probed his, challenging him and killing his smile. She wasn't going to make this easy. She always had before, using her special powers to figure out exactly how to help him navigate.

Not this time. He shifted from foot to foot but couldn't find a comfortable stance. "Because I wanted to give you something that had special significance."

Her expression didn't change. "So it's nothing more than a gift designed to buy your way out of giving me anything emotional."

What did she want from him? A pound of flesh? She held in her hands one of the most emotional things he'd ever done. Somehow he had to make her see that.

"It's not just a gift, like jewelry. It's better than that."

Frozen, she stared at him for an eternity, long enough for him to realize he'd devalued the diamonds he'd given her for the party. Which were in her earlobes at this moment.

This was not going at all how he'd envisioned. She was supposed to make the first move. Fall into his arms and tell him this separation was killing her, too.

At the very least, she should be giving him a choice between two impossible options and then pretending it was okay when he picked the wrong one. The way she always did.

Floundering, he cast about for a lifeboat. "I'm sorry. I didn't mean it that way."

"How did you mean it? Or do you even know?"

"I do know!" At her raised eyebrows, he faltered. It had been an off-the-cuff protest. And a lie. Nothing between them was tangible. Or quantifiable. Which made it impossible to define the bottom line.

This was like a bad joke. What did the guy who had never hung on to a woman longer than a few weeks say to his wife? If only she'd tell him the punch line, they could move past this.

"What do you want me to say?"

"That's for you to figure out. I'll be here when you do. Thank you for the pomegranates."

With that, she closed the door in his face. Because at the end of the day, she knew the truth as well as he did. Jewelry. Pomegranates. Same difference. He still hadn't given her the one thing she really wanted—everything.

If he truly hoped to change their marriage, he had to dig much deeper. And it was going to hurt.

Dannie slid to the ground, the wood of her door biting into her back, and muffled a sob against the heel of her hand. *Pomegranates.*

Why did this have to be so hard?

Her mother was right: love was the stupidest thing of all to base a marriage on. It hurt too much. All Leo had to do was say, "I brought you a gift because I love you."

If his inability to do so wasn't bad enough, she had the awful feeling that the basket was indeed symbolic of his inner turmoil. Only supreme will suppressed her desire to knuckle under.

He'd tried. He really had. It just wasn't good enough, not anymore. Once upon a time, she'd believed they were a good match because they both valued security. It was how they went about achieving it where they differed.

Leo was an intense, focused man who cut himself off from people not because he didn't want to invest emotionally, but as some kind of compensation for what he viewed as a shortcoming of his personality. She couldn't spend a lifetime pretending it was okay that he refused to dive headlong into the game. She'd already compromised to the point of pain.

His mother had warned her how challenging Leo would be to love. Dannie should get a medal. So should Leo's mother.

Sleep did not come easily. She glanced at the time, convinced she'd been lying there for an hour but in reality, only four minutes had passed since the last clock check. She gave up at quarter past two and flipped on the TV to watch a fascinating documentary about the Civil War.

Her favorite historical time period unfolded on the screen. Women in lush hoopskirts danced a quadrille in the Old South before everything fell apart at the hands of General Sherman cutting a swath through Georgia on his way to the sea.

Dannie's heart felt as if it had taken a few rounds from a Yankee musket, too.

But where Scarlett O'Hara had raised a fist to the sky and vowed to persevere, Dannie felt like giving up.

A divorce would be easier. She could take care of her mother, live with Elise and try to forget about the man she'd married who refused to get out from behind the scenes.

But she'd taken vows. Her stomach ached at the thought of going back on her word. Her heart ached over the idea of staying. Which was worse?

All she knew was that she couldn't do this anymore.

In the morning, she took a bleary-eyed shower and spent the day at Elise's working with Juliet. They were both subdued and honestly, Dannie didn't see the point in giving Juliet a makeover when the woman was already beautiful. Besides, it wasn't as though a manicure and hot rollers would give Juliet what she most desired.

Or would it?

"What if your match is someone you can't fall in love with? Would you still marry him?" Dannie asked Juliet as she showed her how to pin the hot roller in place against her scalp. Some people didn't care about love. Some people found happiness and fulfillment in their own pursuits instead of through their husbands.

But Dannie wasn't some people, and she'd lied to herself about which side of the fence she was on, embracing her mother's philosophy as if it were her own.

Juliet made a face. "I would marry a warthog if he had

the means to keep me in America. Arranged marriages are common in Europe. You learn to coexist."

"But is it worth it to become someone else in order to have that means?"

The other woman shot her puzzled glance in the mirror. "I'm still me. With fingernails." She stuck out a hand, where a nail technician had created works of art with acrylic extensions.

Dannie glanced at her own reflection in the mirror. She'd been polished for so long, it was no longer a shock to see the elegant, sophisticated Mrs. Reynolds in the glass instead of Dannie White. Except they were one and the same, with a dash of Scarlett.

Elise had done the makeover first, but the computer had matched her to Leo because she was perfect for him. As she was. Not because Elise had infused Dannie with some special magic and transformed her into someone Leo would like.

I'm still me, too, but better.

Leo provided the foundation for her to excel as his wife and let her be as brazen, outspoken and blunt as she wanted. He was okay with Dannie being herself.

Their personalities were the match. She'd heard it over and over but today, it clicked.

She'd been so focused on whether Leo would kick her out if she screwed up it had blinded her to the real problem. They both had come into this marriage seeking security, but struggled with what they said they wanted versus what they'd actually gotten. And they were *both* trying to balance aspects of their incredibly strong personalities *for no reason*.

They wanted the same thing deep in their hearts—the security of an unending bond so strong it could never be broken.

The open-heart lavaliere around her neck caught the light as she leaned over Juliet's shoulder to arrange her hair. Elise had given Dannie the necklace when she'd agreed to marry Leo, as a gift between friends, she'd assumed.

Now she saw it as a reminder that marriage required exactly that—*two* open hearts.

Had she been too harsh with Leo about the pomegranates? Maybe she should find a way to coexist that didn't involve such absolutes. Security was enough for Juliet. A fulfilling partnership had been enough for Dannie once.

She'd pushed intimacy in an attempt to fulfill Leo's unvoiced needs and ignored the need he'd actually voiced— a wife he could depend on, who would stick with him, no matter what. Even through the pain of a one-sided grand, sweeping love affair.

One thing was for sure. Real life wasn't a fairy tale, but Dannie wanted her happily ever after anyway. Cinderella might have had some help from her fairy godmother, but in the end, she'd walked into that ball with only her brain and a strong drive to make her life better. What was a fairy tale but a story of perseverance, courage and choices?

It was time to be the wife Leo said he needed, not the one she assumed he needed.

Leo's car was in the garage when Dannie got home. She eyed it warily and glanced at her watch. It was three o'clock on a Tuesday. Someone had died. Someone *had* to have died.

Dannie dashed into the house, a lump in her throat as she triple checked her phone. She'd have a call if it was her mother. Wouldn't she?

"Leo!" Her shout echoed in the foyer but he didn't answer.

The study was empty. Her stomach flipped. Now she was really scared.

Neither was he in the pool, the kitchen, the media room, the servants' quarters around the back side of the garage or the workout room over the garage.

Dannie tore off two nails in her haste to turn the knob on

his bedroom door, the last threshold she should ever cross, but he could be lying a pool of his own blood and need help.

Curtains blocked the outside sunlight and the room was dark but for the lone lamp on Leo's dresser. It shone down on him. He sat on the carpet, hunched over a long piece of paper resting on a length of cardboard. Clawlike, he gripped a pencil in his hand, stroking it over the paper swiftly.

"Leo?" She paused just inside the door frame. "Are you okay?"

He glanced up. The light threw his ravaged face into relief, shadowing half of it. "I don't know when to stop. I tried to tell you."

"Tell me what? What are you talking about? What do you need to stop?"

"Drawing." He flipped a limp hand toward the room at large and that's when she realized white papers covered nearly every surface.

"How long have you been in here?" There were hundreds of drawings, slashes and fine lines filling the pages with a mess of shapes she couldn't make out in the semidark. *Hundreds.* Apparently she'd massively misconstrued what he meant by not doing things halfway.

"Since the pomegranates." His voice trembled with what had to be fatigue. He'd been holed up in here since last night?

"But your car was gone this morning."

"Needed a pencil sharpener. Is it enough? Look at the pictures, Daniella. Tell me if it's enough."

Her heart fluttered into her throat. "You want me to see your drawings?"

In response, he gathered a handful and clambered to his feet to bring them to her. The half light glinted off the short stubble lining his jaw and dark hair swept his collar. Not only had he skipped the haircut she'd scheduled, but he'd obviously not shaved in several days. His shirt was untucked and unbuttoned and this undone version of Leo had a devastating, intense edge.

As if presenting a broken baby bird, he gingerly handed off the drawings and waited silently.

She glanced at the first one and every ounce of oxygen in the room vanished.

"It's you," she whispered. She flipped through the pages. "They're all of you."

Gorgeously rendered. Drawn by the hand of a master who knew himself intimately and who was unashamed to show the world all the glorious details of what made up Leonardo Reynolds.

And he was completely naked in every single one.

He shut his eyes. "I stripped myself bare. Emotionally, physically, spiritually. For you. I cannot possibly explain what it cost me to put all of it on the paper. But it's there. Tell me it's enough."

Oh, my God.

"Leo," she croaked through a throat suddenly tight with unshed tears. This had all been for her. "Yes. *Yes.* It's enough."

More than enough. She clutched the pages to her abdomen. It was the deepest expression of his love she could possibly imagine and these pictures were worth far more than a thousand words. They told the story she'd yearned to hear, lifting his shell once and for all, revealing everything important about the man she loved.

Artist Leo touched her deep in her soul with invisible, precious fingers.

He deflated, almost collapsing. But then he opened his eyes and caught her in his arms, binding her to his strong, solid body. Her knees weren't too steady either as she let the drawings flutter to the floor and burrowed up against him.

Warm. Beautiful. Hers.

Her brain was having trouble spitting out anything coherent. And then he kissed her and she stopped thinking at all.

It was hungry, openmouthed, sloppy and so powerful. As he kissed her, he mouthed words she couldn't understand.

He broke away and murmured into her hair. And the phrase crystallized. "I want to be the husband you need."

"Oh, darling, you are." In every sense. He had been from the first moment, providing a safe, secure place for her to bloom into his wife. He was her match every bit as much as she was his.

He shook his head. "I haven't been. I don't deserve you. But I want you. So much."

"You have me. Forever. We're married, remember?" She smiled but he didn't return it.

"Not like this. No more agreement. No separate bedrooms. No separate hearts." He put his palm flat against his breastbone like a pledge. "I could've hired a personal assistant. But I didn't. I went looking for a wife because I needed one. I need a wife who sees past all my faults and loves me anyway. It's not too late, is it?"

She placed her palm on top of his. "Never. But, Leo, you didn't go to work today. You're not throwing away your company's success for me. I won't let you."

"I can't—so tired." His knees buckled and he fell to the carpet, taking her with him. He pulled her into his lap and cupped her jaw in his strong hands, fiercely, passionately, as if he'd never let go. "Like you said. You didn't draw the line. I did. It's what I do."

With a lopsided half smile, he jerked his head at the hundreds of drawings decorating the bedroom behind him. "You weren't trying to force me to make impossible choices. The choices weren't yours to present. You were simply helping me see what options had been there all along. Reynolds Capital Management is a part of me I can't give up. So are you."

"You want both? Me and your company?" Hope warred with reality. The drawings were a big, flashing exhibit A of what happened when Leo focused on something. His preferred spot on the sidelines made troubling sense.

"I want it all." His eyes closed for a beat, a habit she'd noticed he fell into when he struggled with what was going on inside. "I don't know how to balance. But I want to. I have to try."

His voice broke, carving indelible lines in her heart.

This was the open, raw, amazing man she'd fallen in love with. But she and Leo were the same, with facets of their personality that weren't always easy to manage.

"You can do it. We'll do it together." Who better to help him figure it out than the woman standing behind him, supporting him? "I love your intensity and I don't ever want you to feel like you can't be you. If you want to hole up on a Saturday because you've got a hot new investment opportunity to work, do it. Just don't expect to get much sleep that night. Don't ever deny any piece of yourself. I need all of you. As long as we both shall live."

Her job as Mrs. Reynolds was so simple: provide a foundation for him to blossom, the way he'd done for her.

"That sounds promising. If I have to work on a Saturday, will you still make me coffee?" he asked hopefully.

She smiled. "Every time. We'll both give a little and balance will come."

Nodding slowly, he cleared his throat. "I think it must be like when you have children. You love one with all your heart. Then another one comes along. Somehow you make room. Because it's worth it."

Children. Leo was talking about having children in the same breath with trying to balance.

The tears gathered in earnest this time. He'd transformed before her very eyes, but instead of a pirate or Rhett Butler or even a battered Mr. Fourpaws before her, he was wholly Leonardo and 100 percent the love of her life. "Yeah. I think it must be like that. We have stretchy hearts."

"Mine's pretty full. Of you." He was kissing her again

like a starving man, murmuring, but this time, she had no trouble deciphering what he was saying—*I love you*.

Then he said, "My hand hurts."

She laughed as she kissed it. "Wait right here. I have pills to throw in the trash and a red-hot wedding night outfit to wear for you. I guarantee you'll forget all about your sore hand."

Technically, it wasn't her wedding night. But in her book, every night was her wedding night when she was married to a man who loved her as much as Leo.

Epilogue

Leo Reynolds wished he could marry his wife, but they were already married and Daniella refused to divorce him just so he could have the fun of proposing to her in some elaborate fashion.

"Come on, you can't fool me," Leo teased her as they gripped the railing of the observation deck on the third level of the Eiffel Tower. Nine hundred feet below, the city of Paris spread as far as the eye could see. "You missed out on the proposal *and* the wedding of your dreams. You wouldn't like to do it all over again?"

Daniella kissed his cheek with a saucy smile, throwing her loose brown hair over her shoulder. "I'm getting the honeymoon of my dreams. And the husband. All that other stuff pales in comparison."

Sure it did. His wife suffered from an affliction with no cure—overt romanticism. Since he loved her beyond measure, he took personal responsibility for ensuring she never lost it. "Then you'll have to forgive me when I do something pale and lackluster like…this."

He slipped the ring box from his pocket and popped it open to reveal the rare red diamond ring inside. "Daniella Reynolds, I love you. Will you promise to be my wife the rest of our days, always wear that sexy lingerie set and let me make you as happy as you've made me?"

Daniella gasped. "Oh, Leo. I love you, too, and of course I promise that, with or without a ring. But it's beautiful."

"It's one of a kind. Like you. This ring is symbolic of a different sort of marriage, one based on love. The one I want with you. Every time I see it on you, I'll think about how love is the best security and how easily I could have lost it." He pulled the ring from its nest of velvet and gripped his wife's hand, slipping it on her third finger to rest against her wedding ring. And then he grinned. "Plus, the stone is the same color as pomegranates."

A tear slipped down her cheek at the same moment she laughed. "Thank you. Paris was enough but this…" She stuck her hand out and tilted it to admire the ring. "This is amazing. When in the world did you find time to shop for jewelry? You've been cramming for Tommy's product launch for weeks so you could squeeze in this trip."

"Tommy came with me and we strategized in between." Leo rolled his eyes. "Trust me, he was thrilled to be involved. I never imagined when he said he wanted to learn everything that would include how to pick out a diamond for a woman."

Daniella giggled. "With you as his mentor, I'm sure he'll make the future love of his life very happy."

Tommy had trashed Leo's original proposal. Garrett-Reynolds Engineering opened its doors that same week and the payoff for becoming full partners had been immeasurable. Not only did Leo have a lot of fun, but for the first time, his profit flowed directly from his hand instead of via carefully constructed financing agreements. Leo was right in the middle of every aspect of the business and it fulfilled him in ways he could never completely comprehend.

Without Daniella, he never would have taken that step. She'd invested in his potential and given him a makeover from the inside out. He'd gladly spend the rest of his life loving her for it.

"How're things going in there?" Leo spread his hand across Daniella's abdomen and the thought of their child eventually being inside tightened his throat with awe and tenderness.

"Not pregnant yet. Though certainly not from lack of trying." Her grin warmed his heart. Everything about her warmed his heart, touching him in places he didn't even know existed. "It's only a matter of time."

"We must try harder. I insist."

A baby was one of many possibilities he eagerly anticipated, owing to his new perspective on marriage. And life in general.

Leo kissed his wife and it felt like the beginning of something that would take a very long time to finish—forever.

* * * * *

Don't miss the next two books in the
HAPPILY EVER AFTER, INC. *trilogy*
from Kat Cantrell:

MATCHED TO A PRINCE
Available August 2014

MATCHED TO HER RIVAL
Available September 2014

The World of Mills & Boon

There's a Mills & Boon® series that's perfect for you There are ten different series to choose from and new titles every month, so whether you're looking for glamorous seduction, Regency rakes, homespun heroes or sizzling erotica, we'll give you plenty of inspiration for your next read.

By Request
Relive the romance with the best of the best
12 stories every month

Cherish™
Experience the ultimate rush of falling in love.
12 new stories every month

INTRIGUE...
A seductive combination of danger and desire...
7 new stories every month

Desire™
Passionate and dramatic love stories
6 new stories every month

nocturne™
An exhilarating underworld of dark desires
3 new stories every month

For exclusive member offers go to
millsandboon.co.uk/subscribe

Discover more romance at

www.millsandboon.co.uk

- ❤ WIN great prizes in our exclusive competitions
- ❤ BUY new titles before they hit the shops
- ❤ BROWSE new books and REVIEW your favourites
- ❤ SAVE on new books with the Mills & Boon® Bookclub™
- ❤ DISCOVER new authors

PLUS, to chat about your favourite reads, get the latest news and find special offers:

- ❤ Find us on facebook.com/millsandboon
- ❤ Follow us on twitter.com/millsandboonuk
- ❤ Sign up to our newsletter at millsandboon.co.uk

M&B_WEB